Crystal Skull

Rob MacGregor

AN [e-*reads*] BOOK
New York, NY

First e-reads publication 2003
www.e-reads.com
ISBN 0-7592-4920-2

To my parents:
Don and Ione MacGregor

Zeus, the god of gods, who rules according to law, and is able to see into such things, perceiving that an honorable race was in a woeful plight, and wanting to inflict punishment on them, that they might be chastened and improve, collected all the gods into their most holy habitation, which being placed in the centre of the world, beholds all created things. And when he had called them together, he spake as follows . . .

(Plato's *Critias* survives suspended at that point.)

Table of Contents

One

Collins Avenue between Twentieth Street and Twenty-first was a street fair of purposeful chaos. A sweat-stained Bible thumper condemned anyone who heard him. Four men in orange robes and shaved heads stood, with prayer beads threaded through their fingers and a stack of *Return to the Godhead* magazines piled at their sandaled feet, and chanted the "Hare Krishna" in front of a dreary, X-rated movie house. A solitary, tottering old man with a flowing beard followed by a pair of elderly ladies in pancake makeup ambled by. On the corner, two slender men in matching leather pants entered Wolfies as several tourists in shorts hurried across the street toward the ocean.

Typical day on Miami Beach, Nicholas Pierce thought as he emerged from the cultural hodgepodge. He crossed Twenty-first, and strolled toward a building set back from the street on an expansive lawn. He was a tall, lanky man at the cusp of youth and middle age. His hooded hazel eyes gave him a drowsy look, and there was something undeniably vulnerable about his face, as though he registered the world about him as some aspect of a dream, and himself as the dreamer, half-awake.

He moved on up the walk and entered a wide foyer with beige pocked walls made of coral rock. A rush of cool air swept over him, drying the film of sweat on his brow. He ran a hand through his unruly hair, smoothing down the dark brown strands, then tugged self-consciously at the lapel of his jacket and adjusted his tie.

Jesus, he hated wearing suits in the Florida heat. He'd almost dispensed with the convention, but at the last moment he'd remembered the prim tone of Paul Loften's voice and the man's position. Reluctantly he'd tied the noose and donned his jacket, his coat of credibility.

He spotted a long-haired kid in a uniform behind a desk and walked over to him. He was no doubt a security guard, but he reminded Pierce of a theater usher.

"I've got an appointment to see Mr. Loften."

The guard looked up, asked his name. He told him, and the kid lifted his phone and tapped a button.

Pierce looked around as he waited and saw several people filing into a room to his right. He noticed a man in a baggy-looking dark suit with slicked-back hair falling over his collar. He was staring in Pierce's direction.

"Mr. Loften will be with you in a few minutes," the guard said in a soft voice. "You're welcome to take a look at our new Mayan exhibit. It's a preview showing. It doesn't officially open until this evening."

Pierce gazed over toward the exhibit. "I guess I can enrich myself."

The guard handed him a booklet that looked like a theater program. On the front of it was a drawing of a feathered serpent and, below it, the title, "The Blood of Kings: A New Interpretation of Mayan Art." He glanced over it, folded it in half, and slipped it into his coat pocket.

He walked into the exhibition room and glanced around at the displays of ancient clay pots and urns, and small figurines of Mayans with high cheekbones and prominent hooked noses. The stuff didn't do much for him. It seemed remote, out of place. Looking at it here was like listening to music from another culture that sounded great in the country of origin, played by native musicians. But take a record home and it sounded different. That ineffable link with the home turf, the culture, the local color and context was missing.

The exhibition extended into a second room, separated by glass walls. In it stood a series of upright slabs of stone, all of them eight or nine feet high. As he meandered over to the entrance, he saw the baggy-suited man staring his way through the glass wall. There was an obsessive cast to his eyes. Like the guy was an artist. Or a maniac. And a jagged scar sliced across his lantern jaw. As Pierce passed through the entrance, the man moved away.

Pierce focused his attention on the stones. They were covered on the front with a stucco-like substance, and carved with Mayan glyphs and with figures wearing robes, ornate jewelry, and impossibly complex headdresses. It seemed that the artist had wanted to make use of every bit of space available on the stone, and consequently the figures literally floated, one above the other. Pierce noticed a plumed serpent across the top of one of them. He stepped closer, examining the creature. He reached out, and just as his fingertips brushed over the wings, someone spoke from behind him.

"We've saved our prize piece for tonight."

Pierce pulled back his hand, straightened, and turned to see a handsome middle-aged man with a neatly trimmed beard and short gray hair receding from his forehead.

The man smiled, offered a hand. "I'm Paul Loften. I bet you're Nicholas Pierce."

"Glad to meet you."

Loften's grip was firm, and there was a jocular look in his pale blue eyes that suggested an eccentric edge. Nothing prim here. He wore a pair of black jeans, a billowy white shirt, and a string tie with an abalone clasp.

Loften nodded toward the stone slab. "You know, it took some real detective work to solve the puzzle of these glyphs."

Pierce looked at the vertical row of squares with rounded corners and hash marks and odd designs inside. "Yeah, I bet."

"Would you like me to show you around?"

"That's okay, I don't want to waste your time. But what's the prize piece you mentioned?"

Loften grinned, patted him on the back. "You asked the right question. Follow me."

Pierce trailed the museum director through a door off the exhibition room and down a hallway to another door, marked by Loften's name and title. He slowly surveyed the room. The walls were painted black; they matched the carpet. Behind Loften's desk, black wallpaper studded with the Milky Way swept up the wall and across the ceiling. "Interesting office."

"Thanks. I like to redecorate every couple of years. This time I decided on something gelid and soothing." He smiled mischievously. "I guess I took it to an extreme, but I find it very tranquil. My escape from the heat and the chaos."

He should've been a planetarium director, Pierce thought.

Loften gestured for Pierce to sit, then walked over to the Milky Way wall. He pulled open a panel; inside was a wall safe. He twisted the dial back and forth several times, turned the handle, and opened the door. He took out a cylindrical box, shaped like a hatbox, and brought it over to his desk. "Here it is. I think you'll find this intriguing."

Loften removed the top and carefully lifted out a transparent skull. He laid it on the desk. "Our prize piece. A hand-carved crystal skull."

Pierce pulled a pair of round-lensed, wire-framed glasses from his jacket pocket, put them on, and leaned forward. The skull looked luminescent. Diamond-shaped eyes stared impassively at him from deep within their sockets. Two rows of perfect, crystal teeth seemed to grin and grimace at the same time.

"Its history is a bit murky," Loften continued. "Supposedly it was discovered at a Mayan site in Honduras in 1927."

"I'm sure it'll be a big hit." Pierce sat back in his chair, threaded his fingers together, and gazed past the skull at Loften. "So, what can I do for you?"

"I want you to find something for me. A lost artifact."

"I'm not exactly a lost-and-found service. Was the thing stolen?"

"Not exactly. It was hidden some time ago. Probably in South Florida."

"What is it?"

"You're looking at it. It's a twin to this crystal skull."

He looked from Loften to the skull, then back again. "Why was the skull hidden? Who hid it?"

"All I can tell you right now is that I have reason to believe that a man named William Redington is also after it. He lives in Coral Gables."

Loften opened his desk drawer and pulled out a thick envelope. "I'd like you to watch him. I want to know where he goes, and who he sees."

He dropped the envelope onto the edge of the desk in front of Pierce. "There's enough to cover you for a week at three hundred fifty dollars a day — the fee you mentioned."

"Are you hiring me, or is the museum?"

"Good question. Actually, I'm acting at the request of one of the museum's major contributors."

Pierce counted the money, then stuffed it into his coat pocket. "What else can you tell me about Redington?"

"He's a pro — "

Loften stopped in midsentence as the door opened. He looked up, and his eyes widened. Pierce turned, glimpsed a man in dark clothes rushing toward him, a hand raised like a club, lips drawn away from his teeth. A jagged scar sliced across the man's jaw.

Pierce started to raise his arm to block the attack, but it was too late. The hand slammed down and something hard crashed against the side of his head. He slumped in his chair; the light in the room darkened. As he spiraled into the blackness, the crack of gunfire followed him down.

Two

The street in front of the museum was jammed with cop cars and a crowd of onlookers as the body was wheeled out on a stretcher. A white sheet covered it, and only a pair of deck shoes with well-worn soles protruded from one end. He won't need a new pair, Pierce thought morbidly as the body was eased into the back of an ambulance.

"Okay, let's go over it one more time, Mr. Pierce."

He turned to the burly black man, who had been questioning him for the last half hour, and adjusted the ice pack at his temple. "My head's pounding. I hope we can make this fast."

The detective tapped his notebook. His bulk filled an extra large guayabera shirt — the Latin American substitute for a coat and tie. His clothes were rumpled; he looked like he was coming off a twelve-hour shift. "I'm just double checking. You can leave in a couple of minutes."

Pierce's thumb ran nervously back and forth across the raised letters on a business card that read: LIEUTENANT MORRIS CARVER, HOMICIDE DIVISION, METRO-DADE POLICE. He was about fifty, and his short-cropped hair was thinning on top. His eyes were large, deep-set, and almost black, much darker than his skin. Penetrating, skeptical eyes, Pierce thought.

"Okay, Loften called you about a job. You go in the office. He takes the skull out of the safe, and a couple of minutes later, the white guy with greased-back hair and a scar on his jaw bursts in, knocks you on the head, kills Loften, and takes the skull."

"Right."

"Good timing by the bad guy, don't you think?"

"Yeah, good timing."

Carver lowered his notebook and gave him an exasperated look. "Pierce, no offense, but you don't feel like a detective to me. If I saw you on the street, I'd say, 'That guy looks like a college prof masquerading as a used-car salesman.'"

Pierce looked down at his brown polyester slacks, at the lime-green sport jacket that was draped over his arm. He'd bought the outfit a couple of years ago when he was hired by a man who wanted him to look as much like a police detective as possible while inquiring about his missing daughter. He took off his glasses, slipped them in his shirt pocket, and loosened his tie another notch. "I'm dressed like a typical detective."

A furrow formed on the burly detective's forehead. He turned and scanned the lawn. "Hey, Neil," he barked. "Come over here a minute."

A man with reddish-blond hair and an athletic build, who'd been standing a few yards away talking to the security guard, raised his head and ambled over. He wore a stylish sport jacket — an Italian design, or a credible knock-off of one. To Pierce, he looked like a Hollywood actor playing a slick detective.

"Mr. Pierce here seems to have some stereotypes about how cops dress. I just wanted him to know that all of us aren't slobs."

The man grinned, extended a hand. "I'm Neil Bellinger, Mo's partner. How you feeling?" The man's features were boyish. His skin was fair and lightly freckled. His blow-dried hair was photo material for the window of a hairstylist. Spray held every strand in place. He pumped Pierce's hand and leaned forward. "Don't let him get to you." His soft voice was a comforting purr. "You're a P.I., but I gather you're not an ex-cop."

"Ex–travel agent."

"Really." He nodded, considering the career change. "I suppose anything's possible."

Pierce's head throbbed, and the ice in the compress was melting like ice cream on the beach. "Are we through? I'd like to go home now if you guys don't mind."

"Don't blame you." Bellinger glanced at Carver. "Let's go, Mo. Let the man escape this heat and get some rest."

He turned away, but Carver remained a moment. "You want a ride?"

Pierce shook his head. "I've got my car around the corner."

Carver took a step closer. His dark eyes bore in on him as a trickle of water ran down Pierce's neck. "You know, I've been a detective now for twenty-two years. I've learned that you sense things about a person as much as you pay attention to what he actually says."

"I suppose so."

"What I sense about you, Pierce, is that you're hiding something."

"I don't know what else to tell you."

Carver stepped back, regarded him a moment longer. His barrel chest heaved as he sighed and wiped his forehead with the back of his hand. "You better hope that this Redington has some answers."

Pierce watched the detective walk away. He dropped Carver's card in his shirt pocket and slung his coat over his shoulder. He felt the bulge of the cash-stuffed envelope that was in the inside pocket of the coat. Carver was right about him; the cop had savvy.

He lifted the compress from his head, tightened the fabric around it, squeezed out the excess water. He put it back into place and slipped under the yellow crime-scene ribbon. Most of the crowd and police cars had dispersed.

The Bible thumper and Hare Krishnas were nowhere in sight as he reached Twenty-first and Collins. They'd been replaced by a pair of Moonies hawking roses at the stoplight. Two hookers — one white, one black — eyed him as he neared his car. "Need some directions, sorehead?" one of them called out as he passed. "I'm a tourist guide."

"What time you got?" the other one asked.

Pierce kept walking. "Time to get high," a man's voice hissed from a doorway. "Crack, Jack?"

He glanced at a pair of red pants and kept walking. Fucked-up people. Fucked-up day. He spotted a decorative addition to the window of his eight-year-old Saab. He snapped the parking ticket from under the windshield wiper, and patted the fender with his free hand. "Nice going, Swedie."

He drove the dozen blocks to his apartment holding the towel and ice with one hand to his head. As usual, all the parking spaces on the street in front of the apartment building were taken. He slowly circled the block, watching for an opening between the line of cars. He thought he found one, but as he pulled even with it saw a motorcycle filling half the space.

"Shit." He drove ahead as water seeped over his chest. Disgusted, he flung the sopping towel to the floor, then slammed on his brakes as a car pulled out from the curb. He immediately claimed the spot.

The building was a flashy Art Deco prize with racing stripes stretching around its curved corners, porthole windows, and a checkerboard front. He climbed the steps to his second-floor apartment. Inside, the place was less than a prize. The pipes rattled. The electrical system was archaic. His one-bedroom abode had a living room, a tiny dining area, and a standing-room-only kitchen so small that the refrigerator door hit the counter on the opposite wall if it was opened too far. As he entered the apartment, the late afternoon sunshine filtered through the two porthole windows that looked out onto palm trees at the side of the building. Between the portholes was a wall of photos displayed in plastic box frames. Some were of foreign destinations Pierce had visited over the years, others were studies of Miami Beach's Art Deco facade. At the moment, all of them shone with dust.

He immediately stripped to his boxer shorts and turned on the water in his black-enameled bathtub. The sink and toilet were also glossy black enamel, and the ceramic tile formed a black-and-white checkerboard that matched the front of the building.

He walked out to the kitchen and quickly prepared a fresh compress. He held it to his head a moment and noticed that the newspaper on the counter was open to the page with the astrology column. He traced his finger down to Aquarius. "A fine day for making new friends or getting reacquainted with old ones. Enjoy the cultural arts."

Sure. You bet.

He did, however, need to reacquaint himself with an old friend. He picked up the phone and punched a number that was embedded in his memory, like a nail in a coffin.

"Reference desk." The voice had a slight Cuban accent.

"Hi, Tina. How're things?"

"Nicky. I just knew you would call today. Tía Juana read the *Brisca* cards for me last night. She said I would hear from you soon."

In spite of his day, Pierce couldn't help smiling at Tina's mention of her aunt Joan. Just hearing her say the old woman's name again made him remember better days.

"Yeah. It was in the paper, too."

"What?"

"Never mind."

"Why have you been ignoring me?"

"It's been hectic."

"You know that is no excuse. Are you taking me to dinner? You promised."

"I know. Not tonight."

Her voice turned cooler, suspicious. "So why did you call?"

He imagined her seated in her office, probably tapping her long crimson nails against her desktop. She'd be dressed in a tight skirt, silk blouse, high heels, and lots of gold jewelry. Her mane of shiny dark hair would cascade over her shoulders, framing her round face with its unblemished ivory skin and carmine lips.

"I need a list of contributors to the Beach Museum."

"So go to the museum!" she snapped, obviously annoyed with him. "You are only a few blocks away."

Pierce adjusted the ice pack. "I can't do it that way, Tina. Can you help me or not?"

A pause. "Okay. I will bring it by this evening."

"No. I'll pick it up in the morning. I'm not feeling well."

"Are you sick?"

Pierce suddenly remembered the water running in the tub. He stood up and winced. "Listen, I gotta go. My bath is running over. Talk to you tomorrow."

He hung up, then charged across the kitchen and into the steamy bathroom. He shut off the water, which was lapping within an inch of the rim, and eased down onto the edge of the tub and pulled the plug. As he watched the water swirl down the drain, he thought about Tina — him and Tina.

They still played their silly dating game as if they'd just met, as if they hadn't spent ten years of their lives together, as if they hadn't divorced three years ago. But they'd stayed in touch, and oddly, the library was their meeting ground. Her offers to help him with research and his willingness to accept her assistance were the thread that kept them together. The irony was that when they were married she'd never had the time to help him; she'd belittled his moonlighting detective work, which was all it had been at the time. But he'd stubbornly pursued it, and their marriage had split wide open.

He stuck the plug back into place, slipped off his shorts and, still holding the compress in place, settled into the water. He relaxed and tried to forget about his day. It was over. Loften's death was a police matter. Then he remembered the envelope stuffed with cash that was still in his jacket pocket.

It's not over, Nick. It's just beginning.

Three

Pierce leaned close to the mirror the next morning and examined the lump on the side of his forehead. He gently touched the bulging bruise and pressed around the edges searching for the boundaries of the wound. The swelling made him look a bit off balance. He ran a comb through his hair, but it was useless. The lump still stood out.

He squeezed a couple of eye drops under each eyelid. He hadn't slept well. It seemed every time he'd rolled over, his head had throbbed and he'd woken up. He stared at the fine red lines around his hazel eyes. The pupils looked too light, he thought, as though yesterday's heat had bleached the color from them.

He propped open his droopy lids. He let go and they fell. When he was in his twenties, women used to tell him he had bedroom eyes. Now as he approached forty, he worried that he looked as if he had a perpetual hangover, or allergies, or insomnia, or a lack of iron in his diet. Eyelids like his, someone had once told him, were an advantage; they protected his eyes from pollution. Except there wasn't much air pollution in South Florida, not with the sea winds sweeping across the peninsula the way they did.

He walked out of the bathroom and into the bedroom, where he picked up the envelope Loften had given him and took out the cash. He folded the stack of bills in half and stuffed it into his pocket. Then, picking up his sunglasses from the dresser, he headed out of the apartment.

Outside, the air was warm, humid, clean. The sun glinted off a window in the apartment building across the street. The front of the four-story building was a mirror image of his own, its Art Deco facade displaying the same checkerboard pattern of glossy tiles surrounding a porthole window in the center.

He had to think a moment before he remembered where he'd parked, and wondered if Carver had someone watching him. He wouldn't put it past the cop. He'd no sooner contemplated the idea when a figure careened between two cars. Pierce jerked his head and saw a wino staggering into the sun. He watched him a moment, then moved on.

When he reached the Saab and slid onto the soft leather seat, he noticed two elderly men on the curb. They were Hassids dressed in black and white; cotton-candy beards fell over their chests. They hobbled across the street, one leaning on a cane, the other clinging to the arm of his companion. He eyed the pair closely, imagining that their outfits were only disguises.

Nothing like a little paranoia to keep a man on his toes. Jesus, if he was going to worry about Miami Beach retirees and winos spying on him, he should've stayed in bed. Driving away, he nevertheless gazed through the rearview mirror, watching for one of the old men to turn around. Neither of them did.

It seemed there were fewer and fewer old folks wandering the streets, even in the early hours. South Beach, the heart and guts of Miami Beach, was no longer the secure bastion for retirees that it had been in years gone by. There were plenty of them still living here, but their numbers diminished each year. Muggers on the streets kept them at home; rising rents and "yuppification" drove them out of their homes.

Buildings once housing the elderly were renovated, and their tenants were given walking papers as they were displaced by yuppies and yuccas — Young Upward Climbing Cuban-Americans. Nightclubs and art galleries sprung up overnight with the exuberance of mushrooms, and hotels were refurbished. Meanwhile, the international tourist trade was growing as South Beach became Florida's SoHo, returning to its polychromatic, Art Deco roots.

Pierce had moved to South Beach primarily for convenience, when he and Tina had called it quits. She'd kept their house in Kendall and he'd moved to the apartment just four blocks from his office.

He crossed Collins Avenue and turned into the alley behind the Edison Hotel. "Aw, shit," he grumbled as he saw a rental car parked in his reserved space. Tourists were once his livelihood. Now they simply were in his way. He backed out of the drive and pointed Swedie toward the beach.

He waited at the corner for a break in traffic. Across the street, the wide, pale strip of sand stretched toward the shimmering ocean. Palm trees rose straight from the sand along the border of the beach. The best damn beach in Florida, a hundred feet from the door of his office. He turned onto Ocean Drive and tried to remember how long it had been since he'd taken one of his early morning walks as the sun lifted from the sea, or even gone for a swim. Months, he thought.

He drove slowly along an unbroken line of parked cars. He hated parking at a meter all day, but there wasn't much choice. Finally, on his second swing by the Edison, he saw a woman opening her car door and claimed her space. He fed the meter and glanced at his watch. Walking would have been faster, but he needed to keep his car handy. He rarely spent more than a half-day in his office; sometimes he spent only a few hours there over the span of a week.

He stepped into the Edison's restaurant, where he ate breakfast on most mornings. He was about to sit down at his usual table by the window when he heard someone call his name. He looked around and spotted Fuego Ferraro seated in a booth, signaling to him.

"Morning, Nick. I thought I'd find you here," he said as Pierce slid in across from him. "Heard you took in some culture yesterday."

He nodded to the sinewy, pocked-faced Cuban. "How fast word travels. What do you know about it?"

"Just that you were the lucky guy, and a crystal skull got ripped off."

Fuego's downy mustache twitched. He had a tic in his left cheek, a facial stutter — the work of a bullet he'd taken in the back of his neck during a shoot-out. Six years on the front lines for the Miami P.D. had turned Fuego into a police burnout at age twenty-nine. Now, several years later, he lived on the pension he received for wounded officers, and on the work-for-cash jobs he picked up from Pierce and others who needed information. Lately, though, Pierce hadn't offered him any work. He'd barely had enough to keep himself occupied.

"How's the *cabeza*, amigo?"

"Better than yesterday."

Pierce looked up as the waitress arrived with coffee.

"Morning, Mr. Pierce. Let's see — two poached, home fries, whole wheat."

"You got it, Dolly." He smiled at the middle-aged blonde whose swirling bouffant hairstyle was as reminiscent of the past as the Edison itself.

"Did I ever tell you guys how many eggs Jackie Gleason used to eat for breakfast when he stayed at the Fontainbleau?"

"I think you told me a couple of weeks ago," Pierce said softly but firmly. Dolly liked to recall her glory days as a waitress at the once famous Miami Beach hotel.

"I did? Guess my mind's going."

"If you can still remember how many eggs someone ate twenty-five years go, I think your mind's fine," Fuego said. "But don't tell me. I don't want to know."

Dolly was about to leave when she noticed the swelling on Pierce's head. "My God, Mr. Pierce, what happened to you?"

"Bumped into a wall."

She didn't look like she believed a word of it. "You had a safer job when you owned the travel agency," she remarked, and left.

Fuego's cheek twitched. He jerked his shoulders uneasily. "You should rest. Can I help you with anything?"

"I don't think so."

Fuego stirred his coffee. "Listen, Nick. I took a beating at jai alai last night. I really could use some — "

He stopped as he saw Pierce pull a roll of cash from his pocket and peel off two hundred-dollar bills. He slid them across the table.

Fuego made no move to take the money. "Amigo. I don't want no welfare. Give me something to do."

Pierce considered the request a moment. "Okay. William Redington. The dead man mentioned his name. See what you can find on him. He lives in the Gables."

Fuego nodded, slipped the bills in his shirt pocket. "I'll get right on it." He leaned forward, cheek twitching. "Where'd you get the wad?"

"From the dead guy. He hired me just before he was killed."

"Keeping it?"

Pierce shook his head. "Returning it. Soon as I find the sponsor."

"You deserve at least a day's pay."

"Agreed. That's why I didn't turn it over to the cops."

Fuego smiled slyly. "Smart move. You don't want to give it to those guys."

Pierce laughed. "You don't trust them any more than I do, and you were one of them."

"All the more reason."

Fuego took a final swallow of his coffee, dropped some change on the table, and rose to his feet. "Why don't you meet me at the Jack of Clubs around seven? I'll tell you what I've got. By the way, you seen my cousin?"

"Talked to her last night."

"Good. She keeps asking me about you like I see you every day."

Pierce shrugged. "Sometimes I think she forgets we're divorced."

"I know. She's *un poco loco*."

Pierce watched his friend walk away. Of the half dozen or so investigators he worked with on a case-by-case basis, Fuego was the most reliable. A couple of months ago he'd hired him to follow a woman who was divorcing her wealthy husband. Fuego had found a live-in boyfriend, damaging evidence for her case. But the boyfriend, a charter member of the Colombian mafia, had also found Fuego. Instead of saying he was working for a P.I. — and endangering Pierce's life as well as his own — Fuego had confessed he was secretly in love with the woman, but had never approached her because he feared she'd reject him. The woman was a looker, and the Colombian bought it, but not until Fuego had been beaten by two of the man's buddies. The evidence Fuego had gathered had saved the ex-husband seventy-five thousand a year, and Pierce had received a healthy bonus from the man. He'd offered it to Fuego, but he'd refused to take more than half of it.

As soon as he finished breakfast, Pierce crossed the restaurant to the hotel lobby and climbed the steps to the mezzanine. Halfway down the walkway, he opened the door to the Gibson Travel Agency. He walked rapidly past walls of travel posters, a few desks, and down a hallway. He sensed eyes looking his way, but he kept his head down, not wanting to start any conversations that would lead to questions about his injury.

When he sold the agency to his former partner, Walter Gibson, he'd worked out a deal to keep his office. At first, his old employees had acted as if he were still their boss, asking him for advice and telling him the inside gossip. But gradually, as it became apparent that he was really a full-time private investigator, he heard less and less from them. As new travel agents joined the company and others left, he became a curiosity, a relic of the agency's past. Now, only his former partner ever talked at length to him about the travel business, and that was quite enough. Usually too much.

He reached a door labeled PIERCE AGENCY — INVESTIGATIONS, but as his key met the lock he heard a rush of words like a verbal waterfall, the unmistakable signature of Walter Gibson. "Jesus, Nick, I read about it in the paper, it sounded horrible. Are you okay?"

Pierce turned to see his loquacious former partner looking up at him from his wheelchair. His eyes bulged slightly under his head of dark, almost electrically curly hair; he looked perpetually astonished.

"I'm fine, Gibby. It was in the paper?"

Gibby held up a folded newspaper. The headline read: MAYAN EXHIBIT OPENING MARRED BY MURDER. Pierce took the paper, scanned the article. "I can't believe they put my name in here."

"Things certainly haven't been going your way lately."

"You could say that." He handed back the newspaper.

"Here, I've got something else. I'm still getting your mail mixed in with mine. How long has it been, four years since you left the agency?"

Pierce saw that the envelope had already been opened. He stared a moment at the return address, then slipped out the enclosed letter. He scanned it, shaking his head. "These bastards."

"I know," Gibby said. "I couldn't help reading it. How many is that now?"

"Four. This is the last one."

"You've lost all your big clients." Gibby sounded disgusted. "Thanks to me."

"For Christ's sake, Gibby!" They'd discussed the matter too many times already, but Gibby kept bringing it up. "Stop blaming yourself. It was my decision to take your case. I should have known how they'd react."

"It's a damn shame. The faulty steering was a fact. You proved that. Besides, the car wasn't even made by any of your clients."

"Don't worry about it. Losing the business of a few carmakers is nothing compared to losing the use of your legs."

Gibby straightened in his wheelchair. "Well, I've made a decision. When the money comes through, I'm giving you a bonus — ten percent of my share. After the lawyer takes his chunk that still should be over a hundred and fifty grand."

"Just wait till it's over. They're appealing the decision, right?"

"Sure. But I'll get it. You watch."

Pierce gripped Gibby's shoulder. "That's the spirit." He turned, opened his door, and stepped inside his office before Gibby had a chance to start talking about the convention he'd just attended in Arizona.

Even though he was no longer involved in the travel business, his office walls were still decorated with his travel photos, mostly of South American destinations. There were landscape scenes from the Amazon, Machu Picchu, and the Gran Sabana of Venezuela, as well as colorful Indian market scenes from Colombia and Ecuador.

Still, the office felt empty. His secretary had quit a few weeks ago, and he hadn't seen much point in rushing to hire a new one. As a result, he relied on his phone recorder. He was glad to see it blinking now; a new prospect, maybe. He rewound it and played back the recording.

The first three messages were from reporters following up on the murder story. Then he heard a familiar voice. It was Tina, and she sounded frantic. "Nicky. My God, why did you not say something? Are you all right? Call me right away."

"Christ." She'd seen the newspaper story. Even when Tina was excited and talking fast, she still didn't use contractions. He'd tried many times to get her to relax her stilted English, but had finally given up.

He punched her number. "Hi, Tina."

"There you are, Nicky. Are you okay? I opened the newspaper and could not believe my eyes."

"Tina, calm down. I'm okay."

She breathed into the phone. "I do not understand you. You keep everything inside."

Pierce cleared his throat. He was about to say that her mother told her she should have married a Latin man, but held off. He didn't want to get into a discussion of either their failed marriage or his personality traits. "Did you find the list for me?"

"Yes, and now I know why you asked. I hope you are not going to get involved with this murder."

"Don't worry. I want to get *uninvolved*. I need to return some money."

"Well, I have the museum's annual report. There are more than two hundred contributors listed, and that is not all of them. Some did not want their names used."

"Wonderful."

"You coming to get it?"

"No. I've got the feeling that whoever put up the money will find me. I'll just wait."

There was a knock at the door. "Someone's here. I've got to go."

"Maybe your wait is over."

"Yeah. Just call me psychic."

"Be careful, Nicky."

He hung up, walked over to the door. Neil Bellinger stood in the hallway, leaning against the wall with his arms folded over his chest. A model for a fashion magazine. Real psychic, Pierce thought.

"Morning, Nick. Mind if I come in?"

Pierce stepped back, motioned for him to enter. Bellinger jammed his hands into the pockets of his pleated slacks, strolled around the room looking at the travel pictures. "So what kind of investigative work do you do?"

"The usual," Pierce said evasively. "By the way, thanks for giving the press my name."

"I didn't do it," Bellinger said.

"That was *my* doing."

Pierce turned to see Morris Carver's massive frame filling the doorway. "It couldn't be helped."

"I noticed there was no mention of Redington or the skull in the article," Pierce commented.

Carver moved into the room, scanned Pierce's desk. His eyes settled for a moment on the envelope Pierce had dropped next to the telephone. "Had a talk with Professor Redington at Florida International University."

"He's not the murderer, Nick," Bellinger interjected. "At least not the one you described."

"Maybe he hired the guy with the scar."

"Yeah. Maybe he hired you, too." A menacing undercurrent rumbled through Carver's voice.

"Loften hired me. Or was going to."

"So you say."

"You accusing me of something?"

Carver's large, dark eyes glared at him. Stubble shadowed his jaw. "You feeling guilty?"

"No. Not at all."

Carver took a step closer. Suspicion sullied his face. He pointed an index finger. "I don't know what this is all about, but I *will* find out. You can count on it."

"I hope you do."

Carver took another glance at the envelope on Pierce's desk, then walked over to the door. "Don't go making any deals for a free trip with your travel agent friends, either. Stick around."

Bellinger followed Carver as far as the door, where he glanced back. He jerked his thumb over his shoulder toward Carver and smiled. "He's really a nice guy."

Four

His code name was Thor, and he drove a dark blue Mercedes with tinted windows. It was his second car, and he drove it only while performing special duties, the ones that would ensure him a special place in a very special future. This afternoon he was to meet Frey in the parking lot of a Quick Stop Grocery in Coral Gables, and as usual Frey was late.

After waiting five minutes, he got out of the car and stretched his arms. He gazed up at a tall pine tree, and squinted because the sun was directly behind it. He knew it was called a monkey-puzzle tree, and this one stood nearly a hundred feet high.

Out of the corner of his eye he saw a man walk from the Quick Stop to his car, and he imagined the guy stopping and asking him what he thought about the tree. He'd surprise him with his knowledge. He'd tell him that the monkey puzzle was native to the western slopes of the Andes in Chile, and that even though the tropics weren't the ideal environment for the tree, it was plentiful in South Florida.

And if that curious fellow would say he was asking because he was thinking of planting a tree like this one in his yard, he'd tell him to forget it. The evergreen was majestic and symmetrical, but it was trashy and dangerous. Its cones weighed up to ten pounds, and one of them falling from seventy or eighty feet could knock a grown man out cold.

Not to mention what it could do to the hood of a Mercedes, he thought. No need to take a foolish risk. He backed the car out, moved to the next space.

He knew about the monkey puzzle, and lots of other exotic trees that grew in the tropics, because his family owned a nursery out at the edge of the Everglades. He'd worked there from the time he was twelve through high school, and then summers while he was going to college. His father wanted him to take over the business, but that wasn't going to happen. Thor had other plans for himself, and it wouldn't be long till he could own all the nurseries he wanted.

Frey arrived ten minutes later and pulled up next to the Mercedes. Thor slid into the passenger seat of Frey's Camaro, which was still running. The breeze of the air-conditioning blew against his face; he took in a deep breath of the cool air. "No problem. Just as planned."

"Pierce got a make on Gore."

Thor shrugged. "It happens. Orders should've been to kill him, too. He's trouble."

Frey gazed through the window at the towering tree. "Odin has other plans for him."

Frey always thought Odin was right, never questioned him. It was a sign of his weakness. A flaw in his personality. "What plans?"

"I don't know. I'm sure we'll see when the time's right. He wants you to keep an eye on Pierce for the next few days."

Thor's brow knitted in a frown. "Christ, I'm already on surveillance."

"That's hardly surveillance," Frey said quietly.

"It still takes time . . . and I've got other responsibilities, you know."

"You want me to tell Odin it's too much?"

Thor looked out the side window. He didn't want Frey taking advantage of the matter, but most of all he didn't want to offend Odin. He knew Odin stood at the crossroads of the future. He could open doors for him in the new world to come, but he could also close them.

Just then he heard a bang; both men jerked their heads, and Frey reached for his weapon. "What the hell was that?" Frey was looking around for the source of the noise, but Thor was laughing.

"A pinecone hit your hood."

Frey got out, touched the dent in the Camaro's hood, then picked up the cone. It was as large as a loaf of bread and spiky-sharp on the edges. "Biggest fucking pinecone I've ever seen."

"About average for a monkey puzzle."

Five

The Jack of Clubs was a dive, a deuce of a bar. No booths, only a W-shaped bar on one side, and a pool table on the other. Mirrors topped by blue and pink neon stretched around two walls behind the bar. At one end, the neon limned the reclining body of a woman. At the other end, it spelled JACK and formed a club.

Pierce usually dropped by here when he was feeling down. It was a hangout frequented by South Beach lowlifes: drug dealers and con men; pimps and wise guys; down-and-outers; and old-timers on their final binges. When he left the place, he never failed to feel that he wasn't so bad off, after all.

As Pierce ambled over to the bar, he passed a life-sized poster of Bogart in a trench coat. No one wore trench coats on South Beach, except for Bogie. He looked around. Fuego wasn't here yet, so he climbed onto a stool to wait.

He slipped his camera case off his shoulder and lowered it to the floor. He didn't want to stay long. After a beer with Fuego, he was going to walk a few blocks up Collins Avenue, set up his tripod, and work on his collection of night shots of Art Deco hotels. It would relax him, get his mind off the incident at the museum.

Leni, a generously proportioned blonde who tended bar, was mothering one of the locals, an old guy Pierce had seen here more than once. "Absolutely the last one, Jimmy. Then you go home."

She moved over to Pierce, shaking her head as she wiped the bar with a rag. "I'm taking a chance now. Last time I allowed him more than two brews, he pissed on the stool . . . the bar stool."

Pierce ordered a beer and watched the other patrons in the mirror — a kind of voyeuristic portal. A skinny black guy and a beefy, long-haired Anglo in a Hawaiian shirt and a baseball cap were finishing a pool game. A bleached blonde in tight shorts, black nylons, high heels, and a tank top fed quarters into the jukebox and swung her hips as music came on. A slender, dark-haired woman in a T-shirt and draw-string pants walked into the bar. Pierce's eyes followed her as she moved toward the far side of the bar and settled on a stool.

She was definitely out of her element. Probably a tourist. Immediately, the two pool players moved in on either side of her and both offered to buy her a drink. As they argued over who was getting the drink, the woman ignored both of them, leaned forward and ordered from Leni.

He sipped his beer, watching as Hawaiian Shirt told Leni to get the lady whatever she wanted and put it on his tab. Pierce spotted Fuego entering the bar. He raised a hand, and the Cuban walked over and eased onto the next stool.

"What's new?" Pierce asked.

"Redington's a psychology professor at FIU. Back in the late sixties he got in trouble for experimenting with hallucinogenic drugs on his students. He apparently was a user himself. He's a little weird, but not the homicidal sort."

"That so."

Pierce's eyes strayed to the mirror again and watched the woman as she ignored her two new companions, ensconced on either side of her.

"You're not interested?" Fuego asked.

"Suppose I should be. The cops seem to think I'm working with him."

Fuego caught Leni's eye and ordered a beer by pointing at Pierce's bottle. "I sprayed the entire Psychology Department for roaches, and got a peek at the professor's office. And guess what? He's got a skull on his desk. Could be rock crystal, or plain old glass. I don't know."

"On his desk?" Pierce said incredulously. "I'll tell the detectives next time they stop by for a chat."

"What're their names?"

"Ever heard of Morris Carver?"

Fuego's cheek twitched. "He's a *pendejo*. He'll try to intimidate you."

Pierce laughed; Fuego had just called the detective a pubic hair. "His partner's name is Neil Bellinger."

Fuego sipped his beer. "Mr. Threads. He plays nice guy to Carver's tough-guy act. It's all a routine."

"Figures." He looked at the woman's reflection in the mirror. For a moment, she returned the gaze, then Hawaiian Shirt whispered something in her ear.

"A tourist, you think?" Pierce nodded toward the mirror.

"Probably."

"They come down to South Beach, and after a couple of days staring at the big, blue bath wander over here not knowing where the fuck they are."

The black guy stood up and walked over to the rest room, and Hawaiian Shirt wrapped a thick arm around the woman's shoulders. He whispered in her ear again, then pulled her close, tried to kiss her. The woman grimaced, struggled to get away.

Leni immediately moved over and said something to the man. He laughed, pursed his lips, and threw the bartender a kiss.

"Jesus, what a creep," Pierce said.

"Maybe we ought to help the lady," Fuego suggested.

"She'd probably just get mad at us."

Hawaiian Shirt was nuzzling the woman again, and it was obvious she was trying to get away. Without another word, Fuego slid off his stool and made his way toward the man. Before he reached him, the black guy returned from the rest room and stepped in front of Fuego. Pierce thought trouble was about to erupt, but the man slapped Fuego on the back and they shook hands. No doubt another of Fuego's numerous street contacts, Pierce thought.

Hawaiian Shirt turned toward the pair, and the woman slipped out of his grasp. She slid off the stool, and Pierce expected to see her head for the door. Instead, she grabbed her drink, moved around the bar, and took a seat two stools away from him.

Pierce sipped his beer and glanced over at her. "Friend of yours?"

"Hardly."

"Let me guess. You're from New Jersey or New York — one of those 'New' places — and you're staying at the Carlyle."

"You're seven hundred miles off on one — and across the street on the other! It's Chicago, and the Cardoza."

Pierce smiled, moved over to the adjoining stool. "Let me tell you a secret. Stick to Ocean Drive at night. You don't want to be over here, especially by yourself."

The woman smiled, ran a hand through her short-cropped hair. "What are you, a cop?"

"Just a neighborhood guy with some friendly advice for a tourist."

She smiled, held out her hand. "My name's Monica."

Her hand was cool and soft. "Nick Pierce." He saw her glance past him into the mirror. Hawaiian Shirt was lumbering toward them. "You want to leave?"

Before she answered, the man moved in beside her. "Come on, babe. Let's have another drink."

Monica slipped off her stool and hooked her arm around Pierce's elbow. "We were just on our way out the door."

"Why didn't you say you were with him?" Hawaiian Shirt called after her. "Waste my fucking money."

Pierce looked back once and caught Fuego's eye. He shrugged, smiled, then pushed the door open. When they were on the sidewalk, Monica dropped Pierce's arm and laughed. "Thanks. I didn't need any more of that guy."

"Can I walk you to your hotel?"

She looked away, gazed down the street as if she hadn't heard him. "I suppose."

She glanced back, blue eyes smiling, light from the street-lamp chiseling her features. Her skin seemed soft, tanned, touchable. There was also something else he saw in her eyes, something deeper than he expected. Intelligence, he thought, but something more, something he couldn't pinpoint.

"Would you mind joining me for dinner?" she asked.

Suddenly he remembered his camera. "Not at all. But hold on a minute." He reached for the door just as it swung open and Fuego held out his camera bag.

"Forget something, amigo?"

"Thanks, Fuego. This is Monica."

He nodded to her, then glanced at Pierce. "Talk to you later," he said, and ducked back into the bar.

Pierce self-consciously adjusted the strap of his camera bag and smiled sheepishly at Monica.

Monica looked puzzled. "I thought only tourists carried cameras into bars."

"I'm full of surprises."

She laughed, a light, carefree trill. "Where are we going to eat?"

"If you like Italian, there's a good place up Washington a couple of blocks. Make their own pasta."

"Let's go."

They crossed the street and walked in silence until Monica asked where he lived; he told her it was just a few blocks away.

"It must be interesting. I mean, living here."

Pierce glanced over at her. "That's one way of putting it. It's sort of a love-hate relationship."

They veered around a man who staggered along the sidewalk. He babbled something incoherent and lunged for Pierce's arm, but missed it.

"I can see what you mean. You've got this gutsy, urban scene. Danger, violence, drugs. All that stuff. Then there's that beautiful beach and all those lovely Art Deco hotels and the art galleries and nightclubs."

"Character and characters," Pierce summarized.

He explained that after he'd lived here a few months, he realized that it was mostly outsiders who were concerned about Art Deco and preservation. The problem with "hysterical" preservation, as one of his neighbors called it, was that it dealt only with the facade. When you lived here, you saw behind the pastel exteriors. You thought about finding a parking spot, about the leaky pipes in your building that the landlord hadn't fixed, about last month's break-in down the hall. And when you saw the crack dealers and the winos, the hookers and the homeless, you wondered how many more castoffs from the mainstream would float onto the beach before the place simply caved in under the weight of hopelessness.

"But you like it enough to live here."

He shrugged. "I'm just saying it'll take more than a few coats of paint and more trendy nightclubs to make this place really livable again."

"Guess I hadn't looked at it from that perspective," she said thoughtfully.

"So why did you decide to take a trip here in mid-May?"

"I wanted to come during Christmas break, but it didn't work out. So I promised myself I'd leave as soon as classes were finished."

"Classes?"

"I teach Spanish at a small college. That's why I chose Miami. It's sort of like a Latin American country."

He looked over at her. "This *is* Latin America. It just happens to be part of the United States."

A couple of minutes later, they arrived at the restaurant and were led to a table. The floors were ceramic tile; the table was covered with shiny red-and-white-checked tablecloths. A few framed paintings of Venetian scenes with gondolas and gondoliers completed the typical decor.

"God, what happened to your head?" Monica asked after they were seated. "I didn't notice it before."

"Just bumped it. Wasn't looking where I was going. Looks worse than it is."

"You walk into walls very often?"

He laughed. "Not on a regular basis."

Their waiter arrived, and when it was obvious that his English skills were minimal, Monica addressed him in Spanish. Pierce was impressed with her fluency and guessed she'd lived in a Latin country.

"You're right, this is Latin America," she said when the waiter walked off. "I've never ordered spaghetti in Spanish anywhere else in the United States."

"I even know a Chinese restaurant where you can practice your Spanish."

"Really?"

"Yeah, the Chinese owner and his family are from Peru."

"Oh, that's over in the Grove, right?"

Pierce's smile vanished. "You know the place?"

Monica looked confused, disoriented, something, but only for a moment. "Yeah, I spent a few days in Coconut Grove a couple of years ago. I remember eating there. The waiter told me he was from Peru."

Pierce sipped his water. "You come down here often?"

"Just twice. That's all."

"You come by yourself?"

"I was coming with a friend, another teacher, but she canceled out at the last minute."

"Where'd you learn your Spanish?" he asked.

"Jeez, you got a lot of questions. I spent a couple of summers in Guatemala and Mexico. Where'd you learn yours?"

"I've traveled quite a bit in Latin America. In fact, I used to own a travel agency and lead tour groups."

"Sounds interesting."

"To a point. I'd never go on a tour myself," he grinned. "It's not my idea of what travel is about."

She appraised him for a long moment, a slight smile on her lips. "I think most Americans are wary about traveling in Latin America."

"Of course they are."

She gave him a puzzled look. "So why did you lead trips there?"

"Maybe because you never know exactly what to expect, even on guided tours. The unknown factor. That's what travel is about. In Bogota, for instance, sometimes you check your luggage at the airport, then instead of boarding the plane you end up in a basement, and there's your luggage going around the carousel as if you'd just arrived. But you're trying to leave."

"Why do they do that?"

"Native customs," he said dryly. "To search for drugs."

"I bet your clients loved that kind of treatment."

"I tried to instill in them the idea that it was all part of the adventure. I'd warn them in advance that on this tour, they would be travelers, not tourists."

She laughed. "I guess tonight I feel more like a traveler than a tourist."

I bet you do, Pierce thought. A half-formed idea about Monica was slowly taking shape in the back of his mind; a sculpture being carved from stone.

"You still lead tours?" she asked a while later, after their dinners had arrived.

"I sold my travel agency a few years ago, started a new profession."

While they ate, Monica asked him one question after another about his detective work. She seemed fascinated, even though he emphatically told her the work usually wasn't exciting, or even interesting.

"I never realized that auto manufacturers hired detectives," she said. "What would you do if you found out the car company was at fault?"

"Then my job would be to limit the damage as much as possible. You look at the claimant's driving record, find out whether he or she ever sued anyone before — anything that might bring about some doubts in the minds of the jurors."

Monica swallowed a mouthful of spaghetti. "Isn't that kind of like working for the wrong side?"

"Even confessed murderers deserve defense attorneys. It's sort of the same thing."

"How did you get involved with car manufacturers?"

"My old college roommate from Columbia University grew up to be rich and influential. He helped me out. I'm sure you've heard of him. Raymond Andrews."

"You're kidding. The movie producer?"

Pierce didn't think of Andrews as a movie producer, although he certainly was one. "Yeah, that among other things. He's got a lot of connections."

She looked impressed. "Are you two good friends? I mean, can you call him up and say, 'Hey, Ray, let's do lunch,' or whatever?"

Pierce was tempted to say Yeah, sure, he and Andrews were buddies. Instead, he told her the truth. "Not really. Especially not lately. You see, I took a consumer case *against* a car manufacturer. Word got around, and all the car companies dropped me. I'm sure Ray knows about it. He probably thinks I'm an idiot."

Monica nodded. "That's too bad you lost the business. But you're not an idiot and I wouldn't worry about what Ray thinks."

After they finished dinner, Pierce walked Monica to the Cardoza. She stopped outside the lobby and turned to him. The neon light from the hotel sign accented her high cheekbones and her long, graceful neck. Her body was angular, but feminine. Appealingly so, he thought. Her blue eyes were inquiring, but there was also a wariness about her.

"Thanks for going to dinner with me. I hate eating alone." As she spoke, she nervously fiddled with the crystal pendant that hung from a gold chain about her neck.

"My pleasure. Is that quartz?"

"Rose quartz. You like it?"

"I noticed it at dinner. It's nice."

"You believe in crystal power, Nick?"

He shrugged. "It seems to keep my watch running on time, but I'm still usually late."

"Did you know that if you send out loving vibrations to a crystal, it will respond in kind, enhancing your love?"

Pierce reached out, stroked the crystal, touching her hand and neck as he did. "I didn't know that."

Monica smiled, took a step back. "I better go. Thanks again. It was nice."

"Good night."

Pierce watched her cross the lobby and head for the elevator. As soon as the elevator door closed behind her, he crossed to the beach side of Ocean Drive. He took in a deep breath of night air, gazed at the moonlight reflecting off the Atlantic.

After a moment, he leaned against a palm tree, opened his camera bag. He kept his eye on the hotel as he fixed his zoom lens onto the camera body, then put it away. He lowered the bag to the ground and turned his full attention to the hotel. He didn't have to wait long. A couple of minutes later, he saw Monica retrace her steps across the lobby and leave. He wasn't surprised.

Her story didn't ring true to him. He'd realized it when she'd slipped up and said she knew that the Chinese restaurant he'd mentioned was in the Grove. The place had been in Little Havana for years, and had reopened in the Grove only a couple of months ago. He didn't have any idea why she would lie to him, but now he was curious. He wanted to know who she was.

She headed away from the beach, walking at a swift pace. Pierce trailed well behind her, walking on the opposite side of the street. It was still before midnight; plenty of cars and people were around to make it easy for him to remain inconspicuous. He had an idea where she would lead him, and he was right. When she neared the Jack of Clubs, she approached a white VW Cabriolet, unlocked the door, and slid behind the wheel.

Pierce hurried ahead another hundred feet, unlatching the strap on his camera bag as he ran. He ducked inside a doorway a half a block away from the car. Dropping down on one knee, he took out his camera and pulled out the zoom lens to its full extent.

As the car started and the lights came on, he focused on the license plate. He lowered the camera and watched the car pull away. He wouldn't have any trouble remembering what he'd read. Monica had a personalized license plate: MAYA-2.

Six

In the dream, the crystal skull rested in the middle of a table. He was seated on one side of it, Monica on the other. She was dressed like a gypsy and stared intently into the skull, seeking to divine something. The jaws of the skull were moving, speaking. What it said was important, but Pierce couldn't quite hear, couldn't understand.

Suddenly Monica's hand and arm were sliding into the skull's mouth; it was devouring her. He grabbed her other arm and pulled. But the mouth kept swallowing her, and suddenly the jaws clamped onto his own hand and he was being dragged down after her.

The peal of the phone punctured the dream; the reality hissed out of it and he rolled over, blinking hard against the light. He patted the table until he found the receiver and answered in a gravelly voice.

"Good morning, Nicholas."

The voice was cheery and familiar, but Pierce couldn't place it.

"It's Ray Andrews. Hope I didn't wake you."

He cleared his throat, sat up. "Ray, hello. No, it's okay." He rubbed his face, trying to clear the sleep from his head. A vague memory of his dream, something about the crystal skull, jumbled together with the woman he'd met, tracked across his mind.

"You sure?"

He looked over at the clock on his bed stand, saw it was almost eight-thirty. "It's time I got up."

"How are you feeling? I read about what happened to you."

"I'm okay, Ray. Just a lump on the head. Appreciate your concern."

"I'm glad you're all right, because we need to get together as soon as possible."

Pierce cleared his throat again. "What's up?"

"I'm the one who hired you."

An hour later, Pierce was crossing the MacArthur Causeway when traffic slowed to a stop as the drawbridge rose. He knew he'd be stuck for several minutes, suspended above Biscayne Bay. He shifted into neutral and pulled up the emergency brake. He lowered the back of his seat a notch and gazed out over the aquamarine bay. He saw in the distance the vague outline of the Rickenbacker Causeway, which he would take to reach Key Biscayne, where he was to meet Andrews.

His front pocket bulged from the roll of cash. Andrews hadn't asked about the money, and a couple of grand was nothing to him; the man was a multimillionaire. But Pierce was still going to give it back. He didn't like being indebted to anyone, especially Andrews. After all, he was hardly as naive as he'd been when he'd met the man.

That had been the summer of his sophomore year at Columbia. He'd answered an ad in the student newspaper that had said: *"Help wanted, international travel, Spanish required."* The telephone number had been Andrews's. It hadn't taken Pierce long to figure out that the job involved being an accessory to an international marijuana smuggling scheme, and at first he'd wanted nothing to do with it. But Andrews had convinced him that he would act only as an intermediary, setting up the time and place of exchanges, delivering messages. For Pierce, no money and no drugs were involved.

The summer job had meant four trips to Santa Marta, Colombia, and had earned him $3,200 tax-free. That fall, he and Andrews had gotten an apartment together. Those days had been a time of almost childlike innocence, when drugs were new and mysteriously mind-expanding, instead of mind-destroying; when only the cops carried guns; when cocaine was only a rumor; and when those in the business lived by the countercultural motto: You got to be honest to live outside the law.

Andrews had majored in business and philosophy and had continued operating his importation and distribution network while attending classes. He'd reaped windfall profits from his cannabis connections, and by the end of the academic year he was already starting to invest his profits in legitimate businesses, some of them small, high-risk, high-tech ventures involving the manufacture of what was then a virtually unknown product called the microchip.

Pierce remembered Andrews as generous, but obsessed with amassing wealth. He'd once confided to Pierce that it was a mystery to him why so many of their friends seemed ambivalent about seeking their own pots of gold. Pierce knew that Andrews considered him one of them, and that Andrews would soon move on to a new circle of friends.

Maybe it was his unstable childhood that had provoked the search for quick wealth. He remembered Andrews telling him that he was lucky to have grown up with a father who came home from work every day and a mother who stayed at home to raise the family. Andrews's memories were of a father who was in the air force and a mother who worked in a mill. His mother, he'd once told Pierce, had been obsessed with her fading youth and had started drinking after his father walked out for good. By age ten, Andrews was living in the homes of relatives and family friends, and by thirteen he was working his first job after school each day.

The next fall, his senior year, Pierce saw less and less of his former roommate. Andrews arrived on campus driving a new Porsche he'd paid for with cash, and he no longer needed to share the rent with anyone. A couple of years after graduation, Pierce saw an article in *Esquire* listing Raymond Andrews as one of the top twenty-five young millionaires in America. There was little doubt at that point that his old roommate's ambitions were quickly being fulfilled, and that he was no longer relying on New York pot-smokers.

Over the years, he'd read about his success in commodities and foreign currency investments. He'd financed two blockbuster movies and others that had fared well. He had been president and major stockholder of World Cable Network before selling his interest and buying an airline, which he'd taken from insolvency to prosperity in three years, renaming it Tropic Air. He owned a real estate development company, large land holdings, restaurants, a shopping mall, and God knew what else. He was a financial whiz, worth more than three hundred million . . . and counting. But he was much more than just another wealthy, successful businessman. He considered himself a man of vision, one who saw a future in which mankind emerges from conflict and chaos.

Pierce didn't see Andrews in person for almost fifteen years. Then suddenly one day he'd received an engraved invitation to the dedication of the new headquarters of Tropic Air in Miami. He and Tina were still married, and she'd been stunned to find out that he knew Andrews, that they'd been roommates.

He remembered Andrews speaking from a platform in front of the new building. He was in his element, and charisma emanated from him like a hypnotic scent. It was more than his handsome face, the authority in his voice, or his demeanor. Andrews was born to galvanize a crowd. He commanded your attention, made you feel as if he were talking to you and only you and that he was putting into words what you had been thinking yourself. Here was a man, you thought, who could not only put this vision of a better world into words, but who had the ability to carry it out. Even Pierce, who knew him like no one else in the crowd, had been caught up in the talk that day.

"The course I will follow from this day on will be dedicated to building a peaceful and prosperous world, a world community. Some say, why bother, enjoy your wealth. Others say, nothing can be done; the tide of the times is washing us over the edge of the world into oblivion, the end of history.

"But I say, that is the flat-world vision. And I see the world and mankind as multidimensional. With proper guidance to avoid the inevitable pitfalls, we are headed into a holistic future where mankind prospers in a vision larger than the ordinary. In science as well as society, new paradigms, or visions of reality, are emerging. Indeed, the era of the New Enlightenment is almost upon us. Of course, we may see instances of chaos as our vision shifts. But keep in mind that no system can be completely understood by the properties of its parts. I promise you that through it all, the power of the vision, the dynamics of the whole, will radiate through the darkness."

Andrews stepped down from the podium and was immediately surrounded by a throng of reporters and admirers. On the edge of the crowd, Tina urged Pierce to approach him. "Go say hi to him, Nicky. He must want to see you."

"He probably won't even recognize me."

"Of course he will."

Pierce made his way through the crowd with Tina behind him. He wasn't sure why, but he felt ambivalent about talking to Andrews. When he was within a few feet of him, he saw a hulking man who looked like a professional wrestler and realized that it was Andrews's bodyguard.

He ignored the man's cold stare and after a moment caught Andrews's eye. "Hello, Ray."

Andrews looked blankly at him a moment, then his face lit up, and he grinned broadly. "Nicholas Pierce. Great to see you. Hang on a minute, will you?"

He greeted several more people, told them to help themselves to the food and drinks that were being served from long tables on the lawn. Then he excused himself, and motioned for Pierce to follow him. Pierce took Tina by the hand and noticed that the bodyguard stayed close to Andrews.

They stopped near a tall, attractive blond woman, and Andrews introduced her as his wife, Ginger. "Hon, Nicholas is an old college friend, and I bet this is — "

"Tina, my wife," Pierce finished.

"Mr. Andrews, it is so wonderful to meet you. I am a great admirer, and I did not believe it when Nick received your invitation. He never told me you were friends."

Andrews turned to Tina, looked at her as if no one else existed. His eyes glistened, his toothy smile brilliant, affable. At close range, Andrews permeated a sense of vitality, enthusiasm, and undeniable charm. He took Tina's hand, leaned into the introduction giving her a full second of his presence. His voice was smooth as silk. "Very nice, nice to meet you. Nick always had a wonderful eye for beauty," he confided. "I see that attribute of his has only improved with time. You're lovely."

Tina was mesmerized as if Andrews were a snake charmer and she the captivated cobra. She was wide-eyed, dumbfounded. Her mouth opened, but no words came out. Finally, she blurted, "Thank you."

He turned to Pierce as Tina exchanged a few words with Ginger. "We've been out of touch a long time. I happened to see a list of private investigators working in South Florida and saw your name. When I verified that it was you, I couldn't resist sending you an invitation."

Unless Andrews had changed, he didn't simply invite him for the hell of it. There was a reason. "Well, I work as a P.I. only part-time right now. I own a travel agency."

"It is the child in him," Tina interjected. "I keep telling him to stay with the travel business. But his mind wanders."

Andrews nodded, laid a hand on Pierce's shoulder. "Same old Nicholas. Listen, I have to go, but I wanted to mention to you that I have a friend in the auto industry who's looking for a reliable detective to investigate insurance claims in South Florida. If you're interested, I'll recommend you."

The bridge lowered, and traffic was moving again. In the aftermath of that conversation with his old roommate, Pierce's life had shifted from the travel industry to investigations. Within months his income had doubled, and after a year he was taking cases from several auto manufacturers. Andrews had called on occasion to ask him how it was going, and more than once Pierce had wondered if he was being primed for an assignment. But then he'd taken Gibby's case, and he hadn't heard a word from Andrews in more than a year. Not until this morning.

Pierce crossed downtown to the Rickenbacker, where he accelerated back across the bay. He quickly passed through Virginia Key and drove onto Key Biscayne, the verdant stronghold of the wealthy. In spite of the pricey real estate, almost half of the island was dedicated to parks covered with banyans, palms, and wild growths of lush vegetation. Most of the remainder was claimed by mansions and million-dollar condominiums.

He followed Crandon Boulevard, passing a golf course and a small shopping district. The road narrowed as he motored through quiet, tree-lined residential streets. Suddenly, ahead of him, he saw the gate to Cape Florida State Park and realized he'd missed the turn. He backtracked at fifteen miles an hour until he found Mimosa Lane. Andrews lived at the end of it, on the beach — or more precisely, above the beach. He pulled up to a guard booth at the entrance to the high-rise and told its uniformed caretaker who he was visiting.

After jotting down his name and license number, the guard punched a three-digit number on his phone and spoke into it softly, announcing Pierce's arrival. A moment later, the guard told him where to park and motioned him through.

"There you go, Swedie," Pierce said to his car as he closed the door, "a parking spot with an ocean view."

Once inside the lobby, he looked around for the stairs. He walked past the elevator and took the steps two at a time. Heavy metal fire doors separated each flight. He counted eight of them by the time he reached the top floor. Whenever anyone asked him why he took the stairs, he usually said he liked the exercise or he didn't like waiting for the stupid box. The truth was that every time he stepped into an elevator — and he hadn't done it for several years — he experienced a cold-blooded, phobic chill, a sensation that ran up his spine and was accompanied by an irrational terror that he'd be stuck between floors. It had happened once, and he felt a certainty it would happen again.

Andrews's condominium occupied the southeast corner of the top floor. He knocked on the door, and a moment later, the same bodyguard he'd seen four years ago opened the door. His neck was the size of Pierce's thigh and met his shoulders at a forty-five degree slope. He wore a T-shirt that looked as if it would rip at the seams if he flexed his muscles.

"Morning," Pierce said brightly.

The man nodded without speaking, motioned him to enter. Pierce stepped into a spacious living room that afforded a sweeping view of the ocean. He knew that Andrews owned several other homes and that he spent about three months of the year at this residence.

The bodyguard led him through the room, past a dining room, and down a hall to Andrews's study. In the few seconds it took to walk through the apartment, he saw a man and a woman in the kitchen cooking, a maid vacuuming, and several men in suits seated around a table in a meeting room. He had also noticed something else, a blur of cuckoo clocks, grandfather clocks, wall clocks, and table clocks.

He glanced around the study. More clocks. On the wall behind Andrews's desk, clock hands stretched over a metallic world map. Another, the largest he'd seen, was embedded in the face of an octagonal coffee table situated in front of a black leather sofa. Yet another, this one near the door, said *Tempus Abire Tibi Est* on its face. Pierce laughed. It was the same phrase that Andrews had handwritten on the door inside his bedroom when they roomed together. It meant: It is time for you to go away. At least his sense of humor hadn't changed.

"Lots of clocks," he said to the bodyguard, who'd followed him into the study.

The man made a guttural sound and took out a pen and pad. As he scribbled on it. Pierce discreetly studied him: He was blond, had a square jaw, and a handsome, youthful face. He was surprised the man was a mute, but imagined the handicap suited Andrews just fine, an audience who couldn't interrupt. Actually he probably considered him more a roving piece of furniture than a fellow human.

But then again, he wasn't sure what Andrews thought about anything. Not anymore.

He held up the paper to Pierce. On it was written: "A hundred and sixteen clocks plus forty-two watches."

"That's a lot. What's your name?"

He didn't think the man had watched his lips, but wasn't certain. A moment later, he held up his pad and Pierce read the two-letter name.

"K.J., nice to meet you," Pierce said, speaking in a loud, clear voice and shaking the man's huge hand.

K.J. scribbled something again. "Mute, but not deaf."

Pierce grinned, embarrassed. K.J. pointed at the sofa, then backed out of the room, closing the door after him.

He sat down, but only for a moment. He saw a partially opened door behind Andrews's desk; a glow of colored neon emanated from it. He walked over and looked inside. It was a bathroom, and the glow was from the pink and blue tubes of a neon clock on the wall. He leaned over the sink toward the mirror. The swelling on his head was less noticeable, but the skin was turning an ugly purple and looked particularly bad under neon. He ran a hand through his hair, covering the bruise as best he could.

He was about to return to the study when he realized there was another door opposite the sink. It was covered with the same pink and blue geometric designs as the walls and the handle was a latch set into the door. He tugged lightly at it and the door opened. He glanced about quickly. The room was equipped with computers, fax machines, a dozen telephones, and a paper shredder. Andrews's war room, he thought, and retreated into the bathroom.

As he moved back into the study, he saw a photo on Andrews's desk and picked it up. Ginger and Ray were arm in arm on the deck of a yacht, and in the background he could read the name, *Argo-2*, no doubt a reference to Jason and the Argonauts and the search for the Golden Fleece. He focused on Ginger. Even though she was smiling, there was a distant, vacant look on her face. She'd died a year ago; a suicide, the papers said. He'd called Andrews in the aftermath to express his condolences, but had been told he was unavailable.

He put the photo back in place, wondering how long it would be kept on the desk. He didn't think Andrews was the kind to torture himself over a lost love. Pierce remembered a man who quixotically bounded from one affair to the next, never satisfied, always seeking someone new. More than one young woman had been discarded like yesterday's garbage.

He walked over to a wall and examined framed magazine covers of *Time, U.S. News and World Report,* and *Business Week* featuring Andrews. Cover boy. Maybe living in the shadow of Ray Andrews had become too much of a burden for Ginger.

All the articles focused on Andrews's role in the new capitalism sweeping Eastern Europe. While others feared the chaos and played a wait-and-see game, Andrews had immediately begun setting up deals, acting primarily as an intermediary between the new capitalists and the old ones. He was so successful that diplomats on both sides sought him out for advice in political maneuvering. One headline was: AMERICA'S EMISSARY TO EASTERN EUROPE. Another read: MINISTER OF CHANGE. The third: ENVOY OF THE NEW ENLIGHTENMENT.

Pierce turned as the door opened and a middle-aged woman in a business suit entered. "Mr. Pierce, Mr. Andrews is in a meeting right now. He told me to tell you he'll be with you in a few minutes. Would you like something to drink while you wait?"

"Iced tea or a glass of water would be fine."

As the woman left, he walked over to a bookcase and examined the titles on a row at eye level. Most were tomes on philosophy, mysticism, mythology. Andrews's esoteric side, he thought. One leather-bound book stuck out a bit farther than the others. He pulled it off the shelf. The binding was well worn, and it opened to a page that was marked.

The passage was about an incomplete work by Plato called *Critias,* which abruptly ended in midsentence. It was the second of a planned three-part dialogue on Atlantis. The first was called *Timaeus,* and the third was either lost or never written. The author explained that Plato may have stopped writing the dialogues when his patron, Dionysius I, died. He also pointed out that at the time, there were few lengthy descriptions of foreign lands, so Plato might simply have tired of the task of recreating Atlantis.

Andrews had written one word in the margin: BULLSHIT.

Pierce laughed to himself. Same old Ray, still waving his philosophic sword. He remembered how Andrews was always the center of attention at any gathering, especially when the conversation turned to mysticism, a topic in vogue at the time. One day he would attack Castaneda or the *I Ching*, and the next, he would play the opposite side with equal persuasiveness. He could sway you either way. He loved pulling the switch; he relished pulling it off.

When Andrews wasn't around, Pierce and his circle of friends would talk about him, try to figure him out. The conclusion, which conveniently fit their stoned mystical musings, was that Andrews must be the reincarnation of a medieval wizard. Yet, he'd always been more of a fortune hunter than a fortune-teller.

He replaced the book exactly as he'd found it. On the shelf above it, he read a couple of the titles: *The Secret Teachings of All Ages*, and *Occult Symbols in Art*. Both had several bookmarks protruding. He was about to take one down when he heard the door opening.

"Here is your drink, sir." He turned around to see a young woman with long, dark hair holding a silver tray with a tall glass of iced tea and a slice of lemon on the side. She wore a blue uniform and was obviously another hired hand. She set the tray down on an end table next to a couch and quickly left the room.

He'd only taken a couple of sips when the door opened again. "Nicholas, I'm sorry to have kept you waiting so long. I appreciate your effort to get over here so quickly."

Pierce stood and extended his hand. Even at six-one, he had to look up an inch or so to Andrews. His full head of black hair was swept back, and every strand was perfectly in place. He was wearing a white silk shirt and white pants, which accented his tan. He reminded Pierce of a polished Latin playboy without the accent.

"You look the same as ever, Ray." He knew Andrews appreciated the compliment, and the man did appear younger than his years. He hadn't started college until he was twenty-one, and was three years older than Pierce.

"You think so? I'll be forty-three in a couple of months."

"You'd never know it," Pierce said.

Andrews stared at him for a moment. His eyes were deep, dark, compelling. They begged for attention, were at once forceful and compassionate. "I see the swelling. Does it hurt?"

"Not much at all today."

"Why don't we go out on the veranda. It's much more pleasant for talking."

They walked out to an unscreened porch with several comfortable patio chairs and a table. Pierce moved over to the railing and gazed out at the horizon, where the lapis ocean met the pale blue sky. Even though he disliked what the concrete high-rise condominiums had done to the once-pristine South Florida shoreline, he had to admit that from up here the view was pleasant.

"You've had some rough breaks," Andrews said, echoing what Gibby had said to him. "I wish you had told me you were planning to take that consumer case. Christ, I would've warned you. You can't cross lines like that."

Pierce turned, joined Andrews at the table, and set his glass down. "I realize that now."

"You've always got to guard your rear, Nicholas. Especially when you're dealing with high rollers." He jerked his head toward the interior of the house. "I was just talking with my lawyers about a corporate raider who's after Tropic Air. Believe it or not, I loaned this guy five million dollars a few years ago."

"Can you stop him?"

Andrews shrugged, looked out toward the ocean. "I don't know. I feel like Daedalus, trapped in a labyrinth of my own making. And now the Minotaur's going to eat me alive." He laughed. He didn't sound too concerned. "Ah, hell, it'll work out one way or another."

"Just don't fly too close to the sun," Pierce quipped.

"Icarus, I'm not. My wings aren't about to melt." Andrews regarded him a moment, twisting the gold band on his ring finger. "Business loans can always be recovered. Human losses are another matter. It'll be one year next Wednesday, and I still sorely miss Ginger."

"It must be tough."

"I guess I didn't pay enough attention to her. I thought everything was great, but she was hooked on cocaine. I didn't even know it until she overdosed."

The woman in the blue uniform appeared and asked if they'd like anything. Pierce said he was fine, and Andrews dismissed the woman with a wave of his hand. As she left, K.J. walked out on the veranda carrying a video camera and a tripod.

"You've got a lot of helpers."

Andrews counted them off on his fingers. "Two personal assistants, a secretary, two cooks, a housekeeper, and K.J. That doesn't count my help at the office, or the lawyers." He chuckled. "Lots of company."

Andrews's entourage, Pierce mused, and asked, "Isn't a bodyguard sort of confining?"

Andrews glanced over at K.J., who was setting up the tripod in the corner. "I used to have two of them, but they tripped over each other. I kept K.J. because he was the least intrusive." He flashed a grin, gritting his teeth. The smile was at once friendly and aggressive, ingratiating and contradictory — a visual oxymoron. A smile he remembered from the past.

Pierce looked from Andrews to K.J. and back again as the bodyguard aimed the camera at him.

"You don't mind if I tape our session, do you?" Andrews asked. "I like to keep a video record of important matters."

Pierce shrugged, wondering if Andrews really considered the meeting important, or if he was simply trying to impress him. Or intimidate him. "No, I guess not. I just hope I don't blow my lines."

Andrews laughed, then turned to the hulking bodyguard-cameraman. "Make sure we're in focus."

Pierce smiled to himself, remembering the semester Andrews had taken a filmmaking class. He'd made a ten-minute, sixteen-millimeter film called *Anything You Want*, a deliberately sophomoric spoof about the advantages of being rich. Andrews was the only actor, and his nonstop monologue had shifted from settings on Wall Street, to the front of a mansion, to a polo field, and finally to an office where he'd stood behind a desk stacked with cash. He'd ended the film by opening a closet door and piles of money had tumbled out, nearly burying him. He'd stepped back, brushed himself off, and turning to the camera, had said: "What do you do with it all?" When Pierce had asked him what the answer was, Andrews had gotten angry. "It's obvious, Nicholas. Anything you want."

The image of Andrews and the cash reminded him of why he was here. He reached into his pocket and dropped the roll of bills on the table. "I want to return this to you. Ray. It's short a couple hundred for my time and trouble."

Andrews brushed a mote of dust from his silk shirt, then turned his attention to Pierce. "I'd still like to retain you, Nicholas. I want you to find the man who killed Paul Loften . . . and get the skull back."

Pierce reached for his iced tea. The ice was melting, and the glass was sweating in the sunlight. "That's what the police are for."

"They're overworked. It's just one more murder to them. Besides, they don't have a very good record for recovering stolen property."

Pierce knew he could use the work, but he wasn't interested in getting involved in a murder case. It wasn't the sort of case he took, and he told Andrews as much. "Hell, I don't even own a gun."

Andrews smiled and fiddled with his ring. "We go back a long way, Nicholas. I trusted you to handle my business interests in Santa Marta. You were fearless."

"That was the old days," Pierce said, glancing uneasily at the camera.

"Before the Medellín cartel, before pot was snowed under by cocaine," Andrews said. "Back when drugs were enlightening." His smile faded. "Instead of death traps."

"Jesus, you want this on tape?"

Andrews held up a hand. "Don't worry, Nicholas. It's a private tape. I have no plans to play it in front of the grand jury."

Pierce imagined Andrews studying the tape, watching his expression, looking for hints of hidden thoughts. He did his best to relax, sitting back in his chair and folding his arms. "You know, I can't remember you ever smoking a joint. Not once."

"Tell you the truth, I never liked the stuff much. Besides, I was too busy to get high." He reached into his pocket and took out a roll of bills in a silver money clip. "Considering the dangers involved in this case, it's only fair to double your payment."

Pierce watched Andrews count out the cash and lay it next to the other stack. "Ray, I appreciate your generosity, but — "

"Look, Nick. You help me out, and after this is over I'll straighten things out with the clients you lost. You know I can do it."

Andrews was pressing, and Pierce was wavering. "What about the cops? They're already harassing me like they think I'm involved."

"Tell them you're working for me. Whatever you think is appropriate. Besides, now you can prove them wrong. You'll be working in your own best interest."

Pierce mulled it over a moment. "What's your interest in that skull, Ray?"

"My interest is seeing that it's returned to its owner. I'm presently involved in negotiations with him to buy it."

"When Loften hired me, he said something about a William Redington and — "

"Another skull," Andrews finished. "A twin, yes. I'd like to find it, too. But the stolen one is the important one right now. My guess is that Professor Redington had something to do with the theft. He's the key."

Or maybe Monica is, Pierce thought. Maya-2. Two what? Two Mayan crystal skulls?

He looked at the money on the table, then shifted his gaze back to Andrews. "What's so important about these skulls?"

"They're priceless works of art. No one knows how they were made. It's very difficult to cut quartz with such precision and detail without causing serious fractures in the crystalline structure."

Pierce hesitated, then picked up one of the stacks of cash and counted out a grand. "This will cover me for three days. Let's see what I come up with."

Andrews smiled, reached for the cash, peeled off five more hundreds, and handed them to Pierce. "For expenses. Get yourself a gun."

Seven

As Pierce waited for the clerk from the license bureau in Tallahassee to return to the phone, he leaned back in his chair and put his feet up on his desk. The receiver was still glued to his ear, and he wished he owned a speakerphone. He stared absentmindedly at a photo on the wall next to his desk.

He'd taken it in Ecuador, at an Indian market in Quito, several years ago, and had made an eight-by-ten print of the slide. From a distance it looked like a hodgepodge of colorful ponchos and sweaters, fruits and vegetables. But now as he leaned toward the photo, he saw that in the midst of the crowded market a girl of about ten was smiling and standing straight, seeming to pose for the picture. He'd never noticed her and yet there she was, standing in the center of the photo, beaming at him. Perhaps the lesson in that, he thought, was to pay attention to details.

A woman's voice interrupted his thoughts. "Hello, sir."

"Yes, I'm still here."

"That was M-A-Y-A dash 2, correct?" The clerk spoke in a syrupy Southern accent typical of Tallahassee natives. "Is that a personalized license?"

He tapped his pen impatiently against his notepad. "Yes, it is."

"Oh, no wonder I'm having trouble. That's another code. You'll have to excuse me. I'm new. One moment, please."

Yeah, and I'm getting old waiting. Anyone could call Tallahassee and obtain the name and address of a car's owner with only the Florida license number. But sometimes he wished it was more difficult. Oddly enough, if you had the contacts to expedite matters, privileged information was sometimes easier to obtain than so-called public documents, because you sidestepped bureaucratic procedures.

"Okay," she said a moment later. "The vehicle is registered to Elise Simms." She spelled both names for him, then gave him an address.

"Thank you, ma'am." He hung up, rubbed his ear, and stared at the name and address he'd jotted down.

She lived in Coconut Grove. No wonder "Monica" knew about the Chinese restaurant, he thought.

Maybe the license plate was just a coincidence and Elise Simms had nothing to do with the crystal skull and its disappearance. Maybe she played tourist to fulfill some fantasy, or she was married and used a false name when she met someone new. Or she was an heiress and got her kicks slumming on South Beach. Then again, maybe she was like the girl in the photo — shrouded, but right at the center and staring intently at him. If that was the case, he wanted to find out everything he could about her.

He lifted his reverse directory from a metal bookshelf and laid the twenty-pound tome on his desk. He'd paid $150 for it three years ago, and it had paid for itself many times over. He paged through it until he found the address. The entry listed Stephen and Elise Simms as the owners of the property. It also gave their occupations. He was listed as a lawyer, and she was an archaeology professor.

He lugged the directory back to the shelf. Monica, or rather Elise, was getting more interesting by the moment. He picked up his phone and dialed information. "Florida International University, please. Archaeology Department." He was assuming she and Professor Redington were campus colleagues.

"One moment. Checking under FIU, I don't see any Archaeology Department."

"How about Anthropology?"

"Thank you." A recorded voice gave him the number, and he quickly dialed it.

"Do you have an Elise Simms teaching there?" he asked the receptionist.

"No. Are you sure you have the right department?"

"Is there any other university in the area that would have an archaeologist on its teaching staff?"

"The University of Miami has an Anthropology Department. You might try there."

A moment later he had the number, dialed it, and asked for Elise Simms.

"She's not in. Would you like to leave a message?"

"That's okay. Could you just tell me what her specialization is?"

"Of course. She specializes in Mayan studies."

He hung up, walked over to his bedroom closet, and pulled out the suit coat he'd worn the day of his visit to the museum. He reached in the right-hand pocket and smiled as he felt the booklet the guard had given him. He flipped through it and on the back page found what he was looking for. His investigation of William Redington was going to have to wait. Finding out everything he could about Elise Simms was more important. She was listed as a consultant to the exhibit, and he damn well knew that somehow she was entwined with Loften's murder and the theft of the skull.

He spent his afternoon at the courthouse. It was a familiar routine for him, going through huge ledger books of county property records and viewing microfiche documents of civil and criminal records. He found out the Coconut Grove house was valued at $245,000 and the property was now listed solely in her name. She'd been to court in Dade County once, to get a divorce.

He walked down the hall to the marriage and divorce records office and asked for the file on the case. In some of his cases, courthouse checks had yielded mother lodes of suspicious evidence. Once he'd discovered that a bereaved husband who was suing over his wife's fatal accident had filed for divorce a week before the accident, and had withdrawn the divorce procedure the day after the accident and two days before his wife died from the injuries.

In another case, a man claimed that his car slipped out of park on an incline and pinned him against a wall, causing multiple fractures to one of his legs. Pierce's record check uncovered three arrests for check-kiting schemes and one for insurance fraud. Besides that, a half-dozen subcontractors had sued his construction firm. Two days after the information was presented to the defense attorney, the case was dropped. One of the insurance company's attorneys told Pierce that the information he'd obtained would have made it impossible to convince a jury that the man had actually set his car in park.

When the file arrived, he went through it page by page. Even though there was no transcript for the case, he learned a variety of details about Elise Simms's life from the documents that had been filed. She had been raised in Guatemala, the daughter of an archaeologist, and after marrying Stephen Simms, had lived in Chicago and taught at a university until moving to Miami six years ago.

She'd filed for the divorce, and he'd opposed it. She claimed he was obsessed with weight lifting and took steroids. The drugs made him abusive when he was on them, and sexually impotent when he wasn't. He also hated to travel and refused to go to Guatemala with her or even visit her while she was involved in fieldwork at Mayan sites. In the end, she'd been awarded the house in the settlement.

The ex-husband might prove worthwhile later, he decided. But first he wanted to confront Simms in person. He'd drive over to the Grove tonight and arrive unannounced. He couldn't wait to see the expression on her face.

As he left the courthouse a few minutes later, he decided to make one more stop. The library was just a few blocks from the courthouse, and unless she'd changed her schedule, Tina would be still be there. When he arrived, he took the stairs. Her office was located on the top floor, five flights of stairs, ninety-six steps. Pierce's best time was twenty-eight seconds. Today, however, with his head still recovering from its recent blow, he took his time.

Tina was on the phone when he reached her glass-walled office. He tapped on the door, and she glanced briefly at him, signaled him to enter. He made his way between two metal carts stacked with books and stepped over a cardboard box. Somehow, she managed to work amid the clutter.

She hung up and looked him over with an appraising eye — as if he were here to apply for a job or had been caught stealing books. He knew it was her way of saying she hadn't seen him for a while. He simply smiled and looked her over, too. She wore a deep red blouse with a high collar, and matching ruby lipstick. Her thick black hair fell over her shoulders, but didn't hide the half-dozen gold chains that dangled from her neck.

"How is your head?" she finally asked.

"Better."

"Good. Let me guess. You want me to look something up."

"That's your job, right?"

"Yeah. That is my job," she said in a weary tone. "What is it now?"

"You having a bad day?"

"I have had better ones."

"When you get a chance, I'd like you to look for any published works by a William Redington or Elise Simms. He's psychology; she's archaeology. I'm especially looking for anything about a crystal skull."

She jotted down the names. "Does this have something to do with that murder at the museum?"

"Tina, I didn't think cross-examining library patrons was part of your job."

She dropped her pen on the desk. "I want to know about it."

He folded his arms over his chest, and regarded her a moment. "Ray Andrews hired me. It was his money."

"Raymond? I am surprised he even talks to you after you double crossed him."

"I didn't double cross anyone," he said testily. "I was the one who lost the clients, not Ray."

"Well, if it was not for him . . . "

"Yeah, yeah. That's enough, Tina."

"Just do not offend him this time, all right?"

He placed his hands on the edge of her desk and leaned over. "You going to help me or not?"

"Of course, I am. Let me see your head."

He tilted it toward her, made a face. "It's nothing."

She ran her fingers through his hair. "Nothing? It is all black and blue." Her fingers slid down over his cheek. "I wish you would be more careful. I worry about you."

That was Tina. Annoyed with him one moment, sentimental the next. He drew his head back. "There was nothing to be careful about. I had no idea I was in danger."

She rested her chin on her hand. "So tell me about this crystal skull. It sounds very mysterious."

"Not much to tell. That's why I want you to find something on it."

"Was it stolen?"

"Good guess. Listen, I've got to go. Call me when you have something. All right?"

Those big brown eyes fixed on him. "I always do," she said.

He stepped over the box, edged through the carts, and left the office. Jesus, she loved to make him feel guilty. But he knew damn well he asked for it. Even though it was her idea that they should remain friends, he was the one who kept asking her for help. Maybe it worked for some ex-spouses, but it wasn't working for him and Tina. Sooner or later, he would have to end it.

Pierce drove slowly along a quiet residential street in Coconut Grove. A plum-colored ribbon of light bled across the western sky, the last vestige of dusk. Halfway down the block, he pulled to the curb near Elise Simms's house. Nice neighborhood. But when you paid nearly a quarter-million for a forty-year-old, two-bedroom wood-frame house, you'd damn well *better* like the neighborhood.

The house was shrouded in hibiscus and bougainvillea, but he could see that the windows were dark and the driveway leading up to it was empty. He'd wait for her, but while he waited he'd have a chat with her neighbors. No resource had ever proven as fruitful as neighborhood gossip. The things some people divulged about their neighbors never failed to astonish him. It was as if they'd been waiting for someone to ask what so and so did at night, who visited, who else lived there.

Just in case Simms knew his car, he parked it around the corner. He passed under a streetlamp just as the light blinked on for the night, and his shadow veered out in front of him. Pebbles crunched underfoot. As he approached the house next to Simms's place, he took out his notepad, rang the bell.

When the door opened, a man in his early thirties, wearing suspenders and a tie, greeted him with a questioning look. "Can I help you?"

"Evening. My name's Tracy Holmes. I'm a private investigator. I'm just doing a routine insurance company check on your neighbor, Elise Simms. Can I ask you a couple of questions?"

"You got a card?" Suspenders asked warily.

Pierce patted his shirt pocket. "Just gave out my last one. Sorry."

He hadn't used his real name because he didn't want Suspenders warning Simms if he didn't manage to talk to her this evening. He always used Tracy Holmes, because it sounded vaguely familiar, like someone you'd heard of. No one, to his knowledge, had ever realized it was a combination of Dick Tracy and Sherlock Holmes.

"Look, I don't know her very well. We've only lived here a few months. I've said hello once or twice. That's about it."

"She have any friends in the neighborhood?"

Suspenders frowned at him, obviously interested in ending the conversation. "You might ask across the street. The old lady keeps tabs on everyone."

Over the years, he'd developed his own interviewing technique, and usually knew just what balance of authority and friendliness to use to get a person talking. With suspicious types, like Suspenders, he looked for leads while assuring them he'd be on his way any moment now. He noticed the man's smug smile when he mentioned the neighbor lady. Either the woman was going to beat him with a broom, or she'd talk nonstop about everyone on the block. He was hoping for the latter.

He thanked the man, started to turn away, then stopped. "Has Ms. Simms caused you any problems?"

"Like I said, I don't know her well. She's a good neighbor as far as I'm concerned. She's quiet. Real quiet. Like a mouse."

"Seen any visitors over there?" he asked, making one last effort.

"Can't say I've noticed any. But I don't have a good view with all her trees and shrubs, and I really haven't paid much attention. Now if you'll excuse me, my dinner's getting cold."

Pierce walked across the street. Suspenders had been a disappointment, but there were plenty of neighbors, even if he struck out with the old lady. Unlike most of the others on the block, the house the man had pointed out wasn't encased in tropical shrubbery. The front windows offered a clear view of the street, and he could detect a shadowy figure watching him as he stepped along the walk. He glanced over his shoulder as he reached the door; he could see Simms's driveway and part of the house.

As soon as he knocked, an outside light came on. He read the name on the mailbox just as the door opened. He wouldn't have been surprised to see a woman in a loose shift and gray hair tied in a bun, wearing pointy-rimmed glasses — the prototype neighborhood gossip. Instead, he was looking at a spindly woman whose shoulder-length silver hair was streaked with pink. She was dressed in a gaudy outfit with black tights, tennis shoes, vibrant green miniskirt, and paint-splattered baggy white blouse. She might've been dressed by a granddaughter on bad drugs. Her lips were smeared red; she was a nightmare.

"If you're selling something, I've already got one. Or I don't want it."

Pierce smiled, shook his head. "I'm not selling anything, Mrs. Johnson." He told her who he was and what he was interested in talking about. He caught a glint of interest in her eyes. She nodded.

"Well, you look like a nice young man. If we're going to talk, let's not do it on the front step. Please come inside, and you can call me Fanny."

She led the way into a living room that was furnished like a boudoir. She stopped in front of a plush pink couch. "Sit down. You're lucky you caught me. I was just about to leave for the movies. Can I get you a drink?"

"No, I'm fine." He felt a little uneasy as she sat down next to him on the couch.

"Now who'd you say you were with, Mr. Tracy?" She laughed. "This is kind of exciting. Like the movies. Did you see *Dick Tracy*?"

"It's Holmes. Tracy Holmes. Like I said, it's simply a routine check for an insurance company."

"Was it a home invasion? I haven't seen any police cars out here."

"No, it's nothing like that."

"Oh, just a burglary?"

Pierce knew it was important to feed her some information to encourage her to reciprocate. "She's a key witness in a case going to trial, and — "

"Murder?" the woman's eyes widened.

"No, no. It was just a car accident. The insurer wants to know who's going to be on the witness stand to testify against his client."

She gave him a disappointed look. "Oh, what do you want to know?"

"Whatever you can tell me about her, Mrs. John — Fanny."

"Well, she's an odd one."

Pierce nodded. Look who's talking, he thought.

"Know what she does for a living? She's one of these bone diggers."

"An archaeologist," he said evenly.

"Divorced, too. Think she kicked him out. Such a shame. You know, when I was young, it was terrible to have your husband leave you. Now, it's a goddamn ritual. But you know, I still see him poking around the place once in a while. Makes you wonder."

"Notice any other visitors, a boyfriend maybe?"

"There's one." She cackled, reached for his forearm and squeezed it, and gave him a conspiratorial look. "This old fart's gotta be in his seventies, a white-haired man. Long white hair. More my type than hers. Wonder where she dug him up." She laughed again and slapped him on the arm. "Get it? Dug him up?"

Pierce smiled. "Yeah. Maybe it's her father."

"Nope, not her father. A while back, she stopped over here and asked if I'd keep an eye on her place while she was visiting her father. Said he lives somewhere overseas and she hadn't seen him in a while. Think she said her mother is dead. Suppose she doesn't see much of her, either." She cackled.

"So when did you last see the white-haired man?"

"Oh, not long ago. Yesterday, the day before. Can't remember now. These pills the doctor gives me for my ar-thu-ritis get me all confused." She tilted her head, listening. "Wait a minute." She walked over to the window. "That's her now. I always recognize the sound of her car."

Pierce joined her at the window and watched as a slender woman stepped from the white Cabriolet and headed toward the house. It was too dark, and she was too far away. But he knew it was Monica. Elise Simms.

"You've been very helpful. I want to thank you for your time. I hope I didn't keep you from your movie."

"No, not at all, Mr. Holmes. I'm just going to rent one from the video store tonight. You're welcome to join me if you'd like. I make great buttered popcorn."

He couldn't help smiling. "I bet you do. Maybe some other time."

"By the way, Holmes, you ever seen *The Seven-Percent Solution*?"

Time to retire Tracy Holmes, he thought. He wished her good night and headed across the street, preparing to confront Simms. He glanced down the quiet street, preoccupied with his thoughts.

He didn't notice a dark blue Mercedes parked on the street, and even if he had, he wouldn't have been able to see the man behind the dark-tinted window.

Eight

The chain lock stretched as far as it would go and an eye appeared at the narrow opening. "Yes?"

"Evening, Dr. Simms. It's Nick Pierce. I'd like to talk to you."

The door slammed shut in his face. Damn, so much for the direct approach, he thought. He was about to knock again when he heard the metallic jangle of the chain being removed. The door swung open, and the woman he'd known as Monica stared at him.

She looked the same, he thought, lean, sleek, short hair the color of bitter chocolate, high cheekbones. And yet, there were small things about her that were different, nuances in her expression, in the way she stood, as though her physical appearance had been altered to refit the persona of Elise Simms.

If she was surprised, she didn't show it. "Hello, Nick." She paused. "I'm impressed."

"Why?"

"You found me before I even had a chance to contact you."

"I didn't buy your tourist story," he said, stepping inside. The living room was decorated with brightly colored Guatemalan tapestries. There was a bookcase and a fireplace with ceramic pots and a couple of amethyst clusters displayed on the mantel. On the wall above the fireplace was a circular piece of wood carved with glyphs like he'd seen inscribed on the stone tablets at the Mayan exhibit. "So you're a professional grave robber as well as a liar."

"Listen, I'm sorry I misled you, but I had to take precautions. I needed to find out more about you before I asked you for help."

She caught him off-guard. "What do you want from me?"

"Have a seat. I'd like you to listen to a taped telephone conversation between Paul Loften and my friend Bill Redington."

Pierce remained standing and watched her walk over to a bookshelf; her slender hips fit perfectly into a pair of white shorts. Her legs were tawny, long, shapely. She picked up a tape cassette and inserted it in a player. "This was recorded three days before Paul Loften was killed."

She pressed the PLAY switch, walked over and took a seat. Pierce eased down into a chair across from her as he recognized Loften's voice.

"I think Raymond is up to something. He told me he thought you've found the other skull."

"Ha. Wish I was so lucky." Redington sounded gruff, almost surly. "Ray is just frustrated."

"He wants me to hire a private investigator, an old friend of his, to watch you."

"Let him watch," Redington barked. "He'll get very bored."

"Well, that's not all. He was asking about the security of the skull in the exhibit. I think he's going after it."

"For Christ's sake, Paul, I can't see Raymond stealing it. He's got too much to lose."

"Believe me, there's more to his interest than you know." Loften's voice was hushed, serious. "We should get together to talk. There're some things I need to explain to you."

"Fine. About time. How about Saturday evening for dinner at my place?"

"Good. But listen to my plan. Bill, I'm going to hire the detective, but arrange for someone to steal the skull while he's in my office — a simulated robbery. That way we'll be assured Andrews won't get it."

"My God. How in the world did you come up with that wild-ass scheme?"

"I'm working with a well-placed contact in law enforcement. He's going to set up the whole thing. It's like a sting, but nobody gets arrested or hurt."

"Who's this well-placed contact, anyhow?"

"I don't want to be any more specific right now. He's doing it as a favor."

"Jesus. Well, it's clever. But won't the skull be in the exhibit?"

"My plans are not to show it until the official opening Friday evening. I'll meet the detective that afternoon during the preview.

The skull will be in my office safe. I'll take it out to show him, and that's when the robbery will take place. The detective will be my witness."

"You sure you want to go to all this trouble?"

"I do, because I feel partially at fault for accepting your offer to exhibit the skull. I should have known better."

"What'll happen to the skull after this fake theft?"

"Simple. A few days later it'll turn up with some stolen goods in a warehouse. Then it'll go back to its owner."

"I hope it works, Paul."

Simms stopped the tape, ejected it from the machine. "We know now that it didn't," she said, speaking with her back to him. She turned, crossed her arms. "Well?"

"Is that what a consultant for a Mayan exhibit does? Tape conversations?"

"I didn't tape it. Bill did."

"You want to know what I think? It sounds like whoever the cop hired to steal the skull took matters into his own hands. He stole the skull and shot Loften."

"And the cop?"

"Keeping a low profile. He was probably acting outside of regulations to make an extra buck, but the whole thing blew up in his face. If he tells what happened, he turns himself in, he loses his job, and could even serve some time as an accessory."

She walked over to the fireplace, adjusted the Mayan pottery on the mantel. "I don't think it's simply a case of a renegade hired hand."

"What do you mean?"

She turned, met his gaze. "I think the cop set up the murder as well as the theft . . . and he's working for Raymond Andrews."

He noted the caustic tone in her voice when she mentioned Andrews's name. "Why?"

"You heard what Loften said. Andrews wanted that skull — and Paul felt he'd commit a crime to get it."

Pierce shrugged. "You might as well say that I was involved, too. Loften said I was a friend of Ray's."

"At first, I thought you were. That's why I followed you to that seedy bar. I wanted to find out who you are."

"And what did you find out?"

Her answer was succinct. "That you are honest, but somewhat naive in dealing with powerful corporations, and people."

He laughed, not sure whether to be offended or flattered. "You think I'm naive because I lost those contracts?"

She crossed her arms and leaned against the mantel. "I think you're naive because you're willing to work for Andrews even after Loften was killed."

"How do you know that?"

"Why else would you be here?"

She was right. If Andrews hadn't hired him, he probably would've given her name to the police after discovering her identity. She was clever, but she was mistaken about one thing. He wasn't so guileless that he believed everything she was saying was true. It could be a ruse. She and Redington might have set up the whole thing.

"I'm here because — "

"Because you think Bill and I did it. I suppose if we knew the cop Paul was talking about, we could have engineered it." Her eyes narrowed and her voice was terse. "If that's the case, why would we have spared you and killed Loften? Think about it."

He didn't know.

"But Andrews had reason to keep you alive. What better cover-up than to hire you to look for the skull and the killer when he's the guilty party."

What she said was feasible. Andrews was shrewd, no doubt about that. But so was she. Simms fit the pieces together for him in one way, Andrews another.

"Why are you telling me all of this?"

"You can help us find the skull. You've got an inside. You know Andrews."

Wonderful. His suspect also wanted him to find the skull, and his client was *her* suspect. He looked above her head at the circular piece of wood with the Mayan glyphs. "Why don't you work with the police? Let them hear the tape."

"Bill already gave them a copy. But I don't know if they're going to do anything. Andrews is slippery. And influential."

Carver hadn't even mentioned the tape to him, hadn't mentioned Andrews. "So I suppose you're going to ask me not to say anything to Andrews about you."

"I'm not that foolish. You needed to find a lead to keep him happy. I'm hoping that one murder is all he dares to commit."

Would she be so daring if she really thought Andrews was capable of commissioning a murder? And what would prompt her to take such a chance?

"Who owns the stolen skull?"

"A man named John Mahoney. He lives in Scotland. Raymond Andrews has tried to buy it from him several times. His last offer was for three million dollars."

"Three million? What's it worth?"

She shrugged. "What's anything worth? Whatever someone is willing to pay for it. But I've heard two hundred fifty thousand as a realistic figure for the skull."

"And Mahoney passed up three million?"

"He has his reasons."

One other thing bothered him. "What about this twin skull that Andrews supposedly thinks Redington is after?"

"Why don't you ask him about it?"

The approach to Florida International University was a long, straight road surrounded by a barren landscape that had once been part of the Everglades. The place looked more like a private airport than a college campus and, in fact, years ago had been a landing strip for military planes.

He glanced in his rearview mirror. Earlier he'd had the feeling that someone was following, but he couldn't pinpoint the car. Now there was nowhere to hide; but neither was there anyone behind him. He pulled into a parking lot, locked his door, and walked over to a grassy mall with brick buildings on either side. A typical campus layout, except there was no ivy creeping up the walls, and there were far too few trees.

He was several minutes early and slowly ambled across the mall among the students. He thought a moment about his own college days and realized that most of these kids weren't even alive then; all the social upheavals of that time were just history to them.

When he found the building where the Psychology Department was housed, he walked past the elevator, climbed the stairs to the third floor, and found himself in the rear of the department. He moved along a hallway, past several offices, until he came to one with Redington's name on the wall. The door was partially open, and he saw a man seated behind a desk. He was looking for something on a bookshelf and his back was to Pierce. He had snow-white hair tied in a short ponytail that fell over his collar.

He tapped on the door; the man turned, looked up over his half-moon glasses. He appeared to be in his late sixties or early seventies. "Dr. Redington?"

He scowled at Pierce. "Didn't you talk to the receptionist?"

"No, I came in the back way," he said hesitantly.

"So you did. Well, don't just stand there. Come on in."

He stepped into the office. "My name's Nicholas Pierce."

"Of course it is. It's right here. Pierce. Eleven o'clock. You were referred by whom?"

"Elise Simms."

"Is this for hypnosis?"

"Hypnosis, no. It's about the missing skull."

Redington frowned at him. "Oh, yes. Sit down, Pierce. You're the investigator. Elise — er, Dr. Simms — sends students to me for hypnosis to improve their study habits. About this time — near finals — I get a flood of them."

"I see." He took a seat across from Redington. The office was cramped, but the chair was comfortable. The walls were lined with books, except for the wall behind the desk; that was covered with diplomas. Among them was a framed poster of a man holding a baby above his head. Near the bottom, a caption read: "The mythic journey begins here. For instructions, look within."

The desk was crowded with books, papers, files. To one side, amid the disarray, was a thermos, and next to it something round and clear that was partially covered by a psychology journal.

Redington saw his glance and lifted the magazine. Below it was a gleaming skull the size of his fist, a shrunken version of the one stolen from Loften's office.

"It's a plastic paperweight, a trinket. Nothing like the one you saw."

"Mind if I take a look at it?"

"Be my guest."

He turned it over in his hand. "Dr. Simms played me the tape of your telephone conversation with Paul Loften."

Redington stared at him impassively, so Pierce continued. "It sounded as if you knew Paul Loften fairly well."

"I knew him for several years. I've lectured a couple of times at the Beach Museum on the crystal skull."

"Why would a psychology professor lecture about a crystal skull?"

Redington smiled and reached for the thermos. "I'm interested not so much in the object itself as in what it represents." He removed the cup from the thermos, unscrewed the top, and poured himself a cup of steamy hot water. "You see, the relationship between myths and the collective unconscious is what intrigues me."

Pierce expected Redington to open a desk drawer and take out a jar of instant coffee. Instead, he sipped the hot water. "There's a coffee machine in the hall if you'd like some."

"I'm fine. Thanks." Pierce set down the plastic skull.

"Do you know about the legend?"

Pierce shook his head. "I'd like to hear about it, though."

Redington removed his glasses, which were attached to a black elastic band, and they fell against his chest. "If I tell you about it, you'll have to promise me that you'll take what I say as being neither true nor false. Most myths, if not all of them, contain at least a spark of truth. But if you take them to heart, and believe them to be the true word, so to speak, then you create dogma."

Pierce nodded.

"I always preface my remarks on mythology with that comment, for a reason," Redington continued. "Our world is filled with dogmas that are deterring our advancement as a species, and I don't want to lend my support to that process in any way."

"You don't have to worry about me. I'm not real big on dogmas." Especially related to Mayan mythology, he thought.

Redington took another sip of his hot water, cleared his throat, and collected his thoughts. The crystal skull Pierre had seen was called the God of Death by the Mayans. The skull was said to have originated in an ancient kingdom to the east, where it had an identical twin, the God of Life. Both mythical gods abandoned their kingdom before its fall; the God of Death went west to the Mayans, the God of Life to the east.

As he spoke about the legend, the gruffness disappeared from his voice. He sounded like a gentle grandfather telling a bedtime story. "Eventually, the God of Death arrived at a great Mayan city. There, on festival days, he talked to people, advising them how to overcome enemies, when to hold ceremonies in his honor, and even offered personal messages. You see, the skull apparently served as an oracle."

Pierce listened patiently. He didn't see how the legend had anything to do with finding the skull or the killer-thief. He needed hard facts, and he doubted he was going to find them in an ancient myth.

"Anyhow, one day the God of Death mysteriously vanished," Redington continued, "and a strange prophecy followed. It was said the skull would reappear and be reunited with its long-lost twin. The event would foreshadow a new era, and the one who reunited the — "

"When was that supposed to happen?" Pierce interrupted.

Redington looked up sharply at him. "I was getting to that," he groused. "According to the Mayan sacred calendar, the reunion is predicted to take place this year. Soon."

"You believe it'll happen?"

Now Pierce was starting to see the connection between the myth and the crime.

"You remember what I said about myths. A grain of truth, but if you get carried away . . . " He cleared his throat and frowned at Pierce. "Elise, Dr. Simms, tends to believe that there is more truth to this myth than I attribute to it. But we'll see."

"You think the twin actually exists?"

Redington held his glasses up to the light. "It's possible. But I assure you, I don't know where it is."

"Do you know Mahoney?"

He wiped the lenses of his glasses with a handkerchief. "He's an old friend."

Pierce nodded. "And Andrews?"

Redington sighed, a deep, cloying sound, as if he were afflicted with perpetual fatigue. "Of course, I know him. I'm the one who introduced him to Mahoney."

"Really? Tell me about it."

Redington put his glasses back on, sipped his hot water, and told Pierce how Andrews had contacted him ten years ago, after reading a paper Redington had written on the legend. Near the end of the article, he mentioned that the crystal skull owned by Mahoney best fit the perfect skull of the legend, and might very well be the so-called God of Death, since it had been found at a Mayan ruin. He also wrote that he'd seen the skull on several occasions and that it never failed to leave him awestruck.

"Anyhow, Raymond asked me to act as an intermediary between him and the owner. So, you see, I'm right in the middle of it."

"How did the skull become part of the museum exhibit?" Pierce asked.

"Every so often Mahoney has loaned out the skull for special exhibitions. He isn't against letting the skull out of his sight. He just doesn't want to sell it."

"I'd like to know one other thing. What's the story with Elise Simms? Why is she so interested in the skull?"

Redington cleared his throat. "Well, she *is* a Mayan scholar," he said in a cantankerous tone. "The theft of the crystal skull offends her."

Pierce nodded. Redington was protecting her. There was something more. He was sure of it.

As he drove from the campus, Pierce saw a Cuban sandwich shop in a small strip shopping center, and turned Swedie toward it. He found a table near the window and ordered a *medionoche* — grilled ham and cheese on Cuban bread — and an espresso coffee. As he ate, he looked over the other shops. There was a *botánica,* a Cuban religious goods store, whose display window was jammed with statues of saints, Indians with headdresses, and blacks in peasant garb. There were vases of flowers, and he knew that inside the shop a variety of herbs and potions were also sold. It was all for the practice of *Santería,* the Afro-Cuban mystery religion. Tina's aunt Juana was a practitioner, and Pierce had heard numerous stories and had even witnessed ceremonies on a couple of occasions.

A couple doors down was a pet shop. Real handy, he thought. Most Anglos knew very little about *Santería,* except that animal sacrifices, often involving chickens or small birds, were part of some rituals. He knew it was a fact, and he also knew it was blown out of proportion by those who opposed the religion. At one ceremony, he'd seen a chicken's head snapped and its blood drained. It was startling, because no one had warned him, but it hadn't been any crueler than the death of chickens the average American ate for dinner. In fact, after the ceremony was over, the chicken was cooked and eaten.

Next to the pet shop was a store with a sign in the window that read: GUNS, GUNS GUNS. Tina had once told him to get a gun.

Miami was dangerous, she said. He'd laughed and told her he was brave. He took on Miami unarmed. But now, he thought, maybe he should take Andrews's advice. After all, Loften's killer was still loose, and if he kept stirring the embers, he could get burned.

He sipped his espresso and argued the pros and cons with himself. Owning a gun was protection. But it also might lead to situations where its use would be required. A toss-up. A gun could save your ass, and it could get you killed. But now the overriding factor in this case was the skull. He'd witnessed a murder, and he was looking for the killer. That left him vulnerable. Andrews was right. He needed protection.

A few minutes later, he paid his bill and walked over to the gun shop. Handguns and rifles were displayed under glass and on the wall behind the counter. He listened to the clerk talking to a man about a Russian AK-47. He was explaining the particular value of assault rifles for boat owners who frequented the Caribbean.

"In case of trouble on the high seas, it's a show of power, really, and as you know, anything can happen today in those waters." The clerk, who looked like a fullback and wore a T-shirt that said: GUNS ARE US, glanced toward Pierce as if looking for support of his argument, then asked how he could help him.

"I need a gun."

"Good. Be right with you." The boater left, and the clerk moved over to Pierce. "Something for protection?"

"Yeah. I'm a private investigator, and . . . well, what do you recommend?"

The clerk reached under a glass shelf, pulled out an automatic. "Take a look at this one. It's a Sig Sauer P two twenty-six, the ultimate nine-millimeter combat pistol, made for people in law enforcement and defense assignments. It sells for seven hundred eighty dollars."

Pierce didn't take it from him. He wished he hadn't said anything about being an investigator. "That's a little steep for me."

"Okay. Got the perfect solution for you." He put the Sig Sauer back and pulled out another automatic pistol. "This is the Glock seventeen. A fine weapon. Again used by police departments all over the country. It retails for six forty-three fifty, but I'm overstocked. I can give it to you for four ninety-nine plus tax."

Pierce took the weapon in his hand, turned it over. "Nice, but what about the standard issue Smith & Wesson thirty-eight?"

The clerk leaned over the counter. "That's like asking a computer salesman about a manual typewriter. Thirty-eights are no longer considered front-line personal protection devices."

"Yeah, I suppose. But if all you do is type a few invoices now and then, a manual works just fine. My kind of investigations usually aren't dangerous."

The clerk got the message. He nodded, gave him a disappointed look. "Okay, it's up to you." He showed Pierce a Smith & Wesson .38 Chief's Special and a Walther P-38. After a superficial examination, Pierce chose the Smith & Wesson.

"That's a hell of a nice gun with a real tradition. But when you're ready to move up to an automatic, let me know."

"Is there a waiting period?"

"Sure. About five minutes." The clerk grinned. "Fill out this form and pay me."

When Pierce left, he put the gun and ammunition in the trunk and headed for Miami Beach and his office. Armed to kill, he thought. A fighting machine. Sure, that was him. *GUNS, GUNS, GUNS.*

Nine

The Miami skyline reflected off the bay as Pierce crossed the MacArthur Causeway en route to Coconut Grove. No matter how many times he crossed the bay, he never tired of the dramatic view. He felt its scintillating vitality, its seduction. Despite the racial tension, big-city crime, and the nonstop influx of refugees, the city never looked weary, especially at night. On the contrary, it pulsed with a vision of itself that spliced together the intrigue of Casablanca with the allure of the Caribbean and the guts of Latin America.

Pierce was on his way to see Elise Simms again, but this evening was going to be different from the last one. When he'd called and said he wanted to see her, she'd invited him for dinner.

"How about lunch tomorrow? I'm going to jai alai tonight."

"Jai alai? I'll go with you," she'd impulsively answered. "I've never been to jai alai."

He'd thought a moment. The jai alai fronton was the one place he knew he would find Fuego, and that was the main reason for his visit. He had a job for him. But taking Simms wasn't a bad idea. He knew from his experiences with travel groups that getting people away from their routines and familiar environments could bring out their best and their worst traits. Thoughts and feelings that might otherwise remain hidden sometimes erupted to the surface. Some thrived; others regressed to childlike behavior. One evening of foreign sport might not be enough, but then again he just might uncover what Elise Simms was all about.

"Sure. Why not," he'd told her. "See you about eight."

He hadn't mentioned anything about Fuego. He also hadn't told her that he'd talked to Ray Andrews and had set up a meeting with him for tomorrow afternoon. Whatever happened tonight might well determine just what he would say to Andrews.

He arrived at her house a couple of minutes early, and she answered the door dressed in a robe. Her hair was wet. "Oops," he said, "guess I'm a little — "

"No, I'm running behind. C'mon in. I'll just be a minute," she said, and retreated up the staircase.

Pierce wandered from the living room to the dining room. Her books were neatly arranged. They weren't stacked one on top of the other, or in double rows with one hiding the other, and they were divided by category: popular fiction, nonfiction, academic tomes. He paused by a collection of frogs on a shelf in the dining room. Some were stone, others were made of ceramic, brass, or sea shells. One upright frog carried a surfboard under its arm, another wore a cap and had a bag of golf clubs over its frog shoulder. All of them surrounded a foot-high frog who sat in a Buddha-like meditative pose. This fellow was obviously the spiritual leader.

He walked over to the fireplace and was examining the circular piece of wood with Mayan glyphs when Elise descended the stairs. She was dressed in black slacks that accented her slender figure, and a pale violet blouse that matched her eyes. Her hair seemed softer, more lustrous than the last time he'd seen her. He liked what he saw, but reminded himself that he was working on a case and she was a suspect. Elise Simms might look soft and touchable, but so did panthers.

"Sorry it took me so long," she said, reaching the bottom of the stairs.

"No problem." He pointed above the mantel. "I was reading some Mayan."

"Good for you."

"Got stuck on the first word, though. What's 'itsay'?"

As she moved across the room toward him, he was struck by her grace. "Let's go," she said, a distracted look on her face. "We can talk about the Tzolkin later."

"The what?"

She repeated the odd word, then added: "It's also called the Mayan Calendar Round, or the sacred calendar. It happens to be my forte."

"Really. I'm impressed. I think." Pierce remembered that Redington had mentioned the sacred calendar, and the prediction concerning the reunion of the crystal skulls.

They walked out to the car and he unlocked the passenger door, opened it, and she slid inside, the faint scent of her perfume tugging at him. By the time he reached the other side, she'd already unlocked his door. He got in, started the car, backed out of the driveway. "Off to the fronton."

She didn't say anything. As he turned onto U.S. 1 a couple of minutes later, he broke the silence. "You're not much of a chatterer."

"Is that the kind of woman you like?"

He shrugged. "Look, if you don't want to do this, just say so. Don't feel like I'm forcing jai alai on you."

"Hey, I'm sorry. It's not you. I've just got a lot on my mind. It's right near the end of the quarter, and I've got a ton of things to finish up."

"You want to go back?"

"No, of course not."

The silence settled in around them again, until he finally reminded her that she was going to tell him about the Mayan calendar.

She brushed her hair back with her hand; it stirred the fragrance of her perfume again.

"They actually have two of them, a three-hundred-sixty-five-day solar calendar and a sacred calendar of two hundred sixty days. The Tzolkin."

He glanced over at her. "Your forte."

"Right."

"I knew the Mayans were good astronomers and mathematicians, and that they had a written language, but I don't think I could tell a calendar round from a calendar square."

She laughed and her mood seemed to lighten. "Most people have no idea that there was an advanced civilization in the Americas well over a thousand years before Columbus was born, or that it produced a hierarchy of mythical figures comparable to the Greek, Roman, Egyptian, or Norse gods. That really annoyed my father. He . . . "

Her expression was pained; she seemed to be in conflict with herself.

"What did he do?" Pierce asked.

"Oh, nothing . . . " Her voice tapered off, the internal turmoil abated — or buried for the time being.

Her archaeologist father was a sore point. He wondered why. And more importantly, he wondered if the problem was related to the crystal skull.

"Andrews and the Mayans have something in common," Elise suddenly blurted.

"Oh, what's that?"

"An obsession with time."

He mulled over the comment. "I know Ray's got a lot of clocks. What's that have to do with the Mayans?"

"The Mayans have the Tzolkin. It's like a clock wound up to run for five thousand years, and it's still ticking."

"What do you mean?"

"It started in the year 3113 B.C. and ends in 2012."

"Strange clock."

"It's a four-dimensional clock. It foretells future events."

"Tell me more," he said, wondering if she'd mention the prediction concerning the reunion of the crystal skulls.

"Okay." She shifted in her seat so her back was to the door. He was glad she seemed to be loosening up. A talkative suspect was always a bonus. "The Mayans predicted the return of Quetzalcoatl, the Plumed Serpent, as a bearded, white-skinned god in 1519. Hernando Cortés arrived in Mexico on Good Friday, the exact calendar day the event was foretold."

He wanted to ask about the skulls, but decided he'd wait to see what she offered on her own. "How could Quetzalcoatl be both a plumed serpent and a bearded white man?"

"There's a historical Quetzalcoatl and a mythological one. Actually, there have been several historical ones."

"Cortés wasn't much of a savior. Hell, he opened the door to the final destruction of their culture, didn't he?"

"He came in the guise of Quetzalcoatl, but he was actually Tezcatlipoca, the Smoking Mirror."

He stopped at a red light. "Run that by me again."

"In Mayan mythology, he's the deceiver, a god of war and destruction who hides under the cloak of peace. He's both the brother and enemy of the Plumed Serpent, the true god of peace and the arts."

"I don't suppose Cortés knew any of this."

"Cortés played at being Quetzalcoatl because that was who the Mayans and Aztecs wanted him to be. But, of course, he was deceiving them. His true role was the Smoking Mirror, the lord of darkness, death, and destruction. He didn't think of it in those terms, but that's what he brought."

"So the prophecy wasn't exactly right."

Elise shrugged. "Yes and no. The same priests who predicted the return of Quetzalcoatl also said his reappearance in 1519 would mark the beginning of nine fifty-two-year cycles of descending doom. Not exactly a promising future."

"Why fifty-two-year cycles?" Pierce turned onto Thirty-sixth Street, a couple of miles from the fronton.

"When you match day one of the two-hundred-sixty-day calendar with day one of the solar calendar, it takes fifty-two years before the two day-ones coincide again."

"Nine fifty-two-year cycles starting in 1519," Pierce said. "Nine times fifty-two is what?"

"It's four hundred sixty-eight years. The cycles of descending doom ended October sixteenth and seventeenth, 1987. It was known as the Harmonic Convergence. You remember?"

Yeah, he recalled it, all right. "That was when all the space cadets were meditating at Machu Picchu and the pyramids and mountaintops, right?"

"On Miami Beach, too. In fact, I was there with a few of my students."

He smiled to himself. "So was I. I was looking for a runaway. Her father insisted I get up before sunrise and look for her among the heathens. Both mornings!"

Elise laughed. "Did you find her?"

"Hell, no," he grumbled. He turned into the fronton's vast parking lot and slowed to a crawl. He wanted to see what else he could get out of her while she was still talkative. "So what's all this have to do with Andrews and his clocks, anyhow?"

"I don't know about his clocks. But I do know that he's obsessed with the next prediction of the Tzolkin, the reunion of the crystal skulls."

Pierce stopped about a hundred yards from the fronton entrance and considered what she'd said. "That doesn't make him a criminal."

"No, it doesn't."

They locked the car and headed toward the main entrance. The lot was well lit and several faint shadows grew from their feet, stretching in different directions. "So tell me about jai alai," she said, changing the subject from Andrews.

He'd heard enough about the Mayans and their timekeeping and her accusations about Andrews. Jai alai would be a relief. For the moment. "What do you want to know?"

"Do you bet on the games?"

"Sure. That's a big part of it. Gives you a reason to root for one Eskualdunak over another."

"What?"

"Most of the players are Eskualdunaks. They come from Eskual-Herria, and they speak Euskera. In fact, jai alai is an Euskera word."

She looked baffled. "What're you talking about?"

Pierce laughed. The tide had shifted. Now he was the knowledgeable one. Jai alai was probably as obscure to her as the Tzolkin was to him. "I'm talking about the Basques. Most of the players came from the Basque region or Eskual-Herria, as they call it, near the French-Spanish border. That's where the game originated."

They climbed the steps to the entrance. "I knew it was a Basque game. But how come you know so much about the Basques?"

"I led a tour there a few years ago. Once I memorize my material, I don't forget it." He smiled at her and had an urge to take her hand. Bad idea, he told himself, and opened the door for her.

"Tell me something else from your well of material on the Basques." They stopped at the end of the line at the ticket window.

"They're a mysterious people, like your Mayans. Euskera is one of the oldest languages. Of the more than four thousand dialects spoken in the world, it's the only one that's unrelated to any other language. Now, don't I sound like a tour guide?"

"I bet you made a good one."

Pierce took out his money clip to pay for the tickets.

"So what does jai alai mean in Euskera?" Elise asked.

"Merry festival."

He stepped up to the window, bought two box seats and a program, and found out the third game had just started.

"The third game? Are we late?" she asked.

"Don't worry. There're thirteen games."

A moment later, they entered the side door of the arena. A couple of hundred people lined a low wall, watching the action. "This is the general admission area. Let's wait here until this game's over."

From where they stood, they could only see the two players closest to the front wall. Elise watched in mystification as the ball whizzed back and forth — front court to back court to front court.

Her court, my court, Pierce thought. When they talked about the Mayans, it was her game. Now, jai alai was his game, his court. His eyes pursued the ball.

"How many players are there?"

"Two on each team. Eight teams in each game."

"Eight teams play at once?"

"No, only two teams. It's a round-robin rotation," he said, adding that the winner got the point and stayed on the court to take on the next team. The loser went to the end of the rotation. The first team that scored seven points won.

Pierce glanced around, spotted Fuego near the betting counter and nodded to him. He opened his program and studied a table of names and numbers. "It looks complicated," Elise said. "What is it?"

"The records of the players for the season. I'm trying to figure out who has the best chance of winning the next game."

"Need some help?"

He turned and smiled. "Evening, Fuego. I want you to meet Elise Simms."

Fuego nodded; his cheek twitched. "How are you?" he said, without mentioning that he'd met her briefly as Monica.

"You good at betting, Fuego?" she asked.

"Sometimes. I know all the players. I don't have to look at their records."

Just then the game ended. "C'mon, I'm going to place a bet," Pierce said. "Then we'll find our seats." He glanced at Fuego. "You going to be around for a while?"

"Until it's over."

They stepped over to the end of the queue, and when it was Pierce's turn, he bet six dollars on a quiniela box, Two, Five, and Seven.

"Not in a million years," Fuego said from behind him. "You should have gone One, Two, and Six."

"We'll see," Pierce answered.

Elise glanced from one to the other, fascinated.

Just as the players were coming out for the new game, Pierce ushered Elise into the arena and toward a row of box seats close to the court.

"Wasn't Fuego the one you were with at that awful bar?" she asked as they sat down.

"Please, that's the famous Jack of Clubs." He laughed. "You're right. He was there."

Her mention of their first meeting brought home that this wasn't any ordinary outing. They both had reasons for being with the other that had nothing to do with companionship. He knew what his were; he wasn't at all certain about hers.

"Okay, tell me what I'm watching. I'm lost already," Elise said, peering toward the court where the game had begun.

"Well, they catch and throw the ball with those baskets."

"I know that much, for God's sake."

"The baskets are called cestas. Did you know that?"

She shook her head.

"Okay, I'll tell you about them." He glanced down at his program and told her the cestas were made of Spanish chestnut and reeds from the Pyrenees Mountains. The ball consisted of two layers of goat skin over nylon thread. It was covered with tightly wound strands of virgin rubber.

She leaned toward him, and for a moment her cheek rested lightly against his shoulder. "That's cheating. You're reading that."

"You caught me. I can't remember everything." He smiled, enjoying the moment. He felt her closeness stirring his desire, and under different circumstances he would've touched her knee, her arm, maybe her hand.

They turned their attention to the court as the game began. "This is game four. We're starting with Teams One and Two."

The ball shot off the front wall as the game began. The back player for Team Two scooped it on one hop and fired it low against the wall. Team One's front player dashed over, caught it, and fired. The ball rocketed off the wall and arced high and deep. Team Two's back player glided over to the side wall, leaped, braced himself, and hurled it back. The volley continued several more times, until the ball eluded Team One's front player.

Team Three replaced Team One, and the game quickly moved ahead. "You see what happened? Team Two has one point now, and they're playing Team Three."

"Is that good?"

"Sure. Two's my team."

"What was that word you said at the counter when you placed your bet? A quinla?"

"Quiniela. You pick two teams to finish first and second in either order. I bet a quiniela box, that means I pick three teams and win if two of them — Two, Five, or Seven — finish first and second in any order."

"How much can you win?"

"Depends. It's pari-mutuel betting, so the amount you win depends on the amount being bet and the number of winners. The house takes a percentage, and the winners get the rest. I've seen Fuego win twelve hundred dollars on one game, and he's probably done better."

"Really?" Elise leaned forward, alternately watching the game and studying the scoreboard above the court.

"All right," Pierce shouted. "Two won again."

"What's your biggest win?" she asked as Team Four took the court.

"Fifty or sixty bucks. I really don't get down here too often. Not like Fuego."

The ball shot back and forth several times until it was bobbled by the back player for Team Four. "Two again," Pierce said. "See the scoreboard? Two's got three points already."

"They don't waste any time, do they?"

"No time-outs for commercial breaks."

"Come on, Five," Pierce yelled.

"Five? I thought you wanted Two to win."

"Five's my team, too. They need a win here."

"Don't the teams have names?"

"You can call them by the players' names," he said, glancing down at his program, "but it's easier to say, 'C'mon, Five,' then 'C'mon Olasagasti and Arteaga.'"

She laughed. "I see your point."

My court tonight, he thought again. Elise, the archaeologist, was digging through the puzzle of the sport like it was an unknown culture, and Pierce, the insider, was the cultural interpreter, a native son.

Team Five beat Two, then Six ran off five straight points. When it was over, Six won first and Two second. "Well, I didn't win that game; neither did Fuego."

He glanced over at Elise. "You want to stick around?"

"We just got here. I'm still trying to figure out what's going on."

That makes two of us, he thought.

Ten

"We should have at least an hour. But I don't want to be in there more than twenty minutes. Tops."

Gore grinned from the passenger side of Thor's Mercedes, and the scar on his jaw curled into a backward S-shape. "I can do a lot in twenty minutes."

"I bet," Thor muttered, thinking over their plans, testing it for any weak spots. They would approach the house from the back, because he knew about the old woman across the street. The lots of most South Florida neighborhoods backed up against one another, but in Coconut Grove there were alleys and that would make it a simple matter. When they reached the house, they would enter through a side window. It would be easy.

The bushes in the front and along the side would block the view of anyone who happened to pass by. They were mostly bougainvilleas and hibiscus. A quality hedge, Thor thought. Far superior to the ficus, which every second or third homeowner in South Florida seemed to plant around his house. He hated ficus. They were a weed, a scourge. If you let them grow into trees, their roots would strangle everything in the area and would even tear up pavement.

He turned his thoughts away from hedges and back to the matter that awaited them. "When we get in, you start upstairs. I'll work downstairs."

Gore nodded and was about to open the door when he let go of the handle. "I got one question. How come you're going with me? Don't you trust me?"

Thor didn't want to tell him that he had his own job to take care of in the house. It was none of Gore's business. "It'll be faster."

They left the car and hurried away from the streetlight. A gibbous moon overhead cast a faint silvery light as they moved like shadows down the alley. The fragrance of jasmine wafted through the warm night air. They paused for a moment as they heard a car and watched as it passed by the Mercedes.

Gore apparently was still wondering why Thor was going with him. "You think I'm going to steal something? Is that it?"

Thor blew out his breath, exasperated. "The only reason I told you not to take anything," he whispered, "was because we don't want to be seen leaving the house carrying anything. This isn't some goddamn two-bit burglary like you're used to pulling in Tampa."

"I got that impression. What is it? What did the broad do, anyhow?"

Thor led the way into the yard and stopped. He stared at the back side of the dark house. "None of your fucking business."

Eleven

They stayed for several more games, until it was obvious that Elise's interest was waning. Pierce had bet three games and lost eighteen dollars. Elise hadn't been willing to place even a minimal bet because she didn't understand the game well enough, and she'd refused to allow him to bet his own money for her. After game seven, he suggested they stay for just one more.

"I think that'll be plenty for my introduction to jai alai," she agreed.

As they headed to the betting counter, he spotted Fuego working his way through the crowd toward them. "Last chance to bet," he said to Elise as Fuego was waylaid by a friend. He looked down at his program when she didn't respond and silently picked his numbers.

"Why the long faces?" Fuego said as he walked up to them.

"I'm losing," Pierce grumbled.

"I'm hot, on a roll. You should've bet with me. I'm up two thirty-five."

"I'll bet with you on the next game, Fuego," Elise said.

"Now you're talking," he said. "But you've got to bet a trifecta box. You know what that is?"

She shook her head.

"I pick three teams," Fuego explained. "They've got to come in first, second, and third in any order. It's a little tougher than a quiniela box, but it's my bet."

"How much?"

"Minimum of six."

Pierce watched, surprised and a bit annoyed as Elise reach into her purse and handed Fuego a five and a one.

She must have noticed because after Fuego moved toward the counter she told him not to get offended. "I believe in using the advice of experts. You said yourself that Fuego's here a lot more than you."

He shrugged and forced a smile. "I'm not offended. Be right back." He walked away, hoping she wouldn't follow, and got in line behind Fuego. "Listen, I need some help myself."

Fuego laughed and glanced over his shoulder. "You mean you want to go with my bet, too? That's a switch."

"That's not what I'm talking about. I want you to see what you can come up with on the connection between Paul Loften, the dead museum director, and Raymond Andrews."

"Oh, going after a big fish," Fuego said as he approached the window.

"Yeah, the guy I'm working for. Just want to cover my ass." He opened his billfold, peeled off several bills, and stuffed them in Fuego's back pocket.

"You're getting very friendly there, amigo," Fuego said, turning his head.

"Yeah, sure. A friendly payment. See how far you get on four hundred, then get back to me. Good luck."

Pierce bought his quiniela box and rejoined Elise. As they sat down again, she touched his shoulder. "Tell you what. I'll let you in on half my winnings for three bucks."

"Ha. I'll stick with my bet." He regarded her a moment. "You're catching on fast."

As the game began, he wondered if everything for Elise was so black and white. She thought like a man, that's what it was. She'd come here with him, but betting his way wasn't part of the deal. Now she was cheering her teams and glancing between the court and the scoreboard. She'd caught on, all right. She wasn't the type who'd stay in someone else's court for long.

By the middle of the game, Pierce's teams were faring poorly. Elise, however, was still in it, but the baffled look on her face told him she wasn't even aware of that fact.

"Hey, Pierce," she said excitedly as the end of the game neared, "I think I'm winning."

He glanced up at the scoreboard. "You're right. If Six beats Two, you got it. Eight, Six, Three."

"C'mon, Six, kill the bastards," she yelled at the top of her lungs. Her shout was lost among the clamor of the crowd, but he'd heard it clearly, and it gave him pause. Less than a minute later, it was over. Elise leaped to her feet. "I won, didn't I?"

Pierce shook his head, amazed at her luck. "You sure did."

They walked over to the betting area and waited as Fuego collected their winnings.

"God, I've never bet on a game in my life. I can't believe it."

Her enthusiasm was contagious; he couldn't help smiling. "You were right. You went with the expert."

She leaned close to him. "Now you know why I went after you."

Her blue eyes sparkled inches from his own. He inhaled the scent of her perfume. Either this was part of her game, he thought, and she was doing her best to entice him, or this was just how she was. He wasn't in the mood to find out which.

As they drove away from the fronton, Pierce considered what he should do next. He was interested in finding out whatever she would tell him about the crystal skull and her interest in it. If she was involved in the theft and wanted to keep his suspicions to a minimum, she probably would have a story ready for him. He would have to judge it for himself.

"What're you thinking?" she asked.

He wasn't sure what to say and simply shrugged. "Guess I was just thinking how odd it is that I ended up taking you to jai alai."

"Why? Because I won and you didn't?"

"Yeah." He chuckled. "That must be it." But that wasn't it at all. He knew it, and so did she.

He could feel her eyes on him. "Did anyone ever tell you that you look like you're lost in a daydream sometimes? Something about your eyes."

"Maybe it's because I'm a little confused."

"Confused? About what?"

"About why you're so concerned about this crystal skull, and what it is that you've got against Andrews."

"I already told you. I think he stole it."

"What else? There's something more."

She looked down at her hands, didn't respond, then turned her gaze out the window.

"You want to know about Andrews. Let me tell you about him." Her voice was curt, and the edges of her mouth turned down as she spoke. "Your buddy Ray Andrews enticed my father into a business deal several years ago that ruined him."

Pierce glanced over at her, then back to the road. "What kind of business deal?"

"It involved the production of Mayan replicas, mostly ceramic reliefs using the theme of Quetzalcoatl. Each one came with a copy of the legend of the cultural hero. Dad felt the story of the Plumed Serpent should be as well known as the deeds of Zeus. That's why he entered the venture."

"What happened?"

"Andrews and his sales team convinced thousands of people in South America, Europe, and the Orient to pay as much as a hundred grand each for the replicas."

"C'mon, I find that hard to believe."

"No. It happened. The sales pitch was that Mayan shamans had placed spells on the replicas, and that if you bought one before the Harmonic Convergence you'd be protected from natural disasters or attacks by enemies."

"I must have missed that scam."

"That's because there was very little promotion or sales in the United States, which Dad thought was the main point. Then he was astonished when he found out how much people were paying for them and learned about the phony sales pitch that went along with it."

"He hadn't known about it?"

"He had nothing to do with the sales end, and didn't make much himself. Yet, I've seen evidence that total sales in the year and a half period leading up to the Harmonic Convergence exceeded a hundred and sixty-five million dollars."

"Jesus." Pierce slowed for a light. "Well, if Andrews was involved, it's possible. He's always had the Midas touch. So what did your father do?"

Her resentment bubbled like hot soup. "It's not so much what he did, but what happened to him. There were complaints, and investigations in several countries. Everything was in Dad's name. Andrews was never touched, but Dad's reputation was ruined. He lost his credibility, and was driven from the field."

He turned onto Grand Avenue from U.S. 1 and entered Coconut Grove. "Where were you when all this happened?"

"Teaching in Chicago. If I'd known what was going on, Andrews would never have taken advantage of him."

It was guilt and revenge that was driving her, Pierce thought, and maybe that was what the theft was about. Neither spoke as he mulled over what she'd said. As he pulled into her driveway, he had another question. "How did your father meet Andrews?"

"Through Bill. You see, he introduced . . . "

Her voice faded, stopped. She leaned forward, her body tensing as she stared at the house.

"What's wrong?"

"I didn't leave any lights on. I'm sure of it."

There was one on in the living room, and another illuminated an upstairs window. "Anyone else have your keys?"

"No. Except — It better not be him."

"Who?"

"Steve. My ex-husband."

He turned off his engine. "Let's take a look."

They moved swiftly toward the house, their feet whispering through the grass. He tried the door and found it locked. Prowlers rarely entered through a front door, but it wasn't uncommon for them to leave that way. An intruder could still be in the house. She handed him the key and he slipped it into the lock. He turned the knob, pushed open the door. He heard her suck in her breath, and a shiver fanned across his back as he glimpsed the wreckage. The place had been ransacked.

Books and bits of pottery were strewn across the floor, and two armchairs were overturned. Cushions had been torn away from the chairs and couch, and records and tapes had been tossed around. Elise's Mayan calendar lay amid the clutter; it was broken in half. Next to it, a television set lay on its side.

"Oh, God, my pottery."

"Stay right here," he hissed. "I'm getting my gun." He ran to the car, opened the trunk. He took his new .38 from its box and fumbled with the cartridges as he loaded it.

"Hurry," Elise called to him.

"Hold on. Be there in a second."

He hurried to the house and moved in ahead of her. He gripped the gun with both hands as he stepped over piles of books, shattered ceramics, records, and tapes. Holding the gun above his head, he moved carefully toward the back of the house.

He stopped, listened. He heard the honk of a distant horn and the hum of an electrical motor from the next room. He moved ahead, into the kitchen. The refrigerator and freezer doors yawned open, yellow light spilling out over lumpy pools of shadow on the floor and table. He found the light switch, flicked it on. The pantry shelves had been swept clean, and the floor was covered with boxes of pasta and oatmeal dumped over canned goods and bottles of cooking oil and vinegar. Chicken, hamburger, and leftovers were spread across the table.

He stepped over the food and closed the refrigerator and freezer doors. He knelt down and picked up an ice cube tray. The cubes were melting, but still filled the compartments. The place had been trashed within the hour. He set the ice tray down on the kitchen table, walked over to the back door, and turned the handle. It was unlocked.

"Nick!"

Elise stood in the doorway. Her eyes were wide with fear, her voice was a dry croak. "Upstairs. I heard something."

He closed the back door and followed her to the bottom of the staircase. She stopped, her hand lightly touching the railing. "There. Did you hear that?" Her voice was a whisper.

"What?" He froze, listened. Then he heard it, a ripping noise, like clothing being torn apart, coming from upstairs. *The bastard's still here.*

He peered up the shadowy staircase, heard the noise again. It grated at him. Quietly, slowly, he mounted the stairs, the .38 pointing the way.

"Nick," Elise whispered. "Be careful."

He patted the air with his hands and continued up the stairs. He stopped a couple of steps from the top. *Maybe this isn't such a good idea.*

He glanced back over his shoulder and frowned as he saw that Elise was gone. In some odd way, her presence at the foot of the stairs had impelled him forward, had kept him moving toward the noise. Now his courage deserted him. He listened, then heard her voice from somewhere in the living room. She was speaking low, giving her address. She'd called the police.

Just then, a scratching sound drew his attention back to the dark hallway. *What the hell's he doing? Ripping her clothes? The fucker's crazy.*

Cautiously he took another step.

He tried to swallow, but his throat was dry.

He pressed his back against the wall at the top of the stairway. There was a room to the left. The door was open; the room was dark. Quickly he bobbed his head forward and back. The hall to the right was dimly lit and empty. At the end of it, light seeped from under a closed door.

If you're going to do it, then move it.

He crouched low, gripping the gun above his head. He'd rush the bastard, catch him off-guard. But which room was he in? He glanced around the corner again, and was about to rush down the hall toward the light when he caught a flicker of movement out of the corner of his eye. He pulled back, pressed against the wall; his heart pounded. The intruder was in the dark room at the top of the stairs. Just a few feet away.

Pierce's muscles tensed; his palms sweated against the grip of the .38. He waited, but nothing happened. Had he imagined it? Cautiously he poked his head out again.

He's coming.

Pierce aimed, then lowered his gun. "Jesus, cat! You scared the shit out of me!" A furry orange tiger cat sauntered out of the room and down the hall. He took a deep breath, exhaled, then moved down the hall. He stopped outside the room with the light on, turned the knob, inching the door open.

What if the cat wasn't the only one up here? He leaned forward, glimpsed a bedroom with dresser drawers upturned. Clothing — shirts, jeans, blouses, underwear — littered the carpet. Shoeboxes and more clothes were piled on the bed. He pushed the door further open. It squeaked. And just then Elise shouted his name.

Her voice shredded the silence and sliced through him like a hot blade. He turned and raced for the stairs, bounding down them two or three at a time. He spotted Elise backed against a wall next to an open closet door. Her mouth was moving, but nothing was coming out.

"Christ, what happened?"

"He was here. In the closet."

"When? Just now?" He glanced around.

"No. Before. Look." She nodded toward the open door.

He peered into the closet and saw clothes and boxes. Then he saw the inside of the door. Scrawled in red crayon was: YOU CUNT.

Below it was a crude, childlike drawing of a woman with her legs spread, and between them a kitchen knife was jammed into the crimson red, oversized lips. Pierce jerked the knife from the wall. "I'll wash it off."

"No, we better wait for the police." Elise touched his shoulder. "They'll be here any minute."

"All right."

Just then, the orange cat pranced into the room. "There's your upstairs noise. He was scratching a chair or something."

"Mouser, what are you doing in here?" She knelt down and held out her hand. "It's the neighbor's."

The cat took a couple of tentative steps toward her, stopped, hissed at her, then scooted across the room, leaping over a pile of books. Mouser jumped onto a window ledge and disappeared through the opening in the curtains.

Pierce walked over, spread the curtains. "Here's where the creep broke in. He went out the back door." An upper pane of the window was broken and the window was open. He closed it.

Elise was on her way upstairs and he followed her, thinking that she wasn't going to like it. She walked immediately to the room at the top of the stairs and turned the light on. A study, and the intruder hadn't overlooked it. A lamp lay on the floor; nearby was a coffee cup and a telephone. Books were piled in front of an empty bookcase. Stacks of files were strewn from one side of the room to the other, and the drawers of a file cabinet hung open.

She dropped to her knees and ran her fingers over the file folders. "Let me find the *R*s. I've got a file on Andrews. I put it under *Raymond* for this very reason. Here it is." She thumbed through it. "I don't see anything missing."

He craned his neck, trying to see what was in the file. "I didn't tell him about you. I haven't seen him." As soon as he spoke, it occurred to him that Andrews might have hired a detective to watch him.

She snapped the folder shut. "I don't care. He knows." She stood up, looked around. "Oh, God. My bedroom."

She rushed down the hall just as Pierce heard a pounding at the door. "I'll get it." He scrambled down the stairs and was about to open the door when he realized he was still holding his gun. He considered tucking it into the back of his pants, but decided against it. The pounding started again. He looked around, then set the .38 on the overturned television set.

He unlocked the door, opened it. A policewoman quickly looked him over, her hand hovering inches from her holster. "Who're you?"

"Nicholas Pierce."

She was a foot shorter than he was, with blond hair tied in a ponytail. A frown knitted her brow. She was attractive, and would probably be more so if she were wearing something other than a baggy police uniform, he thought. Right now she was all business.

"Where's Elise Simms?"

"That's me," Elise said, hurrying down the stairs. "I was the one who called."

The cop glanced past him, nodded to Elise, then stepped inside. Her eyes suddenly froze on Pierce's .38. "Whose gun?" she asked sharply.

"It's mine. I'm a private investigator."

"Is that right?" Morris Carver walked through the door. "Wrap the gun, Officer. We'll check the registration."

"What are you doing here, Carver? I thought you were a homicide officer."

"I'll ask the questions." He glanced over at the policewoman, who was putting the .38 in a plastic evidence bag. "Check the rest of the house."

"Yes, sir." She handed him the bag and headed upstairs.

"I've had someone tailing you all day," Carver said in a low voice that was like a rumble. "For a change, one arm knew what the other one was doing." He glanced at Elise. "The dispatcher recognized the address when you called as the one we had staked out."

"They should've been here earlier, when the place was getting tossed," Pierce said.

Carver ignored him, moved across the living room, stepped over records, books, tapes. He crossed the dining room with Elise and Pierce behind him and walked into the kitchen. "Anything missing?"

"I don't know," Elise said. "It's hard to tell right now."

Carver walked over to the back door and opened it. "Did you leave this unlocked?" he asked.

"I'm sure I locked it," Elise answered.

"He came in a window and left by that door," Pierce said.

"So you've got it all figured out," Carver muttered, and went about his business.

The cop walked into the kitchen. "Lieutenant, there's something you should see out here." Her face was impassive, but her tone was urgent.

She led them to the closet at the bottom of the stairs and pointed to the scrawling on the inside door.

"So. We've got an artist of sorts," Carver said.

"There's a knife on the floor," the cop said. "I think it was sticking in the wall. There's a hole."

Carver squatted his heavy torso down on one knee. He picked up the knife from the floor, holding it by the edges of the blade, and glanced at Elise.

"I pulled it out of the wall," Pierce said.

Carver stood up, turned on him. "What kind of detective are you, Mr. Pierce? Don't you know enough not to tamper with evidence?"

"I didn't think about it," he said quietly. "She was upset."

No one said anything for a moment. Carver rubbed the nape of his bull neck. "I want to talk to each of you, separately."

While Carver questioned Elise upstairs in her study, Pierce returned all the perishables to the refrigerator and freezer and scoured the obscenity from the closet door with cleanser and a scrub brush. When he was finished, the drawing and words were still visible. Elise would need to paint the door before the image would be completely obliterated. He'd just closed the door when Carver joined him in the living room.

The detective walked immediately to the door and opened it. "Pierce, did I say you could wash the fucking evidence off the door?" Carver let out a long sigh and shook his head. "You do know that cases are sometimes solved by matching handwriting?"

Pierce knew. He ran a hand through his hair. "You can still make it out."

"Sit down."

For the next several minutes, they went over what happened from the time he and Elise arrived at the house. Finally the burly detective put his notebook away, shook his head, and rose from the couch.

"It's funny, Pierce. That's twice now you showed up around trouble in one week. How do you figure that?"

"I don't know, and I don't find it funny."

Carver picked up a broken ceramic frog that still held a surfboard in its remaining arm, examined it a moment. "What do you think this guy was after?"

Pierce shrugged. "No idea. It might have been someone trying to scare her."

Carver laid down the frog. He moved over closer to Pierce and his dark eyes focused on him. "We put a man in the gatehouse at Raymond Andrews's condominium the other day. We couldn't help but notice that you stopped by for a visit. Stayed close to two hours."

"He's an old friend. He asked me to look into the theft of the skull."

"I got the impression from Simms that you were doing the same thing for her."

Pierce gazed down at the floor as if he were looking for something amid the mess. "Then you got the wrong idea. I'm working for Andrews."

Carver stared at him, shook his head. "One way or another, Pierce, you're going to get your ass kicked. I can see it coming. See you around."

Twelve

"Look, maybe you should just drop me off at a motel, Nick. I'll be fine," Elise said as they drove through downtown. It was one-thirty, and the city looked abandoned. The only sign of life was a man shuffling along a dark sidewalk and another huddled in a doorway.

Pierce glanced over at her as he turned on Biscayne. She was slumped in the seat, her arms crossed. "Whatever. But my offer still stands."

"I don't want to put you out."

"You're not."

She would have to make up her mind fast, because he was nearing the turnoff for the causeway.

"You sure?"

"Positive."

"Thanks, I just couldn't stay in the house tonight."

"Understandable. So what do you think of Carver?"

"What do you mean?"

"I don't know. What do you think of him?"

"If you're asking me if I think he's the cop Paul Loften hired, I doubt it."

"Why?"

"For one thing, it would be quite a coincidence that he just happens to investigate the case that he's perpetrated."

He considered her point for a minute. "Maybe he set that up, too. He would probably know where he had to be and what he had to be doing to get it assigned to him. I mean, he *is* a homicide investigator."

"I hadn't thought of it that way." Her voice was flat.

"Did he ask you about the skull?"

"Sure he did — and he asked me about Andrews, too."

Pierce thought it over as they crossed the causeway. If Andrews was behind the theft and murder and Carver was also involved, why would the cop be pursuing Andrews as a suspect? Unless he was trying to cover his ass. Something about it didn't feel right. He somehow couldn't imagine Carver taking orders from Andrews. Not unless Carver owed him for something.

"This is so goddamn typical," he griped after they'd turned from the causeway and slowly cruised his neighborhood. "No place to park."

"Let's go get a drink," Elise suggested. "I could use one. We'll find a spot when we get back."

"It's pretty late. The hotel bars are closing up."

"Then let's not go to a hotel. Take me someplace different. But not the Jack of Clubs, please."

He laughed and drove over to Collins and headed north. He slowed for a red light at Twentieth Street. Even the scene along the string of porno and seedy strip joints was subdued tonight. The sidewalks were deserted, except for a red-wigged woman in a shiny silver miniskirt.

The light changed and he glanced to his left as he passed the Beach Museum. It was dark and silent. Pierce was about to ask her if she'd visited the museum since Loften's death when she pointed at a nightclub on the next corner. "Let's go there."

He turned onto the side street and parked across from the Place Pigalle. "You sure?"

"They serve drinks, don't they?"

"They sure do." He found a parking space with no problem and turned off the ignition. He looked over the nightclub. The engine ticked loudly in the silence.

The Place Pigalle was one of those joints where private eyes were supposed to hang out and absorb the atmosphere. Here, a dick was supposed to find contacts. He'd been here once, and he'd left no wiser.

As they walked across the street, Elise hooked her arm through his. "This a strip joint, isn't it?"

"Sure is."

They were met at the door by a size-sixteen woman in a wraparound leopard skirt, high heels, and a blue wig. She wore thick hexagonal glasses with fish-eye lenses that made him dizzy. He nodded, blinked, and headed into the Pigalle's cool, dark womb.

The nightclub had been around a long time. In its heyday in the fifties, there were shows here, fabulous spectacles with live bands and parades of leggy women wrapped in pink boas. Now, the glamour was tarnished with time, but the show went on.

The stage was straight ahead and lit up. On it, a topless woman was gyrating her belly. The Human Earthquake, Pierce thought. There were about a dozen customers. All but a couple of them sat at the front tables with the best views.

"Attentive group, aren't they?" Elise said as they sat down at a table between the bar and stage.

She watched the dancer on stage peel off the remaining patch of cloth from her crotch as she pranced and strutted for the crowd. "No way in a million years I could do that. Could you?"

Pierce chuckled. "Never occurred to me as an option."

"So you come here often?"

"I met a client here once. A guy who wanted me to find his missing teenage daughter. He was sure she was working as a stripper at one of these places along here."

"Was that the same girl you looked for at the Harmonic Convergence?"

Pierce smiled wryly. "The same. Her father was pursuing every avenue."

"What happened? Did you find her?"

"Naw. She found herself. She came home on her own. Turns out she ran off to a fundamentalist Bible camp near Orlando and didn't want to tell her Jewish father about it."

"I guess he had her all wrong."

"Yeah, he got the pagans and Christians mixed up."

"What'll you have to drink, friends?" a waiter in a bow tie asked.

Elise ordered a Scotch on the rocks, and Pierce asked for a beer. As she turned her attention back to the stage, he watched her surreptitiously — the way her fingers tapped the edge of the table in time to the music, the curve of her jaw, the rich brown of her hair. This was obviously not the sort of place she frequented. She was escaping, he decided, blotting out any thoughts about what had happened this evening, delaying the worries and concern about its meaning.

The stage went dark as the act ended. The music changed to a fast dance beat, and their drinks arrived. Pierce held up his glass and tried to think of an appropriate toast, but she beat him to it. "To better times," she said, and clicked her glass to his.

"I bet you've never gone to a strip joint with Bill Redington."

"Hardly," she replied, with a laugh.

"How do you know him?"

She sipped her drink and regarded him. "You still playing detective with me?"

"I'm just trying to get everything straight. That's all."

"He's an old friend of my father's. He used to visit us in Guatemala and grill my father about his knowledge of the Mayan legends. They'd go off together for days, visiting the old shamans, the keepers of the mythology."

"After my conversation with him at his office, I can believe that."

"Nick, what kind of person do you think I am?"

"Jesus, what kind of question is that?"

"Just tell me."

"You're sort of a chameleon."

She smiled, leaned her elbow on the table, resting her chin on her palm. "Is that your way of saying you don't trust me?"

"I didn't say that."

"Maybe I just don't fit in one of your little boxes." She moved her hands about, making a rectangular shape. "This person fits here. That one fits there. But when someone comes along who doesn't fit into one of them, you get confused. Like that little blond cop tonight. I saw you trying to figure her out. But cute little women and tough cops aren't supposed to fit together, are they?"

Pierce absently ran his fingers over the bump on his head. It was still tender, but not so noticeable now. "I guess I'll have to create a special little box for you, and one for the cop, too."

"Maybe I'm wrong," she replied. "But I think you've already got me in a box — one for people you don't trust."

"That would be a crowded box. In my work, it's not wise to trust too many people."

"That's too bad. If you can't trust people, your life can't be too happy."

"What about you? You certainly haven't got much good to say about Raymond Andrews."

She looked across the room at the stage as another dancer stepped out, dressed in high heels and a miniskirted cowboy getup. As she undulated about the stage, the hat slipped sideways, threatening to fall. She held it in place for a few dips and turns, then flung it to the side.

"I have nothing good to say about him, and for good reason," Elise said, turning back to him.

"So you're holding a grudge."

Her mouth tightened as she leaned forward. "You saw what he did to the house. He was responsible."

"I told you before, I didn't tell him about you."

"Doesn't matter. He knows; he has other ways."

Pierce was puzzled by her insistence on Andrews's guilt. "Why the hell would he want to wreak havoc with your life? Tell me that."

She stared at him as if weighing her next comment. "I guess Bill didn't tell you who owns the skull."

"He said some Scotsman named John Mahoney."

"He's my father."

Wonderful. What else hadn't she told him?

She explained that he'd lived in Scotland part-time for more than twenty years, ever since he spent a year on a fellowship at the University of Edinburgh. After he was discredited as a result of the replica scam, he'd moved there permanently.

He sat back in his chair when she finished and gazed at the dancer whose clothes were slowly falling away. The woman seemed unreal, as if she were a celluloid image on a screen. Elise was real, and what she'd just told him made her interest in the skull all the more understandable. He sipped his beer and felt her watching him.

He leaned forward so he wouldn't have to raise his voice. "Why the hell didn't he take the three million Ray offered?"

"The skull means more to him than money." Elise looked down at the table, lost in thought. Her eyes closed, and for a moment he thought she was about to cry. "Let's get out of here, Nick."

It worked out as Elise had said it would; he found a parking spot near the apartment building with no difficulty. She grabbed her overnight bag and followed him upstairs. As they entered the apartment, he asked if she wanted a nightcap.

"No thanks. I'm really tired now."

"Okay. I'll make up your bed." He took the cushions off the couch, and Elise helped him pull out the sleeper. He stepped back, noticed how she shifted her glance from him to the bed, then back again. "Something wrong?"

"Got any sheets?"

"Oh, yeah." He walked over to the linen closet and returned with sheets and a light blanket.

"How long have you lived here?" she asked as they made the bed.

"Since my ex-wife and I split up. I'm divorced, like you."

She didn't say anything, and he watched her as she tucked the sheet in the corner. He wondered what she looked like naked, and what it would be like in bed with her, and he wondered if she was thinking similar thoughts. But when she spoke he realized that there was something else on her mind.

"I bet you checked the court records," she said. "What else did you find out?"

"You instigated the divorce."

Elise straightened the sheet at the bottom of the bed, then stood up. "We were going in different directions."

"I know what you mean. My marriage went sour when I quit the travel agency."

"You get along now?"

Pierce shrugged, feeling uneasy at the mention of his old life and his present relationship with Tina. "Sort of. You ever see Steve?"

"No, never, and I don't want to see him, either." She dropped her bag on the edge of the bed and unzipped it.

Then why, he wondered, had she blurted that he might be in the house when they arrived from jai alai? And why had the old lady across the street said she saw him visit her regularly? It was time he looked up Steve Simms, he decided. "I'll put some fresh towels in the bathroom for you."

A few minutes later, he said good night and retired to the bedroom. He lay in bed, listening to the sounds of another person in the apartment. He heard the toilet flush, the water running in the sink. Footsteps in the hallway. The sleeper creaking.

Why had she lied to him about her ex-husband, and what else was she lying about? Then he remembered "Monica." She was a lie. And he recalled something else from the court records. Steve spent a lot of time in the gym. A fanatic. He wondered if he also had a scar on his jaw.

He was too tired to think any more about it. He closed his eyes and dozed off with Elise and Monica juxtaposed in his mind like twin sisters. Sisters of suspicion.

Subdued morning light filtered into Pierce's westward-facing bedroom window. He blinked his eyes open, focusing on the pale blue wall of the bedroom. He'd heard something.

Now he heard it again. A voice. He sat up, confused. What the hell? He sniffed, smelling the aroma of coffee.

Elise. He'd forgotten. But who was she talking to? He leaned forward, listening. She said something about eleven o'clock, then he heard a click. The phone.

"Morning," he called out, his voice hoarse with sleep.

"You're awake. Can I open the door?"

"Sure." He tugged the sheet around his waist.

The door swung open, and Elise was holding a steaming coffee mug. She was wearing an oversized T-shirt that reached to the middle of her thighs. Her hair was mussed, falling across her forehead. She raised the mug. "Hope you don't mind. I've been up a while and couldn't wait."

"Not at all."

He noticed the light sprinkling of freckles across her cheeks as she smiled. No makeup on, and she looked great. He cleared his throat.

She made a face and looked apologetic. "Sorry if I woke you."

"No, it was just odd to hear someone else in the apartment. How about going out to breakfast?"

"Fine with me," she answered, and turned away. "But I have to be home by eleven. I just made an appointment with my cleaning service. I've got a big job for them."

It was nearly nine by the time they pulled up to the Edison. "You ever eat breakfast here?" Pierce asked as they stepped out of the car in the alley behind the hotel.

"No, but then I don't have a parking spot here with my name on it, either."

Pierce led the way to the entrance, and they were seated at his usual table. "Must be nice to have your office right above a good restaurant and across the street from the beach."

"I guess I take it too much for granted."

The waitress appeared with menus. "Dolly, this is Elise."

"Nice to meet you."

"Dolly used to work at the Fontainebleu back in its glory days."

"Really?" Elise said.

Dolly waved a hand at her. "You should have seen it. All the big stars — Sinatra, Gleason, Rooney, Martin."

She fixed a hand on her hip, and Pierce knew she was about to tell a story.

"One morning I was carrying two cups of coffee and who do I bump into but Jerry Lewis. I dropped them both, and you know what he did? He went right into the kitchen. I thought he was going to get me fired." She shook her head. Pierce had heard the story several times, but she talked as if it had happened yesterday. "You know what he did? He came out with a mop and cleaned up the whole mess. Jerry Lewis mopping our floor. I couldn't believe it."

"That must have been something," Elise said politely.

"Those were some times. I'll get you guys your coffee, then take your order."

"The local character," Elise remarked when Dolly left.

"You come here often and you'll hear all her stories. Keep coming and you'll hear them all again."

After Dolly returned with their coffee and they'd ordered, Elise asked Pierce what his plans were for the day. He was going to see Andrews, but decided that evasiveness was the best tactic. "I've got a meeting in the Grove at noon. So I can drop you off at home and bum around the Grove for an hour. Unless you'd like me to help with me cleanup."

She shook her head. "Thanks for the offer, but I'll let the cleaning crew handle it." She stirred cream into her coffee. "Let me guess. You're going to see Andrews at his office in Grove Plaza."

He sipped from his cup, watching her over the rim. "You seem to know quite a bit about him."

"More than you, I think."

He doubted it. "Tell me something else."

"He owns Grove Plaza."

Pierce wasn't impressed. "He's the major investor. Tell me something I don't know.

"Okay. He founded Noster Mundus."

"What's that?"

"A secret society. The name is Latin. It means Our World."

"Never heard of it," Pierce said.

"That's not surprising. They don't seek publicity."

"Tell me more."

"It involves a select group of influential people from this country, Europe, Latin America, Asia, and the Mideast. Their goal is to shape world events for their own purposes."

Elise Simms, he decided, was carrying her share of bombshells. Last night it had been her father and his relationship with Ray Andrews. Today it was a secret society. "Sounds ominous."

"Not necessarily. You could compare them to other secret societies like the Knights of Malta, Opus Dei, or the Moral Re-Armament. They're religious-oriented and dedicated to the idea that a small group of people can have a great impact on the world. Quite a few well-known statesmen and industrialists are in their ranks. Lee Iacocca and Alexander Haig, for instance, are members of the Knights of Malta. So are William F. Buckley and Senator Jeremiah Denton."

"And Andrews's group is similar?"

"I'm getting to that."

Dolly arrived with breakfast. "Boy, we're busy this morning. I'll get you refills as soon as I can."

Pierce nodded, but kept his eyes fixed on Elise. As soon as Dolly moved on, he waited for her to continue.

Elise ate a few bites of scrambled eggs. "Noster Mundus is a latter-day version. It's only about ten years old. It's like the others, yet it's not."

Pierce listened as she explained that in some ways the organization more closely resembled a turn-of-the-century secret society called the Golden Dawn.

"How is the Golden Dawn different from the others?"

Dolly stopped by with the coffeepot and refilled their cups. They both ate in silence until she was gone. "The Knights and the others are basically international good-old-boy networks," she explained. "The more international connections members create, the greater the opportunity to mold the world the way they want it. The Golden Dawn and Noster Mundus, on the other hand, are founded on the principle that change in the world is created through change in the individual."

She took a bite of toast, chewed it. "You see, they look at human willpower as a real force that can be trained and put to use to create whatever you want."

He wanted to find out everything he could about the group, and he wanted an independent source. But first he'd see what else she had to say. "What do they want?"

"From what I can tell, their intent is to become a major force that governments will look to for direction on global matters."

"You think this Noster Mundus has anything to do with the crystal skull?"

Elise smiled, stabbed her home fries with her fork, and took a couple of more bites. "Dad says they use the crystal skull in their emblem."

Thirteen

The parking garage below Grove Plaza looked like a salesroom for exotic luxury cars. Among the Mercedes, BMWs, Volvos, Peugeots, and Porsches were a Lamborghini, a Bentley, and a Rolls. Pierce walked past at least half of the cars before he reached the stairway in the corner.

One level up, the courtyard was decorated in ornate bronze sculptures, a bubbling fountain, and lush tropical vegetation. The place bustled with well-heeled shoppers, people with time and money. It was as if no one needed to work anymore; their jobs were simply to find ways to spend their excess money.

He walked around the fountain where Andrews was supposed to meet him. Surrounding the courtyard were two levels of glitzy shops and galleries with swirled stucco walls and stained-glass windows. There were a couple of restaurants, a nightclub, a private club, a health spa. Above the shops was a level of offices, then two levels of condominiums.

Coconut Grove had once been a picturesque village of quaint, tree-shrouded cottages and homey storefront shops, a Bohemian haven. Now, thanks to developers like Ray Andrews, it catered to the chic and trendy. The new Grove thrived on wall-to-wall consumerism and high-rise, high-cost living. You could buy a half-dozen brands of designer ice cream on the central streets of the village, but you'd have to look hard to find a loaf of bread or a hammer. Struggling painters, sculptors, and performing artists now struggled elsewhere.

Andrews was nowhere in sight, so he walked into a clothing store and casually priced some of the items. Two-ten for a shirt, ninety-five for a tie. In a couple of years, a thrift shop could use the same price tags on the item just by changing the dollars to cents. He wandered over to a rack of socks marked at forty dollars a pair. No basement bargains here. Nearby was a kid, about ten or eleven, who was coveting a pair of designer pants.

"They're only a hundred and fifty, Mom."

"You just got a pair last week, Avery."

The kid threw his head back in a nonchalant gesture. "I'll put it on my card."

Wonderful, Pierce thought as he turned and headed for the door. As he did, he spotted a familiar face, which quickly disappeared from sight. He was sure it was Neil Bellinger, but by the time he stepped through the doorway, the not-so-plainclothes cop was nowhere in sight. Scared off by the prices, maybe.

He didn't have much time to think about it, because Andrews was standing with K.J. by the fountain. He walked over and greeted them.

"What do you think of the place?" Andrews asked as K.J. stepped back from the two men.

"Pretty impressive. Now I know what they mean when the press says you're one of those responsible for turning the Grove into a yuppie theme park."

He said it as a joke, but Andrews didn't laugh. He gave him a once-over, taking in his casual khaki pants and cotton pullover. He adjusted his yellow tie and smiled. "All that hippy-dippy shit is history, Nicholas. The Grove is upscale living."

Profitable, too, I bet, he thought. "Well, looks like business is flourishing."

"I won't deny that. The square footage rental cost is at the top of the scale for commercial property, and we've had full occupancy since the second month of operation. I've got an office here myself."

"You've got the Midas touch, Ray."

Andrews nodded. "It's a shame when myths are adopted for commercial use, isn't it? You can't mention Midas or the Wheel of Fortune without a modern-day image imposing on the myth." Then he turned to Pierce, smiled, and clapped a hand on his shoulder. "You see, I've got concerns about protecting the past as well as improving on the present."

He gestured across the plaza toward a gleaming brass-and-glass elevator. "C'mon, let's have some lunch."

A chill nipped at Pierce's lower back as they moved toward the cage. It was the sensation he always felt when he considered riding in an elevator. "I think I'll take the stairs and meet you."

Andrews looked nonplussed. "Wait a minute. You mean, you *still* don't ride elevators?"

"I like the exercise," Pierce hedged, and glanced at K.J., who was staring suspiciously at him.

"Oh, c'mon, Nicholas. It's a roomy glass elevator. You've got to experience it. And I promise we won't get stuck. Christ, we're only going up one floor."

Pierce stared at it. One floor. It can't be that bad for just one lousy floor, he thought. "Okay, let's go."

"I'd forgotten about that time in the library," Andrews said as they stepped into the elevator.

Pierce barely heard him. He watched the doors whisper shut and stared straight ahead. He tried not to think about the incident Andrews had referred to, but the memories marched through him with impunity.

Andrews had used one of the conference rooms in Columbia University's library as a meeting place when his Latin American suppliers were in town. While they'd bargained about the cost and number of shipments, Pierce had studied at a desk outside the room and kept an eye out for anyone approaching the door or acting suspicious. On this particular Sunday night, the negotiations had lasted until a few minutes before the library closed.

Pierce signaled Andrews, tapping his watch. The Colombians left by the stairs, while he and Andrews took an elevator on the other side of the building. When it stopped between floors, there was no one around to help.

Pierce vaguely remembered sitting on the floor, listening to Andrews boast about his deal as they waited for someone to show up. The new scheme involved transporting the twenty or thirty kilos of marijuana a week by boat from Santa Marta to Cartagena, where they were loaded in suitcases aboard a cruise ship that stopped for several hours to fill its water tanks. When the ship docked in New York, crewmembers slipped the extra suitcases through customs, which at the time was lax. No one, after all, suspected that tourists spending a few hours in Cartagena would make drug deals. The cargo was then sent by truck to a warehouse and distributed to a network of dealers.

Andrews, who never touched the pot or made direct payments, told Pierce that he was no longer needed to convey messages. Instead, he wanted him to deliver cash to a contact in Bogota. He could make one trip a month and he'd make enough so he could quit his part-time job and live better than most students. But Pierce just wanted out; smuggling was a dead end, and he sensed trouble. He didn't care how easy Andrews told him it would be. If it was so easy, he could do it himself, and he told him so.

They'd argued — but that was all he could remember. He didn't even recall how they'd gotten out of the elevator; all he knew was that since then he'd never been comfortable in one. But at least Andrews had never asked him to go to Colombia again.

The glass box whispered to a stop and they stepped out. "There, that wasn't so tough, was it?"

Pierce's breath caught in his throat, his legs were rubbery, and he felt as though he'd been in suspended animation while shifting from one time frame to another. But he hadn't let the panic take over, and he hadn't passed out. He could still breathe. On top of it, Andrews had been with him. Maybe that was all he needed, maybe now his fear of elevators had been vanquished forever.

At the entrance of the restaurant, the host greeted Andrews by name. Even though several people were waiting to be seated, they were immediately ushered to a corner table; Andrews was at home in his kingdom.

Twice during the meal, a waiter handed King Raymond a fresh linen napkin and removed the old one, which still looked clean to Pierce. At one point, the tine of Andrews's fork touched the tablecloth and he asked for a replacement. Before allowing the waiter to pour his wine, he held up the Waterford crystal glass and carefully inspected it for water stains. He did the same with his water glass.

Pierce still vividly remembered Andrews's pickiness and his fanatic concern about cleanliness during their year as roommates. He'd changed his bed sheets daily, put name tags on his towels, washed his hands a couple of dozen times a day. He'd even told Pierce that when he was wealthy he'd put on new underwear every day, wear it once and once only, and throw it away.

Andrews chatted throughout the meal, talking about an office building he'd bought in London, a banquet he'd attended in Paris. Pierce nodded, offered a few comments, and across the table K.J. listened to it all, eating his meal and watching. He wondered if there were any women in Andrews's life. He considered asking, but decided against it. If there were, they obviously weren't a big part of it. Something else occurred to him. He recalled what Elise had said about the man's apparent interest in time, and he was curious about what he would say about the topic. When there was a lull in the conversation, he commented on Andrews's watch, an expensive Rolex.

Andrews looked down at his wrist and shrugged. "I've had this one for a few years now. Let me tell you a secret, Nicholas. When you have enough money that you can have anything, you tend to lose your desire for personal material things."

If that was true, Pierce thought, why the hell had he offered three million dollars for a crystal skull? Pierce could see it: the skull on a shelf next to Andrews's clocks, a maid dusting it twice a week. On second thought, maybe Andrews saw the skull as something other than a material possession. "I noticed you had a lot of clocks in your apartment."

Andrews gave him an odd look, a defensive one, Pierce thought, then it was gone, and he was smiling. "I've picked them up here and there over the years. Some people collect coins or stamps. My thing is clocks."

Not until after they finished their meal and coffee and tea had arrived, did Andrews bring up the investigation. "I had a chat with a police detective named Carver this morning. I guess you've met him."

"He knows you hired me."

Andrews lifted his tea bag from his cup. "He said I hired a suspect."

"What does he think, I shot Loften and knocked myself out?" Pierce laughed. "Where's the gun?"

Andrews looked amused, unconcerned. "Don't feel bad. He implied that I was involved, too. Let's not worry about Lieutenant Carver. Tell me what you've found. Maybe we'll give him a lead."

Pierce wiped his mouth with his napkin and set it aside. "You ever heard of a woman named Elise Simms?"

Andrews sat back in his chair and shook his head. "Who is she?"

He told him what he knew about her: her career; her association with the museum's Mayan project; how he met her as Monica; who her father was. He told him about the tape and how they'd returned from jai alai to find the house ransacked. All he left out was her suspicion that Andrews was behind the break-in and her hatred of him.

Andrews twisted the gold band on his finger as he listened. But his face remained inscrutable. Pierce might as well have been telling him the plot of a movie Andrews had already seen. He interrupted once to ask why they'd gone to jai alai.

"It just worked out that way. It wasn't anything I planned." Jesus, what about everything else I just told you? he thought. Andrews hadn't even remarked on the accusations on the tape. Pierce wanted an explanation. He needed one.

Andrews shifted himself in the chair, moving closer to Pierce. "So she knows you're working for me. That's good. What about Redington?"

He touched briefly on his visit to the professor. "He told me he gave the cops a copy of the tape."

"Well, that explains why Lieutenant Carver visited me, but he didn't say anything about a tape."

"Redington also told me that John Mahoney wasn't interested in selling the skull."

"Unfortunately, he has been very reluctant to sell. Until recently, that is."

"What do you mean?"

Andrews brushed a speck of food off the tablecloth in front of him. "A few months ago, we reopened negotiations. We were finally close to a deal. We were keeping it quiet, and I didn't think anyone knew. Then this Loften thing happens. I think you can appreciate my concern . . . and understand why I hired you."

Since Andrews was finally loosening his tongue, Pierce pressed him. "But why did you want the skull?"

"It's more than just unusual, and I can afford it. And its value will continue to escalate. Besides, I wanted to end this silly argument with Mahoney."

"You're saying the fraudulent sales of the replicas never happened?"

Andrews waited as the waiter refilled Pierce's coffee cup and poured fresh water for Andrews's tea. "Sure it did. It was a scheme by a few of the sales reps overseas. I had no idea what was going on."

Pierce crossed his arms over his chest. "Simms thinks it was your idea. She says you ruined her father's reputation."

"He ruined it himself!" Andrews snapped. "He spent so much time studying the Mayan shamans that he adopted their beliefs. He lost his perspective."

Andrews stirred his tea a moment. "Don't let her fool you, Nicholas. I didn't recognize Elise Simms's name, but I knew Mahoney had a daughter. The last time we talked about the skull, he told me she was after it. He said they hadn't talked to each other in years, then suddenly she wants the skull. I think she's behind the theft — and set up the ransacking of her house to protect herself. She wants the cops to think I was behind it."

Pierce shifted his eyes to K.J., who was doing some sort of isometric exercises in his chair, first pressing his hands down on the armrests, then pulling up on the bottom of the chair. When he saw Pierce's gaze, he immediately stopped. Pierce flicked his eyes back to Andrews. "She must really have wanted the skull, to go to that length."

"She's only told her side of the story. My association with her father and Redington goes back to when I formed a service organization called Noster Mundus."

Pierce nodded, realizing that in recounting everything else, he'd forgotten to mention the organization. "She said something about it, but not that her father or Redington were associated with it."

Andrews smiled and leaned back in his chair. "They were charter members."

"What exactly is Noster Mundus?"

"It's basically an international goodwill group."

"Simms called it a secret society," Pierce said.

Andrews laughed and looked over at K.J., who was doing his isometrics again. "We maintain rules of secrecy, sure. But that's traditional for many service organizations. The truth is, most of us in the group take advantage of our contacts for business as well as goodwill purposes. In fact, that's how Mahoney and I got started in business together."

"I guess she only told me whatever would make you look bad. You see, she wanted me to investigate you for her while I'm investigating her for you. That was the gist of it."

"You hear that, K.J.?" The bodyguard took out his notepad, jotted something, and handed it to his boss. Andrews glanced at it, smiled, passed it to Pierce. "Real cute," the message said.

"Let's be frank, Nicholas. You know I've gotten my hands dirty. I was involved in the marijuana trade back in the old days. But hell, I would give away every cent of my fortune before I'd go out and kill anyone for a goddamn chunk of quartz crystal."

Pierce nodded.

"I appreciate you coming forward with this. It's good to know how she thinks. I'm curious, though . . . What did you tell her when she asked if you'd work for her?"

Pierce shrugged. "I said I'd think about it."

Andrews clasped his hands behind his head. "What the hell. Go ahead and play with her. Maybe you can find something out about the twin skull. My feeling is that she has a lead on it, and she wants both of them."

"She hasn't said anything to me about it yet, and Redington talks as if he's not sure it even exists."

Andrews spoke with an unexpected fervency. "It does exist, and it will be found."

He reached inside his coat pocket, slipped out an envelope, and passed it to Pierce. "I think you deserve the rest of the money I offered. You've done a terrific job in such a short time."

Pierce hesitated.

"Go ahead, take it. Put it away. I don't want any argument." He motioned with his hand.

Pierce glanced over at K.J., who was pushing his palms together and gritting his teeth. He stuffed the envelope into his pocket. He didn't like what he was doing, didn't like the awkward situation of playing one side against the other, but it seemed the only available option at the moment. The fact was he didn't know which of them to believe, and that just made it all the worse.

"I'm going to be out of town for a few days," Andrews said. "I'll let you know when I get back." He pushed his chair away from the table and shook Pierce's hand, sealing their agreement. "It's good seeing you again. Kind of like old times."

Yeah, old times, Pierce thought as they left the restaurant. That's exactly what worried him. He didn't want to repeat those old times. Not in any form. They walked as far as the elevator and waited. Andrews was going upstairs to his office, and Pierce hoped the elevator would be going in Andrews's direction; he'd immediately head for the stairs. But a red arrow above the door was pointing down when the door slid open. "Thanks for lunch, Ray," he said, and stepped aboard, his gut sinking.

The door hissed closed. If I came up in it, he told himself, I can go down. He gazed out through the tinted glass, and suddenly his stomach knotted. It wasn't the elevator, though. Standing below him in the courtyard, staring directly at him, was the hulking figure of Morris Carver. He glanced to his right at the staircase, wishing he'd taken it. But then he spotted Neil Bellinger covering the stairs. They must have been there all along, watching and waiting.

As the elevator door slid open, the hulking black man stepped up to him. "Afternoon, Mr. Pierce." He made the greeting sound menacing.

"What're you doing here?"

"That's good, Pierce. Same thing I was going to ask you. But since you asked first, me and Neil came here for lunch. Funny thing — we couldn't afford the prices on the menu of that fancy place upstairs." He turned as Bellinger walked up. "Didn't you think that restaurant was sort of expensive?"

Bellinger smiled at Pierce. "Yeah, I guess, Mo. So what's new today, Nick?" Bellinger sounded as affable as ever.

"Lunch with his old buddy Ray, and a little shopping," Carver answered.

Bellinger adjusted his tie, pointed over his shoulder. "You see that shop over there, Nick? You can get a tie for a hundred thirty-nine ninety-five." He grinned playfully at Pierce. "A damn nice tie, too, and check out their sport coats."

Pierce noticed Carver eyeing the envelope that protruded from the corner of his pocket.

"Hell, you can afford it," Carver chimed in. "You're working for Mr. Big Money."

"Maybe I am," Pierce snapped. "If that's against the law, I want to hear about it."

Carver poked a finger toward Pierce's pocket. "I bet you got a nice cash payment in that envelope."

"Lay off him, Mo," Bellinger snapped.

Carver crossed his arms and sidled up to Pierce like a baseball manager arguing with an umpire. "Maybe you're not working for Andrews. I could accept that. Maybe you've done the job already."

"What are you talking about? You actually think I had something to do with Loften's murder?"

"Here's what I think. Your part was to get Loften to take the skull out of the safe. Then you signaled the killer somehow, and the rest is history."

"Afraid that doesn't hold water, Carver. If that's the case, what am I doing hanging around Andrews in public, trying to implicate both of us?"

"Hey, who said anything about Andrews being involved? Did you, Neil?"

"Not me."

"Let's just say Andrews is behind it, since you brought it up. If that's the case, he must've wanted that skull real bad."

"Think about it," Pierce said. "If he were paying me off today for my part in a murder, don't you think he'd do it a little more discreetly?"

"People do weird shit all the time. One guy in our fine city killed his girlfriend, cut off her head, walked outside naked, and threw the head at a cop. How's that for subtle?"

"Listen, guys. I'd like to stand around the courtyard here and bullshit with you all day, but I'm busy. You mind if I go about my business?"

"Have a real nice day, Mr. Pierce," Carver said dryly.

Bellinger took a step closer. "No offense, Nick, but you ought to take those pants to a dry cleaner's. They'd look a lot nicer with firm creases. If you hang around with guys like Andrews, you want to look a little more polished."

"Thanks for the advice." Pierce walked away, feeling the eyes of the detectives burning into his back.

Fourteen

Intense purple thunderheads were assembling to the west over the Everglades, and even though the sun still shone, there was an ominous purple tint to the afternoon. June was just days away, and the pending storm seemed to announce that summer, the "off-season," the time of torrential downpours, afternoon boomers, and hurricane threats, was about to arrive.

Pierce's windows were rolled up against the heat and humidity, and his air conditioner blew cool air against his face. By the time he reached the Edison and pulled into his parking spot in the alley, large drops splattered his windshield. He hustled around the side of the building, glancing once toward the band of ink-colored ocean. He ducked into the hotel lobby and climbed the stairs to the mezzanine.

The travel agency was deserted, as if summer and the approaching storm had chased everyone away. But then he remembered it was also Saturday. Pierce heard his phone ringing and quickly unlocked the door. By the time he reached his desk, he heard his recorded voice saying he wasn't in the office. He snapped up the phone, shutting off the recorder. "Pierce."

"There you are. You should just say 'hello' or 'Mr. Pierce.' You sound like you are spitting when you answer that way."

"Hi, Tina."

"When are you getting a secretary?"

"I don't know. What do you want?"

"Why do you not return my calls?"

He rolled his eyes toward the ceiling, resisting the urge to hang up and reenter his office. "Tina, I just walked in the door."

"I found two articles in psychology journals by William Redington, and also a book on mythology he edited."

"Good. Can you send the articles?"

"This is not a mailhouse," she said indignantly. "You are trying to avoid me. I know you."

Pierce paced back and forth, twisting the telephone cord around his hand. "I've been busy."

"I talked to Fuego this morning. He said he is working for you."

"He's helping on a case," Pierce said, knowing that Fuego wouldn't tell Tina any details.

"You pay him; you never pay me."

"Tina, the library pays you," Pierce said evenly.

"Yes, and I have to work all weekend."

"Then I'll meet you downtown for lunch tomorrow," he said, making an effort to appease her.

"That is better. Make it brunch at eleven at Paco's."

"Sunday brunch it is. Don't forget the articles."

"Do you want me to look up anything else?"

He wanted to wean himself of his dependence on Tina for research. Yet, he was also curious about Noster Mundus, and anyhow he was already planning on seeing her. "Well, if you're not busy . . . "

When he finally rang off, he sat down at his desk, slipped on his wire-framed glasses, and flipped through his mail. He spent a few minutes calling the two Stephen Simmses and the six S. Simmses listed in the Miami phone book, but didn't have any luck finding Elise's ex-husband. He called the Florida Bar Association, but got a recording. He'd call Monday. Then he'd find the lawyer's number with no problem.

"Nick, I didn't hear you come in. I was about to leave you a message."

He looked up to see Gibby, seated in his wheelchair in the doorway. "What's up, Gibby?"

"I hope you're planning on getting a new secretary pretty soon."

"Don't tell me I'm getting heavy walk-in traffic after four years."

"No, but Tina called me a couple of times."

"I just talked to her a few minutes ago. Why'd she call you?"

Gibby wheeled into the office. "She didn't want me to tell you, but she was asking a lot of questions about you."

"What kind of questions?"

"You know . . . Whether you've been in the office much lately, when you came in, how long you stayed. She even wanted to know if I thought you were seeing anyone else."

"Oh, Christ." Pierce shook his head. He didn't know what irked him more, Tina's nosiness or Gibby's gossipy tone. "Thanks. I'll set her straight when I see her tomorrow. No reason she should be bothering you."

"I just thought you should know. Oh, guess what? There's going to be a hearing on my case in a couple of weeks. This might be it. My ship's finally coming in."

"Great. Good luck. Hope it works out."

When Gibby made no effort to leave, Pierce asked what else was new.

"Oh, God. Let me tell you." Gibby wheeled closer, and Pierce felt edgy. Gibby was going to chatter nonstop until Pierce either interrupted him or he ran out of gossip.

"This group we sent to Paris last week just got back, and Lorraine — she led the tour — had a ton of horror stories. We had the group at a wonderful Parisian hotel, and then this couple and their two kids insisted they stay at a hotel where they had a view of the Eiffel Tower. So she moved them to this two-star hovel with a view, for about the same price. Then a few of the others heard about it and they wanted to change. You know how that goes. It's like the flu. And she said everyone complained about the prices as if *we* were the ones who set the exchange rate. I mean, my God . . . "

Gibby rambled on. Pierce nodded when he was supposed to, smiled, interjected a word here and there, but stopped listening. His thoughts were still on Tina and her questions to Gibby, and now his anger was turning to depression. Something had to give. And soon.

Pierce interrupted. "I need a drink, Gibby."

Gibby stopped in midsentence and looked up at him. "Oh. Okay."

"You want to go over to the Jack with me?"

Gibby made a face. "No way. That place sucks. You feeling down about something?"

Pierce stood up and shrugged as Gibby backed out the door. "Yeah, maybe I am. But I don't want to talk about it now."

Gibby looked worried. "Take care of yourself, Nick."

The street was damp, and the clouds hung low and heavy. Lightning flashed, followed a few seconds later by a crash of thunder.

He could feel the tension of the impending storm as he hurried to his car.

The happy-hour crowd at the Jack of Clubs was not a happy bunch this afternoon. Some looked as if they'd been drinking since morning; others as if they'd just gotten out of bed and this was their first stop. But as long as no one bothered him, Pierce didn't care. He just wanted a couple of beers and some time to think.

He settled on the same stool where he'd met Elise, or rather Monica, and gazed into the mirror, remembering how he'd watched her glide across the room. He ordered a beer from Leni when she walked over. "Twice in the same week," she said, sliding the beer over to him. "Life treating you rough or something?"

"Or something."

She must have sensed he wasn't in any mood to talk, because she nodded and moved on. He tipped the beer, gulped until nearly half of it was gone, then set the bottle down and stared at it.

He'd never had a case like this one. He was conspiring with his client to deceive the subject of his investigation into thinking he was conspiring with her. And still he wasn't even sure what he thought about the case. When he talked to Elise, he sympathized with her. It seemed to him that she actually believed Andrews was behind not only the theft and murder, but the break-in. Andrews told another side, negating her story. But what if he was lying? Then what?

He turned over every aspect of the case in his mind. He prodded and poked at everyone's story, looking for the soft underbelly, the weak points, the duplicity. Then there was the matter of the cop who was involved. Who the hell was that? Was he nearby, keeping track of everything, or was he staying away, out of sight?

He was halfway through his second beer when he felt a hand on his shoulder and slowly turned his head, figuring someone was about to hit him up for a beer, or tell his hard-luck story. He was in no mood for it.

"Amigo, what's going on?"

He smiled, relieved that it was Fuego. "Just enjoying a beer at happy hour."

"You look like happy hour just ended," the slender Cuban said as he slid onto the seat next to Pierce.

"Got a lot on my mind." Pierce reached for his beer and took a deep swallow. "What are you doing here?"

"I stopped by your office. Gibby was just leaving and told me I'd find you here. Said I should cheer you up."

Pierce smiled, shook his head, and picked at the sweating label on his beer bottle. "So what's new?"

"What do you know about Ginger Andrews?"

Pierce lowered his beer. "I know she's dead. Died of an overdose last summer."

Fuego's cheek twitched. "It may not have been accidental or suicide. I'm looking for a woman named Marisol who used to be Loften's girlfiend. She knew Andrews's wife, did some work for her, don't know what. I hear she stopped seeing Loften right after Ginger died. Just sort of disappeared. She may have been supplying Ginger with drugs, maybe even knocked her off with the OD. Don't know why. Or maybe Andrews did it to get rid of her, and this Marisol went into hiding."

Pierce drank the last swallow of the beer. "Sounds like a fishing expedition to me."

"It's the best lead I've got."

"Yeah, well, don't waste your time."

Fuego looked at him suspiciously, his cheek twitching spasmodically. "You telling me to drop it?"

"I'm telling you that's not really relevant."

"What about the money you paid me? I haven't earned all of it."

Pierce waved a hand at him. "Don't worry about it."

Before Fuego could protest, Pierce called out to Leni and ordered another beer for himself and one for Fuego.

"You feeling okay?" Fuego asked as Pierce guzzled his beer.

"Hey, I'm feeling great. I'm happy. It's happy hour, right?"

"Tell me the truth, amigo."

Pierce took another swallow. "Tell you the truth. Okay. No offense, but your cousin, you know, my ex-wife, is driving me nuts."

"Again? If that's how you feel, stop seeing her."

"Yeah."

Fuego motioned toward the crowd around them. "You think you got problems. Look at these guys. *They* got problems."

Lightning flashed in the window, and a clap of thunder followed. "About time that storm hits," Pierce said. "It's been threatening all afternoon."

After finishing his third beer, he decided he'd had enough. Of the Jack, of beer, of his forlorn thoughts. He wished Fuego a good evening, slid off the bar stool, and walked out the door and into a downpour. He was soaked by the time he reached the car and dropped his keys. He couldn't find the lock and kept hitting the handle.

"Fuck it." He only had a few blocks to go. He'd walk. He was wet already. He made no effort to hurry, and didn't even bother to avoid the puddles. The rain pelted him, the wind gusted down the street.

He'd almost reached his building when he heard a car honk twice. He glanced up; the street was empty except for the parked cars. He heard another blast of the horn and realized it was coming from across the street. He stopped, shielded his face from the rain, and saw a blue Mercedes. The windows were too dark to see inside it. He wasn't sure that was the one that had honked, but it caught his attention because he'd never seen it on the block. Maybe one of his neighbors had come upon sudden affluence. Or it was simply a tourist staying with a friend or relative.

Just then a bright bolt of lightning flashed and was followed almost instantly by a deafening crack of thunder. Too close. He turned and hurried into the apartment building.

His deck shoes squeaked as he climbed the stairs to his apartment. Thunder boomed, echoing eerily along the stairway, and the hall light at the landing momentarily blinked off and on. He jammed his hand into his wet pocket, extracted his keys. The walk and the rain had been sobering, and this time the key fit easily into the lock. He flipped on the light switch.

The living room remained dark, except for a ray of light from the hallway. Damn, electricity's out, he thought, then realized something didn't mesh. Why the hell was the hall light still on? He flipped the switch again. Maybe the bulb was burned out.

"Shit," he said aloud as he stumbled over a coffee table. He recovered his footing and moved ahead. Lightning momentarily illuminated the kitchen, but when he turned the switch nothing happened. No lights. He felt his way along the kitchen counter until he found the drawer where he kept his flashlight. He flicked it on and moved to the utility closet. He shone the flashlight on the metal door of the fuse box, opened it, and leaned forward, studying the fuses.

He heard a noise — raspy breathing — inside the closet. He jerked his head, redirected the flashlight beam. He saw a blur of movement, a figure lunging at him, a fist driving toward his head. He flinched and deflected the blow with the flashlight, which flew out of his grasp. The attacker slammed his fist into Pierce's stomach, grabbed him by the collar, jerked him forward, drew back his arm to aim another blow. Pierce's reactions were slowed from the beers, but his adrenaline surged, and his survival instinct drove him to retaliate.

He kneed the man in the crotch. The intruder grunted, fell back, and Pierce scrambled forward, grabbed him under the jaw, and battered his head against the cement floor. Once, twice . . . another blow or two and — A flash of lightning illuminated the man's face. He instantly recognized the jagged scar, and the moment of hesitation was all Scarjaw needed. His hand must have fallen on the flashlight, because he slammed it against Pierce's head, striking him precisely on the spot where he'd been bashed a few days ago. He fell back and blacked out.

He thought he was trying to get up, but maybe he was dreaming. He felt fuzzy, his skin tingled, and his head throbbed. Spittle drooled from his mouth. He was sure his eyes were open now, but there was only darkness.

His hands moved; he felt the cool floor beneath him, and he remembered the fight. But how long ago had it been? Minutes, hours — he didn't know. He couldn't hear the sound of rain any longer, but it was still dark. He pushed off the floor onto his hands and knees, crawled forward until he bumped into a wall. He waved his hand in front of him, patting the wall until he found the doorway and felt the kitchen tile beneath him.

Testing his legs and arms, he rose to his feet and slowly made his way to the bathroom. The light didn't work, which was just as well. He sponged his face and head with cool water. He had a nasty headache, his lip was swollen, but he didn't seem badly injured. He fumbled in the cabinet, found the aspirin, cursed the container when it wouldn't open. Finally he dumped three tablets into his palm, popped them into his mouth, and gulped them down with a splash of water from the faucet.

An hour later, his headache had subsided to a dull throb. He'd flipped the breaker switch and the lights were on. All of the lights. The apartment looked as if the storm had blown right through it, tossing and tearing at his belongings. Scarjaw had trashed the place. The drawers of his desk hung open, their contents strewn on the floor. His photos had been knocked from the wall, shelves swept clean. Drawers had been dumped, his closet pillaged. Pierce had apparently interrupted him before he'd had a chance to attack the kitchen.

He heard a knock and knew it was Carver. He'd found the lieutenant's card lying on the floor and had called him. He didn't like Carver much, but knew he should report the incident. Loften's murderer, after all, had made another appearance.

Carver was alone and looked as if he'd been called from home. He wore tennis shoes, chinos, and a sweatshirt that did nothing to disguise his bulk. His deep-set eyes quickly took in everything around him.

"Well, we're making a real habit of this, aren't we, Mr. Pierce?"

He settled his gaze on Pierce, assessing the extent of his injuries. "You call me because you want a ride to the emergency room?"

Pierce shook his head. "I'll be all right."

"Good. What happened?"

He told him.

"Anything missing?"

"I don't know. Can't tell yet."

"I see a stereo, I see a television." Carver walked into the kitchen. "You've got a microwave."

"I don't think theft was the motivation," Pierce said. "At least not theft of valuables. I've got a little box of gold coins in the bedroom. They were dumped out, but they're all there. I counted them."

Carver moved over to the bedroom and stood in the doorway, quietly studying the room. "You know, it sure does look a helluva lot like what happened to your girlfriend's place."

Pierce didn't answer. He didn't appreciate Carver's calling Elise his girlfriend.

Carver turned, stared at Pierce, and he ran a hand through his thinning, frizzy hair. "You know, I think you're getting me business, Mr. Pierce. Elise Simms is giving you the business."

The way Carver called him Mr. Pierce grated on him. He knew the cop did it for that very effect. "What's that supposed to mean?"

"I'm thinking now that I made a mistake about you and Andrews. You're working for him, which is what he told me in the first place. But you're not killers, or even accomplices or thieves."

"Thanks for the vote of confidence," he said, relieved that Carver was finally seeing clearly.

"Here's the way I figure it. Andrews hired you to look for the stolen crystal skull because he wants it for himself."

"He wants to buy it."

"Right. You stumbled on Simms, who knows something and seems like a nice, reasonable lady. But she's a spider lady, and she's woven the entire web. She and Loften were after the skull for themselves, but Spider Lady worked it out so this Scarjaw fellow not only steals the skull but kills her partner as well. Then he tosses her place and she blames Andrews, hoping to get you on her side."

He shook his head and continued. "And you swallow the whole fucking thing. Christ, she is attractive, and you are as gullible as they come."

Pierce was slow to anger, but Carver was badgering him. And he was ready to fire back. "You're overlooking one thing, Lieutenant."

"What's that?"

"You heard the tape." Pierce winced as a hot stab of pain lanced the side of his head, but he pushed on. "Who's the corrupt cop involved? The middleman — the one who set the whole thing up. And where does he fit?"

Carver's dark, deep-set eyes stared at him; a furrow formed a V on his brow. "I don't know. Wish I did."

Pierce wondered about that.

Fifteen

The kapok tree Thor was standing under rose a hundred and twenty-five feet and was covered with clusters of white flowers. Its buttressed trunk spanned fifteen feet, and its thick, wide-spreading branches were almost horizontal to the ground. Only a tree with immense strength in its limbs could manage that feat.

Thor knew all about the kapok. Its fruit formed in an oblong, leathery casing, and when it matured and dried, the casing cracked open, releasing a cottony fiber. Before synthetic fibers, it was used as a stuffing for pillows and life preservers. He knew the kapok was also called a ceiba, but he didn't like the name. To him it sounded somehow weak, utterly unlike the tree. What impressed Thor more than its flowers or magnificent trunk or useful fiber were the perfect crosses that the branches formed naturally. A symbol of good fortune.

"What's so interesting?" Frey asked, coming up behind him.

Thor had been here for fifteen minutes, and had seen Frey walking across the park toward him. "It's a sacred tree."

Frey frowned and looked up into the leafy canopy. "What are you talking about?"

"Kapoks are good luck."

"They got these up North, too?"

Thor gave Frey a look of disdain. The man was ignorant and unappreciative of his environment. That was another count against him. "They grow only in the tropics," he said condescendingly.

"Okay, listen. This ain't Arbor Day. We've got some business to attend to, and it's something Gore can't handle."

Thor turned his attention fully to Frey and waited for him to continue.

"Odin wants him out of the game. Eliminated. He knows too much, and he's not one of us."

Thor nodded. He wasn't surprised. Frey had brought Gore in for the hands-on work, and it was a mistake. He wasn't the crafty ex-con that Frey had described. He was just another fuck-up, a small-time crook who was asking too many questions. When they were driving to Pierce's apartment, he'd complained that he didn't like being called Gore, and wanted to know what the bullshit was about the weird names. That was the way Gore had put it.

Thor had patiently explained that in Norse mythology Odin is like Zeus, the most important god, a god of war who brought victory and defeat to warriors. Thor is the son of Odin, the second most important god, while Frey is the third-ranked.

"So where's Gore rank?"

"He doesn't," Thor had answered.

"You related to this Odin?"

"No."

"Who is he? What's he want with that skull?"

"Just do your work and don't ask questions," he'd told Gore.

But a few minutes later, just before they had broken into Pierce's apartment, Gore had asked about the relationship between Simms and Pierce, and he'd wanted to know what Thor's real name was. It was more than idle curiosity. He was asking too many questions, and Thor had told Odin.

And he'd also fucked up. Gore had hidden in Pierce's closet and had almost been caught. If he hadn't escaped, Thor would've had no choice but to kill Pierce. And that would've angered Odin, because he was saving Pierce for later.

Odin was right. Gore's days of crime were over. History.

"I'll take care of it," he said calmly.

"Don't wait too long," Frey said. "Odin won't like it."

He looked up at the kapok's strong limbs. He had great respect and reverence for the tree and he quietly asked for its blessing. "I won't wait any longer than necessary," he said again to Frey; but his eyes were on the kapok.

Sixteen

The sweet aroma of frying plantains mixed with the tart smells of black beans and Cuban coffee. The chatter of Spanish seemed to resound around him. He'd never been here on a Sunday, but it was obvious the restaurant was a popular stop for Hispanics coming out of mass from the cathedral down the block.

The place was rapidly filling as families in Sunday dress promenaded along the three aisles in search of empty tables and booths. A sign in Spanish next to the sugar bowl said the booth was reserved for two or more. He tapped his fingers on the Formica tabletop and wished Tina would hurry up. If she didn't show soon, he'd have to move to the counter.

He stuck his head in his newspaper and read a few paragraphs of an article about the cost of police corruption. The gist of it was that the city spent more on covering the salaries of suspended officers under investigation than it spent on providing day care for children. The results of a new investigation of police corruption could push the cost up to more than was spent on sewers and highways in Miami. And that was just to keep the suspected dirty cops on the payroll at full rate while they stayed home; it didn't even include the millions spent on the investigations and trials.

He couldn't concentrate on the article, because he kept thinking of Carver. Just the possibility that one of the detectives investigating Loften's murder might have ordered it made him damn uneasy. All morning, as he'd put his apartment back together, he'd tried to blank out everything. He'd turned the radio on to a rock station and raised the volume until the sound was like a white wave, a cushion that insulated him from his own thoughts. But here he was, stuck on the same thought again.

"Hello, Nicky. I should have figured you would be hiding in the corner with your back to the wall."

He lowered the paper. Tina, as usual, was draped in gold chains. She wore a tight shirt, high heels, and layers of makeup that made her look as if she were auditioning for *Cats*. It was only since they'd separated that she'd taken to wearing heavy makeup and excessive jewelry, and he wondered what it meant. Maybe it was her way of compensating for some deep inner lack. Maybe she felt more attractive. Hell, who cared? He'd stopped trying to figure her out a long time ago.

"You're late."

"I cannot just walk away from my desk like you do." She frowned at him.

Her black leather purse hung from one shoulder and she was clutching a couple of books under her arm. Between them was a large manila envelope. She slid into the booth and set the books down on the table. "What is with the sunglasses?"

He was hoping she wasn't going to notice, but Tina always noticed changes. He tipped his head down and removed the dark glasses.

"God, what happened to you now? You look worse every time I see you."

Pierce licked his swollen lip. His right cheek was bruised and his left eye was blackened. "I had a little trouble last night. I'll survive."

She stared at him, slowly shaking her head. "Are you getting in fights now?"

"I didn't start it."

"You should have just walked away."

"Tina, he was in my apartment. Okay?"

"You caught a burglar in the apartment? Did you call the police?"

"After the burglar got away."

"You should move. Did he get anything?"

"No."

"Good for you. You stopped him."

"Yeah, good for me. So what've you got there?"

"Do not be in such a rush. Let us have lunch and talk. I have hardly talked to you in weeks."

That wasn't exactly true, but he didn't argue. The waitress arrived and they ordered plates of chicken, black beans and rice, Cuban bread, and *café con leche*.

"And please, no sugar in my coffee," Pierce said. "They always do that to me here," he remarked when the waitress moved away.

"Maybe they just want to sweeten up the gringo." She smiled and gave his hand a quick squeeze.

"What do you want to talk about?" He reached for his glass of water.

"Do you notice anything different about me?"

He looked her over. He had no idea what she was talking about. "Let's see . . . A new blouse? A new bracelet? A new kind of makeup?"

She waved a hand at him. "I am not smoking. I quit."

"Again?" He'd lost count of the number of times Tina had given up cigarettes over the years he'd known her.

"It is almost two weeks. Well, ten days tomorrow."

"Congratulations. The tobacco industry must be hurting."

"Oh, shut up. I never smoked more than a pack and a half a day."

He glanced at the books, but Tina had other things on her mind. "Let me see, Nicky. I do not think I told you yet that Consuelo is engaged. I tried to convince her to drop the guy six months ago. He is no good. Now they are getting married. I cannot believe her. And I just found out Tía Juana did a *trabajo* for her, and that is how she got him."

So Aunt Joan had cast a spell, Pierce thought. What else was new?

Consuelo was Tina's younger sister, and Pierce knew he was about to hear a monologue on the conditions of her entire family — the three sisters, two brothers, and parents. Their meals arrived, and he let her talk.

There were two sides to Tina. The warm, caring woman, the one who expressed concern about his bumps and bruises, the one he'd married. Then there was the catty side; the manipulator who tried to control through emotional subterfuge. That was the Tina he'd divorced.

As she talked, a nagging thought occurred to him. Finally he interrupted her. "Say, Tina, have you ever asked Tía Juana to do a *trabajo* on us? You know, like to get us back together?"

She stared at him, her mouth tight, her eyes narrow. "How dare you say that? You do not ask things like that. It is impolite; it is my business."

"Hey, if it involves me, it's my business, too. Right?"

"I thought you did not believe. You always make fun of Tía Juana."

"Tina, for Christ's sake." It was no use trying to explain to her again that he regarded *Santería* as a belief system that seemed to work if you were a part of it. If you thought you could be manipulated by spells, you probably would be. He didn't think that way; plain as that. Still, he was curious to know if good ol' Tía Juana had been invoking the spirits or *orishas* to bring them together again.

"Are you denying that you made fun of her?" Tina demanded.

"So I made jokes. I hereby apologize to all the *orishas* — Changó, Eleggúa, the whole gang. How's that? And besides, you know I like Aunt Joan." He'd actually not made fun of *Santería,* but had joked about Tía Juana's name, saying that she should do her invocations with tequila instead of Florida water. But Tina didn't find it funny.

"You are terrible," she huffed.

Pierce was grateful when their lunches arrived and Tina moved on to the subject of life at the library. When they were almost done eating, she asked about Gibby. "What is wrong with him, anyway? He sounded so cold on the phone."

"Tina, you used to say that you didn't like him because he talked too much."

"Well, he did. He is very self-centered. I mean we all are, but . . . You know what I mean."

"Yeah. You just don't like him. You never did. So what's in the books?"

She shook her head, gave him an exasperated look. "You are so damn critical of me. It is truly amazing I am still a whole person after ten years of marriage to you, Nicky. You must have a high opinion of yourself if you think I would ask Tía Juana to do a *trabajo* for more of the same."

"Sorry I brought it up." He didn't lift his gaze from the books.

"Okay, clean your mess up," she said, turning the two books around. "I do not want to get these dirty."

He moved his plate aside and wiped the table with a paper napkin. Tina slid the smaller of the two tomes over to him. "It is on Mayan mythology and was edited by Redington. I marked a section on the crystal skull myth."

Pierce opened the book to the page with the marker. On it was a photograph of a crystal skull. It looked identical to the one he'd seen in Loften's office. Next to the picture was a section on the myth.

"I bet that crystal skull was stolen when the museum director was killed," she said, leaning over the table.

"That's a good guess."

"Are you looking for it for Raymond?"

He put a finger to his lips as he concentrated on the paragraph below the photo of the skull. The myth of the twin skull was described as a parallel legend to that of the Plumed Serpent and the Smoking Mirror. One skull was a god of life and hope, a counterpart to the Plumed Serpent; the other was a god of death and darkness and correlated with the Smoking Mirror. It went on to explain that both myths invoked the duality principle of man, his inner struggle between the forces of "good" and "evil."

Redington noted that the reunion of the skulls, as described in the myth, symbolized the resolution of the internal war of the human heart. Once freed from this duality, mankind would transform, shedding its old ways and moving to a higher level of existence. He went on to explain that it was the Plumed Serpent, rather than the Smoking Mirror, who could achieve the true union of opposites.

"Hello, Nicky. I do not have all day. I have more to show you."

He looked up, pleased that she wasn't pressing him about the investigation. "What's the other one?"

She rubbed her hand lightly over the cover. "We just got this one in last week. It was not even shelved yet."

Pierce glanced at the cover as she passed it to him. *The Encyclopedia of the Arcane.* "What is it?"

"You wanted something on Noster Mundus, right? This is what I found."

She reached over and opened it to a page she'd marked. It was a color plate labeled EMBLEMS OF SECRET SOCIETIES.

Pierce slipped his wire-framed glasses out of his shirt pocket and put them on. He glanced over the page of emblems; they looked like coats of arms of European families. "What am I supposed to be looking for?"

"Down at the bottom, on the right."

He stared at a drawing of a scroll. On either side of it was a skull. Below the emblem were the words NOSTER MUNDUS.

"That's it, right?" she asked.

He nodded. "Think so."

"Can you read the tiny letters on the scroll?"

Pierce leaned close to the page. "I can't quite make them out."

"Neither could I. Use this." She reached into her purse and handed him a magnifying glass. "I thought detectives were supposed to carry these."

He guffawed. "Sure, Tina. And smoke pipes and wear funny hats."

He leaned closer, at first focusing on one of the skulls. Its eyes were diamond shapes, instead of simply hollow, just as in the crystal skull he'd seen. He turned his attention to the scroll. "J-U-N-G-E-R-E," he spelled out.

"*Jungere.* That is Latin for join, or bind together. I guess it means bind together our sorry world."

"Why do you say that?" He looked up from the page.

"There is one other reference to Noster Mundus in the book." She flipped to another page she'd marked. "It is just a short description."

Pierce leaned forward again and read the passage:

Of more recent origin, little is known about a group called Noster Mundus, which was founded by international financier Raymond Andrews. Their membership is by invitation; their numbers few and their meetings secret. A spokesman for the group, headquartered in Bayonne, France, defined their purpose this way: "We are a group of men and women who are working toward higher standards in public life, improved industrial relations, and a more sensible attitude between nations. Furthermore, we believe that a few individuals can make a significant change in society, but first they must change themselves.

It sounded vaguely like what Elise had told him, except she'd made it seem more ominous. He wondered why Andrews would locate the headquarters of Noster Mundus in Bayonne. Maybe he was planning on investing in a jai alai team, he thought wryly. Bayonne was located in the heart of the Basque region, and was where many of the top players grew up.

"Does that help you?" Tina asked.

"Sort of." He wasn't sure what to think of it. "Can I take it with me?"

She snapped the cover shut. "Reference only." She pulled out the manila envelope from the back of the book. "I made copies of both pages, plus the section on the crystal skull from the other book. And there are also copies of two journal articles by Redington in there. They are both about mythology, and one talks about the crystal skull."

"Good. I'll read them later. You're very efficient."

She smiled coyly. "I did not think you ever noticed."

"Of course I do. I appreciate your help."

She reached out, ran a finger over the back of his hand. "You know, it has been a while since we have spent an evening together."

She meant night, not evening, he thought, and slipped his hand out from under hers.

"Tina, I don't think that's a very good idea. We're divorced, remember?"

She pulled her hand from his side of the table, suddenly indignant. "You do not have to tell me the obvious. I am well aware of that."

"Think about it. You and I are like a broken record that keeps playing the same notes over and over, and I don't think either of us likes the sound of it very well."

Her eyes narrowed again, and her lips turned down as she drew back and glared. "How long did it take for you to come up with that cute line?"

He didn't answer her.

"There is someone else. I was right," she said accusingly.

"What I do is none of your business. That's what divorce means."

He thought for a second that she was going to cry. But then anger tightened her jaw, and he braced himself for an outburst. "Well, I have been seeing someone, too," she hissed. "And you can just get your own goddamn reference material from now on." She swept up the books and the manila envelope as she sprang from the booth.

"Hey, I thought that was for me," he protested, reaching for the envelope.

"I feel sorry for you," she scoffed, drawing away. "You have no feelings for people. You cannot even express the way you feel. You do one thing, say another. It is like you are hiding behind — " She shook her head. "Behind I do not know what." She turned and strutted out.

Pierce gazed glumly after her. *Nice going. Get her mad and send her on her way.* Her theatrics had captured the attention of the foursome at the next booth. He felt like explaining that they were just practicing for a play. In a way, it was true. The scene was a repeat of past performances. Another cycle was completed, and he knew what would follow, if he allowed it.

She'd call him in a day, two days, or a week, apologize; or she'd just stop over and they'd tumble into bed. Or his resolve would weaken and he'd stop by the library to make up. That's how it had happened twice, no, three times since their divorce. Divorce wasn't meant to be another version of a bad marriage. He knew at least that much.

Seventeen

As soon as he left the restaurant, Pierce walked to the phone booth at the corner and dialed Elise's number from a scrap of paper in his pocket. He wanted to talk to her about what happened to him last night, but he also wanted to get Tina out of his mind.

As the phone rang, he fiddled with the coin-return slot. "No one is in right now, but if you — "

He hung up on the recording, paused a moment, then lifted the bulky Miami phone book on his knee and looked up Bill Redington's home number. When he found it, he deposited another quarter and dialed.

A woman answered on the second ring. "Is Dr. Redington in?"

"I'm sorry. I don't expect him until late this afternoon. He's holding classes."

"On Sunday?"

"Yes. At the Coral Castle."

"The tourist place?"

"That's right. In Homestead."

"Why there?"

"I'm just his wife." She laughed. "You'll have to ask him. He should be home about three. Can I take a message?"

"No thanks. I'll talk to him later." He rang off and glanced at his watch. What the hell. He didn't have anything planned this afternoon, and he did want to talk to Redington about Noster Mundus. Besides, he was curious to find out why a psychology class would be held at the Coral Castle.

As he drove to Homestead down U.S. 1, he thought about the break-in again. Scarjaw could have killed him, but didn't. It seemed that getting Nicholas Pierce out of the way would have been the expedient thing to do — unless whoever was behind the break-in needed him. On one hand, Elise and Redington wanted him to keep track of Andrews. On the other, Andrews was using him to pursue Elise and Redington. The break-in, he decided, was simply a warning to him to watch his loyalties. But whose warning?

He glanced out the window at a clown waving to him in front of a car dealership. U.S. 1 stretched through South Miami like a bad dream, a garish commercial corridor devoid of character. The tropics had been buried beneath tons of concrete and only gradually did stretches of open, undeveloped land appear. He passed a billboard advertising the Monkey Jungle, then another for the Coral Castle. One more mile. He parked in the lot, walked to the ticket window, and passed six ones through the slot. He'd driven by the castle a few times on trips to Homestead, a town bordering the Everglades, but had never stopped. Now he felt strangely like a tourist on his home turf.

"Could you tell me where Professor Redington is holding his class, please?"

"Why didn't you say you were with the class? It's only two dollars." She pushed four ones back through the slot. "Go all the way to the back. It's in the garden, on the other side of the revolving door."

"Do you know when the next class is supposed to start?"

She looked to the side, probably at a clock. "In twenty minutes, I believe, sir. He's just finishing up a class now."

"Thanks. Keep it." He shoved the four dollars back to the woman and walked away, following the sidewalk to the corner of the building where several people stood under a speaker listening to a tape-recording about the castle. They were all about the same age, and they looked collegiate, so he assumed they were some of Redington's students who'd arrived early for the second class. Although he'd heard about the castle's history, he listened to the tape, refreshing his memory.

The story was a strange twist on an old plot: a man's dedication to building a monument in memory of his great love — in this case, the young woman who spurned him. In 1913, Edward Leedskalnin was a twenty-six-year-old stonemason living in Latvia and engaged to a girl of sixteen. But the night before the wedding, his young love told him he was too old for her. Heartbroken, Leedskalnin left his homeland and wandered through Canada and the United States for several years. By 1920, he had developed a mild case of tuberculosis and moved to South Florida for the climate. Here, he bought an acre of land for twelve dollars and began carving large blocks of stone from the four-thousand-foot-thick bed of coral rock below him. Using only primitive, handmade tools and with no helpers, Leedskalnin, a hundred-pound, five-foot-tall elf of a man, mined, shaped, and moved eleven hundred tons of coral rock. And it was all dedicated to his lost love.

So love moves coral rock, he thought. Why not?

When the taped history had run its course, he passed through an arch in the castle's coral wall. Inside was a courtyard filled with massive rock tables and chairs, towers and stairs, a stone sundial, a well, and an open-air, coral rock bathtub. Perched atop the far wall was a crescent moon, and spheres like planets. He joined a tour group in progress and heard the guide saying that Leedskalnin worked on the Coral Castle only when alone, usually by lantern at night. "Whenever people came around, he would simply sit down and stop working until they left."

A young man, probably one of Redington's students, raised his hand. "You said that the whole tower is one solid piece of rock and weighs more than twenty-eight tons. How could he raise it by himself? Even if he had hoists, he'd need help."

The guide, a rotund, middle-aged man wearing a Greek sailor cap and a two-day growth of gray-speckled whiskers, smiled. "That's an intriguing mystery, isn't it?"

He led the group along the back wall and stopped where a block of coral rock was inset in an oval hole in the wall. "This door weighs nine tons." He pushed it with one finger, and it revolved on a central axis. For an instant, when the door was perpendicular to him, Pierce caught a glimpse of Redington talking to a group of students who were sitting on a lawn. "It's actually on its second set of gears," the guide continued. "One day several years after Ed died, the old ones underneath broke in half and the door fell over. It took six men and modern tools to put the door back up after they made new gears for it. One of the engineers who examined Ed's holes in the door said it would take a laser beam to drill them."

He led the group over to the well and explained that Leedskalnin had no electricity or running water. Yet, he had developed a coral rock water-filtration system and heated water in his own solar heating system. "He was truly ingenious. And virtually everything here is impregnated with the memory of his Sweet Sixteen. From the valentine-shaped table to the sixteen steps leading to his tower."

They moved over to an L-shaped coral rock near the side wall. Water percolated in a shallow pool on the horizontal surface, and embedded in the upright slab behind it was a trail of shells leading from larger ones at the bottom to the center, where smaller shells formed a vague face. "When Ed himself led tours, he always walked right by here and never said anything about this one. I call it the Bubbling Altar. The water is funneled up through a lead pipe from the spring below and drains back down. Notice the shells leading up to the human face. Some people have said it's symbolic of the evolution of man."

Pierce stared at the altar a moment as the guide pointed to the larger of the two towers. He talked about the stonemason as if he were a dear, old friend. "Ed lived a very ascetic life in his tower. He slept on a swinging bed made of burlap and metal."

"Did his Sweet Sixteen ever find out about the castle?" a young woman asked.

The guide nodded solemnly. "That's a sad story. After Ed died, the family who took over ownership of the castle located the woman. She was a widow in her sixties and still living in Latvia. She had heard of the Coral Castle, but had no interest in seeing it, even if her trip was paid for. A heartbreaker to the end."

As the group headed up the steps to the tower, Pierce saw a stream of students with notebooks filing into the castle through the revolving door. The class was obviously over. A moment later, Redington entered the courtyard accompanied by several students. His half-moon glasses hung over his chest from an elastic band, which disappeared beneath his ponytail, and he carried a thermos bottle under his arm. He stopped at the valentine table, and the students grouped around him.

Pierce ambled over and stood a few feet away from the group. Redington was comparing coral rock to the unconscious mind when he saw Pierce staring at him. The professor looked blankly at him, as if he couldn't figure out where he'd seen him, then scowled. He excused himself from the students and moved over to Pierce.

"What the hell are you doing here?" he said gruffly. A shock of white hair hung over his forehead, which was pimpled in sweat.

Pierce decided to confront him with the break-in. He could be as direct and caustic as Redington. "Someone broke into my place last night. You know anything about it?"

"Why would I know anything about that? You think I did it?"

"I know who did it. I just don't know who put him up to it."

Redington ran a hand through his hair. "You drove all the way out here to accuse me of sending someone to break into your house? You think I was responsible for the break-in at Dr. Simms's house, too?"

Pierce lifted his sunglasses, balancing them on his head and revealing his shiner. "I want some answers. That's all. The same guy who broke into my place killed Loften."

"I don't know what to tell you, except that you're lucky you're still alive."

"Tell me this. Why were you and Elise's father involved in a group called Noster Mundus?"

Astonishment flickered across Redington's features, then melted away as he glanced around and noticed students looking his way. Pierce thought that he was about to deny knowing what he was talking about. Instead, he said: "I have a class now, but sometime soon we should talk about it."

Pierce nodded, and as Redington turned away fired another question. "I hear Elise didn't talk to her father for several years. That true?"

Redington glanced back at Pierce. "I think you should talk to her about that matter. It's none of my business."

"I will," Pierce said, taking the answer as an affirmative reply. He followed him toward the rear of the castle, where Redington's students were gathering. "By the way, why are you holding your class here?"

Redington smiled for the first time since he'd seen Pierce. Either he was more at ease with that question or he was trying to cover up his anxiety. "Why don't you join us and see?" he said jovially. "I always hold one class here each quarter."

Redington stopped at the revolving door and motioned to Pierce. "Give it a shove."

Pierce pushed, and was amazed by how smoothly the huge rock revolved. He looked around the garden. "It's pleasant back here."

"A bit humid this time of year, but the bottlebrush trees and wild almonds are still in bloom," Redington responded as if their earlier, strained conversation hadn't happened. "Now, please excuse me."

When the class began, about twenty students were seated on the grass in the umbra of several date palms. Pierce leaned against a tree by the castle wall barely within hearing range of the class and watched Redington pour himself a steaming cup of water from his thermos. How the hell could he drink that stuff?

He listened as Redington asked who had toured the castle. He nodded at the show of hands. "What would you say is the main factor that attracts people here?"

The man Pierce had heard questioning the guide about the tower spoke up. "It was built by one man with primitive tools."

"It's the only castle in town," another student said, and everyone laughed.

Redington smiled, and Pierce could tell he had good rapport with his students. He wondered what they would think if they knew the professor was a suspect in a case of murder and theft.

"It *is* unique," Redington said. "That can't be denied. And that it was constructed by one man with homemade tools is indeed interesting. However, that's a matter more suited for engineers and physicists than a psychology class.

"We're more concerned with the symbolic aspects of this marvel. Here we have a man who lost the love of his life on the eve of his marriage. So what did he do? He made his love concrete by building a stone castle in her honor from coral rock."

He paused, giving the students a moment to consider the thought. A woman raised her hand. "But Dr. Redington, stone seems so cold and unemotional. Stone doesn't care or love."

"True. But at the same time, something constructed of stone symbolizes the eternal, that which is immortal and unalterable, which is, of course, our little stonemason's love for his Sweet Sixteen."

Redington motioned toward the castle walls. "Edward Leedskalnin said little about what he was building here. But it's all written symbolically in stone. This man, an uneducated contemporary of Carl Jung, understood the archetypes of the unconscious mind without ever taking a single psychology class at any university. New hope for those who skipped today."

Redington grinned as the students laughed. "Leedskalnin apparently tuned into the objective or collective unconscious, our racial memory — which, as you all know by now, was described by Jung as a storehouse of knowledge lying below our individual subconscious minds." He fiddled with the half-moon glasses dangling over his chest, and Pierce had the impression that he was momentarily distracted by another thought. Then he blinked and went on. "Let's list some of the symbols we can see here. I've told you the stone itself is one. Who has another?"

Several students raised their hands and offered ideas: the tower; the planets; the heart-shaped table; the sundial; the well; the solar hearth; the altar.

"Excellent," Redington remarked. "Another one is the four-sided configuration of the castle walls. I could expound on each at length, but instead I'll let you select one for a short paper, your last of the quarter."

The class groaned in unison.

Pierce smiled, recalling his own college days, and remembered something he hadn't thought about for years. Ray Andrews had run a term-paper sales business along with his drug operation. Andrews had considered college a profit-making venture as well as an education, and somehow, he'd made it through his four years without ever getting expelled or arrested, and even though he seemed to skip most of his classes he's graduated with a B+ average.

He decided he'd heard enough. He walked over to the revolving door and pushed through it. As he crossed the courtyard, he glanced up and saw the silhouette of a man's face in the window of the tower. Something about the shadowy image disturbed him. He felt a tingling in his lower spine, the same sensation he experienced when he thought of entering elevators. He kept walking.

He'd nearly reached the exit when he decided not to ignore the eerie feeling about the silhouette. He backtracked, then slowly climbed to the tower. It took a moment for his eyes to adjust to the dim light. He glanced in the corners. No one was there. But the burlap bed, which hung from chains, the bed where Ed Leedskalnin had slept, was gently rocking.

As he walked out to his car, he saw a dark blue Mercedes pull out of the parking lot and quickly accelerate as it headed north on U.S. 1.

Eighteen

Pierce knocked and waited. Knock and wait. Knock and wait. Waiting for people was a big part of his job. He didn't want to think about what percentage of his time over the past several years had been spent standing around or sitting around. Waiting for someone to leave a house, waiting for someone to answer a door, or just waiting for a subject to do something.

He'd called Elise earlier, briefly told her about the break-in, and said he wanted to see her. Her Cabriolet was in the driveway, but the lights in the front of her house were off. Maybe she was in the shower.

He sauntered around to the side of the house and peered up at the window where the intruder had entered. The broken glass had been replaced, but he could see inside and noticed light filtering from the kitchen. He walked to the backyard.

"Elise?" he called out. Lots of tropical shrubbery, as in the front yard, but no sign of her. He approached the back door. He knocked, he pounded, but still no answer. The scent of jasmine from a nearby bush curled through the late May night. A shriek of tires somewhere in the distance made him aware of just how deeply the silence surrounded the house, as though it were encased in silence, frozen in it.

Fuck propriety. He tried the door and it swung open. "Elise?"

His voiced sounded hollow, empty, stripped. There was a mug on the butcher-block table and a newspaper spread out on it. He moved into the dining room; the silence and darkness seemed to seal him off from the rest of the house.

He found a light, turned it on. Everything looked as though it was back in order. He walked over to the stairway. Maybe she was taking a nap. Yeah, that must be it. It had to be it. A sound sleeper might not hear a knock on a downstairs door.

"Hello, you up there?" Would she really take a nap and leave a door unlocked?

He listened, remembering the scratching sounds he'd heard the last time he'd stood here. But there was nothing this time, only the interminable silence. He started up the staircase, into the yawning dark. He ascended, and several of the stairs creaked with his weight. At the top of the stairs, he paused and listened. He heard a click and a hum as the air conditioner turned on.

"Elise?" His voice was soft and less self-assured.

He moved down the hallway and squinted at the darkened doorway to her bedroom. His heart thumped, and it wasn't from the climb up the stairs. He stepped through the doorway and fumbled for a light switch. He found it and saw the room was empty. He quickly checked the rest of the upstairs without finding a clue to her whereabouts. She was probably visiting a neighbor. He tried imagining her talking to the old lady across the street, but couldn't.

He descended the stairs, was halfway down when he heard the front door open. "Nick, you here?" She stood in the doorway, her purse over her shoulder, a shopping bag under her arm. She was wearing jeans and a T-shirt and her short hair looked windblown.

"Up here." He hurried the rest of the way down the stairs. "I was looking for you. The back door was open, and — "

"You decided to snoop around." She looked intently at him.

"No," he said defensively. "I thought something might have happened."

She shrugged. "It's okay. You've already seen everything I own, dumped on the floor for your ease of inspection. You want a glass of wine?"

"Sure." He followed her to the kitchen, trying to remember if he'd seen any grocery stores nearby. He was almost certain the closest one was at least several blocks away. He watched as she put away a loaf of bread and a carton of milk. Then she took a bottle of white wine from the refrigerator and set it on the counter.

She turned, looked at him. "Nice shiner. How are you feeling?"

"Better. I saw your car in the driveway. What'd you do, hike down to a store in the dark?"

She opened a drawer and rummaged around in it. "Shit, where's the stupid corkscrew?"

She opened another drawer; it irritated him that she was ignoring his question. "Here it is."

She held out the corkscrew. "Will you open it?"

Pierce took it, but didn't make a move to open the bottle. Elise saw his inquiring look and snatched the corkscrew away. She turned her back to him and worked on the bottle.

"What's wrong?" he asked.

"Okay." She paused. "Okay, that's enough." Something — anger, suspicion, chagrin — curled in her eyes. "I lied to you."

"About what?" She was going to own up. His eyes darted to the kitchen door as he heard a noise. *Shit, it's a trap.* The kitchen door suddenly swung open and a tall, brawny man with thinning blond hair stared at him.

"This him, Lisie?"

The man had something in his hand, but Pierce kept his gaze on his eyes. They were bloodshot, as if he'd been drinking. "Damn. Looks like you beat him."

Pierce glanced at Elise just as she raised the wine bottle by the neck. He jerked back, raised an arm, but she was moving toward the man in the doorway. "Get the fuck out of here, Steve."

"Hey, I was just giving you an extra filter. Take it easy." His voice was slurred. He weaved from side to side, held up his empty hand, and placed what looked like an air-conditioning filter against the wall. "Christ's sake, Lisie."

Pierce looked between them, baffled, and at the same time relieved that he wasn't the target of the confrontation.

"Bye, Steve." She moved toward him again. He stepped back, then stopped. "I said, Bye, Steve."

He took another step back. "Don't come crying to me next time something goes wrong."

She slammed the door in his face, locked it, and leaned against it. "Sorry," she said. A slight smile curled her lips and she held the bottle out to him. "Will you open it now? I'll tell you all about it."

He took the bottle from her, smiled back. "Your ex-husband, right?"

"You got it. Like I said, I lied to you. I told you I never see him." She crossed her arms, remained leaning against the door. "The truth is, he comes over all the time, always to fix something, or work in the yard. This evening he changed the air-conditioning filter. Then he hung around. As you could see, he'd had a few drinks. I finally asked him to drive me to the store, hoping he'd just drop me off when we got back. He must have seen your car when I got out of his."

"He's a big guy." And, ironically, he was the guy Pierce had planned to look up.

She walked over to the cupboard and took down a couple of wine-glasses. "A big baby."

"He's a weight lifter, right?"

"Yes, and we're lucky he's off steroids. I wouldn't have gotten him out of here so easily."

Pierce poured the wine. "What kind of law practice does he have?"

"Oh, so there's something you didn't find out on your own. He was in private practice in Chicago, but he took a job with the federal prosecutor's office when we moved down here."

Pierce nodded. "Does he get jealous about your seeing other men?"

"Oh, no. Not him." Sarcasm dripped from the words.

Pierce's hope that Steve would be helpful was fading fast. He doubted that the man would be cooperative now that he'd seen Elise and himself together. "Did you tell him about the break-in?"

"You serious? He'd be here every day for the next two weeks installing a five-thousand-dollar electronic security system at his own expense, and making me feel guilty."

Pierce laughed. "He sounds like a male version of my ex-wife."

Elise held up her glass, touched Pierce's. "To our ex-spouses. May they go their own ways."

"May we let them," he added.

They sipped at their wine, and Elise asked if he wanted to move out to the living room or sit at the kitchen table. "Let's just stay here." He pulled out a chair and sat down.

She joined him, stacking the newspapers in a pile on the corner of the table. "Now you've seen me at my worst, threatening Steve with a bottle of wine."

Her sincerity nearly convinced him she was telling the truth. But then he remembered something. "I don't care what you said about your ex-husband. But I wish you'd told me the truth about your father."

"What about him?" A defensive edge laced her voice, her brow knitted in a frown.

"He was a member of Noster Mundus." He paused. "Andrews told me, and Redington verified it. He was a member himself."

"So what?" Her response was quick, too quick. "Dad and Bill both quit when they got wind of the replica fraud."

"It bothers me that you didn't tell me the full story."

She shrugged, looked down at her glass of wine. "I didn't think it was important."

"That's not all. Andrews said you haven't spoken to your father in years. Not until recently, when you expressed interest in the crystal skull."

Color rushed into her cheeks. "That's a goddamn lie. We get along fine." Her fingers raked through her hair. "Don't you see what Andrews is doing? He's trying to stick this theft of the skull and Loften's murder on *me*, just like he stuck my father with the replica fraud."

"Then why did Bill confirm the thing about you and your father?" The question hung there, thick, ugly. He was hoping that by confronting her, she would tell him the whole story, not just her edited version.

"Bill told you I haven't spoken to my father in years?" She sounded incredulous.

"Well, not exactly. But I sensed he was confirming it."

"That's hardly the same thing." She glanced at him, then dropped her gaze, staring into her wine. Her fingers tapped nervously against the glass. "But there were several years when Dad and I didn't talk."

"Why not?"

"When I entered the field, I rebelled against him." Her voice was calmer now, as she acknowledged that Andrews's comment was not completely fallacious. "See, he has a mystical bent. It's really the force behind his work. I tried to forget all of that and take a strict, empirical approach to everything, and it was like a wedge between us."

Pierce sipped his wine, then set his glass aside. "Why didn't you say that before?"

"Because that's the past." She looked up; her eyes were pinched with fatigue. "Things changed after my marriage fell apart. I spent a few months in Guatemala doing fieldwork, and we reconciled. Part of it was that Dad introduced me to a Mayan man who understood the Tzolkin — the sacred calendar — far better than I did. It was through him that I began to come to know its true significance, and what Dad is all about."

"And what's that?"

Her fingers absently touched a pendant through the fabric of her blouse. He saw a glint of light between two buttonholes and realized it was the same crystal she'd worn when he'd met her as Monica. "Basically, he sees the Mayan culture as alive. He's penetrated the hidden part that's linked with the ancient past."

He nodded, but kept his eye on the pendant. He hadn't thought about Monica's crystal since that night. Now, however, he was curious.

"Could I see that?"

She looked surprised. "What?"

"The crystal."

She lifted it from her blouse and held it out to him. "You told me about the power of crystals that night we met. I thought that was just Monica. Was that Elise talking, too?"

She shrugged and looked down at the pendant. "Elise thinks that crystal power exists, yes."

"I thought you were a scientist. How do you explain this so-called power?"

Elise asked if he wanted more wine, then refilled their glasses. "You want to hear more about my thoughts on crystals? Is that what you're saying?"

"Yeah, I would." There might be a connection between Elise's interest in so-called crystal power and the skull, he thought. At this point, he was willing to try anything.

He sat down, and with the crystal pendant now dangling on the outside of her blouse, Elise started talking. Quartz, she explained, consisted of silicon dioxide, the very substance of the human nervous system. When you squeezed quartz or struck it, the crystal discharged piezoelectricity — electricity produced by pressure. A few scientists thought that a similar process took place when sound or even thought waves struck quartz. The crystal resonated the energy.

He wasn't sure he followed her. "So can scientists measure this energy that comes from quartz?"

She shook her head. "Not the kind of energy that's generated by sound or thought. At least, not yet. If it exists, which I think it does, it's a subtle, higher energy. Maybe it emanates from another dimension, a higher plane."

It sounded like mumbo jumbo. "So this is sort of like a spiritual thing."

"You could call it that, but the word *spiritual* has a religious connotation. To me, religion carries the baggage of dogma, restrictions. And worst of all, arrogance and divisiveness. My religion's better than yours. Right? Unfortunately, a lot of people who are fed up with religion decide there's nothing worth believing in that they can't immediately perceive. They become completely materialistic and cynical. I don't like religion, but I do believe in a universal force and life beyond this existence."

"For a lot of people, religion is their only hope."

"Lambs on their way to the slaughter," she said softly.

"So how does your crystal work? What do you do?"

"You can concentrate on a message, anything you want to achieve, and repeat it while you hold the crystal. The idea is that the crystal works like a subliminal tape, sending you positive reinforcement of your message."

She paused, scrutinizing him as if she hoped his thoughts would appear on his face. "Does that sound crazy to you? It certainly does to Steve. He didn't want to hear about it."

"Give me an example."

"Okay. For the past few weeks, I've been concentrating on the idea that I would find the twin crystal skull."

Now we're getting somewhere, he thought. "And?"

"No, I haven't found it — but let me finish. One day while I was focusing on the thought, I sensed the image of a man. I couldn't see his face, because he was looking away from me. But I knew that the man would play a role in finding it, and that I would meet him. Very soon."

Pierce remained silent, waiting for her to continue.

"The next day Bill played me the Loften tape, and I heard about you, the private investigator. I didn't think much of it until the murder and theft of the skull. That was when I decided to follow you, to see who you were."

Pierce took a final swallow of his wine. "You're saying you think I'm going to find the *other* skull, not the one I'm looking for?" He nearly laughed out loud. "C'mon."

Elise ran her fingers over the stack of newspapers on the table. "The day after I met you I focused on the question of whether you were the person I was supposed to meet."

"And?"

"I'd just gotten home. I'd barely spent two minutes on the thought when I heard a knock on the door. It was you."

Maybe she was deranged but functional most of the time, he thought. Maybe she was just trying a strange form of flattery on him. Or, hell, maybe she really believed this stuff. Sure, strange things happened from time to time, but he had to agree with the statisticians, the scientists of probability, that it would be weird if weird happenings — coincidences — never occurred. But he wasn't going to argue.

He remembered Redington talking about the myth of the reunion of the skulls and recalled what he'd read about it while at lunch with Tina. "You said your father told you the Noster Mundus emblem has a crystal skull on it."

She nodded.

"I saw it in a book on secret societies. It's got two crystal skulls, one on either side of a scroll."

"Dad had heard about it, but I don't think he'd ever seen the emblem. He said it was something recent."

"That's not all. There's a Latin word below the scroll. It's *jungere*. It means join, or bind together."

He realized now that it didn't refer to uniting the world, as Tina had suggested; it meant reuniting the skulls, and he told Elise as much.

"Nick, that's the key to Noster Mundus. Andrews must have perverted the organization so it would serve as a vehicle for his goal of getting the skulls. Or actually he probably set it up with that goal in mind and everything else was just a cover."

"But why?"

"It's obvious. He wants to be the one to fulfill the myth. He's obsessed by it."

Pierce nodded, suddenly not sure what he believed. He knew that people with unlimited amounts of money sometimes pursued odd obsessions, but he found it difficult to accept the idea that Andrews would kill and steal to achieve a goal.

"What about your father? Is he also obsessed by the myth?"

"Not in the same sense." Her eyes locked with his. "A long time ago Dad told me why he'd never sell the skull. He said that when the God of Death deserts him, it will mean his own death."

Nineteen

The rows of six-foot-high royal palms seemed to run on forever behind his father's nursery. Thor remembered planting palm seedlings here as a kid; those trees, wherever they stood, must be twenty-five, thirty feet high, he thought. He also remembered walks like this one between the rows, when he'd carried a fishing rod and had been headed for the canal.

"Never seen so many goddamn palm trees," Gore muttered as he walked behind Thor. "How far's the canal, anyhow?"

"Not much farther."

"Orange groves make more sense."

"What?"

"I'm used to seeing orange groves around Tampa. At least you get oranges. But what good is a grove of palm trees?"

Thor turned as Gore swatted a palm frond with his fishing rod. "This isn't a grove, Jim. It's a nursery. These trees are going to be sold. So take it easy on the fronds."

"Sure. Myself I'd rather have an orange tree in my yard."

Fruit trees were fine, but palm trees had aesthetic appeal. But aesthetics had never been one of Gore's strong points.

Thor heard him swat another frond with his rod. "I said take it easy, Jim."

"What's the big deal?"

"My father owns this nursery. That's what. I grew up here."

"Well, why didn't you say so? Okay, now I get it. I mean, I was wondering why you wanted to come out here instead of fish by the road."

They reached the canal a couple of minutes later, attached floating popper lures from Thor's tackle box, and cast their lines. "I love bass fishing," Gore said.

Thor didn't answer. He slowly reeled in his line, jerking the rod lightly so the lure danced across the surface. After a few casts, he opened the box again. "Think I'm going to try something else."

He unsnapped the lure, opened the tackle box, and set it into an empty tray. He reached down to the bottom of the box, moved aside a couple of stringers, and slipped his fingers around the handle of a snub-nosed .38.

"Hey, I got a strike," Gore said. "I got him."

"Good." Thor walked over to Gore as he reeled in the fish and the rod arched toward the water. "Jesus, he's a fighter," Gore said excitedly. "He ain't getting away, either."

Thor aimed the .38 at the back of his head. "Neither are you."

He fired, and Gore's body jerked like the popper lure, then fell forward, tumbling over the canal bank, and splashed into the water. Thor climbed down the bank. He recovered the rod and reel and landed a three-pound-plus bass. Then he pushed Gore's body into the deeper water and watched as it slowly drifted and sank.

He tossed the .38 into the canal. Even if it was found it would never be linked to him. He took one more look at Gore as the body vanished from sight. At least he'd died doing something he liked. That was more than most people could expect.

Twenty

Visiting a morgue was not an auspicious way to start the week, Pierce thought as he followed Neil Bellinger down a flight of stairs along a poorly lit hallway. Bellinger softly hummed a tune and walked with a swagger. He was as upbeat as ever, evidently oblivious to the darker side of his profession, the side that had burned out Fuego. Pierce rubbed his arms; the air-conditioning was frigid. But he was tired, and the chill kept him alert.

He'd lain awake in bed last night for a couple of hours, rehashing his talk with Elise, looking at it from every angle. He'd tossed about, lying first on one side then the other, on his back, on his stomach, his back again. Finally he'd gotten up and started a book Fuego had given him a couple of weeks ago called *The Watcher,* about a man who confused illusion with reality. Sometime after three he finally fell asleep.

Bellinger woke him up at eight with the news and asked him to get to the morgue as soon as possible. He'd showered, dressed, gulped one cup of coffee, and was downtown by eight-thirty.

They stopped at an office and conferred with the weekend morgue attendant, a short, thin man with thick spectacles and a white lab coat. Pierce glanced at his own reflection in the open glass door. His hooded eyes were surrounded by circles. Zombie eyes. He looked as tired as he felt.

The attendant squinted over Bellinger's shoulder at Pierce, then picked up a clipboard from his desk and led the way down the hall. They passed a room dominated by an aluminum autopsy table; a microphone hung over it for the coroner to dictate his findings. The place gave Pierce the creeps.

The attendant pushed through the double doors of the morgue, and they moved into a long room with ice blue walls. Shiny metal drawers climbed the walls. Pierce drank in the noxious odor of formaldehyde, and his stomach heaved. He put a hand to his mouth, tasted an acid mix of bile and coffee.

"Let's see here," murmured the attendant as he perused the clipboard, holding it a couple of inches from his nose.

Bellinger glanced at Pierce and rolled his eyes. The old fart isn't playing with a full deck, said his expression.

"Nine B. Nine B. Right here, gentlemen." He pulled open the drawer and uncovered the face with the care of a mother lovingly turning down a bed sheet for her child.

Pierce glanced at the stone-cold corpse. The face was distorted, bloated; the skin a faint blue. The right eye was shattered as if it had exploded from the inside. Bellinger reached down and turned the head to the side. A jagged scar was visible on the jaw.

"Please, don't touch the corpse," Charlie admonished, sounding like Mr. Whipple talking about his Charmin.

Bellinger ignored him, glanced at Pierce. "This him?"

"Yeah."

"You sure?"

"Positive. He drowned?"

Bellinger's laugh was short and quick, like a cough. "Yeah, after he was shot in the back of the head. He was fished out of a canal last night."

Pierce stepped back. He'd seen enough. Bellinger motioned the attendant to put him away.

"Nightie-night," Charlie said, covering his face and pushing the drawer back in place. He moved past them, back to his desk.

"Who was he?" Pierce asked.

"Bad guy from Tampa with a long record. Guess he won't bother you anymore."

"Why do you think he was killed?"

"Probably became a liability for someone."

That someone, Pierce guessed, carried a badge. But was the cop carrying out someone else's orders or acting on his own? He suddenly remembered that his first thought about the case after Elise played him the tape recording was that the cop Loften hired had taken the matter into his own hands. Maybe he'd ordered the murder and theft and now he'd gotten rid of the perpetrator, the link to his identity.

"You don't look so good, Pierce," Bellinger said. "You feel all right?"

"Just tired."

Bellinger pulled a .38 from his sports jacket. His eyes gleamed as he pointed it at Pierce. "Watch this, Nick. This'll wake you up."

He spun the gun a half-dozen times on his index finger. He pointed it again at Pierce, said "Bang," then gave it a half spin and handed it to him by the barrel. "All yours," he said cheerfully.

Pierce took the .38, which Carver had confiscated, and kept his eyes on Bellinger. "Fancy moves, Neil. But you could get yourself in trouble with that bullshit."

Bellinger raised his hands, laughed. "Give me a break, man. Just a little early morning exercise for the trigger finger. No harm done."

"Yeah, I suppose." But maybe Bellinger had revealed more by his trigger-finger antics than he'd intended. Maybe he was something more than the happy-go-lucky charmer who offset Carver's hard-line tactics. Pierce looked at the gun, uncertain what to do with it, and at the same time alarmed by the possibility that he might be standing in the presence of the killer. He pulled out his shirt and jammed the gun in the waistband of his pants.

"Jesus, I wouldn't do that, Nick. Safety comes off, you could blow your balls off. Give it to me."

Pierce handed the gun back to him. They walked out of the morgue and down the hall to the attendant's desk. Charlie was sipping coffee and reading the paper. "Can I get the sports section from you, Charlie?" Bellinger asked.

"Take it. I never read it," Charlie said, without looking up.

Bellinger picked it up and folded it around the gun. "Here you go. Gift-wrapped. Just don't walk any farther than your car with it or you might get busted, unless you've got a concealed weapon permit."

Bellinger laughed, but Pierce's throat was too dry to join him. "Thanks."

"One more thing," Bellinger said as Pierce started to walk away. He reached into his pocket, then dropped six bullets into Pierce's palm. "Guess you wouldn't have shot your balls off, after all."

"Guess not." Pierce took one last breath of formaldehyde-scented air and headed down the hall.

"See you around," Bellinger called after him.

The light was blinking on the answering machine as he walked into his office an hour later. The first message was brief. It was from one of Raymond Andrews's assistants, who asked him to call his boss. Andrews obviously was back in town. The second one began with the sound of soft breathing, sniffling, and he knew immediately who it was.

"Nicky, do we have to go through this over and over again? Can we just be friends? I am sorry that I stormed away, but it upsets me when you say things like that. You know we have a lot in common. We have a history. You and I should not be mad at each other. Okay? You know, you never call me Tinita anymore. Call me."

A heavy, sickening feeling settled over Pierce. It was the same old story. Get angry, make up, then act like nothing had happened, that everything was all right. But everything wasn't all right. It was all wrong. This time it was going to be different. She could leave all the messages she wanted. He wasn't returning her calls. He'd already told her how he felt. Sooner or later, she'd realize he was serious.

He felt a twinge of guilt as he rewound the tape and argued with himself.

We're divorced.

(She means well.)

The hell she does.

(She loves you.)

Bullshit.

It was just easier to stay in the past than to cut loose into an uncertain future. If she wasn't going to make the move, he would. *Adios, Tina.*

He sat down at his desk, cleared his mind, and punched Andrews's number. The same voice he'd heard on the recorder answered, and when Pierce identified himself the man said he'd transfer the call to the mobile phone. As he waited, he imagined Andrews sitting in the back of a black stretch limo that was as cool as Iceland inside and whispered across town, gliding through traffic as if there were nothing to it. He'd probably be talking to an aide, and K.J. would be at hand.

"Nicholas, how are you?"

"Hi, Ray. How was your trip?"

"Everything went as planned."

What kind of plans? Was the trip related to Noster Mundus? "Glad to hear it. We've had some developments here." He explained about the break-in at his apartment and the body he'd viewed less than an hour ago. Andrews listened until he'd finished, then asked how he was feeling. "I'm fine. Got a shiner, but it's already starting to fade."

"That's too bad, but you're obviously better off than the other guy. Listen, I had a visit first thing this morning from Lieutenant Carver. He seems to think that you might be taking Simms seriously."

Damn that Carver! "Listen, Ray, I'm well aware that she could be behind the whole thing. But there's another possibility. It could've been the cop Loften hired acting alone."

"What makes you think that?"

"Well, it makes sense. He knocks off Scarjaw to protect himself."

"That's a possibility, Nick. But why didn't he have Scarjaw kill you?"

"I don't know," Pierce conceded.

"You see, that's why I think it's Simms's game."

"I can understand how Simms might have turned the blame for her father's problems on you, but why would she have Loften killed?"

"Nicholas, I think she was so set against me that she was ready to consider anything to keep me from owning the skull. She probably knew the cop Loften was hiring; maybe she'd even introduced Loften to him."

"And you think she talked the cop into going along with her scheme." Pierce shook his head. It didn't feel right. "That seems extreme. She'd be taking a big chance." He realized he didn't like that idea any more than he liked it the other way, with Andrews behind it. He wanted the whole thing to be the cop acting alone.

"Not if she was close to the cop. Besides, she *is* an extremist. I've had one of my lawyers make inquiries about her. He's come up with some interesting bits of information. Some of her colleagues say that in the last few years, she's gone off the deep end."

The deep end . . . Hell, that could mean virtually anything. "Did these colleagues give any specifics about what they meant?"

"Simply that she's lost her scientific perspective in favor of some way-out ideas. She's done things like using a dowser on digs to try to locate buried artifacts."

"You mean a dowsing rod?"

"That's right."

"I thought that was for finding water."

The phone line crackled with Andrews's chuckle. "You'll have to ask her about that. Mahoney, her father, is the same way, but worse.

From what I understand, getting involved in the practices of a culture you're studying is not necessarily an unacceptable method of study, but he apparently lost his perspective. Probably drank some concoction the shamans made and never fully recovered."

"I see."

"That's not all. Have you had a chance to look into her financial status?"

"A bit. Not much."

"Did you know she withdrew twenty-five thousand dollars from a money market account last week?"

"No."

"Looks to me like the cop's fee for services."

Maybe Andrews was right. It was hard to imagine Elise spending twenty-five thousand dollars on a shopping spree.

When Pierce didn't say anything, Andrews went on. "So where do we stand? Does she still trust you?"

"I'm not sure she's ever trusted me, but she's still interested in working with me."

"Good. Have you seen Redington?"

"Yesterday, but just briefly."

"He's basically a good fellow," Andrews said, "but he's somehow gotten all caught up in Simms's web. I wouldn't doubt that he actually believes she had nothing to do with Loften's death. That's why I was a little worried by what Carver said. The woman must have a talent for gaining sympathy."

"She hasn't fooled me." He sounded more confident than he felt.

"Well, enough said. I trust your judgment. I know that for you to make any inroads you have to act like you're working with her. Go ahead. Tell her you're on her side."

"But what's the point?"

Pierce listened to the slight buzzing on the line. "I thought I made that clear." A sternness had entered Andrews's voice, as though he were a teacher addressing a troublesome student. "The *point* is finding the skulls. Getting back the stolen one, and finding out what she knows about the other one."

"Okay. I'll see what happens and let you know."

Pierce hung up. For the first time in weeks, he felt like taking a walk on the beach. He needed to sort things out. He kept a swimming suit,

T-shirt, and tennis shoes in a locker in the corner of his office for just such occasions.

He stood up and took two steps toward the locker, when the phone rang again. The recorder was still on. He kept it on and listened.

"Nicky, pick up the phone. . . . Pick up the phone. I know you are there. Your line was just busy."

"Fuck you," Pierce barked, without making an effort to answer the phone.

"Nicky, talk to me. . . . Please. . . . Suit yourself. I will call Gibby and see if he can tell me why you will not answer your phone."

"For Christ's sake." He snapped the receiver out of its cradle and turned off the recorder. "What the fuck do you want?"

"That is no way to talk to me. I do not deserve that. Not after the way you acted in the restaurant."

"The way I acted? You're the one who stormed out."

Softer now: "Nicky. I do not want to fight with you."

"Tina. We're history, and I'm tired of history repeating itself."

"Oh, that is cute. You are so clever, and so damn stubborn."

"Is that all you wanted to say?"

"Look, I am sorry if I embarrassed you at the restaurant. I still have the envelope with the articles and copies from the books."

"Send it to me. I know your library's not a mailhouse, but you could have given it to me at the restaurant."

"No, I want you to come and get it."

"I'm busy." He started to hang up.

"Either you come over here, or I will call Raymond Andrews and have a talk with him about you."

"Leave him out of this, Tina," he said, gritting his teeth.

"I am sure he will be interested in knowing that I have information for his case and you do not have time to pick it up because you have another girlfriend."

He thought a moment, then spoke slowly and calmly. "I'll be there in half an hour."

He slammed down the phone. "Bitch." His anger and frustration propelled him out his chair, out of the office. He knew she'd follow through on her threat if he ignored her, and he didn't need that complication. He'd pick up the envelope and tell her . . . He didn't know what he'd tell her, but he'd tell her something, something that would shut her up, something that would get his message through to her.

As he drove across the causeway to downtown, his anger became a crescive ache at the back of his eyes. He kept hearing Tina's voice on the recorder. "Pick up the phone, Nicky. I know you are there." Her precise, accented English, which he'd once thought cute, now was a burr rubbing his skin.

He veered around a slow-moving car, and his Smith & Wesson rattled in the glove compartment. He glanced into his rearview mirror and noticed a dark blue Mercedes with tinted windows shift lanes. Was it the same one he'd seen at the Coral Castle? And the same one he'd seen parked in front of his apartment the day of the break-in? He remembered a car honking; now it came together. The driver of the Mercedes had been trying to signal Scarjaw that one Nicholas Pierce was coming home.

He pressed on the accelerator and glanced in the mirror to test his notion. But the Mercedes made no effort to catch up. Maybe it was all his imagination. Hell, Miami was full of blue Mercedeses with tinted windows. As he came off the causeway and headed down Biscayne Boulevard, he decided to see if the Mercedes would pass him so he could get its license number. But he lost track of it in the traffic. After a mile or so of stop-and-go driving, he turned into the library parking lot and the .38 rattled again as he moved across the bumpy pavement. He considered waiting to see if the Mercedes showed up, but his thoughts turned to Tina, and his anger crested again.

He literally raced up the five flights to her floor. He was breathing hard as he threaded his way between carrels and shelves. He passed tables, a row of microfiche machines, a copier, and finally reached Tina's office. She was talking with two other librarians. He pounded once against the office window. It shuddered under his fist. All three looked up, startled by his sudden appearance and his grim demeanor.

"Okay, here I am. Where the hell is it?"

"Nicky. Calm down."

"Stop fucking with me."

Tina's eyes flicked nervously toward the other librarians, who were backing away and moving toward the door. "Get out of here before I call security!" she shrieked, reaching for the phone.

Pierce saw the manila envelope on the corner of her desk and snatched it. "You're not calling security. You're not calling anyone."

He yanked the phone from her hand, jerked the cord out of the wall. "No more calls. Got that?"

By the time he reached his car, he imagined that the librarians had sent a team of security guards after him and they were now sealing off the exits. He was about to be arrested for destroying public property, for threatening a library employee, maybe even for assault.

He was in such a hurry to get away that he didn't notice that his car door was unlocked, or that his Smith & Wesson no longer rattled in the glove compartment.

Twenty-One

No one saw Pierce for the rest of the day and half of the next. He spent most of the time reading the novel he'd started. It gave him a chance to forget about Tina and Elise and Andrews and the crystal skull. After reacting as he had to Tina's threat to call Andrews, he needed to get away — if not physically, at least in his mind.

Now and then he went over to his desk, where he'd left the stuff he'd grabbed from Tina, and ran his fingers over the manila envelope, debating with himself. If he didn't open it, his life might improve. If he opened it, the damned thing might prove to be a Pandora's box of unimaginable complications. Repeatedly, he turned from the desk without opening the envelope. But his resolve not to open it grew progressively weaker.

Late in the morning, when he'd finished the book, he picked up the envelope. It occurred to him that Tina had used a carrot-and-stick approach to get his attention. The envelope had been the carrot; the threat to call Andrews the stick. But none of that mattered now; it was over, done.

In the envelope he found copies of the pages from the two books Tina had brought to the restaurant and two articles by Redington. The names of both were a mouthful. One was *A Jungian Interpretation of the Mayan Myth of the Twin Crystal Skulls as Related to the Fountain of Youth Myth*. The other was called *The Study of Anomalous Behavior Related to Obsessions with Mythology*.

He read the title of the second article again, and didn't put the article down until he was finished. Redington claimed that in rare cases a myth could actually possess an individual and lead to bizarre and possibly dangerous behavior. He saw the implications, the parallels to the skull case, and suddenly wanted to talk to Redington face-to-face.

He stuffed the article back in the envelope, slipped it under his arm, and was about to leave when the phone rang. He hoped it was his credit bureau contact, whom he'd belatedly asked to run a check on Elise Simms. He'd specifically asked her to find out about any large withdrawals.

"Hello, Nick. It's Elise."

"Hi," he said coolly.

"I haven't heard from you in a couple of days, and I was wondering what was going on."

He thought for a moment about how he should respond. He knew Andrews wanted him to play along with her, but he just couldn't do it. He told her he knew about the large withdrawal she'd made from her money market account and asked what it was about.

There was a pause, and he wondered if she was making up a story. "Nick, have you seen any documentation of this money market withdrawal?"

"No. It was from an informant."

"An informant. Who? Your friend Fuego? He's working for you, isn't he?"

"Why do you say that?"

"I just got that feeling when I saw you two guys talking at jai alai. I'm right, aren't I? You don't trust me. You never have."

"Just doing my job."

"Well, Fuego must have the wrong account. I haven't taken anything out of my money market for months."

"That's not what I hear."

"Nick, even if I did take out twenty-five grand from an account, that wouldn't mean a damn thing."

The line fairly crackled with tension. "I guess not." Christ, it *is* her, he thought as he hung up and leaned against the kitchen wall. He hadn't said anything about twenty-five grand; she'd blurted the figure.

The phone rang again as he left the apartment, and he hadn't turned on the recorder. Probably Janet at the credit bureau. Hell, he'd talk to her later.

As he drove to Florida International University, he thought more about Redington's article on obsessions with myths. If his guess was right, Elise was seeing Redington as a patient. She was obsessed by the myth of the crystal skulls — no, possessed by it — and Redington, like a priest who protected the confession of a murderer, was inadvertently involved. Redington could deny it, but Pierce was taking the article with him and was ready to put him on the spot.

Possessed by a myth.

Hell, it wouldn't even be the first time he'd dealt with a case involving possession. He'd once been hired by a man who claimed his wife's bizarre behavior was related to possession by a mythological god. Sarah was an heiress, a WASP aristocrat with an opulent lifestyle, but from time to time and under the most embarrassing circumstances, she would slip into a trancelike state and proclaim herself a goddess called Oshun.

When Pierce was hired, Sarah was under treatment at a mental health center, but the doctors were baffled. Most of the time she appeared perfectly normal, and the battery of tests she'd been given revealed no psychotic delusions.

Pierce was surprised that neither the husband nor the doctors had taken the hint in the god's name. He made a couple of inquiries, and it was as he suspected. Oshun was an orisha, a god of *Santeriá.* So he'd gone to Tina's Tía Juana, the only practitioner he knew personally, for elucidation.

She was a plump, spry woman in her midfifties who lived alone in a small cement-block house in Little Havana. She always wore the same perfume (at the request of the spirits, she said, so they could find her through the scent), and ten or twelve beaded necklaces of various colors, and when she worked, she was usually dressed in white — the color for her *trabajos* or spells.

She'd listened to the details of Pierce's case and suggested he bring the woman to her. He'd returned the next day accompanied by Sarah, her doctor, and her husband. They'd followed Juana into a small room devoid of furnishings except for an altar. It was covered with candles and statues of saints, some black, others white, and with figurines of black peasants and American Indians in feathered bonnets.

At first Sarah was reserved as Juana performed a cleansing. She sprinkled Florida water on her and rubbed a bouquet of white flowers up and down her body. Finally she lit a cigar and blew clouds of smoke over her. An odd idea of cleansing, Pierce thought. But by then

Sarah seemed captivated by Juana, who started reciting a spiritist mass. Within a couple of minutes, Sarah began drooling, then convulsing. The doctor moved toward her, but Juana's assistant, a black woman, motioned him back again. At that point, amid the confusion, Sarah stepped to the center of the room and Oshun began speaking in a deep, strong voice.

She addressed each person in the room, saying something personal. She'd stepped close to Pierce, looked in his eyes, then whispered: "You travel in the astral planes." Then she spoke to the group as a whole and said that she meant no harm to her "horse," as she called Sarah, and that in making the unwanted appearances, she was giving her a message. Sarah needed to stop living two lives and join her separate identities together.

When it was over, Sarah confessed that she was keeping an apartment in Little Havana and had become fascinated with *Santería.* At first, she had wanted only to obtain readings about her future. But gradually she became fascinated with the gods themselves and had started going into trance.

Once she had opened up to her husband, Pierce's involvement was over. He later heard that her consuming interest with *Santería* had faded, and as far as he knew, the goddess Oshun never mounted that particular horse again.

Pierce parked his car, crossed the campus, and climbed the back stairs to the Psychology Department. The secretary had told him that she was expecting Redington to be in all afternoon, so he hadn't made an appointment. Pierce preferred it that way. Lost in his thoughts, he nearly bumped into a man descending the stairs. He looked up in surprise and veered to the side. But the man's briefcase still caught him on the hip. Both men excused themselves at the same time and moved on.

As Pierce entered the department offices, the quiet seemed overwhelming. Classes were over for the quarter, and the place looked vacant. But when he reached Redington's office, he saw the professor seated at his desk behind a stack of papers. He was frowning and shaking his head as he wrote a note on a typed page and didn't notice Pierce in the doorway for several seconds.

"Afternoon."

Redington scrutinized him over his half-moon glasses. "You again. What is it now?"

"Sorry to bother you."

"Don't stand there saying you're sorry. Come in and close the door. Look at this," he said, pointing to the stack in front of him. "Term papers. All afternoon I've had a low-grade headache — and have been giving consistently low grades. They can't complete a thought; they can't write a comprehensive paragraph." He shrugged and sighed. "Of course, there are exceptions, and those are the ones who have always kept me going."

Pierce eased himself down into the chair opposite Redington and nodded sympathetically.

"You came up those back stairs again?" Redington asked, then muttered that he was fortunate his students hadn't discovered that direct route to his office. "They'd probably sneak in here and change their grades." He made a halfhearted attempt to straighten the stack of papers on his desk. "So what is it today?"

"I read your journal article on myths and obsessions. Do you really think it's possible to be possessed by a myth?"

"For Christ's sake. I wrote that in 1965. But it's just as true today, I suppose."

"So you can be possessed by a story?"

Redington removed his glasses and let them hang over his chest from their elastic band. "First of all, myths are more than mere stories; they're archetypal experiences. They are part of all of us, of our collective unconscious. Do you understand?"

He nodded. "I wrote a paper back in college on Jung's ideas about mandalas."

Redington smiled, tapped the stack of papers in front of him. "Good. I certainly hope it was better than what I've been reading here. Now as to possession, let me make it clear that myths are not independent entities that creep up on you in your sleep. However, in certain circumstances mythological images can cause numinous experiences, which can result in changes in a person's psychological makeup."

"It sounds dangerous." Pierce smiled, only half joking.

"Only if the archetypal image assaults the conscious mind to the point that the individual is unable to integrate it. Then the consequences can be destructive."

Pierce nodded and tried to think how to phrase his next question. He wanted to know if Redington thought that someone who was functioning in what seemed to be a normal fashion could be possessed by a myth. Then he was going to ask him directly about Elise. "Is it possible for a person who — "

"You worried that the crystal skull myth is getting the better of you?" Redington asked.

Pierce laughed. "Me? Why do you say that?"

"Look, Nick. I understand that the situation you're in isn't very comfortable. Playing both sides never is."

Pierce's spine stiffened. "I don't know if that's true."

Redington put on his glasses and rested his chin on the palm of his hand, studying him. Pierce found the scrutiny annoying and returned his steady gaze.

"You tend to cover up your emotions, because you fear what might happen if you let loose. It's a good personality trait for a detective, but it puts you under a lot of stress."

Pierce's irritation rose another notch. Why was it that shrinks always seemed to feel obligated or entitled to dispense unsolicited psychiatric observations? *Was your childhood happy, Nick? What kind of relationship did you have with your mother? Your father?* Yeah, he could hear it now.

"Mind if I offer you a personal perspective on your situation?" Redington didn't wait for Pierce to answer. "Raymond Andrews is your problem."

I need this.

When he didn't respond, Redington raised his voice.

"You've met Elise. Do you actually think she would set up Paul Loften's murder? Or anyone's murder? Think about it."

"I have been thinking." He was about to reveal the purpose of his visit when Redington spoke up again.

"Only from the point of view of one who's working for Andrews. The last thing you want to believe is that he's the master murderer, and that's your problem. And it's clearly affecting your perception of the case."

"Why are you protecting Elise? What's at stake for you, Bill? Why are you sticking your nose into this matter?"

"The only way I stuck my nose in was by giving the detective the tape of the conversation."

Pierce glanced over Redington's desk. "What made you decide to tape it?"

Redington lifted a newspaper from the corner of his desk. Under it was what looked like a typical answering machine. He wiped a mote of dust off the top. "I can record all my conversations with this model, and I do. I got in the habit when I was department chairman. It was a safety measure. I keep the tapes a month or so, then erase what I don't want to keep."

"Is Elise your patient?"

"No, she's not," Redington said in a huff. "But yes, I am protecting her. I've seen what Raymond Andrews can do to people. Unfortunately, I've inadvertently helped him ruin the career of a very good friend, and I won't allow him to do it again; I hope you don't, either."

The evening news was droning on the TV in the next room as Pierce prepared pasta and clam sauce, and a salad for dinner. Since leaving Redington's office he'd been trying to come up with other reasons Elise Simms might have for withdrawing twenty-five grand from the bank. A new car, an extended trip overseas, the down payment on a piece of real estate . . . None of it felt right. He still hoped that the theft of the skull and Loften's death was the work of the cop and his front man, Scarjaw. But how could he prove it, and who was it — Carver, Bellinger, neither, both?

He drained the pasta shells, and was running cold water over them when the phone rang. He quickly lowered the temperature on his sauce, then answered it. It was Janet, his credit source, with information on Elise's financial status. She told him that Elise had $2,800 in a money market account, but it hadn't been removed. There had been no withdrawals in more than a year.

"You're sure?"

"Positive. But she did withdraw $25,000 from a CD account."

"When?"

"Let's see. Ten days ago. She's got a great credit rating. Pays her bills on time, doesn't charge much on her credit cards. She . . . "

"Thanks Janet. You've told me plenty."

"That's all you want?"

"That's it."

"Do I still get the Carlyle?"

"What size you want?"

"Eight by ten. The one with the old Ford parked in front."

"No problem. You'll have it in a couple of weeks."

Pierce rang off and made a note to himself on the pad next to the phone. He'd met Janet several years ago when he was exhibiting some of his South Beach Art Deco photos at a local gallery. He was just getting started as an investigator, and she became one of his first sources. His ongoing arrangement was to trade one of his photos for each credit check she handled for him.

He stirred the sauce, but he'd lost his appetite. He didn't find any joy in verifying that Elise had lied again. His problem was not Andrews, as Redington had said; it was that he really didn't want to find out that Elise was the schemer behind the theft and the murder. He walked out into the living room and stared at the television. A story about sightings of a fifty-foot-long octopus on Biscayne ended in a humorous vein with the announcer saying that the creature was made of plastic and was a PR gimmick. "That's news?" Pierce muttered. He was about to turn off the set when the announcer turned serious.

"A late-breaking story just in. A former Miami police officer, who was wounded twice in the line of duty, was shot to death this afternoon. Here's our Eyewitness News report."

The picture switched to a reporter talking into a microphone several feet in front of a car where a body lay, draped with a sheet, against the steering wheel. "The victim has been identified as Felix 'Fuego' Ferraro, a former Miami police officer who — "

"Oh, Christ, no," Pierce whispered.

"Several people in the Little Havana neighborhood say they heard shots fired about two o'clock this afternoon," the reporter continued, "but the body was not discovered until less than an hour ago when a teenage boy spotted Ferraro slumped in the seat of his car. Detectives say the assailant may have been seated in the passenger seat of Ferraro's car when he was gunned down at close range."

"Aw, Christ, Fuego."

The newscaster was back on the screen again, sharing "happy talk" with his coanchor. But Pierce didn't hear a word of it. He reached up and snapped off the television. He closed his eyes, blocking out the reality of what he'd heard. He covered his face with a hand. *Not Fuego.*

He wasn't sure how long he stood there without moving, without thinking, trying to blank everything out. But gradually a thought curled through his head: he had to call Tina. She was Fuego's cousin, and she must know by now. And he wanted to say something to her, to make sense of it, for Christ's sake.

He punched her number and listened to the ringing. On the fourth ring, he heard a voice. "Tina? Is Tina there?"

It was Consuelo, Tina's younger sister. She recognized his voice, greeted him, and he could tell from her voice that she knew. But he asked anyhow. "Have you heard about Fuego?"

"Yes, we have. Let me get Tina."

Nearly a full minute passed before he heard a voice. It was Consuelo again. "Listen, Nick. She doesn't want to talk to you now. But thanks for calling."

"Okay. I understand. I'm really sorry about this."

He hung up and smelled his clam sauce burning. He turned off the burner, scraped it from the bottom of the pan, and threw it out.

Why? Who would do it? Did it have anything to do with Loften's murder and the skull? He had to know. He'd taken Fuego off the case, and Scarjaw was dead. But then he remembered that Elise had mentioned Fuego, speculating that he was the one who had given him the information on her withdrawal.

But would she have killed him over that? He doubted it. Unless Fuego knew something else, something that would expose her. What had Fuego told him? He was looking for a woman who had been Loften's girlfriend. But she was Latin. Or was she? Her name was Marisol, but he'd never said she was Latin. Could Elise, who had been Monica, have used still another name? But why? And again a plausible answer came to mind. Maybe she'd befriended and killed Ginger to get back at Andrews, and Fuego had figured it out.

He had to see her. He wanted to watch how she'd respond when he told her that Fuego was dead. If she was guilty, he would know it. He was sure she couldn't hide it from him.

He called her number, but got her machine. He'd try later.

He'd known about Fuego's death for less than an hour when Carver and Bellinger showed up. This time both of them seemed to be in surly moods. "Mind if we come in?" Carver asked.

Pierce stepped aside, watched the two detectives move into the room. Carver looked like his usual disheveled self; Bellinger showed a surprising capacity to look somber.

"Trouble seems to dog you, Mr. Pierce," Carver said. "The man who tailed you the other night saw you talking with Fuego Ferraro at the jai alai fronton."

"I know he's dead. I just saw it on the news." Pierce lowered himself into a chair, but neither of the detectives sat down.

Carver picked at his thumbnail. Rings circled his deep-set eyes. "He is a friend of yours?"

"My ex-wife's cousin. He worked occasionally with me on cases."

"Recently?"

Pierce told them about Fuego's involvement in the skull case. "But I told him to drop it a couple of days ago."

"Why?" Bellinger asked.

"Seemed like a dead end."

Bellinger nodded, but he wasn't through. "Where were you between one and two this afternoon?"

"At Bill Redington's office."

Carver also had a question. "Where's that .38 of yours, Mr. Pierce?"

Pierce looked up at him as he realized he was a suspect in his friend's death. "My car. You don't think I — "

"Ferraro was shot with a .38. We'll want to check your weapon in the ballistics lab."

They walked out to the car and found the gun right where he said it was.

"Just a routine check," Bellinger told him.

Carver picked up the gun with his handkerchief and looked it over. "You been practicing with your new gun?"

"I haven't shot it yet."

"I'm no ballistics expert, but I'd say this gun's been fired."

"Can't be."

"Do me a favor," Carver said. "Stay home tonight. I don't want you getting into any more trouble."

Twenty-Two

The giant crystal skull looked like a transparent Halloween pumpkin. Pierce was trapped inside it; he could see through its eyes, through its hard, clear cheeks. It was devouring him. He clawed at its mouth, struggling to force its jaws open. An invisible fist pounded against its crown and reverberated in his own skull. He slapped his hands over his ears, but the terrible pounding went on and on, driving him out of the dream.

He sat up, looked around, wiped his damp brow. It was morning. The pounding again. It was the door. He glanced at the bedside clock, saw it was seven-thirty.

"Who the hell is it?" he muttered as he quickly pulled on a pair of pants. "I'm coming. Hang on," he yelled as the pounding resumed.

It was Carver again. "Where were you at one-thirty yesterday afternoon?"

"Christ, Carver," Pierce said, running a hand through his mussed hair. "I already told you. I was at Redington's office."

Pierce stepped back from the door. "Come on inside. You'll wake up the whole building talking out there."

"Did anyone else see you?"

"I came up the back stairs and left the same way. Classes were over; there wasn't anyone — No, wait. There was a guy with a briefcase that I bumped into on the stairs. He had a mustache and was in his late twenties, I'd say."

"We'll see if we can find him."

"Just ask Redington."

"He's not around. Neighbor saw him come home yesterday at three and leave a few minutes later with his wife. They were carrying suitcases."

Pierce rubbed the sleep from his face, trying to make sense of what he was hearing. "So what? I didn't do it."

"Lab says the bullet that killed Ferraro was fired from your gun."

"What? That gun never left my car."

"Tell it to the jury. You're under arrest for the murder of Fuego Ferraro."

"That's bullshit," he protested. "He was my friend. I didn't kill him."

"You'll have to do better than that," Carver admonished. "Most murder victims are killed by family or friends."

"Jesus Christ, Carver. You've got to talk to Redington," he pleaded. "I was with him."

"Bellinger is working on that now."

Bellinger, he thought. Great.

Carver didn't waste any more time. He read him his rights from a card he carried next to his badge and told Pierce to put on a shirt and shoes. He followed him into the bedroom.

"Don't you think it's a little premature to throw me in jail?" he asked, pulling on his shoes. "I mean, there're other options."

"You're it, Mr. Pierce. I don't know what your motive was, but your prints are all over the gun."

There were a thousand reasons he shouldn't be arrested. The main one was that he didn't do it. But since when did that stop an arrest if the evidence said otherwise? Besides, Carver wasn't listening. "Can I make a call?"

"You can do that downtown."

As Carver snapped cuffs on his wrists and led him out of the apartment, Pierce felt lightheaded, and about as nauseated as if a ten-pound rock rested in the pit of his stomach. During the drive across town, bits of the dream he'd been having before Carver woke him returned. Hadn't he dreamed about the crystal skull before? All he knew for sure was that he'd been yanked from one nightmare into another.

When they arrived at the courthouse, they parked near the police entrance of the county jail. Pierce was familiar with the courthouse, but he'd never entered this door or walked down this corridor. He was going to jail. But he'd get out; he'd call Gibby, and Gibby would get him a lawyer. Carver stopped in front of an elevator and pressed the button.

"How many floors?"

"What?"

"How many floors are we going up?"

"To the top. The penthouse."

A paroxysm of fear clutched his spine. Oddly, the idea of taking an elevator suddenly overshadowed his anxiety about being arrested and jailed. Hell, he'd climb the stairs in leg irons if he could avoid the elevator. "I want to take the stairs."

"I don't. And you won't."

"Carver, I'm serious. I can't do it." The door opened, and Carver pushed him forward. "Get your ass in there."

Pierce stumbled into the cramped box and sucked in his breath. The door shut and dread tightened around him. He knew instantly he wasn't going to make it. His shoulders trembled, his legs wobbled, the elevator walls pulsed inward. He squeezed his eyes tight; darkness closed around him like a vise. As the elevator rose, an invisible hand cranked the vise harder, pressing down upon him.

He gasped for air, sputtered, coughed. He was suffocating in a black hole, being crushed like an insect. Time was stuck; seconds took hours to pass. A shriek poised at the tip of his tongue. He gripped his throat. Lost his balance. Hands grabbed him, pulling him upright.

The motion stopped. Light and air exploded around him. He gulped for air, filling his lungs with the scent of floor wax. "You motherfucking asshole. You're not going to fall apart on me," Carver said, dragging Pierce from the elevator.

He never thought going to jail would be a relief. But after the elevator ride, it was. Carver turned him over to a guard, and he became official fodder for the legal system, processed like a product passing along an assembly line. No one told him what was going on, and when he asked if he could make a phone call, he was ignored. He was led into a booth and a light flashed in his face. His fingertips were pressed into an inkpad, then printed on paper. He emptied his pockets, and his belongings were inventoried.

He saw Carver and a man in a dark suit step out of an office; they studied him like an insect. Carver'd probably told him he was prone to seizures, that he was a danger to himself and other inmates, that he might need a psychiatric evaluation.

Carver left with no parting word to the new prisoner, and after the processing was finally finished, Pierce was led along a row of cells. Eyes watched him from behind the bars. The guard unlocked the door of a roomy cell. Inside on the right were several smaller cells. He directed Pierce into one of them. "When can I make a phone call?"

"Later." He slammed the door shut.

His cell, about the size of an elevator, was furnished with a wooden bench and a toilet. He'd sat there less than a minute when he heard the door of one of the other small cells sliding open and realized he wasn't alone. He looked over and saw a black kid in his early twenties watching him. He was shirtless and wore jeans; one of his wrists was bandaged.

"You don't have to hang your ass in there, you know. Just open your gate."

He saw that the kid was right. The cell wasn't locked. He slid open the door and stepped out into the larger cell. "Thanks."

"You bust out?"

Pierce frowned, uncertain what he meant. "What?"

"You bust out of another jail?"

"No. Why do you say that?"

"Because this is where they put guys they want to keep an eye on. Guys they think might bust out."

Pierce glanced up and saw a video camera panning the cell. He hadn't thought about escaping, and had no idea how he'd do it. Even if he somehow got out of the cell, he'd still need to get out of the cellblock, and the locked door was right next to the guard station.

"You're on TV day and night, and they never cut the lights. Never."

"How long've you been here?"

"Since last night. I took a walk from Z-Hills."

"From what?"

"Zephyrhills, man. Minimum security playpen. It's been my crib for six months. Had enough."

Pierce nodded. "Think they'll send you back?"

"Not if they wanna keep me around!" He laughed. "I'm going to court this morning, and then I get a new crib at the county detention center until my trial. Least that's what happened last time. They got real beds there, and food that you can eat, you know. Not the crap they shove at you here. You'll like it there."

"Yeah." Like hell, Pierce thought. "I'm Nick. What's your name?"

"Richard."

Pierce extended a hand, but Richard swatted the air above it. "Man, if you be here in jail awhile you gotta learn how to act. Make a fist, and go like this." They knocked knuckles a couple of times. "Now like this." They opened their hands and slapped their palms a couple of times. Pierce figured there was more to it than that, but Richard seemed to think that was enough for his first lesson.

"What happened to your wrist?"

"Fuckers cut me. They wanted blood. What they get you for?"

"Don't know. Probably murder."

The kid reappraised him, nodded. "Who'd you get?"

"No one. I didn't do it."

Richard grinned, flashing his teeth. "Yeah. I didn't escape, either." He laughed and punched fists with Pierce again. This time he jammed his forearm at him after slapping palms. Part three of the fraternal cellmate handshake, he thought, and walked back into the small cell — his crib. He lay down on the bench and stared up at the camera. It was going to be a long wait, no matter how quickly he got out of here.

An hour later, a couple of guards picked up several inmates for arraignment. Richard was one of them. He put on his shirt and, as he left, told Pierce he'd see him in the county detention center.

"When do I get my call?" Pierce asked the guard.

"Just hang on. You get it as soon as these guys are out of here."

It was five to eleven when he made his phone call. He kept it short, explained what had happened, asked Gibby to arrange for a lawyer. He also told him to take his spare key, open his office, and find his address book. In it, he'd find Redington's phone numbers. "You've got to find him, Gib. He's my alibi."

"Jesus Christ, Nick," Gibby said for the third time. "Anybody else you want me to call?"

He thought a moment. "Yeah, if you can't find Redington, call Elise Simms. Her home and office numbers are in the same book. She may know where he is." He didn't know if she'd be any help, but it was worth a try.

"What about Raymond Andrews?" Gibby asked.

"Not yet." Andrews was his last option, his ace in the hole. If Redington didn't show up, he'd turn to Andrews. But for the moment, he hoped to avoid getting him involved.

He'd missed breakfast. Lunch was a salami sandwich, potato chips, and coffee. He devoured it and waited. He tried to rest, but couldn't get comfortable on the bench. Mostly, he paced back and forth in the cell, considering what had happened from every possible angle.

Finally, late in the afternoon, he was taken to a visitor's room. Gibby wheeled over to the doorway and greeted him, shaking his hand and clasping his forearm. Behind him, seated at the table, was a slight, dark-haired man in his middle to late forties. Gibby spun his chair around and introduced Carlos Rodriguez. The man nodded, smiled, shook his hand.

"My lawyer suggested Mr. Rodriguez because he has experience handling criminal cases, and — "

"Because I'm Cuban. Like the victim," Rodriguez said, standing up and shaking Pierce's hand.

He looked Rodriguez in the eye. "I didn't kill Fuego. I want you to know that."

The lawyer sat back down, and Pierce took a seat across from him. "So far no one says that you have, Mr. Pierce. You haven't been charged with anything. The prosecutor's office can hold you for up to seventy-two hours. If formal charges haven't been filed, they must release you."

"You mean they might just be harassing me?"

"Not harassment. That's against the law. They are simply holding you as a suspect while the case is being investigated."

"It's harassment to me, because like I said, I didn't do it."

He turned to Gibby. His curly hair looked even wilder than usual, his eyes even bulgier. When they were partners, Pierce was called the sleepy guy, because of his droopy eyelids, and Gibby was the wide-awake guy.

"Did you find Redington?"

"He's gone. No one's seen him since yesterday afternoon, including Elise Simms."

"I'm not surprised. They set me up."

Gibby looked confused. "Why do you say that?"

"I think Simms is behind the whole thing, and Redington is protecting her. She wanted Fuego killed because he was on to her. That's what I think."

Gibby shook his head. "I don't know if you've got that right, Nick. She was pretty upset when I talked to her."

"Upset about what?"

"About your arrest, about Fuego's murder, and about Redington's disappearance. She thinks he was kidnapped, and that Ray Andrews was behind it."

"Christ. She blames him for everything. I don't buy it. Besides, Redington was seen leaving his house with a suitcase."

"But if Redington didn't want to be your alibi, he didn't have to disappear. All he'd have to do was say you weren't in his office."

Pierce shrugged. "Maybe once I was out of the way, he had other business to attend to." Like turning up the second skull, he thought.

"What other business?" Gibby asked.

"Excuse me," Rodriguez said. "I don't think speculation will do any good right now. Let's wait until you are charged, and see about getting you out of here. Then we'll talk about your defense."

"You think they'll let me out on my own recognizance?" he asked.

"Mr. Pierce. This is a murder case. I can't be sure there will even be any bail."

Twenty-Three

The sunbaked beach spread out in front of him, a mirage of seemingly endless sand, palm trees, and oil-slicked bodies. Several of the women within Thor's view from the veranda of the Sea Horse Hotel wore only string bikini bottoms. He watched with curiosity, but was aware of the irony. The only place on Miami Beach where topless sunbathing was tolerated was directly in front of a hotel known for its homosexual clientele.

The hotel bar was called the Sandscape because fifty yards or so from it, the sand rose in a dune that blocked the view of the ocean, and all you could see from here was a desert, a sandscape specked with near-naked bodies. He tilted his beer to his mouth and knocked back half of it. He was glad he was here, and not in Key West. Maybe Miami Beach was decrepit, but the place at least had some sense of class.

Key West used to have class, but he wasn't so sure anymore. He'd been there last month investigating a particularly violent Miami-based smuggling syndicate that was running an arm of its operation out of a boutique. He didn't have a name, only that the boutique was somewhere on Duval Street. Some help that was. Duval Street was one string of boutiques, broken only by the occasional gallery, restaurant, or bar.

He and one of his investigators had looked for leads at several of the bars, including the unforgettable Kokomo Tiki, which that weekend was offering a "Caribbean-style luau." He'd joked with the bartender, telling him that next week they ought to hold a Caribbean-style dogsled race. At first he thought the guy didn't hear him over the pounding disco beat that was nothing more than a tape loop playing the same synthetic refrain over and over. The bartender heard him, all right; he just didn't get it. Instead, he asked Thor if he was looking for some snow. Bingo.

He looked at the man, smiled at his sidekick. He'd found the lead he'd needed, and now his underlings were doing business with the syndicate. Another major cocaine bust was imminent, but, of course, it wouldn't matter. New syndicates quickly replaced defunct ones. Same drug, new people. And sometimes even the same people, out on bond.

Key West had been tolerable for Thor mainly because of the tropical flora. It was a botanical paradise, an island arboretum, where exotic and bizarre growth was to be found literally at every turn. There were scheffleras with glossy leaves; gumbo limbo trees with peeling red bark that made them look sunburned; massive banyans with aerial roots as thick as his thighs. On one street were flaming blossoms of poinciana trees, on another the night-blooming cereus, a South American cactus that looked as if it belonged in a desert. And, of course, there were the palms, from bushy ones like the Canary Island date palm and the fan palm to the towering Cuban royal and the latania.

"Thor. There you are."

He bolted out of his chair as he realized that Odin was standing next to him. He took pride in his ability to observe without being detected, and was himself rarely surprised by anyone. But he'd been lost in reverie.

"Sit down," Odin said.

"Would you like a drink?" Thor looked around for a waiter as Odin pulled up a chair.

"I've already told the waiter to bring me a spritzer." He grinned as he looked out at the beach. "Enjoying the view?"

"You bet."

He wondered whether Odin liked the view of the topless women on the beach, or whether perhaps he preferred to look at the handsome young men in tight shorts who stood at the bar. Odin had chosen the meeting place. Just as he'd chosen their names. He wondered how he would react if Thor called him by his real name. Probably not well. He'd consider it a deviant act, and Odin didn't tolerate rebels, at least not in his rank. That was why Gore was dead and Pierce was in jail.

The waiter placed the spritzer on the table and Odin carefully stirred it with his swizzle stick, taking his time.

"Thor, we're close now; I feel it in my bones. Very close. Are you ready?"

"What if we can't find the other one?"

"It's not a matter of looking. It's a matter of waiting. It won't be found until the appropriate time."

"That's what worries me," Thor said. "I don't think I'm going to hang on much longer. They're coming down on me. I can feel it."

Odin nodded. "I know. But don't worry. It'll be sooner than you think."

Twenty-Four

The eye of the video camera seemed to follow Pierce as he paced back and forth in the cell. Who monitored it? Did Carver and Bellinger stop by to watch him? Did he look anxious? Neurotic? Guilty?

He stopped in front of the camera and peered up at it. He grinned. Then he continued to pace, until a guard in his early twenties with a Marine-style crew cut slipped his breakfast tray through the slot in the door. "For the guest of honor. Glad to see you're still here," he remarked, and walked away chuckling to himself, as if he'd just cracked a joke and Pierce had missed the punch line.

Breakfast was rubbery scrambled eggs, cold toast, and weak coffee in a plastic mug. It was every bit as bad as the night he'd just spent on the hard bench. His legs were sore and cramped. He'd been given a thin blanket and a pillow, but his back and neck felt bruised. Richard, his short-term cellmate, had been right about the light. It was never turned off, and as if that and the bench weren't enough to keep him from getting much sleep, he was wakened twice during the night by a guard on the boardwalk above the cells.

The first time, he'd bolted awake as someone called his name and a flashlight beam caught his face. He'd remembered where he was and thought he was getting out. He'd leaped up, but the guard just moved on without another word. He'd barely dozed off, maybe an hour later, when it happened again. He'd cringed as the bright light shone in his eyes and shielded his face. But this time, he'd just turned over and pulled the blanket over his head.

"So how was the chow?" Crew Cut asked when he came by to pick up the empty plate.

"About like the bench. Why did they wake me up during the night?"

"Part of our services for the guest of honor."

Pierced listened to him laugh as he walked away. "Real funny guy," he muttered.

A couple of hours later Crew Cut said, "A call for you," holding up a telephone. "Thought you'd like to take it in your office. Just pick it up and say, 'Hellhole.' Get it? Hellhole." Crew Cut cackled at his joke.

Pierce took the phone and sat down on the bench. The phone was a prison special — no dial, no buttons. He lifted the receiver, thinking it was Gibby.

"Yeah," he said.

"Nicholas?"

Aw, shit. It was Andrews. "Uh, Ray. Hi. I — uh . . . I guess you heard what happened."

"Tina called me last night."

"I was set up."

"I suspected as much. I can have a lawyer down there within the hour. I'll get you out."

"I've already got one, but he can't do much until they arraign me."

"You mean you haven't gone to court yet?"

"Not yet."

Andrews was quiet a moment. "I'd like to know what the hell's going on."

Pierce nearly laughed. "You're not alone there."

"Feel free to have your lawyer call me if you need any help. Just hang in there. I'm sure everything will get straightened out."

"Thanks, Ray."

Feel free, he thought as he hung up. He didn't. Not a bit.

Pierce smelled food. Lunchtime. The only way to tell time in here was by the rhythms and rations of the jail itself. He figured he'd been here at least thirty hours, and he still hadn't seen a judge. His life was on hold, and it seemed that the person on the other end of the line had forgotten all about him.

"Still alive, I see," Crew Cut said when he passed him his lunch of two hot dogs, potato salad, and milk.

"Still alive," Pierce repeated as the guard walked off.

He tasted the potato salad; it was the blandest he'd ever eaten. Forty more hours, forty-two tops, he thought. He wished they'd return his watch so he could check the time. He wished someone would tell him something. Get it over with.

Jangling keys. Pierce sat up and dropped his legs over the side of the bench. Maybe this was it, the arraignment.

"You know this is a special cell, Pierce," Crew Cut said, pointing at the camera as he unlocked the door. "And you're a special case."

"You guys really think I'm going to escape?"

"Yeah, sure. Escape through death. You're in the suicide watch."

Pierce remembered the bandages around Richard's wrist. "I'm not suicidal."

"Don't tell me about it. Tell the shrink. C'mon. He's waiting to see you."

"Jesus, now what?" he muttered.

He was taken to the same visitor's room where he'd seen Gibby and the lawyer. To his surprise, Redington was seated at the table. Redington, his ticket out of here.

"Where the fuck have you been?" Pierce hissed as he sat down. "You're my alibi, for Christ's sake."

Redington jabbed a finger at Pierce. "Don't talk to me that way," he groused. "Just listen. I've got a few things to tell you."

"Well, that'd be a great start, Professor."

Redington twisted the elastic band that held his half-moon glasses. He didn't look any different than he did in his office. He wore the same suit coat, and his white hair was tied back. The only thing missing was the thermos of hot water.

"I told Carver you were with me when your friend was killed."

"Good. Since it happens to be the truth. What the hell else did you tell him?"

Redington sat back and started explaining.

About an hour after Pierce had left his office, he said, someone called and told Redington he'd be killed if he told anyone he'd seen Pierce that day. He left the office immediately and went home. He didn't know what it was about, but he figured it had something to do with the investigation of Loften's murder.

"My wife and I were planning on leaving in a few days for our place in the Smokies. It's very private; we don't even have a phone. We decided to leave immediately. The rest of that day and the next, I tried to blank out the incident. I didn't want to think about it, but, of course, it kept coming to mind."

Redington looked down at his hands as he continued. He said that he'd awakened this morning to feelings of guilt, knowing that he was not only ignoring something that could affect another person's life, but was allowing some unknown person to force him into hiding. "Finally, my wife told me to go into town and call Elise. When I did, I was surprised by how concerned she was about me. She told me everything that had happened, and when I heard you were in jail I made up my mind to come back. My wife agreed, and insisted on returning with me."

His story, Pierce thought, sounded genuine; he told Redington he appreciated his returning. The old professor waved a hand, an impatient, almost deprecatory gesture. "I refuse to live in fear that something I do or say is going to get me killed." He paused and glanced over his shoulder toward the door. Bellinger had just stepped in. He ambled over to the table as though he were just passing through and happened to see them.

He nodded to Redington, looked over at Pierce. "You're free to go, Nick. Just pick up your stuff at the desk. Sorry about the mistake. Happens to the best of us." He smiled and glanced conspiratorially at Pierce. "Even Mo Carver."

Surprise, surprise. And wasn't everyone friendly and helpful all of a sudden. Suspicious, he thought, but he didn't ask any questions. He wasn't about to push his luck.

On his way out, he picked up an envelope containing his billfold and a receipt that described his car. Then he heard the bad news. Swedie had been towed in as evidence and wouldn't be ready for him to pick up until tomorrow morning. Redington, who was standing nearby, offered to drive him home and said he'd get the car and meet him in front of the courthouse.

After he'd signed several forms, Crew Cut opened the gate to the cellblock. "You stay alive now," he said, apparently still convinced that Pierce was suicidal.

"You, too," he replied, and headed for the stairs.

Redington's Volvo was the epitome of luxury — lush, comfortable seats, tinted windows, a great air conditioner. Riding through downtown Miami had never been so enjoyable, and Pierce took a renewed interest in everything around him. He looked in the windows of the shops and at the people on the streets. They were young and old, mostly Latin and black, and he listened to the street chatter, feeling like a tourist rather than a longtime resident. For a change, he didn't even mind the long waits at the traffic lights.

Redington hummed along with the radio, allowing Pierce to enjoy his restored freedom and think about what he'd told him. As they crossed Biscayne Bay, he puzzled over the relationship between Elise and Redington. The more he thought, the more confused he felt. Redington had gotten him out of jail — when he could've just as easily stayed away — and was delivering him home. But he also knew that he was protecting Elise; he'd said as much. But was he protecting her from Andrews, or from the law?

"Have you talked to Ray since your arrest?" Redington asked as they neared his apartment.

"He called me earlier today."

"Doesn't surprise me. Are you still working for him?"

The question annoyed Pierce. "Kind of hard to do much work when you're behind bars."

As he got out of the car, he thanked Redington again.

"You're out of jail, Nick. Now what?"

"I'm going to see what I can do to find Fuego's murderer. Right now, nothing else matters."

Pierce had been home about two hours, and had showered and eaten a meal when he heard a knock on the door. It was Carver.

"Now what?"

Carver walked in without answering. "If you think Redington's word means anything to me, you've got another think coming. That doesn't clear you. It makes me even more suspicious. Especially since no one else saw you."

"I told you I bumped into a guy on the steps."

"So you said. What's his name? What's he look like? What was he wearing? For all I know, you made him up."

Pierce crossed his arms. "Is that why you came here, to tell me you think I'm a liar and a killer?"

Carver's dark eyes watched him.

"If you want to find the killer, Lieutenant, why don't you look over your shoulder?"

"What are you talking about?"

"You mean *who* am I talking about. Your partner, Bellinger, that's who."

"What about him?"

"I think he's the dirty cop."

Carver stared at him. "If you've got some evidence, I'm ready to listen."

Pierce looked down at the floor. He didn't have anything on Bellinger; that was the problem. "Does he drive a dark blue Mercedes?"

Carver laughed. "On his salary? Get serious! The guy lives in a dump and drives an old ragtop Cadillac that he bought for fifteen hundred dollars. He never spends money for anything he can't put on his back or comb through his hair."

"I've seen the car following me. It was parked outside my apartment the night I got jumped. . . . I suppose he'd keep quiet about it if he paid for it with tainted money."

"You got a license plate number?"

"No."

"Just what do you have on Bellinger?"

"It's just a hunch."

Carver glared at him. "That's the problem with dicks like you, Mr. Pierce. You've always got hunches and no proof."

Twenty-Five

The morning light slanted through the venetian blinds, forming dark, narrow bars on his ceiling. A fitting metaphor, he thought, for his two days in jail. Fitting and depressing.

He dropped his legs over the side of the bed and went into the bathroom, still groggy despite nine hours of sleep. He stepped into the shower; the hot spray pelted his cheeks, his shoulders, and chest. It washed away the physical vestiges of his incarceration, but didn't touch the emotional wounds of Fuego's murder. It was still hard to believe.

He was toweling himself dry when the phone pealed. He wasn't in the mood to talk to anyone. The way his luck had been running lately, it was probably Carver with more questions and accusations. But after the fifth ring he walked into the bedroom and answered. Elise's voice was soft and concerned, but it didn't comfort him; he wished he hadn't answered.

"I'm glad you're out of jail, Nick."

"So am I."

"I'm really sorry about your friend."

"Yeah." Sorry, and maybe responsible, he thought.

"Would you like to come over for lunch?"

"Can't. I've got to go downtown and get my car back from the police. I don't know how long it's going to take." His tone was brusque, but he didn't want to alienate her, so he added: "How about this evening?"

"That's fine. How about if we order Chinese takeout? What do you like? I'll order ahead of time." When he hung up, his evening was all planned. Tonight, he'd put her on the spot.

He dressed and called Gibby, who picked him up in his customized van and drove him downtown. When he presented the receipt for his car to the attendant in charge of the police garage, he was told to sit down. He waited two hours in a dingy room that smelled like stale smoke before he was finally told it was ready. He signed the release papers, then waited another five minutes until the attendant showed him to the car. He patted the Saab affectionately on the fender. "Hope they weren't too rough with you, Swedie."

Inside, he looked around. Everything looked the same. No ripped upholstery, no missing door panels, nothing destroyed. Even the manila envelope with the copies of articles that Tina had given him were still on the passenger seat. No doubt they'd been copied and examined, but at least they'd been returned. He flipped through the package and realized that he still hadn't read one of Redington's articles. Later, he thought.

Pierce's first stop was his office, to see if there were any messages. To his surprise, his answering machine was turned off and there were no calls on the tape. He thought back, trying to remember the last time he'd left the office. Ever since his secretary had quit, he'd been careful to remember to turn on the machine.

He spent the afternoon on the street, looking up everyone he knew who'd known Fuego, but nobody had talked to him on his last day. He also asked about Bellinger, but didn't get anywhere. It was obvious from the reactions to him that some of them knew Pierce himself was a suspect. Even if they had seen Fuego or knew anything about Bellinger, they might not be willing to talk to him about it.

It was just after five when he stopped at the Jack of Clubs. He ordered a beer and two hard-boiled eggs. His only lead was the dark blue Mercedes, and he didn't even have a single digit of its license number.

"There you go, Nick," Leni said as she slid the beer and eggs across the bar. "How was your day?"

He looked up at her. If she knew about his arrest, she gave no indication. "Sore feet and no answers."

"So what's the question?"

"Who killed Fuego?"

She shook her head. "It's a goddamn shame. I couldn't believe it when I saw it on the tube. I mean, I'd just served him a beer a few hours before."

"You *saw* him that day?"

Lent glanced in the mirror, checking out the half-dozen customers behind her. She turned back to him and leaned forward, her voice hushed. "He was here just before noon. He didn't stay too long."

Pierce took a swallow of beer, trying to contain his excitement. "Who was he with?"

She wiped the bar with a rag. "Nobody."

"What did he say to you?"

She shrugged. "Not much."

"What kind of mood was he in?"

Leni pushed back a strand of her strawlike hair, skewed her pale blue eyes, thinking about it. "He wasn't happy. I mean Fuego was never the ha-ha happy type. He was intense. You know, his cheek twitched, his eyes looked around. That's how he was." She swiped at the bar with her rag. "Of course, he was always sort of that way."

Pierce nodded as he peeled his eggs. "Remember anything else?"

"He made a call."

He glanced over at the pay phone, which was about five feet from the bar, imagined Fuego standing there. "Did you hear what he said?"

"It was too noisy, and I wasn't listening. But now that you mention it, I think he called you."

"Why do you say that?"

"Because when he came back to the bar he complained that you were never in your office, and he had to talk to your machine."

The problem with that, Pierce thought, was that his recorder had been off. "You sure he was talking about me?"

"Pretty sure."

He picked up an egg, cracked it on the bar. He remembered the phone ringing as he left for Redington's office that day. Maybe Fuego had called him at home, too. "What else did he have to say?"

"Nothing much. . . . Well, there was one other thing, now that I think about it. I asked him if he wanted a second beer after he got off the phone, and he said — "

"Hey, Leni."

She glanced to her right as one of the customers — the old guy Pierce had seen here before — rapped his bottle on the bar and called her name again. "All right, Jimmy. I'm coming."

She turned to Pierce. "Be right back. The baby'll have a fit if I ignore him."

Mother-bartender, Pierce thought as he watched her tend to the old man. He mechanically finished peeling his eggs and waited patiently. Maybe what Fuego had said to her would be meaningless, but maybe it was just what he needed. He'd devoured one of the eggs by the time Leni moved back toward him along the bar.

"I swear that old man thinks I'm his old lady."

"So what did he say?"

"Him? He just wanted me to listen to his usual bullshit."

"No. I mean Fuego. You were telling me he said something to you."

"When?"

Pierce hesitated before he spoke. The Jack of Clubs wasn't a place where you drilled people for facts or exact quotes, but he had to get whatever he could. "You remember, after you asked if he wanted another beer."

"Oh, yeah. He says to me no, he's gotta go check out a book."

It didn't make sense. Fuego wasn't a reader.

"You sure it was a book, not a bookie?"

"Yeah, I'm pretty sure he said a book. Check out a book. Least, I think so. Maybe it was bookie."

When he pulled into Elise's driveway, she opened the door and waved. She was dressed casually in a cotton T-shirt and the same white drawstring pants she'd worn the first time he'd met her. He didn't know what was going to happen this evening, but he sensed it would be a turning point. Before he left, he would make up his mind about Elise.

"I asked Bill to join us for dinner," she said as he stepped inside. "I hope you don't mind. He won't be here for a few minutes yet."

"No problem. Hope he's in a good mood."

Elise grinned and wrinkled her nose. "He's always a little grumpy, but that's just his way. Don't be put off by it. He likes you."

He wondered how Redington acted if he *didn't* like you. "That's good to know."

"I already ordered. You want a glass of wine or iced tea?"

"Iced tea's fine."

He watched her as she hurried off to the kitchen. She seemed nervous, too anxious to please, to be a good hostess, he thought as he sat down on the couch. When she returned to the room and handed him his drink, she asked if he'd talked to Andrews since he'd gotten out of jail.

"I don't know if that's any of your business, Elise." It came out more sharply than Pierce intended. Take it easy, he told himself. "But, no, I haven't had a chance."

"Good," she said, sitting down across from him. Seemingly unperturbed by his brusqueness, she added: "Let's hope he still thinks you're licking your wounds from your stint in jail."

He smiled, sat back in his chair. "You think I'm in that much danger from him?"

"I think it's unwise ever to underestimate Andrews. Besides, anything could happen in the next three days."

"Why do you say that?"

"Because according to the Tzolkin, the next three days, June 17–19, 1990, mark the period when the twin skulls will be reunited."

"That so," he said.

Elise shook her head, perplexed. "Don't you understand the significance?"

Pierce had something else on his mind. He set his drink down on a coffee table. He hadn't taken a sip. "Look, you *did* take twenty-five grand out of the bank."

She was caught off guard. She looked startled. Then her shoulders slumped and her features shifted: happy to glum. Her hands moved over her arms in quick, urgent motions, as if to warm them. She averted her eyes, gazing at the floor, and finally muttered, "You said a money market; it came from a CD."

"Big deal."

"I felt like a fool. That's why I didn't tell you about it."

"Why a fool?"

"Because I gave it to Steve."

"What?"

"He told me he'd lost a lot of money in bad investments in the stock market and needed help. I'm just a sucker for his sob stories."

When he didn't respond, she continued: "Besides, you're not the only one who's had some difficulties the last couple of days. Lieutenant Carver tried to get me to confess to this big conspiracy. He even tried to drag Steve into it. Maybe Carver *is* the cop Paul Loften hired."

She made it sound as if her difficulties with Carver explained her lie about the loan. But he let it go for the moment. "His partner, Bellinger, makes a pretty good candidate, too. I'm sure that whoever that bad cop is, he killed Fuego, or he knows who did it."

Elise nodded and when she spoke, her voice was gentle and sympathetic. "Nick, I want to tell you again how bad I feel about Fuego. It's terrible, and I'm partly responsible. I dragged you into all of this."

"You didn't drag me into anything. I was hired by Andrews."

"But I could have warned you to drop the case. Instead, I got you to play along, and look what's happened."

He watched her closely as she spoke. He thought he'd be able to tell right away if she was involved in Fuego's murder. Something in her expression would give her away. But he couldn't see anything clearly, and she seemed sincere. Maybe her lies really were a result of her feelings of shame about her continuing relationship with her divorced husband. If anyone could understand those sentiments, he could.

"You think Steve really needed the money?"

"I believed him."

There was a loud knock at the door and Pierce looked up, startled. "That's either dinner or Bill."

She moved over to the door and let Redington into the house. They greeted each other, and Redington glanced at his watch. "Hope I'm not too late."

"Dinner's not even here yet," she assured him. "You want your usual cranberry spritzer?"

"That'll be fine."

She seemed relieved to have something to do, and hurried off toward the kitchen. Pierce stood and greeted Redington and then, as both men sat down, considered commenting that he was glad to see he drank something besides hot water. But he thought better of that. Instead, he asked if his wife minded his leaving her at home. He was trying to be friendly and conversational, but Redington seemed to take affront.

"I didn't leave her at home," he snapped. "She's staying with her sister for a few days."

"Oh, I see." He fidgeted in his chair and tried to think of something else to say. Redington, meanwhile, peered at him over the rim of his half-moon glasses.

"I hope you've thought more about what I said the other day, Pierce, when you asked about myths and possession."

He nodded, trying to remember what he'd said, then realized he was referring to Elise. *Protective old goat.*

When Elise appeared with Redington's drink, she glanced between the two men, sensing their unease. She grabbed hold of the faltering conversation and steered it toward Pierce's jail experience. Was it awful? How did they treat him? She couldn't imagine what it must have been like.

"Actually, the worst part was taking the jail elevator. I can't ride them."

Elise laughed. "Why's that?"

"Claustrophobia or something. I start feeling like I'm suffocating."

"So what do you do?" she asked. "Take the stairs all the time?"

"Yeah."

"How long has this been a problem for you?" Redington asked.

Playing shrink again; it annoyed Pierce.

"It's a problem only when I get in an elevator. I got stuck in one in college. In fact, if you can believe it, I was with Andrews."

"Really?" Elise said, then shook her head and frowned. "But that was years ago. You shouldn't be affected by those feelings now."

"Doesn't matter."

"What do you remember about being stuck in the elevator with Andrews?" Redington's voice shifted to the professional shrink tone he'd used with him in his office the other day.

"Hardly anything. I remember realizing we were stuck. But nothing after that. I never could remember."

"What did Ray say about it later on?"

"Nothing. It was like it never had happened. So I never asked him about it."

There was a knock at the door, and Elise leaped up. "That's got to be dinner."

"Let me give you some money," Pierce said.

"Nope. It's my treat."

To Pierce's relief, the topic of elevators wasn't mentioned throughout dinner, and he hoped they'd both forgotten about it. He found talking about it somewhat embarrassing. But Elise brought it up again once she'd broken out the Frangelico.

"Hey, Bill, you think it would help Nick with this elevator phobia if you hypnotized him?"

"It's not a phobia," Pierce said.

"Your problem may not even be elevators," Redington said. "It could be that something traumatic occurred in that elevator between you and Andrews. You've blanked it out, but Andrews hasn't forgotten. It might even relate at some level to what's going on right now."

"Well, guess I'll never know."

Redington pointed his glasses at him. "Unless you confront it."

Pierce chuckled and held up his hands. "No thanks to the hypnosis."

"Oh, c'mon, Nick," said Elise. "It might be worthwhile. Bill's really good. I send my students who are having difficulties to him. Not one of them has ever regretted it."

"I don't think so." Who knows what they might try to pull.

Redington cleared his throat. He obviously knew what Pierce was thinking. "Don't worry about my taking control of you and implanting suggestions in your mind that you don't agree with. With hypnosis you never give up control of yourself unless you do so willingly. In fact, I typically include the suggestion that you will maintain control and remember everything."

"What do you say, Nick?" Elise said, giving him a look of encouragement. "Why don't you try it?"

His resistance slowly disintegrated. He was curious about where it would lead, and if he was honest about it, he didn't think anyone could take away his self-control. "I suppose. But only if you record it."

Redington agreed, and they moved back into the living room where Pierce sat down in a reclining chair. While Elise set up the tape recorder, Pierce removed his shoes and made himself comfortable. "Okay, once you're fully relaxed," Redington was saying, "I'm going to lead you into an elevator. Then we'll go back to your experience."

"Is there anything in particular I should do?"

"Just listen to the sound of my voice, and follow my instructions. You're going to get very relaxed."

Redington nodded to Elise, and she started the recorder. "I want you to breathe deeply, count to five as you take in a long, slow breath through your nose, then count to five again as you exhale through your mouth."

Pierce closed his eyes and concentrated on his breathing. All traces of Redington's gruffness disappeared. His voice was soothing, like the sound of water in a brook, as it directed him to relax his muscles and skin, starting from the top of his head and working down. Slowly the tension drained from his body.

He was so at ease that he was hovering on the border of sleep when Redington told him to imagine his body expanding like a balloon. "You're getting lighter and lighter, and you're starting to float. It's a pleasant sensation as you float up through the ceiling and above the house. Glide for a moment slowly over the trees and look around. What do you see?"

He felt lightheaded, and envisioned himself looking down on Elise's gabled roof. Beyond it he could see the house across the street where the nosy old lady lived. The sun was low in the sky and the trees and houses were casting long shadows. But it was just his imagination. He was creating it, not really seeing it, so he didn't say anything.

"Just tell me whatever comes into your head. Some people see images, and for others it's more like thoughts. Whichever way it is for you, that's what you're seeing."

He described the roof.

"Good. Keep going now, higher and higher until you can see all of Miami and the ocean below you. It's beautiful, isn't it?"

Pierce nodded.

"Now you're going even higher. . . . Up, up . . . Past the clouds, away from the earth. You're entering a place that's bright as day and you can see clearly around you. You're on a flat plain that's white and fluffy, and your body is normal again. Your feet sink a little into the soft substance, but you can walk.

"Look out over the plain. In the distance, there's a blue dome, and you're moving toward it. Tell me when you reach it."

Pierce imagined himself walking toward a cerulean dome, his feet kicking up the soft powder below them. It was as if he were walking through sparkling, dry snow, but there was no resistance or coolness to the stuff. He saw himself reaching a massive, seamless dome.

"Okay."

"Place your hands on the walls, and as you do so a doorway opens for you. Step inside. You're in a foyer with a high ceiling now, and before you is a very special elevator. You can go into it whenever you like. There's nothing to fear in this elevator."

Oddly, he not only saw the foyer, but aspects of it that Redington hadn't described. The walls were gold-colored, and gold pipes like those of an organ hung down over his head. The exterior of the elevator was immense; golden lines curved over the door. It made him think of a gigantic old jukebox, and now the door was opening. He took a breath, let it out, and stepped inside.

Redington's voice was gentle and soothing as he continued describing the scene. The elevator was large, airy, and well lit. He was comfortable inside it. The door closed and he felt movement.

He was directed to look above the door, and was told he'd see the number ten. He looked up, but for some reason there were two nines between the one and zero. Instead of ten, it read 1990.

"Now as I count backward, you'll see the numbers changing until we reach number one. Then the elevator will stop and you will have returned to the day when you were temporarily stuck in an elevator with Raymond Andrews. Ten . . . nine . . . eight . . . "

He listened to Redington counting, but the numbers he saw were moving backward faster than Redington's count, and he knew they were years.

"Seven . . . six . . . What you see will be your own impressions. My words will guide you, but won't alter your perception of any past events. You are in control. Five . . . four . . . This experience will not only help you overcome your fear about elevators from this time on, but will also help you to clarify your feelings about Raymond. Three . . . two . . . one."

Even before Redington reached the last digit, Pierce saw the number 1969 above the elevator and felt a sense of apprehension. The elevator was small and cramped. Like it had always been. It was as if he were waking up and realizing where he was.

He forced himself to focus on his surroundings. Andrews was standing across from him. He was younger, and his hair was longer. He seemed tense, as if Pierce had just said something he didn't like. "Nicholas, the Colombians are counting on your help. If you don't go back to Santa Marta, you could be in real danger. Things are starting to get rougher, you know."

"I'll be in danger, but not you, Ray. Right?"

Andrews grinned and gritted his teeth. "That's right, buddy. It's your neck."

"Like hell." Pierce took a step forward and slammed his fist into his roommate's mouth. Andrews stumbled back and grabbed his jaw.

"What do you see?"

The words seemed to come out of nowhere. He was confused a moment, then realized the voice was Redington's. "I hit him."

Andrews wiped the blood from his mouth. His lower lip was split, and he was simmering with anger. "You're fucking crazy, Pierce."

"What's going on now?" Redington asked.

Andrews suddenly rushed him, grabbed him by the shoulders, and slammed his head against the elevator wall. Pierce slumped to the floor, slipping from consciousness. "And don't think you're getting off that easy. Nobody hits me and gets away with it."

He heard Andrews's voice, but at the same time he was looking past him to the numbers above the door. "We're moving. The numbers are changing."

"The elevator is moving?" Redington asked.

Pierce was confused. "It's not the elevator that's moving. The numbers, they're . . . I can't read them. They're moving too fast."

"What do the numbers mean to you?" Redington asked.

"They're not floors, they're years."

"Okay. Keep watching them. Tell me when they stop."

"They're slowing," Pierce said. "I don't know if it's a year. It stopped at one . . . two . . . eight . . . zero."

"Twelve-eighty. The year 1280?"

For a moment, he didn't speak. When he did, his words were slow, his voice a monotone. "Ray's not here anymore."

"Where is he?"

"Don't know. Gone."

"That's okay. What do you see?"

"The door's opening." He took a deep breath, exhaled. He knew he was lying on the couch and his eyes were moving rapidly under their closed lids. But at the same time, he felt himself stepping out of the elevator. "I see a forest. Very green. And mountains. There's a trail ahead of me."

"Where does it lead?"

Instantly he knew . . . and was there. "To a thatched hut. There's a woman sitting in front of it on the ground, doing something, and a child nearby."

"What's the woman look like?"

"She has brown skin, long black hair. She's wearing some sort of loose clothing like a dress. She's fat . . . hmm, maybe pregnant."

"Who is she?"

"I don't — she's . . . I think she's my wife."

"Look down at your feet. What do you see?"

"I'm wearing leather sandals. My feet are brown."

"Step away from yourself. You can do that. Look at yourself. What do you see?"

It was a dream, but not a dream because he was awake. He described a man with thick black hair, high cheekbones, dark eyes. He was muscular, short, brown-skinned.

"What are you wearing?"

"White cotton pants. Thick, raw cotton. They reach about to the middle of my calves. I'm wearing a loose cotton tunic that goes down to the middle of my thighs."

"What is your name?"

He thought a moment. "Atlan."

"Okay, what is the significance of this time for you?"

He answered without hesitating. "I have an aim."

"You mean like a goal, an objective?"

"Yes."

"Okay. Go now to the time when you're attempting to achieve that aim. . . . What do you see?"

"Candles in a cavern. Men are seated in a circle, and I can see myself. I'm lying on my stomach in the center of the circle. But I also see myself floating above everyone."

"Now what?"

"The two bodies are together. My breathing is fast."

"Are you sick?"

"No, I am happy. Very happy. I have returned from the underworld. I am alive, and I have it."

"What do you have?"

Atlan rolled over on his back, and he was clutching something. He grasped it in his hands, held it up. The eyes of several men around him seemed to grow large in the flickering candlelight. They muttered their approval.

"The God of Death. I've captured it from the enemy."

"What does the God of Death look like?"

"Crystal skull."

"Is this important?"

"No one who has tried to get the sacred skull has returned. Now the God of Death will protect us from our enemies."

"How did you get the skull?"

"By the changing."

"What is that?"

"You take the drink and change so you can travel far and fast."

"What do you do with the skull?"

"I take it to the Old One."

"Who is he?"

"Man of power. He guides us. He makes the drink."

"What does the man look like?"

"Lots of wrinkles. Sharp eyes that watch everything."

"What else do you know about him?"

"I don't . . . I'm not supposed to know."

"It's okay now to know."

"I think I am more powerful than he is. I have brought back the sacred skull."

"What else do you know?"

He thought a moment. "No one can be stronger than him. He will try to kill me."

"Look closely at his face again. Is he anyone you know in this lifetime?"

Pierce gazed into the eyes of the old sorcerer who was holding the crystal skull in his hands. Candlelight flickered across his face. He thought of Redington. It didn't fit. Elise, and they weren't her eyes, either. Then he knew. He could see the two faces melding. "Yes. It's Andrews."

Twenty-Six

A black-lacquered coffin gleamed under the bright lights. The top was open, and people were leaving their seats in the chapel to walk by it. Pierce didn't get up; he wanted to remember Fuego alive. So he sat in the pew, conjuring memories, pulling them out like a magician plucking doves from a top hat.

Now and then, he glanced around, astonished by the number of people in the chapel. Fuego had seemed like a loner — a man with contacts, but not a congregation of friends. Several wore police uniforms; others paying their last respects looked like underworld types. It was an odd and somehow fitting combination. He spotted Carver and Bellinger across the aisle and nodded as Carver's gaze slid to the side and fixed on him.

There was also a host of Hispanics, from toddlers to octogenarians. Family members: He recognized several of them, including a couple of Tina's sisters and Tía Juana, who was also Fuego's aunt. She wore a black veil and several strings of red and black beads.

He glimpsed the figure of a woman dressed in black walking up the aisle. Even from the rear and with her raven hair piled on her head, there was no mistaking Tina's petite figure. She paused at the casket, then returned down the aisle, her eyes glistening with tears. She stared straight ahead until she was a couple of rows in front of him. Her eyes shifted, settled on him. Then she was past him.

The service began, and the minister murmured the expected aphorisms — that death was a new beginning and not the end, and God in His infinite wisdom had chosen to take Felix Ferraro from his friends and family. Such bland confidence would not be Pierce's lot. Fuego was dead, and he was going to find out who was behind it;

that was all he felt. The minister, who most likely didn't know Fuego, was making his death sound like justified homicide: God needed his servant elsewhere.

That was about par with the reality of his hypnotic regression. It had the mark of a dream, melding recent events and circumstances in his life into an outrageous fantasy. After it was over, he'd told Redington and Elise that he'd found the experience interesting, but didn't know what it meant, except that he had a fertile imagination.

Redington, naturally, had analyzed it symbolically, suggesting that the cave represented his unconscious mind, and the skull stood for the wisdom and answers he was seeking. "But your search is fettered by the old sorcerer who is symbolic of your feelings about Andrews."

"But what happened in the elevator?"

"You were probably so sure that Andrews would retaliate against you for striking him that you blocked out the incident. When you woke up, you didn't remember what had happened."

"I don't even remember having a sore head, but I must have had at least a lump."

"Again, you didn't want to know about it."

Elise's interpretation was somewhat more esoteric — that the regression could be an actual recollection of a past life. Redington's response to that was a shrug.

"You can call it that if you like." He'd glanced at Pierce. "But it's the symbolism — not whether it was or was not an actual past life — that was important. Working for Raymond seemed like it was to your benefit. But the story you told revealed that you know you've been playing right into his hands."

"But there's another message, too, Nick," Elise had said. "You found you're stronger than he is, and that you can overcome him."

He wasn't so sure about that. Nothing in the experience had indicated that the Indian, Atlan, had overcome the sorcerer. And he wasn't so sure that Redington hadn't pressed him into identifying the sorcerer as Andrews. Sure, the eyes did seem to match, but wasn't it possible that his subconscious mind had created what he knew Redington and Elise wanted him to see? This morning he'd played the tape, and listened closely. But he was no wiser. He didn't know; he wasn't ready to pass judgment.

A shrill wail shattered Pierce's ruminations, and he glanced over to see several people pressing around a matronly woman who sat near Tía Juana. Probably Fuego's mother, he thought. She was still weeping softly when, a few minutes later, the minister brought the service to a close.

Pierce remained seated while a clutch of people surrounding the woman passed by. Suddenly Tía Juana was standing next to him. "Take this, Nicholas. *Es para su protección.*"

She pressed something into his hand and moved away. As he stood and joined the flow of people filing out of the chapel, he looked down and saw that she'd handed him a tiny white cloth bag that was tied with a red thread at the top. The bag was light and probably filled with dried herbs.

He dropped it into his coat pocket and looked for Tina. He wanted to tell her how sorry he was about Fuego, but he didn't see her. He'd reached the lobby when he felt a finger poke him in the back. He turned, expecting to see Tina. Instead, he stared at Morris Carver's thick neck. He raised his eyes until he met the detective's stare.

"I want to talk to you. Outside."

Pierce nodded and worked his way through the crowd. Carver followed him onto the lawn, away from the clusters forming in front of the chapel. Bellinger was close behind him.

Carver loosened the knot in his tie. He looked hot and uncomfortable in his black suit, while Bellinger seemed as at ease as always in the dark blue one he wore. "Did you know that customs has a file on your boss?"

"On who?"

"Andrews."

"No. I didn't."

Carver took out a handkerchief from his pocket and wiped the perspiration from his forehead. "It's got some interesting stuff about his past. Apparently, he was a fairly big drug dealer back in his college days."

He waited a beat, eyeing Pierce intently. "Funny thing, your name is there, too, as an associate."

"That's bullshit. We were roommates, not associates. I was a college student." Not exactly the full truth, but he was having enough trouble with the present, and wasn't about to launch into ancient history.

"He's just telling you what's in the file," Bellinger said. If the detective knew about Pierce's accusation, he didn't show it.

He looked at Carver, who'd taken a step closer. "If they knew so much about Ray Andrews, why wasn't he ever arrested?"

"Because, Mr. Pierce, he was working undercover for the feds. Did you know that?"

Pierce moved back as Carver's face loomed inches from his. He saw Tina standing near the front of the church, watching him. "No. I didn't know."

"Your old roommate played quite a part in the collapse of the Santa Marta pot business. Made it so rough that the business moved from those Colombian mountains to California almost overnight."

"I don't know anything about it."

"Now you do," Bellinger said, and grinned.

Pierce shrugged and glanced past the detectives again. Tina was no longer in front of the chapel. "So what's that got to do with anything?"

"That's just a prelude, Mr. Pierce. Tropic Air, your boss's airline, is under investigation for the importation of cocaine in its cargo hold."

"What else is new? Cocaine has been smuggled aboard every commercial line that flies to South America."

"Yeah," Carver said, dabbing at his forehead again. "But this time they've found a direct link between Raymond Andrews and a certain corrupt federal investigator who happens to be buddies with him."

"What's this got to do with me?"

"Just this: The bad guy is Steve Simms."

"Christ," Pierce said.

"Yeah, you can imagine the implications," Bellinger said.

That, in fact, was exactly what Pierce was doing. If Steve Simms was connected with Andrews, then it looked like Elise and Redington were right. They just hadn't known her ex-husband was involved.

"Then I'd guess he was the one Loften made the mistake of hiring to set up Andrews. A prosecutor, not a cop."

"Bingo! My guess, too. Loften made a poor choice of partners," Carver said.

"Sorry, Nick." Bellinger grinned. "It wasn't me."

"My mistake. When are they going to make arrests?" Pierce asked.

"When they think their case is solid, but we're not waiting for customs to move," Carver said. "We've got our own case. We're watching both of them."

"Can't you arrest them?"

"Not yet. Only reason I'm telling you about it is that I owe you one for locking you up. I wasn't convinced by Redington's story until we found a teaching assistant in the Sociology Department on the second floor of the building who identified your picture. He was the one you bumped into on the back stairway, and he knew the exact time when he left his office."

Pierce nodded, relieved, but worried.

"Watch yourself," Carver said, and turned away.

Bellinger nodded to him. "We'll get 'em." He joined his partner, and they headed to their car.

Pierce had parked on the other side of the building, and as he moved around the side of the chapel, he saw Tina standing beside his car. He sensed another confrontation in the offing, and that was the last thing he wanted. He didn't need it, not now, not ever.

"I heard you were in jail," she said coolly.

"I didn't do it; I've been cleared."

She shook her dark mane of hair off her shoulder, and her brown eyes met his gaze. Her black dress hugged her hourglass figure; Pierce found her strangely alluring. He felt the temptation to patch things up and begin the same old cycle one more time. "You just expect me to take your word for it?" she said.

"That and the fact that I was released with no charges filed." He reached into his coat pocket, took out the white bag and held it up. "Juana must believe me. She gave me this for protection."

He smiled, but Tina didn't laugh. She stared at the bag, then shifted her focus to him. "Put it away. And do not make fun of it. If Tía Juana prepared that for you, she must know you are in danger."

He looked at the bag, felt it again, then dropped it back into his pocket. "What's in it?"

"For protection? Probably *ajo, yerbabuena, perejil.*"

Just common herbs, he thought; garlic, peppermint leaves, and parsley.

"Keep it on you all the time, even if you do not believe."

"Okay. I'll even believe I'll be protected. How's that?"

She nodded. "Nicky, listen, I know you did not kill Fuego. He stopped by the library the day he was killed."

"What?"

She reached into her purse and took out an envelope. "I did not see him, but he must have dropped this in the book-return slot. It was found there."

The envelope had been torn open and taped closed. Tina's name was written on the front, and suddenly Pierce knew what Fuego meant when he told Leni he was going to check out a book. He was going to the library to deliver the envelope. "What time was that?"

"I got it about an hour after you ripped my phone off the wall. I thought it was from you, and almost threw it away I was so mad." She glared at him as she spoke. "You really embarrassed me with that stunt."

He didn't respond. "Can I see it?"

"If you promise me something."

"What?" He didn't want to make any promises.

"That you won't be mad at me for not turning the letter over to the police. I don't want the police bothering Tía Juana with questions, and I wanted to give it to you in person."

"Yeah." Another one of her carrots.

She handed him the envelope, and he carefully pulled back the tape and slipped out a sheet of paper. He read the note.

TINA — GIVE THIS TO NICK. IT'S IMPORTANT.

Nick — Left a message on your recorder. This is just in case something happens, and it might. I'm being followed. A long time ago, Juana, you know my aunt, the *santera,* told me to watch out when a dark woman named Mercedes followed me. Never knew until now what she meant. The dark woman's a car. Anyhow, I didn't give up on the Andrews stuff. You know how I am. I kept looking for the connection. Found it, too. You've got to talk to her.

The message ended with a name and address. Pierce refolded the paper and slipped it into the envelope. Now he knew that someone must have broken into his office and erased his messages.

"You ever heard of this woman, Marisol Puente?" he asked Tina.

She shook her head. "I was tempted to go see her myself, but I thought it was better to leave it to you."

He nodded, starting to feel uneasy as she moved closer to him.

"Are we still going to be friends, Nicky? I do not want you mad at me."

"I'm not mad at you."

She reached for his hand, squeezed his fingers. "We worked things out before, you know."

He glanced up as a party of mourners passed by and looked curiously at them. "No, we didn't. We just buried it, Tina, and acted like everything was okay. It wasn't. It's not. It's over."

Tina dropped his hand. Her eyes went cold and hard; the corners of her mouth plunged. He expected another outburst. She would blast him about his behavior in the library. She would scream about his insensitivity. He looked around to see who would hear her. But she surprised him.

"Suit yourself." Her voice was calm. "I do not need this abuse anymore. You have had your last chance." She turned on her heel and walked away.

Well, this was the place to end it, he thought — at a funeral, with both of them dressed in black.

Half an hour later, Pierce stood in the doorway of Elise's office at the University of Miami. There was no mistaking the origin of her focus of study. The office was decorated with colorful woven *huipiles*. Ceramic artifacts lined a shelf, and a circular wooden Mayan calendar, like the one that had been destroyed in her house, hung on the wall.

She was seated at her desk, which looked orderly in comparison to Redington's. She was finished with classes for the quarter, but had told him she still had administrative work to complete. The look on her face said she didn't appreciate being interrupted. But she was in danger; he had to warn her.

"Funeral's over?"

He nodded, closed the door, and quickly explained what Carver had told him. She listened quietly until he was finished. "Of course, I knew Steve was working with the DEA on drug-related cases, but . . . " Her voice wavered as she attempted to maintain her composure, but tears welled in her eyes. Her lower lip quivered.

"Oh, Christ, Nick. The bastard." She looked down, raised a hand to her forehead.

He moved around her desk, wanted to touch her, stroke her hair, something. But he didn't. "I'm sorry."

"God, I've been such an idiot."

So have I. "It's better that you know."

"Of course it is. It's just that I feel like I've been assaulted."

You have been, and in more ways than one. "I know what you mean. I figured you wrong."

She stood up, smiled, and wiped her eyes. "God, what am I going to do if Steve shows up?"

"Don't let on that you know anything." He thought a moment. "How about if I come over again tonight? You mind?"

"Of course not."

He reached out, touched her arm. "I'll call you."

She hugged him, pressing her face into the nook of his shoulder and neck. Her body, snug against his, felt like a missing part that had suddenly found its home. They held the embrace long past a friendly good-bye; and when they separated, Pierce felt slightly flushed. His heart pounded and ached for what wasn't yet. But still might be.

Twenty-Seven

Pierce almost missed Marisol Puente's house. It was set back from the road under the folds of a pair of trees whose branches were weighted with mangos. Even though she lived just a few blocks from Calle Ocho, the busy commercial hub of Miami's Little Havana, you'd never know it here. Her backyard was a tropical garden, a lush, verdant sanctuary. A self-contained world, Pierce thought as he knocked at the side door.

The dark-eyed woman who answered gazed warily at him. Her frizzy black hair flowed over her shoulders. She wore khaki shorts and a black T-shirt and a gold necklace with a cross dangling from it. She was broad-shouldered, large-boned, neither slender nor chunky. Her skin was a deep tan, and it was difficult to tell her age. She could be thirty-five or a dozen years older.

"Are you Marisol Puente?"

"What can I do for you?"

"My name is Nicholas Pierce. I'm here about Fuego."

"Who? I don't understand." She spoke with a slight Spanish accent, and he sensed fear in her voice.

"Felix Ferraro. I think you know him."

She took a step back and started to close the door. "I don't think I want to talk to you, Mr. Pierce."

"Wait, please." He stuck his foot in the door. "It's important. Fuego is dead; I went to his funeral this morning."

"I know he's dead, and it's because he was snoopy. For your own good, please leave. Now."

"Listen, I'm a private investigator. I hired Fuego to investigate Raymond Andrews. I want to know what you told him."

She paused, considered what he said. "Why? Why did you hire him to do that?"

"I've been working for Andrews, and now I've got a lot of questions about him. I need to know what you told Fuego. It's very important."

She looked uncertain, then resigned. "Oh, God. I don't know. Guess it doesn't matter now. I knew Andrews would find me someday."

"This conversation will go no further than the two of us."

She stepped back from the door, then led him into a tidy living room the size of a postage stamp. It was packed with odds and ends — books, a collection of dolls, paintings, sculptures. Everything was crowded together, yet somehow orderly.

She perched at the edge of a wooden chair and watched him like a predator. Her feet were bare, her back was as rigid as an iron bar, and her hands rested lightly in her lap. She had the grace of a dancer. He, on the other hand, felt like an oaf as he lowered himself into a rocker and nearly toppled over backward. "Be careful in that chair," she said. Then: "So what do you know about me?"

"The day Fuego died he left your name and address in an envelope for me. That's all I know, except that he'd been looking for someone named Marisol who had known Andrews's wife."

He decided not to mention that he'd heard about Puente's relationship with Loften. Not yet. "What did you tell Fuego that he thought was so important?"

"That Ginger died because she knew too much."

"What do you mean?"

Puente didn't reply immediately. She breathed deeply, exhaled; he was reminded of Redington's relaxation exercise. "Ginger hired me to find out how her husband spent his time away from home."

"Hired you?"

"Yes, I was a private investigator."

"But no longer?"

"I quit after that case. I had had enough."

Pierce looked down at several painted stones that lay on end tables next to him. He picked up one of them and saw the eyes and nose and realized it was an animal. "So you're an exile from your homeland as well as your profession."

"I don't consider myself an exile in either sense. Miami is my home. As for the P.I. work" — she shook her head — "that case convinced me it was time for me to move on. I'm a commercial artist."

"If Mrs. Andrews died because she knew too much, you must also know too much. How come you're alive and she isn't?"

"Because I'm cautious. I respect the threat that Raymond Andrews represents. Something you apparently aren't concerned about."

"But you talked to Fuego."

"Yes. I confided in him. Maybe it was because we both grew up in Santa Clara, and shared memories of our childhood in Cuba."

"You knew him in Cuba?"

"No, and we probably would never have met, either. My father was a doctor, his was a storekeeper. But look what happened to him." She touched the gold cross dangling from her neck and bowed her head. *"Dios lo bendiga."*

When she looked up. Pierce asked why Ginger had wanted her husband followed.

"He was a secretive man, always going off on trips, and rarely taking her. She was sure he was having an affair and wanted to document it for a divorce case."

"Did you find another woman?"

"No, I did not." She was answering his questions, but offering nothing beyond a minimal response.

"Did you find anything suspicious?"

"I found a lot that was suspicious about him. But there was no other woman as far as I could tell. I told Mrs. Andrews that."

"Was she satisfied?"

"For a short time, yes. Then one day, she took a telephone call for her husband from an antique dealer in Edinburgh, Scotland. He told her to tell Mr. Andrews that his three-million-dollar offer for the skull did not interest him. That baffled her, because she'd never heard him say a word about spending millions on a skull."

Pierce nodded, doing his best to avoid indicating that he knew anything about the skull. "Did she ask him about the call?"

"Yes. He acted like he didn't know what she was talking about. A couple of days later she asked me to see what I could find out."

"And what did you find?"

"I visited the antique dealer and told him I was there about the skull. He assumed I represented Andrews and got angry. He said he wasn't selling the crystal skull for any price, and to tell Andrews to stop bothering him. By the time I left, I realized that owning this skull was the consuming passion of Mr. Andrews's life. *That* was the other woman."

"Why did he want it?"

"What're you going to do with this information? Get me killed, get yourself killed, or get both of us killed?"

Some choice, he thought. "If I get enough evidence that he's involved in a murder, I'll take it to the authorities."

She stood up, pacing the room. She stopped in front of him; her features were relaxed, resigned. "I don't know if that'll do any good at all, but I'll help you. I've been blessed that I've lived this long in peace without him finding me."

"Like I said, I'm not going to tell Andrews, and I made sure I wasn't followed. If he's guilty of murder, the police will protect you."

She nodded, but didn't look convinced. "The reason he wants the skull is that he feels it's powerful, that it would keep him from growing old."

He gazed after her as she meandered about the room. "How would it do that?"

"There's a legend that involves two skulls. He and his inner circle are set on obtaining both. He believes that by fulfilling this legend he will conquer death like the ancient gods. In fact, you could say he expects to become one of them himself."

Possessed by a myth, Pierce thought, recalling Redington's paper. "What is this inner circle?"

"It's part of a secret organization. They go by the name Noster Mundus."

"I've heard about it."

"Well, the inner circle is like a group of alchemists. That's the only way I can describe them. Their main work, they call it the *opus alchemicum,* is transformation to god-man through the *prima materia* — the first matter — the crystal skulls." She touched her cross again. "I am a religious person, and to me what they are doing is the devil's work."

"How did you find out about it?"

"Partly on my own, and through the help of someone in the inner circle."

"Who?"

"Someone I met through Ginger. She thought he might know something about the skull."

"Would this person talk to me, or the police?"

"No, Paul is dead. He was murdered."

"Paul Loften?"

"You know him?"

"I was in his office when he was shot," he said, and explained the circumstances.

Puente sat down again, closed her eyes as she spoke. "My God. Now I understand why Andrews didn't kill him earlier. He used him to get the skull."

"I don't understand. Why would he have killed him earlier?"

"Because he thought Paul had told Ginger too much about the scroll."

Pierce frowned, shook his head. "The scroll? What scroll?"

She studied him a moment. "You don't know about it? It's a silver scroll, an ancient document. Paul showed it to Andrews. That was ten years ago, and a short time later, Noster Mundus was formed and Andrews became interested in crystal skulls."

He remembered the scroll in the Noster Mundus emblem. "What does the scroll say?"

"It's devil's work about the two crystal skulls and immortality."

"Where is it?"

"Paul told me it was kept in Europe, somewhere near Bayonne, or just over the border, in Spain."

"Why would Andrews believe that what the scroll said was valid?"

"Maybe because of the source. Paul said that he'd become convinced the scroll was written by Plato — that no one else could have written so beautifully. He said it was a lost dialogue, and that it was incredibly important."

"Plato?"

"That's right."

Pierce recalled the book on Plato he'd seen in Andrews's study and his scrawlings in the margin of the one he'd taken off the shelf. "But did Loften also believe this stuff about immortality?"

"Paul's interests were professional. He wanted to make the scroll public, but he promised Andrews that he wouldn't reveal its contents until the two skulls were together. In return, Andrews became a major donor to the museum."

"Why did Loften tell you all this?"

She picked up one of the painted rocks, nervously brushed the dust from it. "I got to know him by forming a liaison with him."

Pierce assumed she meant she'd had an affair with him.

"Gradually, he confided in me. I told Ginger everything. Her mistake was in confronting her husband with some of it. Andrews knew the information must have come from Paul — and since he knew Paul was having a love affair, he wrongly assumed it was with his own wife."

"Christ. She kept you out of it?"

"She denied having an affair with Loften when Andrews accused her of it. But he didn't believe her. I was very fortunate, because she never told him anything about me. She didn't care if he believed her or not. She just wanted out of the marriage. She didn't want to be married to someone who had such a strange and secret life, and who was so heedless of her existence."

"Then she gave herself a fatal injection," Pierce said.

"I don't believe that. She called me at ten the morning after he accused her of adultery. She said she was fine, but was afraid of him. She'd told him the marriage was over. I advised her to get out of there, to meet me for lunch. She agreed, but never showed up. She died before noon."

"If you thought he did it, how could you let him get away with it?"

Her glance was sharp. "You think I'm proud of that, Mr. Pierce? I was terrified. I kept thinking he was going to find out from Paul that I'd told Ginger about her husband's secret life. But nothing happened. He never confronted Paul. He was saving him."

"You stopped seeing Loften?"

"Of course. It was too dangerous. I never saw him again. I tried to forget about all of it. But I've always felt that someone like Fuego or you would show up at my door someday and Andrews would find out." She smiled ruefully. "I'm not surprised it happened now. For some reason, Andrews always thought that his quest would be completed this year. In fact, this very week."

Twenty-Eight

Thor huddled amid the thick undergrowth of elephant ears and cabbage palms, remaining as still as possible. From his position he could see through the sliding glass doors into the living room, where Pierce and the woman were talking.

He couldn't hear a word, of course, but he knew from the woman's behavior that Pierce hadn't dropped by for a friendly chat. He was on to something, and that something was whatever Fuego had discovered.

Odin had turned livid when he'd heard that Fuego was asking questions about him, and that the Cuban had been hired by Pierce. Thor had followed the twitching, tic-faced snoop around town for a couple of days. But he couldn't watch him constantly, and he'd lost half a day when he'd snuffed out Gore.

He would never have known that Fuego had found the missing link to Odin's past had he not been electronically monitoring Pierce's answering machine. With a telephone and a gizmo the size of his palm he could not only listen to his messages, but erase them and even turn off the machine. The marvels of high technology.

His gaze wandered from time to time to the garden. He could spend the entire day ensconced here with the philodendrons, bromeliads, and scheffleras. He was particularly drawn to the vibrant orange, trumpet-shaped flowers of the birds of paradise plants. This garden, he thought, compared favorably to his own backyard, which he'd landscaped with such close attention to the mix of plants. The average person didn't know that certain plants were more compatible to some, less compatible to others. The average person didn't know shit about the plant world. But his own backyard was not his any longer, not since the bitch had kicked him out. She had just ignored the yard, hadn't even watered the plants during the dry winter months. If it wasn't for his weekly trips to the house, the garden would be shriveled and overrun with weeds.

Lisie had never thanked him. Not once. She didn't appreciate him. Never did. But she would pay. Oh, she would pay. She was still scheming against him. He was sure of that. He'd followed Pierce in a rented red Chevette — instead of his Mercedes — from the funeral, where he'd watched Pierce's ex-wife hand him an envelope, to the university where Pierce had visited the bitch.

When Pierce left her office, Thor was sure he would lead him to the missing link Fuego had talked about in his recorded call. He could tell Pierce was watching for someone tailing him, so he'd driven in front of him — a tactic he'd learned from his chief investigator, an old hand at surveillance in the agency. Usually drivers gave away their intentions of turning far enough in advance to allow a lead driver time to make the turn first. He'd only once missed a turn. But that time he'd cut across a parking lot and quickly passed the suspect again.

He would show Lisie what he thought of her scheming. And he would show Pierce what he thought of his moving into Thor's territory. Married or not, Lisie was still his. He'd proven that when he'd convinced her to loan him twenty-five grand to cover bad investments. There'd been no bad investments, though. The money was part of his extra cushion for his exile. He was already out of the DEA, suspended while under investigation. Let them investigate. That was inevitable, and it didn't matter.

His future was elsewhere, as Odin's chief aide and confidant. He was proving himself by his willingness to do the dirty work. He was well aware of the power and wealth of the chiefs of outlaw empires, like the drug lords, and he knew how well he would live. He made Odin think that he went along with all the crap about immortality and the crystal skulls, but he kept his own counsel. Later, when the time was right, he would show Odin — Raymond Andrews — just how mortal he was. He'd snuff him out and take control of the empire.

He saw Pierce standing up, shaking the woman's hand, patting her on the arm. He'd find out soon enough what they'd been talking about. This woman wasn't going to be like Fuego, who'd been too tight-mouthed, useless. It would have taken days to get him to talk, and now they did not have days. It was his idea to waste him if he didn't talk, and let Pierce take the rap. And it had almost worked.

With this woman, it would be different. She would sing for him. Oh, how she would sing. Just like Lisie would sing.

Twenty-Nine

Ignoring Andrews any longer was only going to arouse suspicion, Pierce thought as he dialed the number from a pay phone booth on Calle Ocho. The man who answered asked him to hold while he was connected to Andrews's Grove Plaza office. He knew he had one impressive advantage with Andrews. He knew about Marisol Puente, and Andrews didn't. He wouldn't give away her identity, but he could put to use what he now knew.

"Ray, sorry it's taken me so long to get back to you," he said when he heard Andrews's voice. "It's been a little crazy since I got out."

"Well, I'm glad you're out, Nicholas."

"I'd like to talk to you. Is there any way that I can see you this afternoon?"

"Of course. Please come right over. I'll wait for you. My office is on the third floor."

Before he left the phone booth, he called Elise and asked her to call him from another line. He didn't know how far Andrews would go, but he didn't want to take any chances that her phone was tapped. When the call came through a minute later, he briefly told her what had happened.

"Why didn't you say something about her when you were here?"

"You had enough to think about. What time should I come over?"

"Nick, let's meet at Bill's. I'll feel safer over there."

"That's fine," he said.

"I've already talked to Bill. He said to come at seven and bring your appetite."

He hung up; once again he'd avoided mentioning his immediate destination. When he arrived at Grove Plaza, the glass elevator gave him an idea. He'd test Redington's hypnotic suggestion that elevators would no longer bother him. He stepped into it confidently, pressed the button for the third floor. He only had two levels to ascend, and even if the elevator stopped at the second floor, he'd be off in less than thirty seconds.

As the door started to close, a hand reached out, reopening it, and he was joined by a man in his twenties wearing dark glasses and a lightweight sport coat over a dark brown T-shirt. Pierce glanced once at him, then turned his attention to the courtyard on the other side of the glass enclosure. The elevator slowly rose, and he focused his thoughts on the spacious interior of the complex. It was open, airy, well lit, and he was on an observation deck, he told himself.

The elevator stopped at the second floor; the door opened and three women with packages crowded in. "You're going down, I hope," one of them said.

"One floor up," the other man said.

Pierce looked over his shoulder as one of the women jabbed a package in his back. Then he turned his attention back to the window, trying not to think about how crowded the elevator was.

"Up? We want to go down," the woman said.

"Oh, come on, let's just stay on," a saccharine voice answered.

As the door closed and the elevator started to rise, he felt the press of the woman. "There's that restaurant Trudy told me about. She said they have great ceviche."

"Delores, I'm sure she said the ceviche was in the Mayfair," the saccharine voice said.

"Maybe you're right. We should try this place just for the fun of it next time."

"Well, just don't count on ceviche."

The elevator jerked to a sudden stop, but the door didn't open. "Okay, what happened?" one of the woman said, panic rising in her throat. "Why're we stopped?"

Pierce closed his eyes. *Oh, Christ, get this glass madhouse moving.* Nothing happened. He opened his eyes and turned around, seeing for the first time how crowded it was. "What're you doing over there?" one of the women asked the man at the control panel.

"We're stuck, ladies. I'm just pushing the buttons."

One of the women groaned. Another murmured something about claustrophobia and needing a restroom, and the man at the control panel kept playing the buttons.

Pierce's stomach churned. He would have made it easily, no problem, if the elevator hadn't stopped. But now chills shot up his spine, heat flushed his cheeks, and his body didn't seem to know whether to shiver or sweat. He pressed his forehead and hands to the glass to steady himself. Cloying perfume mixed with the stench of someone's flatulence. Hysteria bubbled in his throat. *We're stuck and someone farts. Swell, just swell, I'm going to puke or pass out, I'm going to —*

"Goddamn it, mister, hit the alarm button." The saccharine voice was turning nasty. "It's right there."

A ringing like a fire alarm ripped through the capsule and across the plaza. People below stared up at Pierce. The courtyard started to spin, his stomach began to heave. He was about to pass out.

But then the elevator lurched upward, the alarm fell silent, and the nausea in his gut plummeted. "Can you believe it? The emergency stop was switched on," one of the women exploded.

"Sorry, ladies," the man apologized. "I must have leaned against it."

"God, that scared the you-know-what out of me, Delores. I mean, if we would . . . " The purr of the rising elevator muffled their voices.

Pierce closed his eyes and regulated his breathing, taking deep, even breaths. An image from the hypnosis bled across the insides of his eyes: The old sorcerer was staring at him, grinning, those ageless eyes burning into his soul.

A hand touched his shoulder, and his eyes fluttered open. One of the women was saying, "You getting out, mister, or going back down with us?"

"Out. Getting out. Thanks." He forced himself forward between the gauntlet of packages, suffocating perfume, and staring eyes. He made it out and stopped to catch his breath. He felt as if he'd scrambled up a dozen flights of stairs.

"He didn't look so good, that one," a voice from the elevator said as the door closed.

He looked around, saw a sign for a rest room, and headed for the door. He walked to a sink, bent over, and splashed water on his face.

"Hey, that was quite a ride, wasn't it?"

Pierce looked up into the mirror to see the man from the elevator standing behind him, combing his wavy hair. "I thought those broads were going to shit in their pants. It smelled like one of them did."

The man's laugh was a high-pitched cackle. "You okay?"

Pierce patted his face with a paper towel and ran a hand through his hair. "Yeah, I'm fine." He hurried toward the door.

"Hey, you know you looked a little fucked up when you came in here," the man called after him. "I guess you didn't like it much, either."

Up yours, buddy, he thought as he walked down the corridor. He passed a commercial art studio and a law firm before he came to Andrews International, Inc.

He stepped inside and looked around. Andrews hadn't spared anything in the decoration of his offices. It could have been the interior of a French mansion instead of a corporate office in a shopping plaza. From the plush carpeting, chandeliers, and mahogany desks, to the Renaissance paintings with their ornate frames, the place had a feel of European splendor and old wealth.

"Can I help you, sir?" the receptionist asked. He told her his name and she called Andrews's office, announcing his arrival.

"He'll be right with you, Mr. Pierce. Would you like a cup of coffee or iced tea?"

"No, thanks." He sat down, and the cushions of the couch seemed to mold themselves around the contours of his body. It was the softest, most comfortable couch he'd ever sat on. If Redington had hypnotized him here, he would've just fallen asleep.

A couple of minutes later, Pierce looked up to see K.J. He nodded to Pierce, motioned to him. "C'mon."

What the hell? For a moment, as he followed the bodyguard down the hall, he couldn't believe what he'd heard. The mute had spoken. But there was no time to think about what that meant.

"There he is," Andrews said as Pierce stepped into the office. "How are you, Nicholas?" He grinned, gritting his teeth, and glanced at the black suit Pierce wore. "You look very nice today."

"My funeral suit," he said, and inadvertently touched the pocket that held the amulet Tía Juana had given him.

Andrews nodded solemnly. "I'm sorry about your friend, but I'm glad you're not paying the consequences for his death."

Pierce glanced around the office. Two of the walls of the office were glass. One overlooked the courtyard, the other faced a tall condominium. In the corner, a video camera rested on a tripod, the lens facing Andrews's desk.

"How did you know he was my friend, Ray?"

Andrews looked surprised. "Well, I talked to your former partner. We had a frank discussion about the case. I hope you don't mind."

"No, of course not." Damn that Gibby and his mouth.

"How about a drink to celebrate your freedom?" Andrews asked as he walked over to a liquor cabinet. "I'm going to have a Jack Daniels and water. How about you?"

"Just a Perrier would be fine."

"Suit yourself."

Pierce stepped over to the glass wall facing the courtyard and gazed down. "Nice view, isn't it?"

"Very nice."

Andrews poured his drink, crossed the room, and handed Pierce his glass of water. "Listen, Nicholas, I know you're probably grateful to Redington for getting you out of jail, but don't be tricked by him."

Pierce shook his head. "Don't worry about that. I'm on my guard."

Andrews nodded and was silent a moment. "Was there something specific you wanted to talk to me about?"

"There is something I should tell you, Ray. I've been avoiding it, but I think now is the time."

"Oh?" Andrews abruptly turned to K.J., who was seated in a chair by the door like an oversized potted plant. Andrews snapped his fingers and flipped his index finger in Pierce's direction.

Christ, now what?

Immediately the bodyguard crossed the office, brushed by Pierce, and adjusted the lens of the video camera. A red light came on, indicating the camera was running.

"Please, go ahead."

"Before Paul Loften was killed he told me a strange story. He made me promise to keep quiet about it, but now that he's dead, I guess it's okay."

Something flickered in Andrews's eyes, an emotion Pierce couldn't decipher. But it passed as he smiled. "Tell me about it."

Pierce looked at K.J., saw he'd swiveled the camera so that the lens pointed at him.

"Don't feel intimidated by the camera. You don't have to look at it." Andrews sat on the edge of his desk. "So what did Loften say?"

Pierce's throat constricted. "Ray, turn that goddamn thing off. It makes me nervous." It wasn't the camera as much as the circumstances that made him feel uneasy. But the camera served as a way of deflecting his nervousness.

Andrews looked surprised. "Of course." He snapped his fingers again. "I didn't think you minded." The light blinked out. "There, that better?"

"Yeah." He paused, culling his thoughts.

"So go on about Loften."

"Well, the truth is, he told me that you were the one who was actually hiring me. Then he started talking about some sort of document relating to crystal skulls that was written on a silver scroll."

Andrews's smile disappeared.

"He said that if the scroll was real, it was not only an important artifact, but the most important historical and philosophical document to appear since the Dead Sea scrolls."

Andrews tipped his drink to his lips. Pierce wasn't sure, but it seemed as if he'd accepted the story. He didn't particularly like lying about a dead man, but it was better than telling him about Marisol Puente.

"What was his point in telling you the story?" Andrews asked.

"I don't know if there was a point, other than that it provided me with a reason to explain your interest in the skulls."

Andrews stepped close enough to Pierce so he could smell alcohol on his breath. "Why are you telling me about this now?"

"Because I don't think you've told me everything that's going on. I think you've got another agenda. I want to know what it is, or I can't work with you any longer."

"What?" Andrews laughed. "What other agenda? The scroll? Loften was telling you the truth. It does mention the skulls. But I didn't think the philosophical underpinning of these matters had much to do with finding the skulls. That's why I didn't bother going into any of that with you."

Pierce considered asking him what the skulls had to do with Noster Mundus, but decided to stop while he was ahead. He'd pushed hard enough. He wanted Andrews to think he was confused and curious about what was going on — but not that he'd realized what Andrews was all about, or that he suspected he was as expendable as Fuego.

He tried to think of something else to say. "I'd be very interested in seeing this silver scroll . . . and finding out all about it. Do you think it's real?"

Andrews's smile was condescending. "I don't have any doubt about that. I'd enjoy telling you all about it sometime. But right now, I think it's more important for you to see as much of Elise Simms as possible." Andrews's mesmeric eyes held his gaze, held it too long. "My feeling is that something big is going to break in the next day or two. I feel it in my bones."

Pierce nodded. He'd heard enough.

As he left Andrews's office and headed for the door, he saw a figure leaning over the receptionist's desk. The man straightened suddenly, glanced his way, and vanished out the door. Pierce hadn't seen him for more than a couple of seconds, but it was long enough to recognize him as the man from the elevator who'd leaned against the emergency stop button.

Well, well, he thought. There hadn't been any accident at all. Somehow, that didn't really surprise him.

Thirty

They sat outside by Redington's pool, sipping coffee and watching the sunset. The gentian sky was streaked with soft pinks, yellows, and ribbons of lavender. A flock of green parrots swept in low over the tops of the trees behind the house, their cries ringing out in the stillness. Despite the tranquil setting and the sumptuous shrimp scampi dinner Redington had prepared, Pierce remained on edge. He'd done most of the talking since he'd arrived, holding nothing back; Elise and Redington had said little aside from asking occasional questions.

"It sounds like you had a busy day, Nick," Redington said.

"And when you phoned, you didn't tell me half of what was going on," Elise added. "Do you think Marisol would talk to the police?"

Pierce shrugged. "It would be her word against Andrews's, and you can guess who would win that one."

"It would probably get her killed," Redington said. "What she told you must have been what Paul was planning to tell me before he died. He'd realized a bit too late how far Raymond would go to get the skull."

No one spoke for a moment, and Pierce watched Redington's black cat munching on a leftover piece of shrimp near the pool.

"He's an evil bastard," Elise muttered, venting her frustration.

Redington's lips pursed in a sour look. "I doubt that he sees himself that way. He's a pragmatist, an amoral one. He's taken the holistic philosophy, which he espouses, and perverted it. In other words, since you can't understand the whole by only examining its parts, it's okay if some of the parts are corrupted by despicable deeds."

Elise shook her head. "That's not any different than believing that the end justifies the means."

"Exactly. He's just given it an updated twist."

Pierce sat back, listening to Redington's succinct and unemotional way of looking at Andrews. But analyzing his personality, as far as he could tell, wasn't going to prevent him from killing someone else. "The only way I see that Ray is going to be stopped is by obtaining clear-cut evidence. But how are we going to get it?"

"I would speculate that Andrews has inadvertently cued you on the whereabouts of the skull," Redington said.

"I'm not aware of any cues."

"You may be aware of them only at an unconscious level."

"It's like how you knew what had happened on the elevator," Elise said.

"That's right," Redington agreed. "We could dig for the cues."

"Hypnosis again?"

Redington cleared his throat. "It would be very much like what I do with students to improve their ability to recall what they've studied. Except in this case we would be dealing with events — and instead of *preparing* you for an exam, we'd take it right now."

"What are you suggesting, that I go back to my meetings with Ray and look for one of these cues?"

"No. The unconscious mind works best if you give it free rein. It'll create its own scenario and speak through metaphors. The trick is to interpret them."

"I think you should do it," Elise said. "Bill knows what he's doing, and you might trigger something important."

Then again, I might shoot a blank, he thought. But what the hell. Another hypnosis? Sure. He was game.

They moved to Redington's den, which was dark and quiet, insulated from outside noises. A small table lamp was the only illumination. As Redington prepared to record the session, Pierce settled into a comfortable chair. He closed his eyes, took a deep breath, and let it out slowly as Redington began leading him through the same head-to-toe relaxation method.

Redington told him it wouldn't take as long this time, and he was right. Pierce followed his words, drifting with them, slipping deeper and deeper into the embryonic waters of his own being until suddenly something flopped across his thighs. He blinked his eyes open, and there was the black cat, perched on his lap, licking a paw.

"Come on, Comus, old boy." Redington snatched him up, and Pierce heard the door softly close. "Comus was letting you know you're in his favorite chair," Redington explained in the same soft voice. "But he won't bother you now. I told him he'd have to share it this evening."

Pierce smiled, still feeling relaxed and unconcerned. Redington picked up where he'd left off, and in a couple of minutes Pierce was passing through the now familiar blue dome and approaching the elevator. Once again, Redington described the elevator as roomy, comfortable, and well lit. He told him he wouldn't be adversely affected by elevators again, and said that whatever happened during the session would result in only positive effects for him. Finally he started counting backward from ten, explaining that when he reached one, the elevator door would open. Pierce would then enter into an experience that would lead him to the place where the stolen crystal skull was hidden.

Pierce's body felt heavy, weighted, yet his mind was alert. He could see the inside of the elevator clearly. He looked above the door and was startled to once again see a blur of numbers.

"Three . . . two . . . one. Now the door is opening. You can step out." After a moment, he asked what Pierce saw.

He didn't respond.

He waited . . . and wondered if anything was going to happen. Then all at once the numbers stopped, the door opened, and the elevator vanished. But all he saw were vague forms against a jumble of light and colors swirling around.

"What do you see?" Redington's voice was mellifluous, like music suited to a dream, a priestly incantation. It reminded him that he was lying on a couch hypnotized. Yet, his awareness was elsewhere, in an in-between place, and he didn't know if he would see anything that would make sense to him.

Then the particles congealed. He was standing in a plaza watching as a line of men dressed in loose cotton pants and tunics climbed the steps on a stone temple. He knew he was back again, in that same time in the green mountains. It was as if he'd been there all along, but hadn't been able to see the obvious.

He described the plaza and the pyramid. At the peak was an altar draped in a black mantle and on top of it was a crystal skull. As he watched, he knew exactly what was taking place. The people were interested not just in seeing the skull, but in hearing it speak to them. He knew that the Old One was beneath the altar, manipulating the jaw with a stick. He was the one speaking, offering the messages to ensure the servitude of his subjects. His powers were false. A craftsman had altered the sacred skull. The jaw had been cut loose and hinged. A small hollow had been carved at its base so a stick could fit into it from below.

"How do you feel?"

"Sad and angry. Tonight I will expose the Old One."

"How will you do that?"

"Steal it. Steal the skull."

"Are you no longer the Old One's student?"

"I am his enemy. He has tried to kill me."

"Can your enemy or anyone else see you now?"

He was confused by the questions, but then he knew no one could see him. "I would be killed. I can see, but I'm not here in the ordinary way."

"Okay. Move ahead now to the next significant event. Take your time, and when you're ready, tell me what you see."

For a moment, he couldn't see anything. Then he realized he was waiting in the dark. He'd waited for hours, and now he heard a noise. He whistled; a responding whistle punctured the air. He knew it was the men who had sided with him, the ones who had fled to the mountains where he was hiding.

"What's going on?" The voice again, gentle, reassuring.

"I have the skull. It disappeared two days ago from the altar before everyone's eyes."

"What are you going to do with it?"

"Take it where the Old One's men cannot find it. He is not a true leader; he deceives. He steals the powers of those he controls."

"How do you know that?"

"Because he does not drink the sacred juice. He only makes it."

"Why doesn't he drink it?"

"He knows it's poison and kills. That is why the warriors never live to old age."

"Don't the warriors question why they die young?"

"The Old One says they get lost on the other side."

"What about you?"

He thought a moment. "Maybe I will die, too. Soon I will take more."

"Now go to that time."

Atlan was lying under the shelter of a rock. He'd drunk the juice and was waiting. Four men were sitting around him, and their eyes were on the skull.

He heard a hissing noise like a snake behind him, and jumped up. The others paid no attention to it. He looked around and instead of seeing a snake, he saw his body. It astonished him at first, then he saw the skull and began to understand what was happening. It was glowing brightly, illuminating the tired faces of the men. He picked it up — and again saw that they didn't notice. He realized the hissing sound was familiar. He'd heard it the other times he'd slipped from his body. It was something within him signaling the departure.

The skull was in his hands, yet he knew what he held was its essence, that its physical presence was still there by the men. He also knew that when he reached his destination and let it go, the skull would vanish from under the rock and appear in its hiding place. It would be safe, away from the Old One, whose weakness would be revealed because neither he nor his warriors would be able to retrieve it.

"Now move ahead to that time when the skull is being hidden."

Pierce's body jerked on the couch. Simultaneously he sensed he was someplace else, a place that Atlan couldn't comprehend. He was crammed against a wall, baffled, terrified. He was no longer in the mountains, but in a nightmarish place filled with strange four-legged creatures with large heads and bodies covered with hair. The rear part of them was even larger and was partly human and whirled along without legs. The terrible creatures moved rapidly, clattering on the wide stone path, and didn't seem to notice him or the skull he clutched.

None of Atlan's trips through the underworld had taken him to such a terrifying place. He knew he must be in the heartland of Xibalba, the center of the underworld. This was where he'd leave the skull. The creatures here would protect it.

He saw a man who was not one of the creatures walking toward him. His face was hairy, but he was dressed like a woman. When he was just a few steps away from him, he swung open a door and disappeared from sight. Atlan followed him into the building and found himself inside a strange room. Along the walls were row after row of odd rectangular wedges. He watched the man pull out one of the wedges and unfold it. There were three other men in the room, all wearing odd clothing, but different from the one with the woman's clothes.

"Where have you gone with the skull?" The voice again. It confused him, and he didn't answer.

He walked to the rear of the room to avoid the men and found a smaller room. Its walls were also covered with wedges. Then he saw something familiar, a burial urn, and knew that was the place for the skull. He lowered it into the urn and let go. The skull was no longer glowing. He knew it was physically here in Xibalba, and immediately he wished himself out of this alien place and back to the mountains.

"Where are you now?"

"Waking, feeling groggy. The men are talking; they're excited. They're saying the skull is gone, and arguing about who was awake, watching."

"Okay, you're going to return to the present. Step back into the elevator."

At first he didn't understand, but then Pierce sensed himself apart from the Indian. The elevator door opened, and he stepped inside.

"You're feeling a bit lightheaded, but you'll remember everything that happened to you. I'm going to start counting, and when I reach five you can open your eyes anytime you like."

Pierce rubbed his face as Redington finished counting. He saw Elise sitting on the couch next to him, smiling. "How do you feel?"

"A little confused, but otherwise fine."

"What happened?" she asked. "You didn't say anything for a long time."

"God, I was really gone. It was like I was living that guy's life. Wherever I took that skull, it was a long way from his home. It was — You know where I think it was?" He shook his head. "Now it makes sense, but *he* couldn't figure it out. He was terrified half to death of horses and buggies. He thought they were monsters. It was an alien world to him."

"Where was it?" Elise asked.

"I think it was Scotland. The man he saw was wearing a kilt. He followed him into a bookshop and left the skull in an umbrella stand in the back room. The stand looked like a burial urn. It was the only thing that made any kind of sense to him."

"So you found where the skull was hidden." Redington spoke the words slowly as he considered what Pierce had just said.

Pierce ran a hand through his hair. "I'm afraid that's not going to help us much. I seriously doubt we'd find it in an umbrella stand in Scotland. Hell, it wasn't even the present. It was like Victorian times, or maybe even earlier."

Redington shut off the tape player. "Your experience doesn't seem to lend itself to an easy interpretation. . . . Unless the Scotsman is John Mahoney."

"That's what I was wondering," Elise said. She gazed off, a distracted look on her face.

"Well, that doesn't get us anywhere," Pierce said. "We know he doesn't have the skull."

After they left Redington's house. Pierce followed Elise's car, sometimes dropping back two or three blocks. He was watching for any indication that they were being followed. He was particularly looking for a dark blue Mercedes, but he kept his eyes on all the cars that were following them.

As he drove, he puzzled over the hypnosis session, trying to make sense of it. He'd definitely accomplished the objective of the session, but what did it mean? What did any of it mean? Why was Andrews so obsessed with the idea that the skulls would give him eternal youth?

He remembered the articles that Tina had packaged for him. He still hadn't read the one on the crystal skull myth, the one that had something to do with the Fountain of Youth myth. The envelope was in the glove compartment, and he promised himself he'd look it over.

Twice, Elise took side routes to see if they would draw a car off the main streets. None followed, but he wasn't convinced they were alone. After all, if Steve had been watching Redington's place, he would have a pretty good idea where Elise was headed.

Finally, when she turned into her driveway, he cruised slowly around the block another time. As he pulled in behind her, Elise was still seated in the car, just as they'd planned it.

Before going inside, they walked around the house together. He took a flashlight from his car and shone it into the shrubs and at the trees. Her hand was inside her purse, clutching a .22-caliber pistol. Unless it was fired at close range, a shot from the gun would probably just piss off the attacker. But it might be enough to give them time to get away.

As he looked around, he realized for the first time how extensive the landscaping was in her backyard. When he mentioned the lush growth, she told him that was Steve's handiwork. He'd spent most of his spare time during their marriage either working out with weights or working in the yard.

When they'd completed their patrol of the yard and were in front of the house again, he asked if she wanted him to take a look inside. She nodded, and her apprehensive look told him that she dreaded even the thought of encountering Steve in the house.

They walked from room to room and as he followed her up the stairs, he couldn't help but notice how gracefully she moved and his eyes lingered on the curve of her buttocks. The last room they checked was her bedroom. He opened the closet door, turned on the light, looked carefully into the corners. They were alone.

"Thanks, Nick. I appreciate it."

"Don't mention it." He tilted his head down and kissed her lightly on the lips. She drew her head back, smiled, then wrapped her arms around his neck and pressed her mouth tightly against his. Once again he felt the snug fit of her body against his, but this time there was no mistaking the intentions. Her thigh pressed against his groin, which grew hard with desire, and her breathing quickened.

She stepped back toward the bed, breaking the kiss, drawing him toward her. His hand slid over the front of her blouse and he fumbled with the buttons. She pulled his shirt from his pants and slid her hands up over his belly and across his bare chest. Clothes dropped away, Elise pulled back the covers, and they tumbled into bed. Her skin was as soft and cool as the sheets, a world to travel in, to get lost in.

"When we first met, Nick, were you hoping I'd invite you to my hotel room?" She moved away from him a little, regarded him in the dim light that issued from the closet. Her hands didn't leave him; they stroked and caressed.

"I was pretty sure you didn't have a room, but I was sort of hoping you'd prove me wrong." His breathing quickened as she kept touching him.

"You know what? *I* was wishing I really had a room."

For a long time, there was only the heat of their fever, the slickness of skin, the tangle of limbs, and the fury of their bodies. Slow, shallow strokes, soft moans, the bite of Elise's nails against his shoulders, her murmurs, the thrust of her hips, her sharp, startled gasps as she came, and a moment later, the explosion of his own breath.

Pierce collapsed next to her, his arm around her waist. He dozed, and came awake when she rolled away and got up. He heard the bathroom door close, and in the distance, the squeal of car tires. He imagined Steve outside the house, watching now, as the bathroom light shined through the window. Steve watching, waiting.

Thirty-One

"That does it," Elise said as she walked into the kitchen. "Still no answer. If I don't reach him today, I'm calling Scotland Yard."

"Sounds drastic." Pierce looked up from the article he was reading. "He's probably enjoying himself in a country house somewhere."

Elise refilled her coffee cup and dropped down in the chair next to him. "I hope so."

"When was the last time you talked to him?"

"A couple of weeks ago."

"You ever read this article on the skull myth that Bill wrote?"

"Yeah," she said, with a sigh, her thoughts still on her father.

"Is it true that — "

The phone rang, cutting off Pierce. Elise literally leaped to her feet and answered it. "Oh, hi. Let me go up to my study. I've got my grade book up there."

She set the phone down and glanced at Pierce. "Will you hang it up for me? It's my teaching assistant."

"Sure."

She hurried off, and when Pierce heard her voice, he dropped the phone into its cradle. He turned his attention back to the article, which he'd brought from the car when he picked up the morning paper.

Although Redington had told him about the legend, his article contained considerably more detail, and related it to Ponce de León's search for the Fountain of Youth. According to the legend, the twin skulls had been taken in opposite directions from their homeland. The one known as the God of Death eventually fell into the hands of the Mayans, while the God of Life went to "River Land." The twin gods, who were brothers and enemies, would eventually reunite after the "Fountain of Transformation" was found.

Most of the article dealt with an analysis of the symbols within the tale, equating the search for the skulls with man's search for meaning and wisdom, and for resolution of his duality. River Land was symbolic of the flow of history. The fountain was a metaphor for the expansion of human awareness, the rejuvenated man — the famed Fountain of Youth. The reunion of the twin skulls signified the merging of man's dual nature of good and evil, the next evolutionary step.

When he came to a section on the reappearance of the skulls, he read each sentence carefully. Before their reunion, the two gods would traverse the great sea. The Mayan skull, the God of Death, would be found on an island. The River Land skull, the God of Life, would be discovered in the Fountain of Transformation, which was located between the place of wisdom and purification and the place of death and transformation.

Some help that is, he thought.

"So what were you asking me about the article?" Elise walked back into the kitchen and sat down.

"I was just wondering if you agreed with Bill that Ponce de Leon heard a bastardized version of the crystal skull myth when he went in search of the Fountain of Youth."

Elise sipped her coffee, shrugged. "That's speculation."

"Why'd he look in Florida?"

"It wasn't that he said he was going to Florida to look for it. He was the first recorded European to discover Florida. But he may have found the peninsula by following the directions in the myth."

Pierce frowned at the article. "These directions?" He pointed to a paragraph in the article. "Christ, it sounds like directions to heaven."

"Not really. The Mayans ascribed certain properties to the cardinal points. North was considered the direction of wisdom and purification, and west the direction of death and transformation. In other words, when the legend says the skull will be found between those attributes, it was referring to the northwest."

"I suppose that's one way of looking at it."

"It makes sense. Go northwest from the Mayan Empire in the Yucatan and Guatemala and you'll run directly into South Florida."

"It says here that the skull that ended up in this Fountain of Transformation — the God of Life — came from River Land. Where's that?"

Elise rested an elbow on the table and propped her chin with the palm of her hand. "Maybe River Land is Egypt. The river's the Nile."

"Why do you say that?"

"The scroll. If it actually is Plato's missing dialogue, then I think it's possible."

"Plato was Greek."

"Yes, but he spent time in Egypt. He was even initiated into a secret society in a ceremony in the Great Pyramid." Her tone sounded professional; he guessed it was her teaching voice. "Maybe he obtained the skull from Egyptian priests and that's where he heard about Atlantis."

"So how did Plato's skull get to Florida?"

"Good question. Since no one's ever found the Fountain of Youth, we don't know that it did."

"What about the other skull? According to the myth, it was supposed to be found on an island."

"Great Britain's an island," she answered.

"Paul Loften told me that the skull was found in a Mayan ruin in the 1920s."

"There's some question about that. A couple of researchers who looked into the origin of the skull found evidence that the adventurer who supposedly found it and sold it to Dad may have actually bought it from an English art dealer and only claimed he'd found it."

"Then where did the art dealer get it?" Pierce quizzed.

A hint of a smile appeared on her lips. "Maybe he found it in an umbrella stand."

"I like that." Pierce laughed and picked up the article. On the last page was a drawing of the fountain. It looked like an upright block of stone on a rock platform. Water spouted from the platform, and in the center of the upright piece of stone was a crude outline of a skull.

"This isn't a very impressive fountain. No wonder Ponce de León never found it. It looks like . . . You know what it looks like?"

"What?"

"There's something called the Bubbling Altar at the Coral Castle. It's the same shape, and right where this skull is drawn is a human face made of shells."

"Are you serious?"

"Positive." He shrugged. "But, of course, that couldn't be it. The altar is fifty or sixty years old, at best."

Elise shook her head. "Doesn't matter. No one said the skull was hidden in ancient times."

Pierce was confused. "What are you talking about? The Mayan myth is hundreds of years old, right?"

"Nick, remember what I said about Tzolkin, the four-dimensional clock? The legend is prophecy, not history."

"You think the skull could be there?"

She rose from the chair. "I think it's worth a look. I'm going to call Bill."

"Okay, but just ask if he'll stop by. Don't say anything else."

By the time they walked through the coral rock arch after taking a circuitous route to their destination, the afternoon sun was burning down on the oversized rock furniture. The air was still, scorched. The same guide Pierce had seen on his first trip here stood in front of a pack of tourists at the rear of the courtyard and demonstrated how easily the massive revolving door opened.

"Here it is. Not much to look at, is it?" Pierce said.

Elise gazed at the Bubbling Altar. "It does look like the drawing."

"My God," Redington muttered. "I don't know how many times I've walked by here. At some level, I must have known. Why else was I drawn back here so many times?"

Pierce squatted down and touched the base where the upright and horizontal blocks were cemented together. The old cement crumbled to his touch. "You know, if you had a chisel and a hammer, it wouldn't be too difficult to take a look inside."

"What if we're wrong?"

"There wouldn't be any damage. They need to repair that cement anyway."

"This place is privately owned, Nick," Redington said. "Even if we convinced them to let us do it and were successful, they'd have every right to claim the skull."

"They'd probably sell it to Andrews for a paltry fifty thousand and count their blessings," Elise chimed in.

Pierce stood up, brushed his hands. "Then we've got to try something else."

The group with the guide was moving in their direction, and Pierce motioned for Elise and Redington to follow him. They walked over to the well, and Pierce looked down it as he spoke. "Bill, do you know what the security situation is here at night?"

Redington glanced up at him, frowning. "No, I don't. And if you're thinking of — "

"Bill, give him a chance," Elise said. "Let's hear Nick's idea."

Pierce touched the white bag in his pants pocket — the amulet. When he'd changed clothes from his funeral dress after visiting Andrews, he'd transferred the bag to the khaki pants he'd worn to Redington's house for dinner and was still wearing today. "I'm just speculating on the possibility of taking a look on our own."

"Sorry for jumping on you, Nick. Come to think of it, I do recall one of the guides telling a story about several kids getting caught crawling out over the wall one night. They admitted trying to turn over the furniture, but couldn't budge it. The point he was making was that there was no need for security systems other than a wedge in the revolving door and a nightly check by a cop."

"Any idea what time he comes by?" Pierce asked.

"As a matter of fact, he said the cop swings by after the bars close."

Pierce stepped back from the well. "Let's go outside and take a look around."

As they walked along the wall after leaving through the main entrance, Elise began to fidget. She nervously glanced over her shoulder to see if anyone was watching them. "I don't know. This could be dangerous."

"Elise, Nick's right. It's time to take a chance," Redington said firmly, flipping his white ponytail over his shirt collar. "If we find the skull, we'll have some bargaining power over Andrews. Maybe enough to draw him into a trap and take advantage of his obsession."

"I agree," Pierce said. "If I tell Ray I know where the other skull is, I'm sure he'll go after it."

"How would we do it and not get ourselves killed?" Elise asked warily.

"Let's think on it. We'll figure something out," Pierce said.

"Well, the timing couldn't be better," she conceded. "Exactly in line with Tzolkin."

Thirty-Two

Thor adjusted his legs as he tried to get comfortable. His perch on a lower branch of a massive banyan tree provided an excellent view of the street and Marisol Puente's house. It was dusk, and flocks of green parrots were making a racket on the limbs above him as they settled in for the night. But he filtered out the distraction and concentrated on the brown Ford that had pulled up about ten minutes after he'd arrived with Odin and Frey.

The brown Ford with Carver in it.

Carver was trouble. Thor knew he'd been following them, and Odin had told him to wait outside and take care of the cop. That's the way he'd put it. The same thing he'd said about Fuego. *Take care of him.* Killing Fuego was one thing, but knocking off a cop was something else. If Carver's body was found before they'd made their escape, there'd be hell to pay.

It was all arranged; they'd leave at sunrise tomorrow. With the two skulls or with only one. If it was up to him, they'd forget about the other skull and lay low until morning. But he knew it wasn't going to be that way. There was a long night ahead.

Thor glanced at his watch. It was time. If he waited any longer and Odin and Frey came out with Marisol, he had no doubt Carver would stop the Mercedes. They had to take control of the situation. There was no choice.

He sprang to the ground and moved in a crouch toward the rear of the Ford. Up along the driver's side now. Mach 10 out of his shoulder holster. Tight in his hands. Cool and deadly, this weapon. He jabbed the end of it into Carver's temple. "Hands flat on the dash. Don't blink, don't breathe too hard, don't turn your head. Very good, Detective."

Thor pulled the weapon away from Carver's temple long enough to open the door, then ordered the detective to move over. He didn't trust him, not for a second, and as Carver inched toward the passenger side, Thor slammed the butt of the pistol against the back of his head, knocking him out. He crumpled forward, and Thor shoved him over.

When he was behind the wheel, he tapped the horn twice, then twice again. It meant the trouble outside was under control. A moment later, Odin and Frey appeared, Marisol between them. Thor waved; Frey slid behind the wheel of the Mercedes. Thor didn't like Frey driving his car, but they weren't going far.

Several blocks away, Thor turned into the parking lot behind an abandoned warehouse. No one was around. Frey pulled up next to him. He and Frey quickly moved Carver to the back seat of the Mercedes, then Frey scooted in beside him. Andrews and Marisol were in the front as Thor took the wheel.

He popped the Mercedes into gear and glanced at his watch. Goddamn. Four and a half minutes. Not bad.

Thirty-Three

Pierce pulled into Elise's driveway at ten. He'd spent the evening preparing for their sojourn, and now in the trunk of his car was a backpack stuffed with everything he thought they'd need. Elise's expression as she let him in the house warned him that she'd been thinking things over. Thinking and fretting.

"Well, I'm going to call him now," he said.

"Nick, listen, I don't know if it's such a good idea. Maybe we should just postpone doing anything until we have it in our hands."

"No. It's safer this way. We've got to be prepared to act. I don't want to give Andrews even one extra hour."

She turned away. "Go ahead then."

"Elise . . . "

"I said, go ahead."

He shrugged, moved into the kitchen, and punched Andrews's number. "He's not available," a man's voice said.

"Tell him it's Nick Pierce."

"I said he's not available."

Damn it. He'd waited too long. "Okay, tell him I made a breakthrough." He spoke slowly, clearly. "I should have what he's looking for tonight. Tell him to meet me at my office at two. . . . That's right, two A.M."

He hung up and met Elise's gaze. "Well, that's over."

She still looked worried. "God, but if we don't find it — "

"Don't even think about it. We're going to get it."

"You keep saying that, but what if we don't?"

"Okay, I've got an alternate plan."

"What alternate plan? You didn't say anything to me about it."

"I didn't want you worrying, but I guess you were doing it anyhow."

"You should be worrying, too."

"All right, listen. Even if we don't get the skull, we'll still get Andrews. Once he's at the office, we'll say we've got it but not with us. Chances are he'll give himself away. He'll demand to see it, and say something about the timing of the reunion of the skulls."

"I wouldn't be so sure about that."

"Look, even if he doesn't, we're going to count on Carver and Bellinger having enough evidence to bust him right there."

"You're counting on a lot. What if Bill can't get Carver to go to your office with him? What if Carver's asleep and won't answer his phone?"

Pierce smiled, shook his head. "Not likely. Not Carver. He's too committed to this case to sleep through the ending."

The phone rang, and Pierce snapped it up. He heard Redington's voice.

"I was hoping you'd be there, Nick. Listen, I want to show you both something that I know you're going to be very interested in seeing. Can you meet me at my office in an hour?"

"Well, I guess so." Pierce hoped he sounded mystified. "What is it, Bill?"

Redington cleared his throat. "I'd rather wait. I don't trust the phone."

"Okay. We'll be there."

They left the house a few minutes later and headed in the direction of Redington's office. After driving a couple of miles, Pierce turned into a residential neighborhood and made a series of figure eights until it was virtually impossible for anyone to stay on their trail without being detected. Finally, he returned to U.S. 1 and headed south, en route to the Coral Castle.

Although Redington had wanted to be there when they opened up the altar, he'd agreed that it was best if he dealt with Carver. Right now, he was driving to the Miami Beach precinct, not his office. His call had been a diversion in case the phone was tapped. From the precinct, Redington would contact Carver, and together they would go to Pierce's office and prepare for the 2 A.M. meeting.

They parked the car in a dark corner of a vacant lot and walked a block and a half along U.S. 1 before they reached the castle. Pierce carried his backpack over his shoulder and wore a pair of threadbare jeans; Elise had donned a floppy hat and wore her favorite dungarees from her digs. Anyone who took notice of them would probably think they looked like a pair of street people searching for a place to crash.

When they reached the castle, they skirted the edge of the parking lot and hurried past the gift shop, toward the side wall. They had about two hours, maybe two and a half, before the beat cop stopped by. That is, if he still made his nightly check *after* the bars closed.

As they approached the wall at the spot they'd found earlier, Pierce slipped off his backpack, removed a pair of gloves from a side pocket, and tossed the pack over the wall. It hit the ground with a thud and a clatter of steel. "Well, now we're committed," he said. "I'll go over and let you in through the revolving door."

"No. Just give me a boost." She took the gloves from him, slipped them on, and turned to the wall.

"Suit yourself."

The coral rock was deeply pitted, and she had no difficulty finding footholds. She took several short steps as Pierce balanced her from below, then she swung a leg over the top. "Oh, God. I think I'm stuck," she whispered.

"Just swing your other leg over and drop down."

"Yeah. Right." Slowly she pulled her leg over and lowered herself, until he could see only her hands. Then she let go.

"You okay?"

A glove hit him in the head, and the other one fell at his feet. I guess that's a yes, he thought, and pulled on the gloves. On his first two tries, he lost his balance and fell off the wall. In spite of the gloves and his long-sleeved shirt, the rough-edged coral rock scraped his skin. On the third try he made it to the top. In the pale light, the place looked like something out of a fairy tale. He almost expected elves or gnomes or the ghost of Ed Leedskalnin to dance out of the shadows. But the castle remained silent and still. To his right, the silhouettes of the coral rock moon, Saturn, and Mars seemed suspended above the wall like astrological symbols carved into the night sky. To his left, the tower loomed, a sentry in the moon glow.

"Hurry up," Elise called to him from the shadows below. He shifted around until he faced the wall, lowered himself, and dropped to the ground. He brushed the gritty coral rock from his pants and asked Elise if she was all right.

"Fine. Let's get this over with." She handed him the pack. And they headed across the moon-washed courtyard toward the altar. The great hulking shapes seemed to press in on him, quivering with a life of their own, whispering of the past. He felt like a dwarf in a land peopled by alien giants who were shaped like coral furniture, and imagined that on certain nights they came awake and communed among themselves, laughing and dancing. As they passed the valentine-shaped stone table, a breeze strummed the branches of the trees in the courtyard. In his mind, its melody became the soft, pathetic moans of Ed's broken heart.

When they reached the altar, he shrugged off his backpack. Even though Elise had enthusiastically told him about her numerous archaeological digs, he knew that her help in moving the blocks was going to be limited. He just hoped he had enough strength to do it. But the first task was removing the cement filling between the blocks.

Pierce shone his flashlight over the altar, paused a moment on the bubbling water, then moved the beam upward along the vertical surface until he reached the face made of shells. The white eyes stared back at him, giving no hint of what might lie hidden within the fountain. He tracked downward again, directing the light along the cemented area between the rocks. "Keep it pointed right there," he said, handing the flashlight to Elise.

He slipped on a pair of goggles after taking out a mallet and chisel from the pack and stabbed the chisel at the cracked joint. It stuck like a knife in melon. "See how weak it is? This'll be easy."

Her face was in shadow above him, but he could sense her unease. "Let's just get on with it."

Pierce struck the chisel squarely with the mallet. It sank several inches as bits of concrete flashed through the light. He wrenched it free and struck the joint again, then again. After several strokes the chisel wedged solidly into the crack, and he couldn't pull it out. "Shit, I can't get a grip."

"How about the crowbar?"

"Good idea." He took out the bar and, using the vertical block for leverage, loosened the chisel.

He resumed the tedious pounding, chipping away at the joint. When he finally stopped to catch his breath, he examined the opening he'd created. Several narrow bridges of concrete still connected the two blocks of coral rock. "This'll just take another minute or two."

"Then what?" Elise asked as she stooped over and examined his work.

"Then I'll move the rear slab away from the front one. That way we don't have to mess with the lead pipes that go down to the spring."

Pierce picked up the crowbar and attacked the remaining links of concrete. When the two rocks were parted, he dropped the crowbar. "Okay, here goes."

He pressed his shoulder against the upright block of rock. It stood a few inches shorter than he and was about two feet in thickness, but wider at the base. He strained and groaned and pushed, and slowly the rock edged backward.

"Jesus," he said when he stopped to rest. He'd been worried about tipping it over and shattering it and possibly destroying the skull, but that didn't seem likely now. "I wish I knew what old Ed's secret was. This is like moving a refrigerator filled with rocks."

"Better you than me. I'm going to go up to the tower and take a look around. Make sure everything's okay."

"Good idea."

Pierce continued battling with the block of stone, fighting for every inch. Once, he stopped and looked over his shoulder and saw Elise's moonlit face in the window. Now and then he thought he heard noises behind him and his head snapped back, eyes roaming across the mammoth structures. But, of course, nothing was there. Nothing but the coral monsters communing in the night, he thought.

When he'd moved the block more than a foot, he knelt down to look inside. He patted the ground for the flashlight, but realized Elise had taken it. "Shit." He glanced up at the tower to signal her, but she wasn't in the window.

He walked over to the steps of the tower and called her name in a harsh whisper. No answer. Only the vast silence, the dark, and an uneasy something that bristled in the air. He called her name again, louder this time. "Damn, what the hell's she doing?" he muttered.

A shadow filled the doorway, then Elise was flying down the steps, her hair a dark penumbra around her head. He grabbed hold of her hand. "What happened? You all right?"

She sucked in a deep breath, tipped her head toward the tower. "Nick, I swear that hanging bed started swinging by itself. I couldn't take my eyes off it. I couldn't move. I couldn't even turn on the flashlight. It was like ol' Ed was lying there watching me."

Like the furniture watches me, he thought. "C'mon. You just got spooked."

"No, it was like I was . . . I don't know. I was overcome by this forlorn feeling. God, it was creepy."

"You see anything else around of a more substantial nature?"

"Nothing. How's it going?"

"Let's take a look with the flashlight."

Pierce dropped down on his hands and knees as Elise shone the beam on the inner surfaces of both coral blocks. He'd hoped to see a hollow space in one of them and the crystal skull resting there, waiting to be rediscovered. But he couldn't see anything except the rough coral surface.

"Nothing," he said.

"Try opening it a little further so we can work inside. Maybe the hole has been covered and we can't see it yet."

He gripped the upright block of coral with both hands and pressed his chest to it again. Rocking back and forth, he nudged it inch by inch until the space between the block had expanded to about eighteen inches. He stepped back, caught his breath. In spite of the gloves, the palms of his hands were bruised and scraped from the sharp coral rock. He took a swallow from the canteen of water he'd brought along, then held it out to Elise.

She shook her head, and instead crawled as far as she could into the opening and closely surveyed the inner surfaces with the flashlight beam.

"See anything?"

She was quiet a moment, then backed out. She shook her head. "It doesn't look promising."

"Damn, it's got to be here." Pierce picked up the crowbar and jabbed it at random against the rock surfaces inside the opening. Chips of rock ricocheted about, and the resounding thud of each thrust echoed across the courtyard.

Elise grabbed him by the shoulder. "Nick, you're making too much noise."

He stepped back, frustrated, and hurled the crowbar into the ground between the two blocks. "Christ, what a fucking waste of time."

But Elise ignored him. She was staring at the crowbar. It had penetrated the ground and was standing upright. She loosened it and scraped at the dirt, then stabbed, digging a hole several inches deep.

"What are you doing?" he asked.

"Didn't you hear the guide today? There's hardly any ground soil around here, except in the garden where it's been added. The coral rock bed should be right near the surface, but it's not."

"Maybe dirt was added here, too."

She took several more jabs. "My guess is that the coral bed has been hollowed out and covered. That means something could be buried here."

"Let me see."

"Be careful, and stop if you hit anything. We don't want to damage it." She handed him the crowbar, and he gouged at the ground for a couple of minutes until the hole was almost a foot deep. "I think you're right, and the one thing I didn't bring was a shovel."

"We'll have to do our best."

The dirt from the hole quickly formed a small mound beside the altar. They took turns working the earth with the crowbar and chisel and carrying it out by the handful. The hole was elbow-deep when Pierce struck something. He reached down and scraped with his finger.

"Shit," Pierce muttered.

"What is it?" She dropped down to his side.

"That's it. I hit rock."

But Elise was unperturbed. "Then we've just got to widen it more. Dig toward the back, underneath the block."

Pierce nodded and redirected his blows. They switched places a couple more times — until one of Pierce's thrusts struck a solid surface again. "Ah, Christ. More rock."

He dropped the crowbar and backed out. Elise moved into his place and reached into the opening. He wondered how much longer they should stay. The bars closed in a few minutes, and the cop would be due.

"Nick, it's not rock. It's smooth and flat. It feels like metal."

"You're kidding!" He slipped his hand deep into the hole. He clawed at the dirt until he could feel more of the smooth surface. Then he touched something else.

"I think I've got a latch. It's a container, a metal case!"

They took turns working with the chisel, loosening the dirt around the container, scooping it out. After a few minutes, Pierce's fingers found something new. "I've got a handle, a leather grip."

"Good. We've got to hurry."

He scraped away the dirt. "I'm going to pull it out." Just as he spoke, he tumbled backward, the rotted leather strap in his hand.

Elise couldn't help laughing.

"Now what if I had landed on the crowbar . . . or hit my head on the chisel?"

"You didn't, though."

"I think I loosened it."

He reached into the hole again, pressing his face against the coral block. "I've got my hand under it. It's moving. Give me the crowbar."

He slid the hooked end of the bar underneath the case and managed to get one of the prongs against the back side. He pulled, and the metal case slid forward to the lip of the hole. He grasped it with both hands. "Gotcha."

Elise brushed dirt from the box as Pierce set it on the ground. "I sure hope you're what we think you are," he announced to the box.

"Let's open it," Elise said.

He glanced around, feeling uneasy. "No. Let's get out of here."

"You're right. It's late. Besides, we should open it with Bill. It's only fair."

"Let's go out the revolving door," Pierce said. "It'll be easier."

They crossed the courtyard, glancing one more time at the coral monsters. Pierce bent down as they reached the door. "That's odd. No wedge."

He stood up and pushed the door. It wouldn't budge. It felt as if the wedge was on the wrong side.

"Hold it!" a voice shouted sharply from behind him.

Oh, God, the cop, he thought. He heard the click of a gun, turned, peered into the gloom. For a moment he didn't see anything. Then a figure stepped out from the shadow of a herculean-sized chair.

"Evening, Nick. And if it isn't Lisie playing in the dirt."

"Steve, what the hell are you doing here?" Elise demanded.

"Oh, I don't know. Just out for a little fun. What're you doing? Archaeological stuff, huh?"

"None of your business. Just leave me alone."

Fat chance of that, Pierce thought, eyeing the sleek, deadly Mach 10 under his arm.

"'Fraid I can't do that, Lisie. By the way, you can call me Thor tonight, sweetheart."

Pierce heard a creak of gears and turned his head as the revolving stone door opened and K.J. stepped inside. No wonder the door wouldn't move, he thought.

"Hello, Nick," he said, speaking as casually as if he'd always spoken. He aimed a .357 at Pierce and grinned. "You can call me Frey."

Thirty-Four

"Real careful now, Pierce. I want you to lay that box on the ground," Simms said, pointing the machine pistol at the metallic case. "Then the pack."

Pierce glanced between the two men. There wasn't much he could do but follow orders. Besides being armed, both were enormous, muscular men. A corrupt lawyer and a fake mute. What a pair.

"Get over to the wall and put your hands against it," Thor ordered, prodding the Mach 10 at him, and Pierce moved.

"You, too, Lisie."

"How did you know we were here, Steve?" she asked, holding her ground.

"Just a simple directional microphone outside the house this morning," he answered. "You said it all. Now get over to the wall."

"Why're you doing this?" If she was afraid of him, her voice didn't reveal it.

"I'm disappointed in you, Lisie," he said, disregarding her question. "I really am. Trespassing, breaking and entering, destroying private property, and theft. Shame on you."

"Cut the crap, Steve. You're crooked. You're working for Raymond Andrews. You've lost all sense of what's right and decent. You're not the person I married. You're a monster."

"I'm not working for Andrews. I'm working with Odin. And I want you to call me Thor, honey. Let's hear you say it."

When she didn't respond, he grabbed her arm and twisted it behind her back, pushed her next to Pierce. "Talk to me, Lisie. You know I don't like being ignored. Did you like my drawing on your closet door, Lisie?"

"You bastard!"

"Come on. Call me Thor. Say it."

She winced in pain and struggled to get away. "Thor . . . Thor."

"Let her go, Simms," Pierce barked.

Simms jammed the Mach 10 against his ear. "What was that, Pierce? Did I hear you say something?"

Pierce didn't answer.

Simms lowered the weapon and snapped on handcuffs, squeezing them tight on Pierce's wrist. "You like fucking each other so much I'll hook you two together."

"Hey, what's this?" K.J. said. Pierce looked back and saw that he'd found Elise's .22 in the pack. "You couldn't kill a squirrel with that thing, Pierce."

"Hurry up, Frey. Open the goddamn box. And you two keep your eyes on the wall."

Pierce heard K.J. banging the chisel against the latch.

"Careful," Simms cautioned.

"I know what I'm doing," K.J. said. "I got it open."

"Let me take a look. You watch them."

Pierce stole a glance over his shoulder as Simms reached into the box. He turned back to the wall as K.J. pointed the .357 at him.

"Yeah, that looks like it," Simms said after a moment. "Let's move out. You take the box. I'll handle these two."

He walked over to the wall, grabbed Elise by the arm, and pulled her and Pierce several steps. "I'm going through first. Follow me." He slowly backed through the door.

"Move," K.J. said when Simms was out of sight.

Just as they pushed their way through the door, Pierce saw a silhouette, a figure partially hidden behind the well. Then they were through the wall and standing in the garden.

Please, be the cop, be the cop, Pierce said over and over to himself.

"Over there." Simms pointed the gun toward a hedge.

Jesus Christ, they were going to kill them right here, Pierce thought. You better hurry, he mentally told the man in the courtyard, the man who had to be the cop.

"It's a beautiful garden in the moonlight, isn't it, Lisie?" Simms said.

They skirted the hedge until they came to an opening. In front of him, as though it were just another piece of coral furniture, was the dark blue Mercedes, the same Mercedes he'd seen following him. The car had been shielded by the shrubbery, parked not fifty feet from where he'd heard Redington lecture his students.

"See, we were waiting for you. We've been here all along," Simms said. "Lisie, you know who my partner here is? Don't you?"

"Frey," she spat.

Simms laughed. "Very good. He's also my workout partner and Andrews's bodyguard. You getting the picture now?"

Pierce heard the faint groan of the revolving door and tried to cover the sound with a question. "So why didn't you get the box yourself if you knew where it was?"

"That wasn't the plan."

"So Andrews makes all your decisions now," Elise snapped.

Simms cast an irritated glance her way. "Get in the back seat."

"Hold it right there," boomed a voice from the corner of the hedge. Pierce gaped as the man stepped out into the moonlight. He never thought he would be pleased to see Neil Bellinger.

"Who are you?" Simms barked.

Bellinger sneered. "Sorry guys. The hundred grand was tempting, but your boss bribed the wrong cop tonight. Now drop those guns and back off."

Simms lowered his Mach 10. K.J. dropped his, and stepped back. "I'm Steve Simms. I'm a prosecutor for the Drug Enforcement Administration."

"Drop it, I said."

"This man with me is an undercover agent. I'm going to reach for my identification card."

"The hell you are."

Simms lowered himself onto one knee, set the machine pistol on the ground, and kept talking. "This is a drop-off point. The box is full of cocaine, and you're fucking up my bust."

"Don't bullshit me. I know who you are, Simms. Where's Carver?"

"I don't know what you're talking about."

The revolving door creaked again, and a commanding voice rang out. "Police. What's going on here?"

Bellinger turned. "It's okay."

"Drop it!" the cop yelled.

The moment of confusion was all Simms needed. He scooped up his Mach 10 and sprayed a dozen bullets. Bellinger was knocked back against the hedge. He hung there a moment, then flopped to the ground. The cop lay several feet behind him.

Simms walked over to Bellinger, pumped another bullet into him, and did the same to the cop. "Get in the car," K.J. said, hustling them into the back seat. Simms slid in behind the wheel, and K.J. joined him in front.

"God, you killed him!" Elise shouted.

"Too bad about that, Lisie. Couldn't be helped." Simms started the engine and eased the big car out of its hiding place and across the lawn to the parking lot.

"Where're we going?" Pierce asked.

"You guys are going for a little ride. Got someone who wants to see you two."

Pierce looked out the window as they cut through the parking lot and headed north on U.S. 1. The tint was so dark he could barely see. For the first time in his life he sensed the proximity of death, his death. He heard it whistling through the air, a bullet with his name on it, a blade K.J. or Simms would sink into his heart, his body dumped into a canal like Scarjaw.... No telling what form it would take. Bad thoughts. He touched his pants pocket with his free hand and felt the amulet. He heard Tía Juana's voice in his head saying: *protección.*

He clasped Elise's hand, squeezed it. He glanced over at her and saw she was staring intently at the back of Simms's head. "Why did you do it, Steve?"

"Do what, Lisie?" he called back.

"Sell out to Andrews. You knew what he'd done to my father, you knew what I thought of him."

"Sure I did, and I took advantage of it. The divorce was over, and you'd burned me. So I decided to get you at your weak spot. I knew K.J. — Frey — from the gym. So it wasn't hard to get to see Andrews. He was happy to meet me. He introduced me to a whole new world, you could say."

They'd been on the road for thirty or forty minutes when Pierce heard the sound of steel grating under the car. They were crossing the Rickenbacker Causeway on their way to Key Biscayne. That was fine with Pierce. In fact, it couldn't be better. If they were going to Andrews's condo, Carver should have the place staked out. Then again, Bellinger had asked Simms where Carver was. What the hell did that mean?

But they weren't going to Andrews's place. Simms passed the turnoff to Mimosa Drive, and several blocks later pulled off the road. There were no lights outside now, and Pierce could barely see out the windows. He knew they must be near the state park at the end of the key.

"If either of you makes a sound, you're dead," Simms said. "You got that?"

The front doors opened and warm, pungent night air wafted over them. K.J. opened the back door, and his beefy arm reached in and jerked them out. They were led down to a canal with a half-dozen slips filled with boats. The state park was on their left, and private homes to their right. But the houses were too far away, Pierce realized as they were hustled over to a streamlined Cigarette boat. Nobody could see them.

Death at sea, he thought grimly, and saw an image of Scarjaw's bloated body in the morgue. He touched the amulet through his pants pocket. *Protección.* But the little bag offered faint hope — hope that faded with each second that they moved closer to their destination.

"Get in," Simms said. K.J. took the wheel of the boat and fired the engine. Simms released the guide ropes and they eased out of the slip. K.J. and Simms were seated in comfortable swivel chairs while Pierce and Elise sat side by side in the bow on a bench covered by a thin cushion.

K.J. guided the boat through the canal toward Biscayne Bay, keeping the speed low so as not to attract attention. As they reached the mouth of the canal, they passed close to a house, but the place was dark. And even if they yelled, it wouldn't have mattered, because K.J. pulled back on the throttle. The Cigarette whined as it picked up speed. It barely skimmed the surface of the water as though it were a creature of the air, not the sea, and they were soaked with the spray.

Pierce looked over his shoulder and saw the lights of downtown Miami twinkling in the distance. To his right he momentarily glimpsed the shadowy houses of Stiltsville that stood like sentries in the moonlight on the bay. Then they were beyond the tiny water community and out into the glistening ocean.

They were heading south along the keys, but the ride lasted only another ten minutes. They pulled up to a white yacht that rested quietly on the placid waters. ARGO-2 was painted in bold, black letters on the side. Pierce remembered seeing a photo of the yacht in Andrews's study. There was no doubt who was waiting for them. He saw a couple of men on the deck; then a spotlight flooded over them, bleaching out everything.

They were taken aboard and into a plush, wood-paneled salon that was larger than his living room. Simms pointed his Mach 10 at a leather couch in the corner and told them to sit down. Across from them was a large-screen television set.

"We going to watch a movie? Is that what we're going to do? Eh, Steve?" Elise emphasized his name as she spoke it.

"Sure, Lisie. Wait till you see the main feature. Gripping stuff."

Pierce looked around and noticed that the walls were mahogany and decorated with nautical clocks. To his right was a grandfather clock, and he noticed it was bolted to the wall. At the other end of the salon was a dining area and bar. In the center of the salon was a high-backed captain's chair, obviously awaiting their host, and next to the television was a video camera on a tripod. The camera was turned on, its red light glowing and its lens aimed directly at them.

Simms said something to K.J., took the box, and tapped lightly on a door. It opened, and for an instant Pierce glimpsed a stateroom with gold-painted walls. Then Simms closed the door behind him.

He looked over at Elise. Her clothes, like his, were wet and soiled; her face streaked with dirt. Her eyes were red and troubled. "You okay?"

She bit at her lower lip, whispered: "What're we going to do?"

"Shut up," K.J. barked.

Their plan to trap Andrews had backfired before they'd even had a chance to set it in motion, Pierce thought. And now he didn't even know if anyone was looking for them. When Redington heard Carver was missing, he must have told Bellinger about the Coral Castle. Now Bellinger was dead, and he didn't have much hope for Carver. Redington would have no idea where to look for them now.

"Well, we're all ready, aren't we?" said a voice from across the salon.

Pierce saw Andrews step through the door of the stateroom, Simms behind him carrying the box. Andrews beamed at them a moment, then motioned for Simms to set the box on the bar. Andrews was dressed in a navy blue blazer with an open white shirt, navy pants, and white shoes. His yachting attire, Pierce thought.

"Welcome aboard, Nicholas. I thought this would be much nicer than your office." He smiled as if there was nothing out of the ordinary about their meeting. "And Dr. Simms. I don't believe we've ever met."

"I've heard about you." As if they'd just dropped by for cocktails, Pierce thought.

Andrews laughed. "Oh, a little humor. I like that." He settled into the captain's chair and swiveled toward them.

"How about explaining what's going on, Ray?" said Pierce.

"All in time." Andrews's smile turned to a frown as he noticed the handcuffs and their clothing. He turned to K.J., who was cleaning the salt spray from his .357. "Frey, please come and take these handcuffs off, and keep the gun out of sight."

He stuffed it in a shoulder holster and unlocked the cuffs. Pierce rubbed his wrist; it felt bruised from the tight grip of the cuff.

"Why did you call them Frey and Thor?" Elise asked. She still maintained her casual, conversational tone, but her hands were trembling.

"If you aspire to godliness, it helps to identify with the gods of the past. Let me formally introduce myself. You can think of me as Odin. You, of course, know Thor, and Nicholas knows Frey as my mute bodyguard. He can speak, but he usually prefers not to do so in my presence, which I find suitable."

He's a madman, Pierce thought. Their only hope was that somehow they could turn his obsession to their advantage. The yacht's engines revved; they started to move. "Where're you taking us, Ray?"

"No place special. Just the cruise of your life, that's all. It won't be boring. I'll keep you entertained." His eyes flicked over them; an expression of disdain claimed his features. "You two are terribly dirty. Why don't you wash up and change clothes. I think we can find something for both of you."

"We're fine," Pierce said.

"No. Really, I'd prefer it. Frey, show Dr. Simms to the master head, and Thor, please take Nicholas to the other one, then find them something to wear."

A few minutes later, they were back on the couch. Elise wore a pair of baggy shorts and a loose sweatshirt, and Pierce wore cotton drawstring pants and a T-shirt. The clothes they'd been given were not only clean, but neatly pressed.

"Now, that's better," Andrews said. "You look much more comfortable." His dark eyes focused on Elise. "See, I'm not such a bad guy, am I? And, Nicholas, I want to thank you for completing your job with such efficiency. But then I'm not really surprised that the missing skull turned up when it did. Not at all. It fits." Andrews rubbed his chin; he looked pensive. "It's just too bad you didn't have the guts to stick with me."

Here it comes, Pierce thought. Things were about to turn nasty.

"So he could die like your wife?" Elise snapped.

Andrews looked amused. "You think I killed her, do you?"

"Nick found out the truth. You can't hide it any longer."

"I'm not hiding anything, Dr. Simms. Let me show you something." He took a remote control device out of his pocket and clicked on a VCR. The large screen was blank a moment, then Marisol Puente's face appeared; she looked distraught. He hit the fast-forward and her head jerked around, then dropped into her hands. Andrews switched it to normal speed.

"Just get it over with," Marisol said, shaking her head. "Kill me. I know that's what you're going to do."

Andrews turned off the tape. "Marisol Puente was as much a surprise to me as she was to you, Nicholas. But we've taken care of her."

"Is destroying people your favorite pastime, Raymond?" Elise's tone was thick with vitriol.

"I'm like you, Dr. Simms. When someone acts against you, you want them to pay the price. It's a matter of balance." He slipped off the chair, walked over to the VCR, and changed tapes. He turned it on. The screen filled with the image of a man with a bushy, gray-streaked beard who stood behind a cluttered counter. Andrews froze the frame.

"What did you do to him?" Elise screamed, and suddenly bounded off the couch toward Andrews. But Simms grabbed her and tossed her back onto the couch.

"Stay seated and you'll find out," Andrews admonished. "Nicholas, this is John Mahoney, Elise's father, in his junk store. Excuse me, antique shop." He smiled. "I made this tape a few days ago."

Pierce realized he was going to see what Andrews's recent business trip had been about, and he wasn't looking forward to it. As the tape began again, he heard the man speak. "Get that goddamn camera out of my face, Raymond. What're you doing here?"

Mahoney's features were strong, like Elise's, but his eyes were melancholy, almost painful to look at. He took a step back. His gaze shifted to one side, as if he were watching someone else who was out of the camera's view. "What do you want from me? You've already got my skull."

"Where's the other one hidden?"

"I don't know. Nobody does."

Andrews stepped up to the counter and into the picture. He set a suitcase down, opened it, and lifted out a gleaming crystal skull. "I'll return your skull if you tell me where the other one is hidden."

"Your deal is a lie."

"You've got ten seconds."

Mahoney stared impassively at him, accepting his fate calmly.

A figure with a gun appeared in the corner of the picture. The muzzle was thrust out at Mahoney's head.

"Five more seconds, old man."

"I've told you the truth."

"I believe you're lying. Shoot him."

The report of the gun rang out. Mahoney's head snapped back, and he collapsed. Elise screamed and struggled against Simms, who grabbed her by the hair and shoved her face toward the screen. "Look, Lisie, look!" He jabbed his finger toward the screen.

The camera relentlessly followed the body to the floor. It zoomed in, focusing on the bleeding head as her father died. "He's dead, dead, dead. Andrews killed your daddy." Simms's voice echoed in the silence, punctuated only by Elise's sobs.

Pierce pulled Elise into his arms and glared at Andrews. But Andrews's gaze was riveted on Simms, and his eyes were cold and hard.

Thirty-Five

The TV screen was black; the show was over. Andrews ordered the engine cut, and now the yacht rocked gently in the tranquil sea. He sat back in his captain's chair and watched as Pierce tried to calm Elise. Her head was buried in her hands and she was weeping, shaking her head.

"I admire your outspoken attitude, Dr. Simms. I really do. But living your life for a vendetta is a misguided use of your talents," Andrews chided. "Look where it's gotten you."

"So is a life devoted to chasing a myth at all costs," Pierce countered.

"I'm not chasing a myth, Nicholas. I'm fulfilling it. There's a difference. And you two are very fortunate to be here to witness the event. It's too bad Dr. Bill couldn't be with us, too. But you can't expect everything to work smoothly. Who would have guessed Mr. Slick was an honest cop? But my shore crew will mop things up before the night's over. Now why don't we take a look at the skull you found?"

Andrews glanced at K.J. "Frey, bring it here, please." The bodyguard carried the box over to him and held it out. Andrews made no effort to take the container from him.

Elise raised her head; her eyes were red, and tears stained her cheeks. "I hope it's full of dirt," she rasped.

He laughed and raised the top of the box, reached inside, and lifted out a leather drawstring bag that was stiff and cracked with age. He rested the bag on his lap and, as K.J. moved aside, carefully loosened the strings, then peeled back the bag. First the top of the skull showed, then Pierce saw the diamond-shaped eyes, the nose hole, and finally the jaw and gleaming teeth. Andrews lifted it up, turned it slowly around, admiring it.

Pierce couldn't wrench his eyes from the skull. It's enigmatic diamond-shaped eyes begged attention, called to him. It was an artifact, a relic, a work of art. Yet, it was also an image from the dream world of hypnosis that suddenly and irrevocably existed here and now.

"You two really have fulfilled my highest expectations." Andrews's voice was hushed, reverent. He gazed at them over the top of the skull. "It's too bad you won't be around to see what will happen."

There was a certain finality in his comment, and Pierce reacted by touching the amulet, which he'd taken from his jeans when he'd changed pants. He glanced at Elise, who sat rigid, chewing at her lower lip, worrying her hands, revulsion contorting her face.

"What are you going to do with it?" Pierce asked.

"Don't worry. I plan to tell you all about it. You do deserve that much for your help, deceitful though it was."

He walked over to the couch and knelt down on one knee in front of them. "Dr. Simms, how would you say this skull compares with the other one?"

Pierce had an overwhelming urge to snatch the skull from Andrews's hands and crack him over the head with it. But Simms must have read his thoughts. He moved in close and kept his eyes on him.

"Well, Dr. Simms?" Andrews repeated.

Elise kept her head lowered, refusing to look at it. Simms grabbed a handful of hair and jerked her head back. "Yes," she screeched.

"Yes, what?" Simms asked, tugging her hair.

"It resembles the other one." Her voice wavered and broke.

"I'll ask the questions, Thor." Andrews waited patiently for her to pull herself together. "Is it an exact likeness?"

She wiped her eyes and focused on the skull as though she was looking at it for the first time.

"Tell me, Elise," Andrews persisted, and Simms tugged on her hair again.

"I'd have to see them both," she said, and sniffled.

Andrews smiled. "I can do that for you. But first things first."

He stood up, reached into his pocket, and pulled out an old copper coin the size of a half-dollar. He held it up in front of him. "This is a commemorative coin," he said, turning it over in his hand. "Its inscription says, 'They Took Cartagena, 1741.'" He looked from Pierce to Elise and back again. "That probably doesn't mean anything to you, but this coin is related to the skull."

He looked over at K.J. "Frey, move my chair closer, please."

Andrews rocked from side to side in the captain's chair — his goddamn throne, Pierce thought. K.J. and Simms were standing on either side of him: the king and his knights. "A short time after we graduated from college, Nicholas, I inherited some family documents from my grandfather. One of them was a letter written by my fifth-generation ancestor, William Andrews, and with the letter was this coin."

William was a British soldier who fought under the command of Vernon Washington, the brother of George, and survived the disastrous British loss in Colombia. Washington was so certain of victory at Cartagena that coins like the one he'd shown them were minted before the battle. In his letter, William Andrews wrote that when he'd left home, he was angry at his father for paying more attention to his collection of gems and antiques than to his family. To spite the elder Andrews, he'd taken with him a metal box that contained his father's prize possession, an ancient crystal skull. William's father had inherited it from his mother, who was of Basque ancestry. Not long after the battle of Cartagena, William jumped ship in Jamaica. He made his way across the Caribbean to North America and became a homesteader in the Florida wilderness.

Andrews flipped the souvenir coin, snatched it out of the air. "At the time, I thought that someday, maybe when I was retired, I'd look for the skull," Andrews continued. "It would be a challenging pastime, since the only clue William left was that the artifact was hidden near the tip of Florida, and, of course, I didn't have the slightest idea where. Now we know that an immigrant stonemason — the man who built the Coral Castle — must have found the buried skull and put it to his own strange use."

Andrews surveyed his audience as he repocketed the coin. Then he told them that a decade ago, he'd changed his mind about the importance of the search, after mentioning the subject to an acquaintance of Basque ancestry. Over dinner the two men had discussed their heritage, and pondered the mysterious and puzzling history of the Basque people, when Andrews had mentioned the letter from William and the tale of the Basque skull. A few weeks later they met again, and the man showed him a document from his own family library, a silver scroll written in ancient Greek. The man claimed that it was written by Plato, that it was his missing dialogue on Atlantis. In part, it dealt with the tale of the two ancient crystal skulls.

"He told me that each succeeding head of the family had pledged not to reveal the existence of the scroll to a soul until approached by someone with knowledge of a lost crystal skull. The scroll was to be made known to the world only when the two crystal skulls were reunited.

"I studied the interpretation of the scroll, and you can imagine my surprise to learn that Plato once owned the skull that had been in my family. It was given to him in Egypt during his initiation into the mysteries."

Andrews paused and looked down at the skull again. He touched it; the caress, thought Pierce, was almost sexual. "Plato spent three days in the Great Pyramid, and during that time the priests taught him the secret to withdrawing the knowledge that had been psychically programmed into the crystal in the time of Atlantis. At that point, I knew that my life was tied with the destiny of the skull. I became partners with the man who owned the scroll, and together we formed a fellowship of searchers — Noster Mundus."

"And you killed him, too," Elise accused. "It was Paul Loften."

Andrews's dark eyes widened. When he spoke, Pierce heard a barely subdued rage in his voice. "Loften betrayed me."

"What did Plato do with the skull?" Pierce asked, anxious to keep Andrews talking to buy them some time.

"He learned from it. He wrote the third dialogue on Atlantis."

"What about the first two?" Pierce asked.

Andrews smiled. "I'm glad you asked. It was because of the first two that he was initiated into the secret priesthood of the Great Pyramid and given the skull. The priests realized that his dialogues were so accurate, as far as they went, that they knew Plato was the 'speaker,' the chosen Atlantean descendant they had been seeking, who would take the message of the skull to the world."

"How did the Basques get it?" Pierce asked.

"It was stolen from Plato along with the third dialogue and the final pages of the second one. Both were taken north, to the Basque region. Fitting, I think, since in their folklore the Basques are called descendants of Atlanteans."

"The scroll is probably a fake," Elise muttered.

Andrews shrugged. "Think what you like. It doesn't matter. Besides, in a way you are right."

He admitted that Plato didn't write his dialogue on the silver scroll. It was inscribed by someone else, the one who had stolen it from the philosopher. At the beginning of the scroll, the anonymous thief — a dissident priest — confessed his crime and explained it. Plato was betraying secret teachings, making too many of the mysteries public. The skull dialogue, called *Solon*, which was related to two earlier ones, *Timaeus* and *Critias*, was stolen to protect the knowledge. The skull was taken as punishment.

"I'm sure you know, Dr. Simms, that *Critias* ends in the middle of a sentence, which has puzzled scholars for centuries. The thief admits on the scroll that when he stole *Solon*, he also took the ending of *Critias*. He may actually have done so accidentally."

"What's the scroll say about the reunion of the skulls? That you're not going to age? Is that it?" Pierce was incredulous. "How could you believe that?"

Andrews closed his eyes, took in a deep breath. It was like a prelude to prayer. He explained that both the scroll and the Mayan legend proclaimed that the reunion of the skulls would impel the world into an era when mankind would again be ruled by immortals.

"You see, the god-men are returning. Plato wrote that the reunion will mark the time of the New Man. I call it the New Enlightenment, as you know." He stopped, leaned toward them. "'He awakens the old gods within him. And he becomes one with them.'"

He sounded like an evangelist. "So what's the lure of immortality?" Elise's voice reeked sarcasm.

Andrews didn't hesitate to answer. "For a man who possesses abundant power and wealth, what greater interest is there than to stop the aging process, to extend life indefinitely?"

"You're misinterpreting the dialogue," Elise said. "You're deceiving yourself, just like you deceived my father."

Andrews's smile was laced with hubris. "Oh, really, Dr. Simms? And just how am I deceiving myself? Please tell me about it."

"The old gods were actually initiates, advanced men and women. Plato, or whoever wrote the dialogue, knew that. They only seemed immortal because the average man lacked their knowledge and understanding."

"'The betrayer struggles to the end, and opens the way for the New Man,'" Andrews said. "You are following Plato so faithfully." He nodded to K.J. and glanced toward the bar. Then, turning back to Pierce and Elise, he told them that they would now have the privilege of witnessing the reunion of the crystal skulls.

"A fitting last memory, don't you think? Myth and reality, life and death intermingling, and from it will rise the new legion."

K.J. walked around the bar and brought out a suitcase, the same one they had seen in the videotape of Mahoney's murder. Andrews motioned for him to set it at his feet. "Elise, please do me the honor of handing me the partner."

"Fuck you. Pick it up yourself."

Simms took her by the arm and started to pull her forward. "Let go of me, you bastard," she shouted, trying to twist away.

Pierce lunged forward and punched Simms in the gut. Simms grunted, dropped Elise's arm, and slammed his fist into Pierce's jaw.

His head snapped back against the couch and everything went black. When Pierce opened his eyes, he was dazed and wasn't sure whether he was conscious or dreaming. He saw Elise bend over, and for a moment she was an altar boy lifting a sacred chalice. He saw her passing a crystal skull to the high priest.

As he held the two skulls, the priest stared ahead and recited some ancient rite in a sort of dreamy tone.

"The king sees the stone, the first treasure of Atlantis, but makes his claim good only after the long struggle. Soon thereafter the allies of the betrayer lead the way to the second stone. The same as the first, it is veiled from sight under the watery altar. So captured, the First Matter and the Second Matter are now before him, and the Great Work begins under the sign of Gemini. The dominion of death is over, the feathered dragon shuns the light, and the king reigns immortal."

For an instant, Pierce focused on Andrews's face. It was a moment of clarity. He no longer saw the suave, elegant man he knew. Instead, he glimpsed the dark, necromantic eyes of the aged sorcerer from the realms of hypnotic vision, the Old One — the Smoking Mirror.

Thirty-Six

"Now, the remainder of the night is reserved for what I'll politely call an exhibition of your mortality," Andrews said as he led the way onto the deck. The skulls had been carefully packed in an aluminum case with a foam-cushioned interior and ballasts on either end, and Andrews carried his precious cargo himself.

"If they try anything, shoot them in the legs." His tone was as cold as the Arctic. Pierce was still woozy from Steve's knockout punch. He wobbled unsteadily behind Elise, and inhaled the night air to clear his head. Simms stalked from the rear, fingering his Mach 10; K.J. followed, carrying video equipment in a backpack.

Andrews opened a door below the bridge, flipped on a light switch, and stepped aside. "The lady first."

When she didn't move, Simms pushed Pierce and he bumped into her. He felt the muzzle of the Mach 10 at his back and followed her down a half-dozen steps. A rush of heat and diesel fumes pressed against him; no plush interior here, just a bare steel frame. They were apparently in a storage room near the engine.

"Visitors to see you," Andrews called after them.

For a moment, Pierce didn't know what Andrews meant. Then he heard Elise gasp and saw Marisol Puente, hands tied to a low overhead beam, a gag stuffed in her mouth, her feet barely brushing the floor.

"Doesn't she look nice? I find her very seductive all tied up like that." Andrews's voice seemed to fill the room. "She's been that way for three, almost four hours now. The beginning of her penance for betraying me."

Elise hurried over to the woman, pulling the gag from her mouth.

"You can untie her. It doesn't matter now. Just pull on the dangling rope and she'll come undone."

Pierce helped Elise lower Marisol to the floor. Her eyes were wide with terror, her lips parched. He heard a murmur from across the room, turned and saw Morris Carver bound and gagged on the floor.

"Another surprise," Andrews said. "I've left a bottle of water in the corner. Go ahead and revive them. I want all of you to be aware of what's going to happen next."

Elise picked up the bottle, took off the top, smelled it. She splashed water on Marisol's face, then held the bottle to the woman's lips. Pierce, meanwhile, untied Carver, and Elise gave him water.

Andrews rapped on the wall. "Now listen closely, friends. Just down the hall, locked in a storage room, are ninety pounds of dynamite. As soon as you hear the engine of the powerboat fire, you'll know I'm activating a remote timing device. You'll have twenty minutes to contemplate your deaths. Then you'll be blown to chunk-sized pieces of shark meat."

"You can't get away with this, Andrews!" Carver rasped. "You'll be arrested for murder as soon as you go back to shore."

"I don't think so, Detective. I've been preparing for this day for some time. I've known that once I had the skulls, my life would transform. That's what Noster Mundus is all about — transformation of the individual and society. I won't be as visible as I am now. Not for some time. But I will reemerge and stronger than ever. Far stronger. You can count on that."

"You're fucked, Ray," Pierce blustered.

Andrews laughed. "No, you are."

Simms stuck his head in the doorway and leveled the machine pistol at Pierce. "I'll take care of that bastard right now, Ray."

Andrews glanced sharply at Simms. "We'll do it my way. I want him to think about his death." He grinned at Pierce; his gritted teeth flashed white, like pearls. "Just think of yourself as being trapped in your last elevator, Nicholas. This one won't go up or down, just apart."

"The bomb might not detonate, Ray," Simms argued. "I say finish them off now."

Andrews swung around and fixed his eyes on Simms. "You will never address me by that name again. And the bomb will explode.

Enough talk. Now it's time to finish our chores and be on our way." He took one more look back. *"Adios, mis amigos."*

"Wait," Pierce said, his mind racing, seeking some excuse to keep Andrews here, to buy them more time.

"Nicholas, Nicholas. Please don't make this unpleasant. I gave you your insurance clients, and I took them away when you betrayed my trust. I gave you another chance with this case, and you blew it again. Now I'm taking your life. It's as simple as that. Besides, you don't remember, but I've got an old bone to pick with you from that time we were stuck in the elevator."

"I know. I hit you. I remember. It felt good. Real good, Ray."

Andrews's dark eyes seemed to bore a hole through him, but Pierce didn't care anymore. He smiled and watched as Andrews turned and the steel door slammed shut with a ringing finality.

"Cabrón!" Marisol shouted. "I never should have talked to you!"

Pierce looked over at her. "I'm sorry. I don't know how they found you."

"It's too late for apologies, *idiota,*" she scoffed, but her voice broke and she covered her face with her hands and began to weep.

Pierce vaulted up the stairs and grabbed hold of the knob. Rattled it. He raced down the stairs and across the compartment from wall to wall. No doors, no windows, no way out. He felt like a rat trapped in a maze, with dead ends in every direction.

"It's no use, Pierce." Carver shook his head and leaned against the wall. "You heard him. It'll all be over in a few minutes."

"Jesus," Elise whispered, running her hands over her arms again and again, faster and faster. "We've got to do something. We can't just — just *stand* here."

"We pray," said Marisol. "There is nothing left. Pray to the Lord, our savior."

"You do that." Pierce shoved his hand into the loose-fitting pants Steve had given him. He felt the amulet. Shit. What good was it? It was like Marisol's prayers. Something to cling to for hope, but there was nothing to cling to anymore.

He pulled out the amulet, and was about to hurl it against the door when he heard a popping sound. Then another, and another. Three muffled pops, then a fourth, like the backfire of a car in the distance.

"What was that?" Elise asked.

"I don't know. Probably the powerboat starting up." He listened, heard the roar of the Cigarette's outboard engine. "They're leaving."

He glanced at his watch. Twenty minutes. The sound of the boat's engine rose to a high whine, then slowly faded. He saw Carver watching him, his arms crossed over his chest, his back against the wall. Elise sat down next to Marisol, who was muttering prayers under her breath.

"Sit down, Nick. There's nothing to do. We've lost the skulls. We're locked in a room next to enough explosives to tear the ship to shreds." Her eyes filled with tears. "I've lost my father." Her voice trailed off, and she buried her head in her arms.

He lowered himself to the floor next to her, reached for her hand. "I wish it could have been different, Elise."

She was quiet for a moment, then squeezed his hand. "I know. So do I."

"Pray for your soul," Marisol said.

He looked at Marisol — and did a double take as he realized she was sitting on a door in the floor. "Hey, move! Get up! It's a door."

She moved aside, and Pierce saw a padlock. He jerked at it, kicked it. Useless.

"Nick, it just leads to the engine room." Elise's eyes were red, but she looked drained of emotion. "That's not going to get us out of here. We're not getting out." Then, more softly: "Not that way."

Seventeen minutes. The hot air and fumes nauseated him. His body was bathed in sweat. *Not that way.*

He closed his eyes and a surge of anger that seemed to start at his feet and rise up his body ripped through him like an electric current. He ran up the steps and battered the door with his hands and feet, like a kid having a tantrum. He started to reach for the handle, but he'd lost his strength. His body felt limp, and he backed down the stairs and sat in the middle of the floor. It must be the fumes, he thought, and closed his eyes.

Images, words, sensations, reeled through his head. He saw the stripper with the cowboy hat tottering on her head; Gibby wheeling into his office; Fuego at jai alai; Fuego's funeral; Elise at the Jack of Clubs; Elise tumbling into bed with him; Redington in his office, the plastic skull on his desk; Andrews holding up the two crystal skulls. The images blurred and melded together.

He felt the familiar chill needling his lower back as he saw himself shoved into the elevator with Carver. He squeezed his head, fought off the panic that pressed against him, clogged his throat. He slid his hands down his face, opened his eyes. *The elevator's stuck. The walls are shrinking.* He felt as if he were spinning, tumbling to hell. Out of control. He was losing it. You'll die insane, a voice said. Andrews's voice.

No! I control the elevator.

He forced himself to look up at the door. Now it was an elevator door. Move the numbers. But there were no numbers above the door. Just a word: *Escape.*

From death? From life? Was he already dead? Maybe it was over . . . and he didn't even know it.

Get out of the elevator. *Escape.* But the door remained sealed.

I'm trapped, stuck.

No, I can get out.

Escape. He said it over and over. A chant, a mantra. Still nothing happened. Something was wrong. Escape, but how? Open, escape, he ordered. Open up. But the elevator remained closed.

He heard a scratching noise. It didn't fit, didn't make sense. He tried to blot it out. *Escape, open, out.*

He heard it again, louder this time.

What was it?

He rubbed his eyes, blinked, looked around. He was still inside the hot room with the others. Nothing had changed.

"I thought I heard something." It was Carver's voice, but it sounded as if it were inside his head.

Pierce rose to his feet. He heard the sound again. It was like sandpaper being rubbed against a wall. Where was it coming from?

He trotted up the stairs to the door. He started to grasp the handle and realized he still was holding the amulet. He jammed it back in his pocket, grasped the handle, closed his eyes, squeezed it. Prayed it would open.

The scratching noise abraded his nerves. He turned the knob. It didn't move.

He let it go, opened his eyes, and stared at his watch. Twelve minutes. Almost halfway through hell.

He heard a sound, but now it was like a rattle. Was he delirious, imagining it? He looked at the doorknob. Concentrated on it. *Open. Escape.*

It was moving, vibrating. He was sure of it. *Escape. Open. Escape. Open. Damn it.*

He grabbed it, squeezed. This time he felt it move in his hand. Move on its own. *Open. Escape.* It moved again, and his heart leaped. He heard a click. Slowly he turned the knob. It kept turning. He sucked in his breath, then pulled with all his strength.

The door swung in; a body toppled forward into his arms and he nearly tumbled down the stairs. Carver moved to his side and together they pushed the man onto the deck. Pierce's hand came away bloody.

"Oh, Christ," Elise said from behind him, and Pierce realized it was Simms. He emitted low, broken groans; he was saying something. His groans became words: "Raff, raff, raff."

Marisol moved out onto the deck. "What's he saying?"

Pierce motioned for her to be quiet.

"Raff," Simms gasped.

"Raff . . . Raft! He said raft!" Carver exclaimed.

Pierce leaned forward. "Where is it?"

Simms was sitting up with the help of Pierce on one side and Carver on the other. He pointed toward the bow.

Pierce glanced at Elise. "Find it. Hurry!"

Her eyes were hard, unforgiving, as she stared at the man who was once her husband. "Leave him, Nick. We can't do anything for him."

She swept past them; Marisol hugged her heels. Their footfalls echoed along the deck. Pierce looked at Carver. "He opened the door."

"And he's going to be my number one witness if he lives," Carver said.

They lugged him forward. He was badly hurt, but he was still moving his legs; somehow he was walking. The warm night swam around Pierce, and he drew in deep lungfuls of air as he moved across the deck. Then his foot struck something and he crashed to the deck under Steve's weight.

He looked around and saw he'd tripped on another body. He looked into the man's eyes. They were glassy, vacuous. He saw two more bodies. "Christ, they killed the crew."

The popping sounds had been gunfire. Simms shot the crew for Andrews, Pierce guessed, then K.J. shot Simms. And he knew why. Simms was too defiant, a potential threat to Andrews.

"Nick, help us. There's no time." It was Elise.

Simms was on his hands and knees, crawling over the bodies toward the raft. A bib of blood spread over the back of his shirt.

"Go on," Carver said. "I'll get him."

Pierce hurried to the bow, where Elise and Marisol were struggling to get the self-inflating raft over a low rail. He lifted and shoved, and it skidded over the side.

"Jump! There's no time!" Elise screamed.

The raft landed upright and bobbed in the sea. Marisol leaped, landed in the raft on her hands and knees. Elise followed her, hitting the water next to the raft. Pierce was about to hurl himself over the railing when he saw Simms's bloody hand on it. Carver was trying to get him over the side, and Pierce ran over to help.

They lifted him by the shoulders to the top of the rail, grabbed his legs, and pushed. The burly man plunged headfirst toward the water and the raft. He smacked against the edge of it, landing just inches from Elise. The raft stood on end, flipping Marisol into the water.

Pierce vaulted the railing. As he fell, he glimpsed the moon low on the horizon, its milky illumination shattering against the choppy seas. He was like the moon, hanging in midair. Then there was only the dark, the sting of the salt water, and his body plunging. He popped to the surface, treaded water, turning in circles.

He saw Carver swimming frantically toward the raft, which looked like a whale painted in moonlight, and Marisol was crawling aboard it. But he didn't spot Elise or Simms. Pierce kicked his screaming legs and propelled his weary arms, shooting toward the raft. As he grabbed the side, the raft suddenly tilted as Carver hoisted himself aboard.

"Where's Simms?" Carver bellowed, hanging over the side.

Where the hell *was* Elise? Pierce shouted for her, listened, waited, shouted again. Nothing.

"Paddle," Carver hollered. "Hurry. It's going to blow!"

The cop grabbed one of the paddles and thrust it into the water as Marisol clutched the other. Pierce shouted for Elise again, desperately searching the dark waters for a glimpse of her. They couldn't paddle away and just leave her here, they couldn't. . . .

The yacht suddenly blew, lighting up the sky. A wave of heat and water flipped the raft and tossed them into the black sea like a handful of pennies.

He tumbled over and over, the turbulence of the explosion tossing him about until he couldn't tell which way was up. He swallowed mouthfuls of salt water. The stuff swirled up his nostrils.

I'm not going to die, not going to die, not going to —

His head broke the surface amid flaming patches of sinking wreckage. He gasped for air. *Not going to die.* He saw flames nearby, and oil-stained water all around him. He sucked air, dived, and swam until his lungs were fairly bursting.

He didn't know if the fire was above him, but now he desperately needed air. He shot to the surface, filled his lungs. Something bobbed in front of him. It was a cushion, and he seized it, clutched it, hugged it. It was life itself.

He gazed over the burning water around him. There was no sign of the raft. No sign of the others. No sign of Elise. He called her name, thought he heard a distant cry. A woman's voice. Elise? Marisol?

Then he heard Carver, closer. He kept shouting for Elise, but didn't hear any more answering calls. Maybe he'd imagined the woman's voice. Maybe it had only been the wind, the water, a trick of the sea. The fire on the oil slick was dying when he spotted Carver, clutching another floating object. He called to him, but his voice was lost in the blast of a ship's horn.

A light in the distance. Was it moving toward him? Yeah . . . yeah it was. He was sure of it. He thought he heard the voice again, a woman's voice, it had to be. He swam toward the light. The voice was inside it, speaking to him, tugging at him. And then the light was on top of him and hands were pulling him out of the water and he clearly heard his name called. But it wasn't a woman's voice.

"Pierce, for chrissakes, about time you got here."

He looked up, blinked, and saw Redington smiling broadly. Two Coast Guardsmen lifted Pierce onto the deck, and carried him away into a cabin. Then he saw her; she was wrapped in a blanket sitting on a cot. Her hair wet and sticking to her face.

"Nick, Nick. I knew you'd make it."

Thirty-Seven

CAPTIVA ISLAND, FLORIDA

It was before nine and the sun was still low above the Gulf. Just ahead of him, teams of determined sandpipers scooted to the edge of the water, picking for their breakfast amid the shells, then quickly backtracked on their impossibly thin stick legs as the surf rolled in. Gulls shrieked overhead and pinwheeled through the clear blue sky. Broken waves eddied over the warm sand, rising to Pierce's ankles and receding again. Like the tide, his thoughts rushed, fled, rose again, both reluctant and anxious to dwell on Ray Andrews.

He had obviously planned all along to disappear once he had the skulls; the world would presume that he had perished with the others on the yacht. He hadn't counted on anyone surviving to tell the story, or that Redington would alert the Coast Guard when he discovered the *Argo-II* missing from its slip.

"I know that look." Elise reached for his hand as they walked along the beach. "You're thinking about him again, aren't you?"

Pierce bent down, picked up an oval-shaped shell and examined its swirling lines, which spiraled inward to a central point. Like his life, spiraling inward, avoiding the world outside his immediate surroundings. "He's hard to forget."

"He's gone now," she said, but he knew she wasn't any more convinced than he was that they'd heard the last of Andrews. After all, they'd betrayed him, and Andrews did not tolerate betrayal.

"Yeah, gone." He tossed the shell into the water, watched it disappear, knowing it would again wash up on the shore. "But they should've caught him by now."

"It takes time, Nick. He's got a lot of money and a lot of connections. Look at the tough time they have catching the big drug smugglers in the Medellín cartel. They're wanted in this country, just like Andrews. But they live like kings, and most of them have avoided getting caught for years now."

Pierce smiled as he thought about the telephone conversation he'd had recently with Morris Carver. If all those "big-time cops" who were after Andrews came home empty-handed, he was going after the "mofo" himself. He had a lot of vacation time saved up, and no one could stop him from doing what he wanted with it.

Pierce believed he'd do it, too. He was tenacious as hell.

"Who knows. Maybe he's hiding out on Miami Beach right now," Elise said when he didn't reply.

"I doubt it. My guess is he's hiding somewhere in the Pyrenees on the border of France and Spain. Basque territory."

"Could be."

"It's no secret that the Medellín cartel has connections with the Basque Separatists, and for a price they'd probably hide Andrews."

Wealth and connections, Pierce thought, could enable Andrews not only to find a secure residence, but would allow him to easily create a new identity. With plastic surgery, he could move about at will without concern about being identified. Transformed.

But where was the New Enlightenment portended by the reunion of the skulls? He asked Elise about it.

"I'm not sure it's something that happens in a flash, but don't belittle the predictions of the Mayan calendar. Just look at what's happened since the Harmonic Convergence. The Cold War died, and the Soviet Union became America's partner. The entire Eastern Block of communist governments collapsed. The Berlin Wall fell without any violence. East Germans are spending deutsche marks, and Gorbachev is trying to build a free-market economy in the Soviet Union. It's incredible."

"I can't deny any of that. And I do remember the people on the beach those two mornings saying that all sorts of changes in the world were about to take place. I thought they were nuts."

She laughed. "I can't really say I believed it was possible myself. I just hoped it was."

"Okay. But what kind of future does this reunion of the skulls portend?"

"Look at how the reunion was achieved, and you'll have an idea. I'd say we can expect more big changes, but with a heavy dose of violence. And I wouldn't be surprised if Andrews somehow emerges out of the chaos as some sort of New Enlightenment prophet, preaching peace and stability."

"I'd like to say there's no way in hell that he's ever going to do anything public again, but then we've just been talking about unbelievable things that did happen."

"And we both know Andrews all too well," she added, grimly.

Pierce paused and stared at the house they were renting. It was a hundred yards away, set back from the beach and partially veiled by Australian pines. He opened the flap of his canvas camera case and lifted out his Nikon F-3 with its 300-mm lens. He aimed it at the front porch, extending the lens to its full focal length.

"What do you see?" Elise asked, gazing over his shoulder.

"Visitors."

"What? Who?"

He adjusted the focus. "Two snowy egrets perched on the porch railing."

She laughed. "You scared me."

Pierce lowered the camera and wrapped an arm around her shoulders. "I think we're safe." He nuzzled her neck, kissed her.

He set the camera back into the case, closed the flap, and took her hand again. They walked in silence toward the house. Every day they were together seemed like a miracle to him. Until he'd been lifted aboard the Coast Guard cutter that had spotted the fiery explosion, he'd thought he'd lost Elise. She'd been trapped beneath the raft after Simms's falling body had knocked her off. But, as Carver and Marisol had started paddling, she'd grasped a guide rope on one side and managed to get a breathful of air before the explosion. She'd never let go of the raft and had been the first found.

She'd told the guardsmen about the others in the water, but they'd only found Pierce and Carver. Pierce was more than a quarter of a mile from where she'd been picked up, and oddly enough, he'd been clinging to the back cushion of Andrews's captain's chair. Carver was found floating on an airtight container that held a collection of Andrews's videotapes.

Marisol and Simms were lost. Simms probably would've died, anyhow, from the bullet wound. But why Marisol? Why did she have to die? He felt a twinge of pain every time he thought about her. After all, she'd been safe from Andrews, until he'd found her.

A week later, Elise had left for Edinburgh, where she spent two weeks attending to her father's affairs after his funeral, and when she'd returned, he'd sensed the change in her. Rather than embittered, she seemed more balanced, and no longer driven by vendetta. It was over. That was all she said about it.

Over for now, he thought.

As for himself, his life had also changed. Ten days after the night on the yacht, Gibby's multimillion-dollar settlement came through, and he'd kept his word. He'd written Pierce a check for $185,000. His bonus, and well deserved, Gibby had said. When Elise had returned, he told her the news and that he'd rented a house for a month on a certain serene Gulf coast island, and asked whether she would consider joining him. Her answer was brief and to the point. "Let's start packing."

The relationship with Elise had blossomed, and everything was taking on new meaning. They were spending their days and nights talking about a life together, what they would do, where they would go. He gazed out into the blueness, which was like their future, vast and awaiting their discovery.

"Another great day ahead," Elise said as they climbed the steps to the porch of the two-story wood-frame house. "And I don't want to hear that man's name again today, or tomorrow, or the next day. You got that?"

"But we lost and he won."

Elise tugged on his hand as they reached the top of the steps. He turned, and she slipped her hands around his waist. "Look on the bright side of it," she said. "You've got your life, a big bonus from another case, and — for better or worse — me."

Pierce pulled her close, smiling. She was right. He had gotten the girl and the money. Just like in the movies.

Biography

Rob MacGregor

(Rob MacGregor is an Edgar-winning author of seventeen novels, four non-fiction books, and numerous magazine and newspaper articles. In addition to writing his own novels, he has teamed with George Lucas, Peter Benchley, and Billy Dee Williams. His latest efforts include JUST/IN TIME, a psychic thriller, co-authored with Billy Dee Williams, and THE GHOST TRIBE: PETER BENCHLEY'S AMAZON. In his spare time, he windsurfs and teaches yoga.)

Printed in the United Kingdom
by Lightning Source UK Ltd.
107935UKS00001B/42

9 780759 249202